H16

Slough Library Services

Please return this book on or before the H34
date shown on your receipt.

To renew go to:
Website: **www.slough.gov.uk/libraries**
Phone: **01753 535166**

LIB/6198

ALL I HAVE TO GIVE

It is 1916 and Edith Mellor is one of the few female surgeons in Britain. She travels to the Somme, where she is confronted with the horrors at the front. Yet amongst the bloodshed on the battlefield, there is a ray of light in the form of the working class Albert, a corporal from the East End of London. Meanwhile in Bradford, strong-minded Ada is left heartbroken when her only remaining son Jimmy heads off to fight in the war. She then discovers that her mentally unstable sister Beryl is pregnant with her husband Paddy's child. Can Edith help her to turn her life around?

ALL I HAVE TO GIVE

ALL I HAVE TO GIVE

by

Mary Wood

Magna Large Print Books
Long Preston, North Yorkshire,
BD23 4ND, England.

British Library Cataloguing in Publication Data.

Wood, Mary
    All I have to give.

    A catalogue record of this book is
    available from the British Library

    ISBN   978-0-7505-4328-6

First published in Great Britain in 2015 by Pan Books,
an imprint of Pan Macmillan.

Published in Large Print 2016 by arrangement with
Macmillan Publishers trading as Pan Macmillan Publishers Ltd.

Magna Large Print is an imprint of Library Magna Books Ltd.

Printed and bound in Great Britain by
T.J. (International) Ltd., Cornwall, PL28 8RW

Dedicated to the memory of the woman who
also helped end the war.

Elsie Inglis, a doctor who travelled to France at
the beginning of the First World War, despite
opposition from the government of the day, and
set up a hospital to tend to the wounded.

To the women who worked in the Barnbow and
Low Moor Munition Factories, especially those
killed in the line of duty.

And to all women who took up the challenge
set them during the 1914–1918 war, either on
the front line or on the home front.

All of these women left a legacy of unselfishness
in the courage they showed and the sacrifices
they made. They did not falter. We will remember
them.

1

Ada

Low Moor, Bradford, Yorkshire, January 1916
A torn heart

'You're not going, our Jimmy. I'm telling you, lad. Get all idea of it out of your head. I couldn't bear it. I've given our Bobby and our Jack to this bloody war. That letter from the King himself said they would ask no more of me. And that me youngest would be exempt.'

Ada clung onto the pot-sink for support and closed her eyes, as the pain of her loss seared through her. She was a woman whose thirty-six years had dealt her many a hard blow, none of which had broken her yet. As she looked out of the window, the view of the cobbled street with its rows of terraced houses blurred through her tears. Fear caused her stomach to clench tightly.

It had seemed as though her world had come to an end when the telegram saying that both her lads had been killed in action had arrived fifteen months ago. But then she'd felt safe in still having her Jimmy. She wouldn't lose him. The King's letter, saying that he and the country thanked her for her sacrifice, had assured her they would not ask her third son to enlist.

'I have to go, Ma. All the lads have joined up. I'd have looked like I was a coward or sommat if I hadn't done the same. Besides, I have to go for our Bobby and our Jack. I have to honour their memory. I have to kill some of them bastard Germans as killed me brothers.'

She couldn't find the words to answer him. As she turned towards him, it seemed to her that Jimmy had grown in stature. Whilst he'd always been a small lad – smaller than his brothers had been, something she'd put down to the difficult time she'd had birthing and raising him – he now stood to his full height, his pride in himself evident.

As her third child, Jimmy had also been her last, as the damage his breech-birth had caused her had stopped everything working as it should, and she'd never seen a period since. Though perhaps that was as well in some ways, as her Paddy never left her be and would have knocked a dozen out of her by now, if he could.

Given to swilling the drink down, Paddy spent most of what he earned through one scam or another, or through the odd job that came his way, on drink. And he gave a good bit of what was left to the bookie's runner. He'd never kept a permanent job. The gasworks, where most men in the area worked, sacked him for poor attendance, and his stint down the mine hadn't lasted long, either. With his record, he couldn't even get taken on in the munitions factory, at a time when they were crying out for workers. By, they'd have been made, if he had, for them workers were earning a fortune.

If it hadn't been for her Beryl helping out,

they'd have starved by now, as Paddy wouldn't hear of letting Ada go out to work. It was against his principles, he'd say.

Beryl was her elder sister, and she'd never had any children. It was said that Bill, her husband, didn't have it in him. He'd been married before and his first wife, who'd died of the typhus, had been childless.

Beryl and Bill had doted on Ada's three. Bobby's and Jack's passing had broken their hearts. How they would take this news, Ada didn't know.

'Eric's going, and so is Arthur.' Jimmy's voice held a quiver, a nervousness, and she didn't think this was just because of telling her this news. Perhaps the possible consequences of what he'd done were dawning on him.

'Oh God, naw! Not them as well. What are their mams going to think? Mabel dotes on her Eric, and Agatha's only got the one lad.'

'They were shocked, but also proud of them, and told all the neighbours. I thought you would be proud an' all, our Mam.'

'Well, you thought wrong, Jimmy. You're not going, and that's an end to the matter!'

'It's too late, Ma, I signed...'

'You haven't, lad! Naw! But how?'

'A bloke came into the mill. He said he wanted volunteers and would be at the social club all afternoon. He told us that pals like us three – and a few more from around here who'd joined us – were all going together, to support each other and keep each other safe. Aye, and he said that lads like us were dying because there aren't enough of us, and they need our help and we should stand shoulder-to-shoulder with them, to fight for free-dom.'

'And you signed up? Well, you can just un-sign, Jimmy; for God's sake, you're not yet turned seventeen! Did you tell him your age?'

'I lied, Mam.'

'Oh, Jimmy, Jimmy...'

The weight of her grief, and the unbearable truth that she could do nothing to stop him going, set Ada's body trembling. Reaching for the fireside chair, she slumped into it. Taking a deep breath, she lifted her head. Her son needed her to be strong for him. 'Reet, lad, what's done is done. I'll see as your stuff's all sorted. You go round the street and tell them we're having a send-off party tonight. We'll see that all the lads that volunteered with you have a good time before they go. Tell everyone to bring what they have in the way of food, and say as I'll be playing me mam's piano, so there will be a sing-song.'

'Aw, Mam, naw...'

'Never mind about "Naw", our Jimmy. You're off to war, and you're not going without a send-off. Bobby and Jack went amidst a lot of tears, and that's not going to happen for you. I want you to remember your send-off and how proud we were of you. Go on, lad, I've got cakes to bake.'

His grin tugged at her heart strings as he ran out of the door. Swallowing hard, Ada took her bag down from the hook on the back of the door where it always hung and rummaged through it for her purse. Her hands touched the soft felt wal-let that she'd made, which was blue, with a neat blanket-stich around the edges; she had embroi-

14

dered her sons' names, Jack and Bobby, in scroll-like writing on the front of it. Tom Garrinton, the grocer along the road, had written it out for her. She'd always admired the lovely signs he'd made for his shop and had asked him to make the names look special. Using what he'd written as a template, she'd lovingly stitched each name in a golden silk thread and then set them in entwining hearts. Pulling it out, she opened the wallet and looked on the smiling faces of Jack and Bobby: both in uniform, both with a likeness to Jimmy. Holding their pictures to her breast, she prayed to them: *Look after Jimmy for me, me lads.*

Wiping her tears with her pinny, she tucked the wallet back into her bag and took out her purse. It felt lighter than it should and the clasp was open. As she emptied it onto the table, the few coppers that rolled out spun with an empty, rattling sound before settling. Staring at them brought a feeling of anger and frustration to her. Paddy had been at her bag again – she'd swing for him yet! She'd had five bob in there, money built up over time from the odd copper here and there that she'd squir-relled away for a rainy day. She'd thought to use it to buy a few jugs of beer to help things along tonight, but now she'd be lucky to get a quarter of a jug, and that wouldn't be any use.

Weary of it all, she hung the bag back on the hook, catching sight of herself in the mirror that hung next to it. The curls she'd never been able to tame had dampened into ringlets. A deep auburn colour, her hair had been what had attracted Paddy to her in the first place. He'd said it reminded him of a flaming fire. And he'd loved her

15

freckled face and huge brown eyes. It surprised her to see that same young girl looking back at her now. She'd aged well. Not that she was a grand age, but she'd had a lot to cope with over the years, and that should have taken more of a toll on her than it had. But then her mam had been youthful-looking, too, right up until her death three years ago: at fifty-five, she'd only looked forty.

The suddenness of the door swinging open cata-pulted Ada out of her reminiscing. She stepped back just in time to save herself from being knocked off her pins, and landed with her back to the table.

Paddy stood in the open doorway with a face like thunder. Still handsome and, aye, still sought-after by many a lass, he glared at her. The door framed his tall, strong body. Her husband of twenty years, she'd met him when she'd been just a lass of fifteen. His Irish charm, coupled with his dark good looks and twinkling blue eyes, had taken her heart. It hadn't been long, though, before he'd taken much more, and she'd found herself pregnant with their Bobby.

'Is it right, what I hear? Have they signed up me young Jimmy?'

'Aye, it's reet, Paddy. Come on in – I've a pot on the go.'

'It's not tea I'm after wanting. How can you stand there and offer such a thing, when our son has signed his own death-warrant? There's some-thing cold about you, Ada. Something that makes you hard against these things and stops them affecting you. I put this all down to you and your ways.'

His movement towards her wasn't one of a loving husband about to comfort his wife. His hand was raised. Cringing away from him, Ada twisted her body and managed to dodge the blow he would have landed across her face. Skipping over to the fireplace, she picked up the poker. 'Just you try it, Paddy, and I'll beat the life out of you with this!'

'Ha, me red-headed devil, you would an' all. Come here!'

His tone and stance had changed in a flash. Now his eyes smouldered with a burning desire. That was her Paddy. He only had two reactions to bad situations: anger and lust. And either emotion could trigger the other. Well, she preferred his lust. Putting the poker down, she went into his arms.

There was a comfort in his holding her, and she could sense his need to find some for himself. Pulling his head away from her neck, he motioned towards the steps that led to the shelf-like loft.

This tiny house stood in a row of back-to-back cottages, all with one large scullery-cum-living room downstairs and a loft space under the roof that was reached by a ladder. This was where she and Paddy had their bed. A large trunk, holding their own and their sons' clothes and what linen they had, was the only other piece of furniture up there. Jimmy slept on a shake-me-down – a soft, horsehair mattress that could be rolled up in the daytime. He put this on the floor and, with a blanket to cover him, was kept warm by the embers glowing in the fire grate.

The sound of the lock clicking into place as she went towards the ladder increased the feeling of

17

anticipation in her belly. The muscles that had tightened with Paddy's kissing and nipping of her neck clenched even harder, causing her to feel sensations that needed sating. So much so that she shunned the self-disgust that niggled at her, making her ask herself how she could give in to such feelings at such a time?

She knew how: it was all they had – emotions; all they could tap into, to help them cope. Aye, it could mean feeling anger, or cause tears and wails because of the sadness of her situation, but more often than not, for her and Paddy, it meant satisfying the need they both had in them.

Willingly giving herself to Paddy's skilful love-making blotted out all that she had to face. His caressing of every part of her made her feel beautiful. The sensation of his lips brushing her nipples, before taking them gently – one at a time – into his mouth, and at the same time stroking the heart of her womanhood left her begging him to enter her. When he did, she felt every part of her clench onto him, as spasm after spasm rippled through her.

With this release, her body betrayed her, wrenching deep sobs from her that left her limp beneath him. Paddy connected to this unburdening of her soul by coming deep into her, then slumping beside her.

His sobs gave her strength. His need created in her a place that could give him comfort and so soothe her own pain. Taking him in her arms, she whispered, 'It'll be reet, Paddy, love. The King promised us. I'll go and see the authorities and explain. They'll have to release our Jimmy. I'll take the letter with me. They can't deny what our own King has said.'

'No.' His hand found her discarded pinny. Using it to wipe his face, he lifted himself on his elbow and gently wiped hers, too. ''Tis as Jimmy is his own man. He's made his decision. We have to stand by him on that, so we do.'

'You're reet, Paddy. We do. Come on, we've a "do" to arrange. We have to give our lad a good send-off.' Grabbing her clothes, Ada began to dress, but she felt a trickle of worry at Paddy's protest, as the sound of his voice showed that his anger was returning.

'That's taking things too far for me. I see it as a mockery, and it's what makes me angry more than anything. How is it that you, his mammy, could rejoice at Jimmy's going? It makes me sick to me stomach.'

Ada hadn't meant to make him angry again. She'd wanted to hold on to the love they had just shared. 'It's not a celebration, Paddy. It's to say we are proud of him. Aye, and to help our Beryl, and them lasses in the street that are sending their lads off, too. And Betsy – young Betsy is in love with our Jimmy, and she will miss him more than any-one. Us having a bit of a do will help them all take their minds off the fear of it, at least for a couple of hours. Mind, it'll be a dry do, because you've had me nest-egg again, Paddy. Eeh, how you can take from your own wife, like you do, beggars belief. You can be a pig at times, Paddy O'Flynn!'

'A pig, is it? And haven't I just given you the loving of your life, bringing you more joy than is known to man, and you call me a pig!'

19

He'd risen and was pulling on his trousers. Normally such talk would put a fear into her. Paddy lived a fine balance between being the man every woman desired and a monster who would knock nine bells out of her. But his tone didn't hold anger. He spoke with a curious insinuation that he knew something she didn't.

'If it is a party you want, and the spirit of it is as you say, then take a look at this. Won't some of that get you a party to tell of, eh?' Paddy produced ten one-pound notes from the pocket of his trousers.

'Oh my God, Paddy, what have you done? Have you robbed a bank?'

'Ha, no. It is the horses that came in for me. I bet a double and a treble, and they came romping in. This is what I did with the four bob I took from your purse. I went forth and multiplied, just as the good Lord said we should.'

'Oh, Paddy!'

'Ha! Is it a pig you think I am now?'

She laughed at him, hitting him with the pinny she'd picked up, then snatched the three one-pound notes that he held out towards her. 'A generous pig, but a pig all the same!'

As he went to grab her, she wriggled out of his reach and clambered for the ladder. She needed to busy herself because, party or no party, she had to face the reality of their Jimmy going to war.

2

Edith

Nice, southern France and the Somme, May–July 1916
In the footsteps of her heroine

From her window seat in Marianne's apartment overlooking the Promenade des Anglais in Nice, Edith found it hard to believe there was a war on, let alone that she had left the family home in London's Holland Park to do her bit.

It was strange, she thought, that she was sitting here, watching the world go by, when soon she would be using her skills to tend the wounded and help the dying to pass over with dignity.

Her plans had been met with opposition from her mother. She understood, of course. Poor Mama. Born Lady Muriel Daverly, Mama had lost a lot of the status that went with her birth by marrying a second son, and not a lord. She did, however, hold a special place in social standing as she had inherited her family's country-estate in Leicestershire, along with a considerable fortune – something that rarely happened to a woman, but there had been no male member left in her entire family line.

A socialite at heart, Mama had tried hard not to acknowledge that there was a war on at all, and had carried on, business as usual. The business in question had been several desperate attempts to marry Edith off to a suitable beau. But she didn't want to be married off, suitable or otherwise! Her first love was her career. Something she realized was quite a shocking thing for a young lady to pursue.

How much better for Mama if she'd had a daughter of the ilk of Lady Eloise, or Lady Andrina. Daughters of her uncle, Lord Mellor, and his French wife, Lady Felicity, they were a lovable but frivolous pair of girls. It was through them that Edith knew and had become close to Marianne, as Marianne was their aunt – sister to Lady Felicity.

Edith had to admit, though, that wanting her married off wasn't the only reason behind her mama's objections. Mama had already seen her two sons off to war: Douglas, who loved nothing more than managing their mother's Leicestershire estate, but whose innate patriotism and sense of duty had driven him to volunteer; and Christian, a student of medical science, driven by the same values as Douglas. They were now both commissioned officers fighting in the Somme area, the same region that Edith planned to go to.

It had been Christian's letter that had alerted Edith to the desperate need for doctors. He'd told her how much he admired a Scottish woman doctor, Elsie Inglis, who, at twenty-eight – the same age as Edith – had gone to the Somme and set up a hospital, despite opposition from the War Office.

Edith's own accomplishment in becoming a surgeon had been an easier path than the one

Elsie had taken. Elsie had been driven to set up her own medical school in order to study, but Edith's father being a top surgeon himself meant that doors had opened that wouldn't normally have done so for a woman. It was strange, she thought, how she had been the one to take up the profession and not her two brothers, though of course Christian's calling was in another very important medical field, so some of their father's genes must be in him, too.

But for all her qualifications, the same fate befell her as had happened to Elsie – the War Office refused Edith's application for a post in the war zone, in the same condescending way that Elsie had encountered. Edith was indignant at the manner of the refusal. How dare they say her place was at home? They seemed to be ignoring the fact that hundreds of women were already in war zones, all over the world: nurses, voluntary aid workers and First Aid Nursing Yeomanry, given the ridiculous acronym of FANYs! And all of them were doing a sterling job.

She'd had no joy with the British Red Cross, either. They'd said they would contact her if they found they needed more personnel, but at present they felt they had enough medical staff. With attempts to provide her services thwarted, Edith had taken a leaf out of Elsie Inglis's book and had gone it alone. She'd arranged to come and stay with Marianne in the South of France, so that she could also apply to the French Red Cross, as Elsie had done in the first instance. Edith's thinking had been that, being in France, her application would have a little more weight, besides which, Marianne had influence in some very useful quarters.

Bringing her attention back to the view she had from her window seat, Edith gazed down on the people wandering along the Promenade des Anglais. She loved the story of how the promenade got its name, and imagined the poor beggars of the 1820s sweating away at their labour – put to work by the wealthy English to make a walkway for them along the beach. A humble beginning had expanded to become the beautiful promenade she now looked down on.

None of the folk ambling along or popping in and out of the couture, art and jewellery shops, or those taking a leisurely coffee or glass of wine in the pavement cafes below the apartment block, looked as though they had a care in the world. But Marianne had told her of her many friends who had sons in the French Army, fighting in the raging battle of Verdun. Many of them had been injured or killed, and their families lived in fear of hearing sad news. So she imagined that some of the men and women she could see from her vantage point had worries that didn't show in their demeanour. Yet war hadn't touched Nice in any other way. Food was plentiful, and even the socializing continued.

The scene altered as she gazed beyond the ever-changing kaleidoscope of the promenade to the turquoise sea, gently lapping onto the sands. On the horizon, boats – some with fishermen in, others with graceful sails – bobbed about, in and out of the line of jewels thrown onto the water by the glistening sun.

Edith's thoughts were startled by the door opening. Marianne entered the sitting room. The fixed, pretend smile on her face ran counter to the usual air of wealth and happiness that she emanated, and sparked a feeling of trepidation in Edith.

'Edith, darling, it is here. The letter you have been waiting for. It has arrived. I hope it has the news you want to hear, but only because you want it so much. For me, *ma chérie*, I would prefer it to be a "no".' Marianne floated towards her, holding not one, but two letters. 'And there is another letter, and a more welcome one, I hope. It is from your mother. I know her handwriting well. Maybe in it we will hear some good news.'

Floating was the only way you could describe the way Marianne walked. She reminded Edith of the mechanical doll she'd had as a child, which, when wound up, moved on little wheels hidden under its long skirt. Marianne's blue silk skirt hid her shoes and brushed along the thick carpet in much the same way. Held in at the waist with a cummerbund, where the skirt joined her cream, frilly blouse, her attire showed off her very slight figure. She wore her gleaming black hair piled high on her head and coiled in a chignon at the back, which saved her from looking as tiny as she was as the style gave her some perceived height. Tendrils of hair fell around her pretty face – a face with chiselled features set off by her huge eyes, the colour of which were difficult to describe, as sometimes they looked the deepest blue and at other times more of a misty grey.

Taking the letters, Edith stared at the brown one for a moment. It *was* what she had been waiting for: the insignia of the French Red Cross was unmistakable. Her heart thudded. *Please don't let the answer be 'no'.*

Translating the French and simplifying it, Edith read just the opposite. The Red Cross would be very pleased to have her. *At last!*

'Good news?'

'I think so. I am to be in Boulogne at the beginning of June, and will be taken to the front from there.'

'Oh no, *ma chérie* – the fighting there is so intense! With the battle in Ypres failing, the Germans are advancing on France, and the news is that the hold at Verdun is failing, too!'

'But where else would I be needed than where the fighting is? Please don't worry, dear Marianne. Medical staff are safe; they are covered by a treaty that allows Red Cross workers to carry out their duty without being attacked.'

Reading on, Edith realized that changes were afoot. 'It says I am initially to go to Verdun, but that the hospital may be on the move. There must be a new offensive. Perhaps I will eventually go somewhere near Christian and Douglas. Oh, I'm so excited to be going at last!'

Opening the second letter, she read that her mother was missing her and hoped that Edith had changed her mind. But, if she hadn't, then would she contact the British Red Cross, as they now needed her urgently!

'Good gracious! First of all nobody wants me, and now everyone does!' Reading Marianne the contents of the letter, she had no doubt which offer she would take up. 'I will contact both, and let them know that I will attach myself to the British Red Cross. I want to help my fellow countrymen more than anything.'

'I admire you so much, Edith, but I...' Marianne paused for a moment. 'Promise me you will visit me as often as you can?'

'I promise. And thank you. To have your admiration means a lot to me. Now I must write to Mama. She won't like it that I am carrying on with my plans, and I cannot blame her, but before I left she gave me her blessing and told me she was proud of me. And in her letter she says her love goes with me, so I think she has resigned herself to it.'

'Poor Muriel, it must be very difficult for her: first the boys, and now you.' Before Edith could answer this, Marianne changed her tone, and the subject. 'But we all have to deal with the situation as it is, and there are things to arrange. Your train ticket for one, and clothes...'

'Now you are being frivolous, Marianne! I do not need any more clothes. I will be in uniform most of the time, and I have some practical pieces with me that will do, when I'm not working.'

Being frivolous was so unlike Marianne. She was a political animal who spoke up for the rights of women. Even in her calling as an author, her books – though categorized as 'romance novels' – held a message. It was very subtle, but still there, in the hope of rallying women to the cause, as her heroines often did.

It was funny that she should write romances, thought Edith, when she'd never known Marianne to be courted by a man. She had many male friends, but that is all they were: friends. When she hosted dinner parties, she would debate with her friends for hours on the war, politics and women's rights, but no one ever flirted with her. Her closest friend was a woman – a handsome woman, in a manly way – who used the male form of her name, shortening Georgette to George. Edith wondered about the implications of this, especially as Marianne often stayed over at George's apartment, but it didn't worry her. Marianne was her own woman, a passionate person who cared deeply about everything. The way in which her sexuality lay was her own business.

The weeks of waiting for her deployment dragged by for Edith. Occasional communications came through by letter briefing her of the plans for the tent hospital that was to be erected in Abbeville, a town on the mouth of the Somme, in northern France. This would be her base. And though nothing was said as to why, she was informed that she would need to be there by mid-June, to organize the hospital.

This seemed a daunting task for her, especially as there was no indication of whether there would be other doctors there or not. Nurses were mentioned. A contingent of very experienced nurses pulled back from Belgium were being sent to Abbeville, as well as many Voluntary Aid Detachment personnel with various skills that she would find useful.

When at last the day came for her to leave, Edith felt a mixture of excitement and trepidation. The day of her departure had been delayed from the original plan as it was already the 25th of June and she was to set off the next day. A confusing number of communications had arrived in the last few days, but the last one by courier spoke of the urgency of her getting to Abbeville and asked whether she could set off immediately for Boulogne.

Marianne accompanied her to the station to begin her journey. They found it was crammed with soldiers. Some Edith wanted to comfort and tend to as their bandaged wounds showed signs of seeping blood and weren't too clean. Others were freshly uniformed and excited, saying their good-byes to weeping wives and girlfriends. There was a strange mix of emotions, which gave a sense that something big was going to happen. She supposed the wounded had returned from Verdun and that the new young soldiers were to replace them.

When her train pulled in amidst a screeching of steel and clouds of smoke, Edith found it difficult to say her goodbyes to Marianne. The atmosphere had frightened her, but pulling her shoulders back she tried not to look as vulnerable as she felt.

Arriving in Boulogne enforced the feeling that the South of France had given Edith. Nothing about it spoke of a war going on, making her situation feel impossibly unreal and had her questioning how it could be that so many were losing their lives just a few hundred miles from here.

A flustered man of around fifty met her. His armband identified him as a Red Cross official. Not stopping to introduce himself, but only confirming who she was, he gave her hurried instructions. 'The ambulances are ready to take you on to Abbeville, but prepare yourself, as an offensive on a massive scale is starting. We are hardly ready, but we will get you there as quickly as we can.'

As she turned a corner to follow the route he'd given her to the beach front, with its grassed area and hotels and shops, seagulls swooped above her and people taking a leisurely stroll walked past her. Was she really going to the front, where she had been warned in her briefing that casualties could be very high? It didn't seem possible, when here, as in Nice, life carried on as normal all around her.

This feeling of disbelief left her as, two hours later, her body bumped and jolted against the sides of the ambulance. The journey of fifty or so miles seemed to be mostly over rough terrain: farmers' lanes, for the most part, and make-do roads that had sprung up in preparation of the need to transport supplies and ammunition. Feeling that her bones would rattle out of her skin, it was a relief when one of her fellow travellers spoke to her. 'Cheer up, love. It ain't 'alf as bad as yer think.' A hand came out to her. 'Me name's Connie. I'm a trained nurse. Been working in Belgium. Not that I'm saying it's a picnic working in a war 'ospital – it certainly ain't that – but there's plenty of fun to be 'ad, besides all the work and sadness. You'll get used to it.'

Connie's words gave a small amount of hope to Edith. She took the outstretched hand. 'Pleased to meet you. I'm Doctor Edith Mellor. And, yes, I am nervous. This is my first time, and I don't know quite what to expect.'

'Blood and gore by the bucketload – and more

buckets of tears, love. But there's also another side. The blokes we save, the pranks some of them get up to, the courage, and... Oh, it's all 'ard to explain, but it's something you come to love – the way of life, that is, not the suffering. So you're a doctor? I had you down as a voluntary aid worker.'

Edith didn't miss Connie's tone of admiration when she found out that she was a doctor, or the note of disdain given to the words 'voluntary aid worker'. But she just smiled, not sure that she wanted to engage in conversation and feeling totally out of control of her movements, sensing that she would throw up any minute. But then the sounds coming to her now told her they were nearing the front, as blast after blast of distant explosions assaulted her ears, setting up a fear in her that she wanted to block out. Holding her hands in tight fists, she answered Connie. 'Yes, a doctor – a qualified surgeon, like my father. They say the hospital tents are up, and all the equipment we'll need is there. We'll just have to put it together and fit it where we want it. Jolly glad about the tents being up, though. Gosh, I have no idea how to pitch a tent!'

Connie looked amused. 'As long as yer can fix a wounded man – and it sounds as though yer can – then you'll be fine. I'll stay close to yer and 'elp yer settle. Where yer from? I'm from Stepney in the East End.'

Chatting about ordinary things helped and, as the other girls joined in, the explosions took a back seat to their laughter, as Nancy, another experienced nurse, and Connie related stories of their time in Belgium, and here in France. It seemed that most of them had been together throughout the war, moving with the action to wherever they were needed.

After telling a tale about a Voluntary Aid Detachment worker who had fainted at the sight of blood, Connie said, 'You'll fit in with the VADs, Doctor – posh lot they are, and mostly very willing, though some of them are as much use as a chocolate Yule log on a fire!'

A girl who had sat quietly throughout the conversation, and who seemed just as new to this as Edith, looked down at her hands, clasped tightly in her lap. A blush spread up from her neck and beads of sweat trickled down her face. *No doubt a VAD,* thought Edith. But saying anything would only increase her discomfort.

The differences between trained nurses and Voluntary Aid Detachment workers was something that Edith had heard of, but it seemed it wasn't as bad as it had been painted. Connie and Nancy sounded quite accepting of them, if a little derisive. For herself, she didn't think it mattered whether those around her were a posh lot or not, trained or not, as long as they all pitched in and did their best. And she'd be just as happy being friends with the Connies and Nancys of this world as with her own class. They were salt-of-the-earth types, and funny with it – just what she needed at the moment.

Both were good-looking girls and sported the same hairstyle, scraped up into a bun on top of their heads. Although this was practical, and would fit under the veil-like hats that all nurses wore on duty, it also looked very pretty.

Connie had a strong-looking figure and was tall and buxom, with features that were more handsome than pretty, but her lovely blue eyes softened her looks and made you feel relaxed with her – and safe that she would have your back and would know the answer to anything.

Nancy, on the other hand, was about Edith's own height, at around five-foot-two. She had a dainty figure and was fairer-looking than the olive-skinned Connie. Her blonde hair was given to curls, one or two of which had escaped the many pins that she had pushed into it to keep it neat, and now hung around her face. She, too, had blue eyes, but hers were more piercing.

Although Edith had detected from Nancy's accent that she came from Leicestershire, it was a surprise to learn that she actually lived quite near Lutterworth, Edith's country home It seemed they had even been at the same church functions, though in different capacities: Edith as local 'royalty', accompanying the dignitaries and cutting ribbons to open events, and Nancy running one of the stalls, or just enjoying the visiting fair or circus with her family.

As the stories came to an end, Nancy asked, 'Have you left a fellow behind then, Doctor?'

'Good gracious, no. No time for such nonsense when you have had to study as hard as I have – but not for the want of my mother trying.'

'Ha, I heard how it was for you high-born girls. Mother invites eligible men around, and daughter dutifully marries the pick of the bunch. Not like that for us, is it, Connie?'

At that moment gunshots and blasts bombarded their ears, taking their focus back to the terrifying reality of where they were. Debris catapulted into the air, landing on the roof of the ambulance with a sound of a million hailstones – a storm holding a fear that stiffened Edith's body.

'We're 'ere. Bloody Kaiser 'ad a gun salute ready to welcome us. Look, you can see the tents... Bleedin' 'ell, look at that convoy coming the other way! I reckon we should 'urry and stake our claim on the best beds. But wait a minute...'

Edith saw what had dawned on Connie. These were not more medical staff arriving, but casualties – the convoy of six comprised of ambulances. Dust puffed into the air as they came to a halt, just feet away from where Edith alighted.

Doors flew open and stretchers emerged as if vomited from the truck. Shouts of 'Have the medics arrived?' and 'We need a doctor over here!' vied with the screams of pain and the hollers of death. *God! How had it come about that casualties arrived before the hospital was even ready?*

With no time to ponder this, Edith bent her head against the onslaught of rain that was now bucketing from the rolling sky. Forgetting all her fears, she hurried as fast as she could through mud that sucked her feet into its squelchy ruts, as she desperately made her way towards the largest of the tents.

Getting there before the stretcher-bearers, she was appalled to see an empty space, with stacks of beds to one side, and boxes and boxes of supplies piled high next to them. Realizing that she was the most senior person present, she began to shout orders.

Trying to do what she could for the men lying on the damp floor wherever the stretcher-bearers could lay them, she shouted, 'Make a line of beds here and here. Then put those tables along here. Oh God, we need lights!'

'I can fix the lights up, Ma'am. Me job before this lot was...'

Edith turned towards the soldier who had said this and, like him, had a moment's hesitation. It seemed to her that for a second or so the noise of the war, and the clatter of beds being assembled, faded into the distance as her heart jolted and she found herself looking into the most beautiful face she had ever seen. *Can a man be beautiful?* As her mind asked this question, she felt a blush sweep her face, but still she didn't look away. In such a short space of time she registered his golden hair and how it waved back from his forehead, his freckled skin and his green-grey eyes, which held a look of astonishment as he stared back at her. A look that told her he had felt the same connection to her as she had to him. But then his words jarred her and didn't fit their situation. 'Corporal Albert Price, Ma'am. I was a mechanic before the war. I've seen a generator outside. I'll have it going in no time.'

Dragged back to reality, she lowered her gaze to compose herself, before answering him, 'Thank you. That would be spiffing.' *Spiffing! Bother – did I really say that! When what I wanted to say had nothing to do with the war, or generators, or the sick or dying... Oh God, what is the matter with me?*

As he turned from her, he winked. Rather than offend her, it made her feel as if someone had brushed her skin with a feather. It was the kind of wink that said he knew how she felt, and this made her even more flustered, giving her the sense that she was a young girl instead of an adult woman – and a doctor at that.

Cross with herself, Edith shook the thoughts from her. How could she have allowed her focus to shift from the important job at hand for even one second? The answer was simple. She'd not been given a choice, for the impact had happened without her bidding it to.

Albert's 'no time' took half an hour, during which time a minor miracle occurred, as the first signs of a hospital ward began to take shape, speeded up by another soldier who had come up to Edith. 'I'm Private Walter Hermon, Ma'am. Over the last few days me and others assigned to get things shipshape have managed to get a wooden floor down in the next tent, but we were told the medical staff were to put the beds up and unpack the equipment, so we didn't touch it. I can get the men to help, if you like?'

'Good. Yes, set to. Thank you. I'll utilize the wooden-floored tent as an operating theatre. And I have been informed there is an Australian hospital nearby that has been coping on its own. Would you send someone over there and ask them if they can take some of our cases? Tell them we are not fully up and running yet, and only have one surgeon at the moment, but more are expected any day.'

'I'll try, Ma'am, but those we have here are an overflow from that hospital, as it is. I think they thought we were ready.'

'Well, tell them we are not; and if they cannot take any patients back, ask them to at least spare us a surgeon, as we are desperate!'

Assessing patient after patient, Edith methodically labelled each according to what they would need, mentally working out an order of priority. The nurses working alongside her were putting her requests into action as best they could.

'Connie, have you come across an operating table yet?'

'Yes, and much more for a theatre, Doc, and I have them all sorted.'

Edith set Connie the task of grabbing one of the helpers to get the wooden-floored tent ready for that purpose, while shouting, 'Nurses, get all the patients onto beds now, quickly! And has anyone located drugs and dressings?'

'I have. They're all in this case here, Doctor Edith. And may I say, listening to you on the drive here, I worried that you were as green as me. But, hey-ho, you're top-hole! What shall I do with this stuff? Oh, by the way, I'm Jennifer Roxley, of London. I think you guessed that I am with the Voluntary Aid Detachment. Pleased to meet you.'

'I know of the Roxleys: you must be a younger sister of Allen, who is in my social set. I'm pleased to meet you, too. Locate either Nurse Connie or Nurse Nancy – they will know where to put everything. Just follow their direction to the letter. You heard what they said about VADs: prove them wrong, for all the posh-girl brigade. And, Jennifer – thank you, and well done.'

Darkness had fallen before Edith's lips touched a drop of liquid. Sipping on the delicious hot tea, which the strange feel of a tin mug didn't diminish, she leant back on the tent post. Thank goodness another team of doctors and nurses was expected soon, to work alongside her team, as she doubted any of them could keep up the pace that had been set today.

An eerie silence clothed the site and the surrounding area with an atmosphere of delicate peace. Some of the tension left her body, if not her mind, as she reflected on what this first day had brought. Men with horrific wounds, some so badly hurt that it had been beyond her power to save them. She'd had to cut out bullets and shrapnel and stitching and ... and saw off a leg of a young man not much older than twenty! Then, amidst all this, there was the effect that Albert had had on her. Throughout all she'd done, his presence had lingered with her, and his wink and his smile had revisited her mind at the most unexpected moments. *What is the matter with me? Have I fallen in love?* No, that couldn't be right, for Albert was far below her in standing. It was ridiculous – they would have nothing in common. *It must be the situation we are all in, playing with our emotions. I have to put him out of my mind!* Somehow, though, she knew she couldn't do that. With these thoughts confusing her, weariness crept into each limb, and tears plopped unbidden onto her cheeks.

"Ere, love, you have a good cry – we all do it. Shows we're 'uman. You did a fantastic job or, as you would probably say, "an absolutely spiffing job"!'

Edith had an urge to giggle at Connie's mimicking of her but, instead, deep rasping sobs racked her body. Connie stood by, waiting, not speaking. At last the deluge calmed. As Edith wiped her face on the apron she'd not yet discarded, the blood of a dozen men mingled with her tears, bringing home to her the pity of it all. Connie's cheery cockney voice saved her from descending once more into a pit of despair.

'Now you've made a right mess of yerself. Come on, there's a shower tent with hot water. Gawd knows yer could do with one. Go and 'ave a quick swill. But hurry back, as we'll need yer in a mo.'

As Edith washed the muck of the day from her face and arms and donned the clean overall that Connie had brought to her, she wondered why she would be needed. Yes, there were one or two cases that the nurses might have to call her to, but Connie had hinted that there was a greater reason for why she was required – a reason Edith hadn't yet been made aware of.

It didn't take long before the rumble of vehicles made the ground shudder, and grated on her ears. Leaving the tent and turning in the direction of the noise, she found Connie already outside. 'Okay, Doctor, ready for the final task of the day? These will be the dead. They collect them at night. They'll need identifying and certifying. Then the men will bury them. Nancy will help you.'

'Oh God!'

'Don't worry, me duck.' Nancy's flat Leicestershire tones soothed her. How often she'd heard the gardeners and stable hands of their country home use that expression. Not to herself of course, but still it gave her comfort, as Nancy continued, 'It's been a hard day – the first of many – but you've coped. And when we get ourselves sorted, we'll find ways of dealing with the horror. In the meantime I'll help you with this lot. I had one of the men fix up that tent over there to use as a morgue. And there'll be an officer with them, to do the paperwork. All must be done with the dignity that the boys deserve, and I know you'll do that.'

These last words from Nancy pulled her up. Yes, she would do this last thing for the soldiers, and she would do it keeping their pride and dignity in mind. But the sadness of it wrenched her heart, as for the umpteenth time she wrote 'Killed in Action' and watched the little pile of belongings, with an identifying tag resting on top, being packed away. Another life reduced to the size of a brown paper bag.

'Well, that's all done. When I emptied the last bucket, I saw Connie. She's done the rounds, and everyone is as best they can be. She was laughing, as one of them posh lot has set to and made us all some cocoa. Bet you could do with some, although I don't think it'll taste much better than ditch-water. Bloody hopeless, the VADs are.'

'Oh, I don't know – she may surprise you. Our nannies were very good at teaching us to fend for ourselves... Oh, I'm sorry, I sounded a bit off. Didn't mean to, I...'

'No, I've been around your class of people long enough now to take what you say as the way you mean it. You're used to different ways, that's all. I'm for a shower first. How about you?'

'Thanks, Nancy. It's nice to know I won't have to be on my guard all the time and that we'll get along. You're a jolly nice sort. And, yes, I'll take another quick shower before I tackle that cocoa.'

Lying on a camp-bed for the first time surprised Edith. It felt very similar to lying on a hammock and gave relief to her aching bones. For a moment she thought of her home in London, and of lazy days spent resting in the garden.

Hammocks would be slung between the trees, and she and her cousins would lie for hours chatting about their future. Well, *she* wouldn't chat exactly, but she would listen to Eloise and Andrina talking about how they would marry amazing men and throw wonderful parties. Why their heads were full of such stuff, she couldn't imagine.

For all their frivolity, they were intelligent young women; especially Eloise, whom Edith knew would secretly love a career. If only she had the courage to pursue her dream, rather than thinking it was hopeless to do so. Well, it wasn't, as she herself had proved. Women were fighting all the time for the right to live their lives as they chose, and to have a say in the politics of their country. She would do the same, once this was over, but not in the way Emmeline Pankhurst advocated. Becoming an arsonist, smashing windows and serving time in prison just wasn't her style. No, her way would be more along the lines that Elsie Inglis, her newfound hero, had taken.

Edith had found out more about this Scottish

lady after the arrival of her brother Christian's letter, and had liked what she'd learned. A supporter of women's suffrage, before her hospital war work Elsie had given talks and had shown by example what women could achieve. But Edith did agree with Mrs Pankhurst on one thing: change could only come about if women were given the right to vote. Everything had to start with that.

However, her thoughts didn't stay long with the part of her that would campaign. Instead, the image of Albert came into her mind. She hadn't seen him again, and when she'd asked where he'd gone, one of the ambulance men had said that Albert would be back in the trenches. It appeared that whenever he had a break, he'd offer to help the crew who had been assigned to erect the tents for the medical camp.

Her body shuddered at the thought of Albert in the trenches; and maybe even, at first light, going over the top to attack. Curling herself into a ball as she thought of this, she prayed: *Dear God, please keep him safe.*

3

Ada

Low Moor, July 1916
Decisions and retributions

Pacing up and down tired her and the cold slabs made her feet ache, but the restlessness didn't leave Ada, no matter what she did. Shaking her head in an effort to clear the heavy fog that clouded her mind, she felt as if she was sinking into madness.

It had been like this since the day Jimmy had left for France. He'd been home after a short leave in March, once his training was over – *if you could call it training: six weeks is all he'd had; six bloody weeks!* It seems they had shown him how to fire a rifle and not much else, by the sound of what Jimmy had told her. Then he'd been shipped out to fight. *The poor lad hardly knows one end of a gun from the other!* This thought made her blood run cold. *How will he cope? How will he keep from getting killed?*

Pulling herself up, Ada stopped her pacing and leant heavily on the wooden table. As she stared down at the many impressions crayons and pencils had made on it over the years, tears began to well up in her eyes. Running her finger over the indentations brought back memories of rainy days when her three lads had sat at this table, scribbling

43

away. *Oh God! I can't go on like this!* Folding her arms around as if to ward off the unbearable pain, she turned away from the table and stamped her foot in frustration. *I need a distraction. I have to do something with my time. I have to!*

Never a curtain twitcher in the past, Ada now found herself lifting the net from the window above her pot-sink and staring out. She did that now, and saw Mabel and Agatha, arms linked, making their way from the station. Mabel, the mother of Eric, and Agatha, the mother of Arthur – the two lads who had gone with Jimmy – hadn't stayed at home moping about; they'd got themselves a job. *That's it!*

Her cardigan resisted her tug as she dashed out of the door, so she left it hanging on the hook. Though she'd found it a chilly day when she'd hung a few bits out on her line earlier, she'd risk getting cold, rather than miss catching up with Mabel and Agatha. Seeing them had given her a solution, and she wanted to sort things before she lost her nerve.

'Hey! Mabel, Agatha, hold on a mo!'

'Eeh, Ada, you gave me a reet fright. What's wrong, lass?'

'Everything, Mabel. Where do I start? But it ain't me troubles I want to talk to you and Agatha about – it's a job. I've heard Low Moor hasn't got owt going. Not that I have enquired for meself, but my Paddy hears stuff, and he was saying that Low Moor was fully staffed. D'you know if there's any jobs going at the munitions factory you work at in Leeds?'

'It's called Barnbow. And, aye, there's a few.

But it ain't no cushy number…'

'Since when have I ever shied away from hard work, eh? The bloody cheek of you, Agatha Ark-wright!'

'Eeh, Ada, don't take on – I didn't mean that. I were just going to say as it's hard work, and I reckon you could find sommat a bit easier, if you were serious about it.'

'I'm sorry, lass, I shouldn't have taken offence. But, look, I don't want easy. I want sommat as'll take all me energy and keep me mind occupied in the day, and drain me so that I fall asleep at night.'

'By, working in the munitions will do that alreet, lass. Me and Mabel can hardly keep awake on the train going to, or coming home from, the factory. I'm dead on me feet now. We've been on early shift and started at five this morning, and that meant catching the train at four.'

'Aye, I can see as you're tired. Look, come in and have a cuppa. I've a pot on. I want to ask you more about it, and whether you think I stand a chance of getting set on.'

'I'll pass on the cuppa, if you don't mind…'

'Aye, and me too. Look, Ada, all me and Agatha want to do is get home. But, aye, you'd get set on. Crying out for workers, they are. I'll put a word in for you tomorrow and stop by tomorrow afternoon and let you know. But I reckon as you'll be on that train with us the next morning, so prepare yourself.'

Some of her despair lifted with this and made her step lighter. Closing the door once she was inside, Ada leant heavily on it. *What have I done? But then, Paddy will have to lump it. It's Barnbow*

Munitions Factory for me, no matter what he says!

A proud man, Paddy maintained that *he* was the breadwinner in the family. *Huh, I've yet to see the day!* She'd never known a time without worry over money, though it had eased a little when her lads had found work... No, she mustn't think of that time. They were gone, and that was that.

Even to her own mind that sounded harsh, but it was the only way she could cope.

Taking her cardigan and coat down from the peg behind the door, she pulled them on. It might be a bit chilly down here, but up the hill where her sister Beryl lived, it could fair cut you in two at times. But she needed to go there to talk about her plans.

The houses at the top of the hill were superior to the rows where Ada lived. The folk up there had jobs – or, rather, *positions*. Beryl's Bill was a bank clerk, and he was forward-thinking, in that he allowed Beryl to work. She managed the local grocery store for the owner, who had retired.

This meant they could have holidays each year and go to places like Llandudno. Beryl said that was in Wales, so it was like going abroad. *Eeh, what does it feel like to have a holiday and to see such places?* Nevertheless, Ada would not have swapped her life with Beryl's. Never to have had young 'uns? Naw, that was sommat as she wouldn't have wanted to miss out on.

As she neared Beryl's house, Ada saw her sister just going into her front gate. Looking at Beryl was like looking at herself, except that Beryl's figure was slighter and almost boyish-looking and she wore her hair short, whilst Paddy made Ada keep hers long. Not that Beryl's bob tamed her curls; if anything, they were worse than Ada's long ringlet ones, especially now, when the wind caught and ruffled them. A smile formed around Ada's lips at the thought of Beryl's hair looking like a dozen coiled red springs, stuck on her head. *Eeh, it must be the new hope in me, as that's the first time I've spread me face in a smile for a long time!*

Calling out to Beryl made her sister wave and beckon Ada over. When she reached the door Beryl said, 'Come in, love. Eeh, our Ada, I feel your sorrow every time I see you, lass, and it wakens up me own. Have you heard from Jimmy? Has he got there yet?'

'Naw. Lad won't write for a while, I shouldn't think. And if he did, it would take weeks to reach me.'

'I wonder how he is – if he's scared, bless him. I mean, he's bound to be really, when you think...'

'That's enough of that talk, Beryl. I can't take it. We have to keep thinking of him having the time of his life with his mates, and of them keeping each other safe. Now, open your door and let me in, and let's get a cuppa. There's som-mat as I want to talk to you about.'

Shaking her head, Beryl looked incredulous at this, but Ada ignored her. They say that talking of doom and gloom brings it down on you, and she had only managed to lift that feeling an inch high off her with the thought of her new plans, so she wasn't about to tempt fate and invite it back in.

Beryl's kitchen gleamed, as if a dozen women had set to and given it a spring-clean, but Ada knew that her sister kept it like that on her own.

She went over-the-top with her cleanliness, and scrubbed her house from floor to ceiling for most of the hours she was at home. Everywhere Beryl had control of was the same: pristine and in order.

'Sit yourself down, lass. Let me take your coat, and then I'll get you that pot of tea.'

'Naw, I'll see to the tea. You can take me coat, though, and then get yourself changed. You don't want to sit around in that overall.'

Making tea in Beryl's kitchen wasn't a chore. The sound of the water hitting the bottom of the gleaming copper kettle was like no other, and it was much easier from a brass-knobbed tap than ladled from a bucket filled from the communal water pump, as Ada and the lasses who lived around her had to do.

Once she'd put the kettle on the stand over the gas ring, she sat at the table, careful not to disturb the whiter-than-white lace cloth. It was one of a set of two that their mam had crocheted. She had the other, though hers was packed away and only came out on high days and holidays. She couldn't risk it being spoiled. It was all she had of her mam's. *Oh, Mam, if only you were here.* Tears stung her eyes at this thought.

A noise pulled her up and made her blink the tears away. She knew what it was, but it still sounded unfamiliar: Beryl had flushed her inside lav. *Eeh, I never thought I would see the like. A lav inside the house!* There was no going out to the bog in the yard and sharing it with a neighbour at the back, when you lived on the hill. No, Beryl only had to cross the hall. And her lav didn't have to be emptied by the cart at night, either, because you

48

could flush the contents away by pulling a chain with a fancy pot-handle on the end of it. *Eeh, whatever next?*

But then everything around her was a marvel to Ada. This kitchen of Beryl's was like something from another world, compared to her own scullery-cum-living room. The red-tiled floor was polished till it gleamed, and yet it wasn't slippery. That was in contrast to her own brick-stone floor, with dirt so ground into the grooves that even taking a wire brush to them never shifted it. Here, the blue-painted cupboards stretched along under the window and butted up to the pot-sink, with its checked blue-and-white curtain looking fresh and pretty. They were nothing like the wooden bench-table she had, with its shelf underneath for storage. And then there was the dresser made of dark oak. Its deep polish gave it a rich texture that provided a lovely backdrop to the beautiful blue china plates displayed on it. She had just four of her own plates, as Paddy had broken his and now used the one their Bobby had used; they were stacked on a shelf next to the stove, along with the few other bits of china she possessed. *But then these are only possessions and, much as I'd like to own them, I'd still not trade places with Beryl.*

The whistle of the kettle brought Ada out of her thoughts and coincided with Beryl's return to the kitchen, giving her no time to look busy. Her sister had a jibe at her, as was her way, laughing as she did. 'Eeh, our Ada, you haven't the pot ready, nor the cups. By, lass, I can't trust you to do owt right.' With this, Beryl took the tea towel from its hook and hit out at her with it. Ada ducked and giggled,

49

and the last of the sad feelings that had taken her earlier disappeared.

They made the tea together. Ada set out the china cups and Beryl scooped three spoons of tea from the caddy into the pot. As Beryl poured the boiling water onto the tea leaves she said, 'Reet, let's have it. Tell me what's on your mind, while the tea brews. If you need owt to tide you over, just say how much – it's there for you, you know that.'

'Ta, Beryl, I could do with half a crown, if you have it to spare. Paddy lost on the horses again. But that isn't what I came for. I need your help with Paddy. I want to go out to work, and I'm wondering if you would talk to him.'

'Ha, Ada, that's a relief. I thought you were going to ask me to help you cope with his antics; stand in for you, or sommat!'

'You daft ha'porth! Ha, you wouldn't stand a chance with him. I told you it ain't like I imagine your Bill is, when he beds you – all gentleness and thoughtfulness.'

'Oh, don't tell me any more or you'll have me blushing. So, you want me to help you persuade Paddy to let you go to work. By, we've a job on there. Look, all I can think of to do is turn a bit nasty with him. Tell him I'm calling in all the loans he's had....'

'Oh, Beryl, he hasn't been at that game, has he?'

'Aye, he's up here regular, but don't let it worry you. He don't allus get what he comes for. I can handle him. I stopped him that time you had a black eye and told him if he did it again, he'd get nothing. And that worked.'

Ada was aghast; she'd had no idea. But Beryl

wasn't right in thinking she'd helped to stop Paddy's violence. Oh, aye, he avoided her face lately, but she had bruises to tell the story of many a beating when he was in a foul mood. Hidden bruises.

'So, lass. What do you think then, eh? I'll tell him he can't have any more, until he has paid what he owes. Then you tell him you've a chance of bringing in some earnings.'

'It could work – it's worth a try, anyroad. Thanks, Beryl, and I'm sorry you've been bothered by Paddy. I didn't know of it. And I feel ashamed at you giving handouts to me an' all, and on a regular basis.'

'Don't – you've no need. I just fell lucky, that's all. I got a good 'un in Bill, and you fell for a ne'er-do-well. Though a charming one, I have to say.'

This last triggered a worry in Ada. How come Beryl felt so confident that cutting off Paddy's loans would make a difference? She couldn't see it herself. If one source of income dried up for Paddy, he found another. And why hadn't Beryl ever said about him getting money from her in the first place? It felt like a betrayal. *Me own sister in cahoots with me husband, behind me back. And the way she said as Paddy was charming... Don't say – no, she wouldn't... He wouldn't ... would they?* Disgust at the thought made Ada shiver.

'You alreet, sis? You've gone quiet.'

'Aye, I'm fine. I just hate me situation, that's all. Having to beg money from you and then finding that Paddy's been doing the same. I think I'll get off home. I've a queasy feeling in me belly. Forget the half a crown. I didn't come up here for

51

money, so I can do without it. I'll see you in a few days. When will you see Paddy?'

'He'll be up later, no doubt. It's usually a Thursday when he comes, as he knows that's the night Bill works late. Mind, Bill doesn't know owt about Paddy's loans, and I don't want him knowing. Look, take the half a crown – you must need it or you wouldn't have taken me offer. Go on. I'd feel better if you did.'

Taking the coin further sickened Ada, but she didn't have a choice. She didn't want Beryl to think she was upset about anything other than her situation. Or to suspect what was going on in her mind. No, she'd let things be as they would normally be. But one thing she knew: she'd a job to do tonight. She'd follow Paddy and see just what was going on.

The awfulness of her thoughts hit Ada when she reached her home. Taking her coat off, she slumped onto a chair and rested her arms on the table, putting her head down onto them. Unable to stop the tears, she let them flow. How could she even have considered Beryl and Paddy together? Beryl wouldn't do such a thing to her. Oh, aye, Paddy would. She'd caught him out many a time and, though he denied it, she knew he was putting himself about. Why did it hurt so much, after all these years? She wasn't even sure she loved him any more. But he was hers. Her man. They were good together and, despite everything, she didn't want to lose that. The passion they shared was all she had left. It was something to look forward to. Why did he need to do it with others?

Though these thoughts caused her pain, she knew they were not all she was crying about. She needed a release from the thoughts and feelings about her sons, which she kept cooped up inside her.

Each tick of the clock on the mantel shelf filled the silent space she sat in, marking the time since she'd arrived home from Beryl's. Now the seven chimes it gave out reverberated around the room like a bell-ringer tolling the death-knell. Paddy still hadn't returned home.

He'd gone out that morning saying that he was going to see if there was a chance of a morning's work, and had then sent her a message to say he'd been given an afternoon's tatting with Mick Smith, the rag-and-bone man. Mick often took Paddy on his rounds looking for scrap metal. He reckoned Paddy could charm anything out of those who would hoard it forever, rather than part with it: old iron bedsteads and bicycle frames, that sort of thing. Come to think of it, it was usually a Thursday when Paddy went with Mick, and Paddy always came in late and smelling of beer, saying he'd had to wash the muck of the job from his throat. While she was thinking about it, he always tipped up a couple of bob to her. Not that it was every Thursday, but every couple of weeks or so. And Thursday was Beryl's half-day! But if he *did* spend his Thursdays visiting Beryl, why did he come in covered in muck? *Oh, stop it!* It was as if she had no control of where her mind went these days. Paddy would be down the Black Horse, she was sure of it.

Despite these thoughts, her body rose up in defiance. Standing still for a moment, she fought with herself: *Don't do this, lass, you'll make a fool of yourself.* But the voice inside her wasn't listened to, and once more she donned her coat and put on her felt, cloche-style hat, tugging on the brim to make sure it sat securely on her head before leaving her cottage.

Passing the Black Horse, she stood on tiptoe to look over the frosted glass bottom-half of the window. She could see a few heads of men she recognized, and knew others would be sitting down and out of sight, but she couldn't see Paddy. She couldn't go in. Women didn't go into pubs. Well, not nice women. Whores did. And if any woman decided to – even just to get her man – she was classed as one of them.

The door opening caused the smell of beer and tobacco to waft over towards her. She quickened her step and scurried on past the pub, hoping that whoever it was hadn't seen her peeping through the window. 'Ada? Is that you? Are you alreet, lass?'

Mick Smith! 'Aye, I am. I'm short of a bit of sugar and Lucy Freeman owes me a cup, so I'm just going to see if she has any. I need to get back before Paddy comes in. Is he still in the bar?'

'I've not seen him all day, lass. He's not in there. Happen he's gone up to the Black Dog. He plays cards up there sometimes.'

Her heart sank with these words, but she held herself together. 'No matter. I'm not looking for him – he'll come home when he's ready. Night, Mick.'

'See you around. Oh, and tell Paddy I might have a day for him on Monday.'

Keeping her footsteps steady, Ada walked in the direction of Lucy Freeman's house. It didn't take long for Mick to come from around the back of the pub with his horse and cart. He would have kept it in the yard of the pub whilst he had his pint. The clip-clopping of the horse's hooves and the grinding of the wheels of the cart on the cobbled road grated on her nerves.

Glad when he'd gone from sight, Ada slipped into the ginnel and slumped against the wall of the corner house. *Oh God, no.* But what other explanation could there be? Paddy had lied about going out with Mick. Beryl had never said, before today, that she gave money to him. Paddy went there on a Thursday. Beryl had an early-closing day on a Thursday, and Bill worked late. *And Beryl was for getting me gone today, whereas usually she keeps me as long as she can, gossiping and such. Not that there can be much in that. Her half-day is when she does her washing ... or was she wanting me out because...? No – it can't be!*

Pulling her shaking body up, Ada turned with determination towards the hill. She'd go there – she had to. She had to know.

Beryl's house looked as it always did. The gas-lights were lit downstairs, and a light showed from an upstairs window. This one was unsteady and gave off the flickering light of an oil lamp. Barely discernible, moving shadows danced and then disappeared, then formed again on the closed, cream-coloured curtains.

Ada's world, which was resting precariously on a fine needle-point, rocked as it dawned on her what the shadows might mean. Despite her warm coat, her limbs trembled and what felt like ice-cold fingers clutched at her heart. A deep moan that seemed to start in her bowel rumbled through her. When it reached her throat it emerged as a piercing scream, over which she had no control.

Windows and doors opened. Voices shouted, 'What's going on?' and 'Who's there?'

The scream died, leaving her throat sore and aching. Opening her eyes, she watched what she knew was an oil lamp being carried, as its light left the bedroom, swung past the porthole window on the landing, then appeared bit by bit at the bottom of the stairs, until it flooded the porch and the front door opened. Paddy stood there without a shirt, holding the lamp aloft.

'Nooooo!'

Without realizing she had moved, Ada found herself in front of Paddy, clawing at him as if she were a wild animal. Her nails gouged deep scratches into his cheeks. Hot, stinging tears rained down her face, the salt hitting her tongue. Slimy snot ran from her nose, but she didn't care. The hurt within her strangled her, and left her incapable of feeling or caring about anything other than bringing this man as low as he had brought her.

Hands tried to hold her. Voices – those of Paddy and Beryl, and of strangers – implored her to stop, but she couldn't.

Escaping the hands, she flung herself at Beryl. Beryl the betrayer, the deceiver, the husband-stealer. Well, she'd make sure she stole no one else's husband. She'd rip that pretty smile off her sister's face and tear her red curls from her head.

'Stop it. Ada, please stop it. You're hurting me, and you're making a fool of us all. Stop it!'

'Stop it! Making a fool of meself ... of you!' Turning to face the small crowd that had gathered, Ada pulled herself to her full height. 'Well, lovely posh neighbours, what d'you think of me sister then, eh? Doesn't really fit in with you all, does she? Well, watch out, or she'll shag all of your men! She's already started with mine. Seen him, have you? Coming to visit on a Thursday? Aye, well, he won't be coming any more, so take a good look at him while you can. Go on, you snooty-nosed–'

A blow caught the side of her head, sending her reeling backwards. Her body catapulted in the air, as though she'd been shot from the barrel of a cannon, before landing on the ground as if it were a bag of rags. Her teeth clamped onto her tongue, spittle ran from the side of her mouth, and blood seeped down her throat.

A voice – a posh male voice – shouted, 'Now then, there is no need for that. Someone go and fetch the police.'

Only one of her eyes would open, but with it she stared with hatred at Beryl. Lit by the light of the lamp that Paddy had retrieved, Beryl's face was a river of tears and blood. 'I'm sorry, our Ada, I'm reet sorry. I didn't think as you'd care. You never had a good word for Paddy, and I ... well, I never get owt from Bill, he ... he can't do it.'

'Sorry? You bitch! You have all of this and you

try to take Paddy an' all. How could you? Such as he is, he is all that I have...' Ada's voice had gone from a nasty grating tone to whimpering the last few words.

'She was for paying me, Ada. It wasn't that I was for wanting to do it – it was nothing to me. I just wanted to bring some money home to you.'

Beryl turned on Paddy, hitting out, but he caught her fist and snarled, at her, 'Isn't it that you're just a whore in reverse? You're not for selling it; you're for buying a cock to satisfy yourself with. And I was easy pickings – me being in need of the money.' With this, he flung her away from him.

A moment's silence was shattered by a high-pitched scream from Beryl, and with it words that Ada wished she'd never have to hear: 'I'm having your babby. I'm five months gone, you stinking sod! You said you would leave Ada for me, so I let you go all the way! Oh God... Bill can't have kids, so he'll know!'

Getting up off the floor, Ada felt the pity of the situation. Some of that pity was for this sister of hers, who had everything and yet nothing; and for Bill, poor Bill... But most of what she felt wasn't pity at all, but loneliness. That her own sister could plot to take her man. That she should be carrying a babby, which she herself could no longer give him. That all the babbies she had given Paddy should be taken from her – for surely that is what would happen to Jimmy? The bloody Germans would shoot him, or blow him up. She'd resigned herself to that.

Turning away, she mustered all the strength and

dignity she could and limped off down the hill. Life had changed. It was not her life any more. She was not herself any more. But she would have to get on with it. Whatever Paddy decided to do, she would go and get that job at the munitions factory. That would save her. She would work hard, and not give herself time to think of all that used to be. Instead she would put away as much money as she could – and in a safer place than her bag – and get herself out and away from it all.

4

Eloise and Andrina

Rossworth Hall, Leicestershire, July 1916
An unbearable life

'I'm so bored, Eloise. Nothing fun happens any more. It's all the fault of this bloody war!' Andrina's sigh travelled heavily around the room. She and Eloise were engaged in embroidering cushion covers that would be sent to a local fete, which was being held to help raise funds for the war effort.

They sat facing each other on dainty Queen Anne chairs, one each side of the French windows that overlooked the croquet lawn of Rossworth Hall. It was a pleasant room decorated in restful colours – beiges and pale greens – and, besides the chairs, which were covered in a light-green velvet, two pink-and-green Regency striped sofas (also in Queen Anne style) stood against the walls opposite each other and facing the centre of the room. Ornate occasional tables were placed in handy positions and held writing cases and pens, and workboxes with silk threads and needles inside, and one was piled high with books. It was a room reserved for quiet activities such as they were doing now, or for reading – something Eloise did a lot of, but Andrina rarely bothered with. Unless, of course, it was *The Queen* magazine, and then she liked to catch up on the latest gossip and fashions; but of late even that had been full of doom and gloom and 'Your country needs you' type of jargon.

'Don't you ever feel a little guilty about that – the war, I mean? Well, and us being bored, while it rages? I know I do. I was talking to Mama about it and she was going to look into what more we could all do to help.'

This appalled Andrina. 'Us? Help? What – more than we are at the moment, by making these bloody awful cushion covers! Oh, Eloise, you don't mean you think we should go to France, do you?'

'Why not? Edith has, and cousins Christian and Douglas; and our friends Martha and Jennifer have too.'

'Oh, but Edith is a different case. She has a skill that is needed. And the boys had to enlist – it was the honourable thing to do. But what on earth have Martha and Jennifer gone for? What can they do?'

'They are voluntary aid workers, and they help out wherever they are needed. I'm seriously thinking of joining myself.'

For a moment Andrina was shocked into silence. This wasn't what she'd expected. Yes, life was unbearable, with hardly any social activities to distract them, but to go and join in and ... well, *help!* No, nothing could be further from what she wanted to do. Oh, it was all so unfair. Why should there be a war now? Just as she and Eloise had reached the age when life should be fun.

'Please don't join, Eloise. I couldn't bear it. Anyway, what can you do that could possibly be of any help?'

'I can drive. I can sew. And write – I love to write. I could go as a news correspondent, or help out in the stores doing inventories. Anything, really.'

Pushing her embroidery stand away from her, Andrina rose. Her world of boredom had suddenly become a world of fear. Eloise couldn't go – she wouldn't let her. What would life be like without her? Even more unbearable than it was now. 'Have you spoken to Mama about this? I'm sure she would have something to say... Look, I bet it is just the boredom of it all that is persuading you. It is better when we are in London. Let's talk to Mama about us going back there. At least something goes on there, even if it is just tea at the Ritz.'

Going to the window, Andrina looked out at the view. The rolling green landscape of the gardens was beautifully laid out, to a design by Capability Brown himself; clutches of trees – some standing as tall as the house and others miniatures, with dark-red and gold leaves – surrounded by flowers of every colour made a beautiful picture. As a young child she had loved this home in Leicester-shire: horse-riding, playing games on the vast lawns, and feeling as free as a bird. But now the horses had been taken, as they were needed by the Horse Guards – God knows what fate would be-come them. And playing games just didn't appeal to her any more. She felt like a caged animal. Eloise hadn't answered her. She had this madden-ing habit of staying quiet if there was even a hint of confrontation.

Oh, I've had enough. I have to get out in the fresh air. I feel stifled! As this thought died, Andrina saw Jay Tattumby cross the bottom of the lawn, pushing a wheelbarrow into the kitchen garden. A strange young man, he fascinated her, and had done since the early days when he hung around the estate as a small boy, stone-deaf and unable to communicate with anyone except their old gardener, who had taken Jay everywhere with him and had somehow found a way of getting through to him.

That had changed over the years, as Jay had mastered the knack of lip-reading and had patiently been taught how to speak by Mrs Tat-tumby, his adoptive mother.

His dark good looks told of the fact that he must have come from the gypsies. But no one knew for sure. The mystery surrounding him piqued her curiosity. Florrie, her maid, had told her it was said that Jay had powers and could tell the future. The story went that he had been left on the doorstep of Mrs Tattumby, the local butcher's wife, when he was just a baby, only hours old. A gypsy camp had been in the area at the time and the gypsies had disappeared, so everyone assumed it had been them who had dumped him.

Florrie had spoken of Jay being unable to go to war, but wanting to, with a note in her voice that told of her attraction to him.

Andrina had to admit to feeling a ridiculous attraction to him herself. There was something about him. It was a magnetism she couldn't explain. Lately she had made it her mission on several occasions to 'bump' into Jay, and the attraction she'd felt had warmed into a desire. Damn it, she'd even fantasized about him, and had experienced a nice feeling in her groin as she did so. Shame washed over her as she remembered exploring herself and intensifying the feeling, until she'd come to her senses and had risen from her bed, summoning Florrie and asking her maid to pour her a glass of water. This action had calmed her.

Women were not meant to have such feelings and, on many occasions since, she'd had to resist the temptation to invoke them again. It had been the mystery of it all that had frightened her and stopped her. Oh, she realized there was something to be done with a man when she married, but what it was she did not know. No one ever talked about it, not even when her monthlies started. But, along with instructions on how to care for herself, she had been told by Nanny that, now she was blossoming into a woman, she would be able to have children of her own in the future.

She also knew that the parts she had touched were involved in this process, but how? She hadn't ever looked at them. Not really – just a quick glance on one occasion when her robe had slipped as she stood in front of the mirror. She'd been so afraid of being caught and looked upon as a shameful person that she had covered up very quickly.

Her fear had stemmed from the fact that Nanny had never allowed the girls to uncover themselves. They always had to wear a shift when they bathed, and a large tent-like garment that Nanny had made would be put over their heads and draped over them whilst they dressed. Then, at school, there had been strict rules and chaperoning, and nothing had ever been said between her and her friends. Even now she still wore a shift whilst her maid attended to her, washing and dressing her.

'You've gone very quiet, Andrina. Are you all right, dear?'

A blush flushed her face as it seemed that her soul had been laid bare. 'Y – yes, of course. I – I was being silly. I just don't like the thought of change. I think I will go out to the garden and get some air.'

Relieved that Eloise hadn't suggested coming with her, Andrina left it until she was in the hall before she summoned the butler to bring her wrap.

Strolling across the lawn, she was shocked to realize that her heartbeat was racing with a mixture of fear at the impropriety of what she intended, and the anticipation of being near to Jay.

The flowers gave off a heady scent as she passed each bed, but none as strong as the lilies that grew in clumps around the pond and nestled in the ripples of the water. Hesitating here for a moment, she smiled as she saw a frog on the slate surround. His neck puffed up as he pursued and tried to lure a lady frog, who was on the base of the stone fountain looking unimpressed.

I'm like you two in reverse, as in my case it's the female after the male! What was she thinking? Oh God! She ought to go back – this was a silly thing to do. Turning, she was about to march back to the house when she heard a cough. Swivelling back round and seeing Jay standing by the wall tightened the muscles in her throat. He looked more handsome than ever as the sun gleamed on his hair, picking out the blue lights in the black-ness of it, with his smile shining in his eyes.

'I knew you would come.'

Embarrassment tinged her cheeks. 'Are you talking to me? If so, please address me correctly.' Oh dear, that wasn't what she had wanted to say. She'd wanted to say, *Yes, I have come. I could not help myself.*

His grin widened, showing his remarkably white teeth. Most people of his class had dirty teeth and an unkempt appearance. Jay always looked clean and … well, almost aristocratic. His stance held an arrogance that would normally be seen in a gentleman of means.

'I beg your pardon, M'lady.' His exaggerated bow made a mockery of his words. 'I forget my manners, in my eagerness to see you.'

Again that hint of a cultured person – not in his heavily pronounced voice, which gave away his deafness, but in his choice of words. Who was he really? Who had left him on the doorstep of one of the kindest people in the village? Andrina somehow didn't think it was a gypsy girl.

'I forgive you. And it is nice to see you again. I was on my way to the kitchen garden. I wanted to pick some strawberries for myself and my sister. I know I shouldn't pick them, but I enjoy being in the garden, and I prefer strawberries to the usual fruitcake that we have in the afternoons.' *What am I babbling on about? He must think me a pompous idiot!*

'I will help you, M'lady.' Opening the gate behind him, Jay bowed to her in a gesture that said she should pass through. Her arm brushed his as she did so, enhancing the nervous excitement she felt.

'Thank you. But I can manage.'

Without taking any heed of her, he followed her through.

Looking at him, she said, 'I said I can manage, thank you.' He pointed to his ears. Her stupid forgetfulness flustered her. 'I – I'm sorry. I forgot.'

'Thank you, M'lady. When people forget, I feel that I am normal.'

'Oh, you are! I – I mean, why shouldn't you be? Please leave me now.' His nearness was too much for her.

'I don't think you want me to leave, M'lady.' A mixture of fear and excitement shivered through her body. She couldn't take her eyes from his. His voice caressed her. 'Don't be afraid of me. I would never hurt you. You are all I think about. My life is nothing when you are away.'

'Oh dear, I…'

His body swayed towards her. She froze. Half of

her wanted him to kiss her, but the other half screamed out in protest that be had the temerity to do so. Her hesitation lost her the battle. His lips touched hers. Sinking into his body, she allowed the kiss, drank it in, felt the world become a different place and knew herself to be changed forever.

When he released her, he made no apology. His eyes told her what was in his heart. And she knew that hers gave back all the love he had for her.

'Andrina, where are you?'

Eloise! Oh no. Shrinking back from Jay, she looked over towards the closed gate. Her sister was not yet in sight. 'Go, Jay, please go.' Mouthing the words did not matter, for he knew what she had said. Anger flickered in his eyes, but he said nothing, just turned and walked away.

The hinge of the garden gate squealed its protest at being opened. It was funny that she hadn't heard it do that when she had passed through it.

'I'm here. I'm just going to get a basket to fill with strawberries. I thought I would prepare them for you in the summerhouse and we could have them for our tea instead of cake.'

'You are a strange one at times. Oh, is that Jay? I haven't seen him yet. Did you speak to him? Is everything all right with him?'

Thank goodness Eloise didn't see what passed between us.

'Why do you say I'm a strange one? I was bored, so I thought I would do something different – that's all.'

'But to come into the kitchen garden and pick your own strawberries? That isn't like you at all. Even when you are looking for something

67

different to do, you have never chosen to do what one of the servants could do for you. What are you up to, Andrina? You worry me sometimes.'

Eloise's glance went to Jay's retreating back and then came back to Andrina. Holding her breath, Andrina hoped there was no hint in her demeanour of what had just taken place and was mortified when the blush that had started to creep up from her neck flushed her face. Eloise's eyes narrowed and she asked, 'You wouldn't do anything improper, would you, Andrina? The servants and gardeners are our responsibility. We must treat them with respect and in a proper manner at all times. If you have stepped over the line, you had better put things right immediately. Am I to call Jay back?'

'No! No, please don't. We conversed, and he forgot his manners. I chastised him. That is all. He is embarrassed, but he's back in his place. You mustn't put him through it twice. *Please!*'

'Very well. Come on – let's forget it. I'll help you pick the strawberries; it will be fun.'

Able to breathe more freely at last, Andrina wiped away the beads of sweat that had formed on her brow and was glad of the distraction of turning her back on Eloise and crossing to the pile of baskets stacked near the greenhouse. Taking one of them back to Eloise, she found herself thinking about Jay's background once more.

'Don't you find Jay a bit of a mystery? I mean, it is thought he belonged to the gypsies, but from what I have heard, they are more likely to steal a baby than give one away. And Jay has this air about him. Sometimes he appears to be more of a gentleman than a working-class man.'

'Is that wishful thinking, dear sister? Look, I've seen how you are attracted to him. Please don't be. Please put all thoughts of him out of your mind, for it can only end in heartache for you, and worse for him.'

'That is nonsense. How dare you suggest such a thing? I'm disgusted with you, Eloise!'

'Well, just be careful. It is easy to fall for someone who is out of bounds. It's the excitement of it. Look, why don't we look into doing some war work? It would be wonderful to be with Edith, or some of the others who have gone. And it cannot possibly be as bad as everyone is saying. What do you think?'

What did she think! She hated the thought of anything that would take her away from Jay. Now that they had declared, by way of a kiss, how they felt for each other, she didn't even want to go back to London again. It was ironic, given that only half an hour ago she'd been longing to go back there.

'That was a big sigh. Sorry, old thing – I didn't mean to badger you. I understand. But, for me, I have to do my bit for the war.'

And I have to pursue my impossible love, thought Andrina. *That will mean a war in itself, and being ostracized from society. Will I be able to bear that?*

At this moment she did not know.

5

Albert and Jimmy

The Battle of Albert, the Somme, July 1916
Another disastrous day

A corporal in General Allenby's Third Army, Albert Price knew he'd done well. A volunteer, he'd taken to the scant training that he'd been given and had come out with flying colours. Keen to do his duty to the best of his ability, he'd made it his business to learn all he could from the regular-army blokes. Now he had the sort of responsibility he probably wouldn't be given if there hadn't been a war on. But, with so many killed, he had been the only choice the officers had. Albert hoped he had the qualities that would be needed. It had seemed strange to him that the battle they were engaged in was called the Battle of Albert – oh, he knew that it was pronounced differently to his name, as this place sounded more like 'Albear', but it was spelt the same. Not that it made any difference what the battle was called; the hardship and terror of it never left them. With every day it became more difficult to follow the order of the whistle and send his young boys over the top of the trench; and even to go over himself, as each time he was certain a bullet had his name on it.

Sometimes he wished it had, because life in the trenches worsened with every passing hour. Incessant rain turned the ground into a bog that sucked everything into it. His feet were constantly wet and bitterly cold. But today, the 10th of July, was different: the sun was up, the sky was blue and some of the ruts in the ground were beginning to crust over. He hoped it wasn't an omen that things were going to go badly; it had been like this on the first day of the Somme offensive and that had been a disastrous day.

Not used to the warm, humid atmosphere, Albert ran his finger around his collar to allow the air to circulate. As he did so, he noticed one or two of the boys fanning themselves. Some of them he'd never seen before, as the faces around him changed daily and diminished in number. Frightened boys, too young to be here, came and died. He shuddered to think how many faces he'd helped to cover with the death-wrap and had shoved dirt on, in the mass graves. But worse than that were the injured. He always helped to move them to the clearing stations, and sometimes, if he could get permission, helped those that he knew would die get to the hospital, so that he could be with them when they took their last breath. Promising impossible things to them, then helping to bury them.

Why? Why, in the course of the Earth's history, were they the chosen ones to do this job? Through lack of food and being eaten alive by lice and rats, they were like corpses themselves; they were not up to the job. But he would not show that.

Looking along the line of kids he would have to

71

shove over to their almost certain death, he caught the eye of young Jimmy O'Flynn. Jimmy had only joined them this week, but already he had found a place in Albert's heart. A bright kid, he'd shown intelligence in the way he picked up new skills quickly, and his cheeky manner made for a bit of light-hearted banter. But that was slowly diminishing, as the reality of war took hold. After trudging for nearly one hundred miles, Jimmy and his pals had arrived exhausted. One battle – their first – had halved their number. That was a lot for a kid to take.

On his first trip up the ladder to the top of the trench and over into no-man's-land, Jimmy had turned, just before disappearing, and had given a wink, saying, 'I'll show them.' The lad had come here with spirit in his belly, wanting to avenge the deaths of his brothers. His spirit was now in his socks. At this moment it seemed to have deserted him altogether, as his huge eyes stared out of sunken sockets. Eyes that held despair.

All Albert could do was nod at Jimmy in a fatherly way, as no words would be heard over the barrage of explosions that made your ears sing and hurt your throat; not that he knew how a father would react in any given situation. He'd been brought up in an orphanage – a prison for children whom no one loved. Shaking this thought from him, he hooked on to the hope they all had for this attack.

The strategy had been to bombard the enemy line, and hope to make a hole in the Germans' barbed-wire defences and take out some of their powerful guns, leaving the way clear for a final assault that should result in wiping out the Germans and bring a swift end to the war, or at least create a defining moment towards that goal.

Forgetting Jimmy and the rest of the lads for a moment, Albert allowed himself to think of Edith. He couldn't believe that he would ever meet someone like her. She was well above his station in life and very beautiful, in a calm sort of a way, with a loveliness that shone from her. No, that was too soppy a way to describe her, as she had guts and a determination that he hadn't come across in many men, let alone in a woman.

To think, though, that there was a chance she returned his feelings! It was an impossible thought, but when he'd been at the hospital with a badly injured lad a couple of days ago, they'd had a moment together. He'd used every ounce of his courage and told her, 'I 'ope I'm not speaking out of turn, as I wouldn't want to offend yer, but I think I am falling in love with yer.' Ha! Imagine him using such fancy words. If she had been one of his own kind, he'd have said, 'Cor, I don't 'alf fancy you, girl' in the good old London way. But she wasn't, and he knew how to speak proper when it was called for.

She'd blushed and looked down at the ground.

He'd been mortified and tried to explain. 'I'm sorry, Edith, I 'ad no right to speak out. Yer come from a different world ter me, but I might die any day and I'd do so a lot 'appier knowing you knew 'ow I felt.'

She'd raised those lovely hazel eyes of hers and told him, 'Albert, I am very attracted to you, but it is difficult.'

He'd nearly jumped for joy. She'd said she was attracted to him! But her saying it was difficult had dampened his spirits, as it had highlighted the gulf between them. And that was as wide and almost as hard to cross as the Somme. But then, what did all that matter now? Leaning towards her, he'd said, 'Love can conquer all, they say, Edith. Besides, people are changing – all this is changing us. And it's likely that me being a cockney lad and you a lady won't make a difference. Go with your feelings, Edith, not with bloody convention.'

Still looking into his eyes and stumbling over her words, she'd sealed his happiness by saying, 'I – I'm not used to baring my soul, Albert, but I do have feelings for you. I can't explain it, and it is something I never dreamed would happen, but I can't stop thinking about you. I ... it's just. Oh, I don't know, I...'

His heart had hurt with the way he longed to take her in his arms. But he couldn't. He didn't care what would happen to himself, but he couldn't bring that trouble down on Edith. No fraternizing was the rule; and, besides, she might have been upset by such an action. He had to remember that she wasn't his usual type. He had to act differently with her. Take his time.

But he hadn't left her without gaining something. Besides knowing she had feelings for him, she'd agreed to a date with him! He'd told her his rest period was due and had asked her if she would meet up with him. He had three days owing to him, and they were scheduled for the last week of July – a time that seemed would never come and now felt like years away, as his longing for them had increased, knowing that he was to spend some of it with Edith. Well, at least she had said she would like to, and would try to arrange a day off. He was ignoring the fact that she'd added, 'But only as a friend. Please do not read any more into this, and you must understand that it has to be a secret, as my reputation is at stake.'

Albert had taken her acceptance as confirmation that her feelings were deeper than she'd admit to. *God, please let me live to make that meeting. Just this one is all I ask, as I've no right to ask you to spare me. Not when so many around me are dying. But while I'm speaking to you, can you look after me lads today? Bring them all back and in one piece.* His 'Amen' went into the sound of an almighty crash, the biggest blast of the offensive. As it died away, the shrill sound of a whistle pierced the air around him. *This is it!*

Waving the lads up the ladder, he told each one, 'Good luck is with yer today. The Germans 'ave 'ad their defences blown to kingdom come, so go get 'em, son.'

They went over without protest. Some didn't get far before they were caught in machine-gun crossfire and had the life blasted out of their bodies. Others made a few yards' progress before they too fell; dead or injured, he did not know, but by the time he went over the top himself, he knew his face to be awash with tears, as his feet trod the bodies of his lads deeper into the caked mud. But there was no time to zigzag between them.

Those still standing were moving slowly forward, snipers picking them off as they went. This wasn't

75

supposed to be happening! The barrage of bombs should have given them an easy walk across. 'Take all you can' had been the order. Some of the packs loaded onto the lads' backs must weigh around fifty pounds. 'And walk,' they'd been told. 'Conserve your energy' *It was madness, bloody madness.* His own bloody pack weighed a ton! Sometimes he questioned the mentality of his superiors, for they could have made sure they'd gained ground and a new strategic point, and then sent parties back for their supplies.

'Keep your heads low, lads. Keep pushing forward.'

Enemy fire whizzed past him as he shouted this. *Please, God, don't let me name be on a bullet today!*

An order of 'Fire at will' came to him. Looking to the east and west, he saw very few young men still on their feet, but to those that were he shouted, 'Keep firing. It may just stop the bastards from raising their 'eads. And keep close to me.'

The words had hardly died when a body catapulted into the air and landed in front of him, tripping him up. His hand squelched into the pulp of the body's chest as he tried to pull himself up. Sickened, he screamed, 'You fucking bastards – I'll kill the lot of you.' But his words were lost in another explosion to the left of him.

Stones and clods of mud hit him, bruising and cutting his skin. Then a bigger object hit his shoulder, sending him off-balance again. It landed at his feet. He stared at the hideous sight of a boot with a leg that had a shattered bone, hanging sinews and a bulging muscle protruding from it as though it was vomiting them out of its severed end. His tears mingled with his snot as he felt for his ammunition.

Reloading his rifle, he shook his head to try and clear the muffled effect the last explosion had had on his hearing – not that he wanted to hear the screams or the cries for help from his comrades, but not doing so made him feel as though the world had deserted him, as a lonely feeling took him.

Ready to battle again, he charged forward. There were lads with him, but he couldn't say how many or who they were. As he squinted through the fog of smoke and dust, what he saw made his heart sink into his boots. *Christ, the barbed-wire barrier is still intact!* The barrage of bombs hadn't cut through it. They were doomed.

A bugle sounding the retreat came through the fog in his head. Would he get back to the trench alive? His eyes seared with pain as they took in the sight of a field of bodies. His feet squelched in a river of blood.

Looking towards the German trenches, he focused on where most of the fire had come from. A machine-gun barrel protruded from a gap in the sandbag wall, but to the right of it he spotted a gaping hole. A bomb must have had a direct hit. 'Get rid of your packs and follow me,' he said to those remaining.

Rolling under the twisted wire, he had to tug himself free more than once, ripping his grey coat to shreds. 'Come on – do it. We have to take that machine gun out.' As he spoke, the gun swung towards them. 'Lay low, lads.'

But the gun swung away and fired into a group

of retreating soldiers. The Germans must not have seen him and his men.

They were at the sandbag wall now. Looking through the hole, Albert could see no movement and not a German in sight. Motioning to his men, he scrambled through, rolling down and clambering up the other side. They were behind the German lines!

In front of them was a scene not unlike the one he'd left: bodies in hideous positions strewn along the bottom of the trench, and the backs of a dozen or so German soldiers intent on shooting ahead at the retreating Allied forces. Still on their bellies, and above and behind the enemy, Albert knew they had to take them out in one assault, if any of them were to get back to their own trench. 'Right, lads, get your Mills bombs at the ready. When I say "go", all get up together, pull the pins and throw and run like hell. You'll have seconds to get out of range. Right, ready? Go!'

The blast rivalled any that had been heard during the bombardment of the last few days. Stones, mud and bits of human body parts pelted Albert. But when the dust settled and he looked up, what he saw made him want to cheer. He opened his mouth to do so, but only a croaking sound came from him, rasping in his throat and choking him. There wasn't a German soldier alive for as far as he could see, and their killing machine was blown to smithereens.

Getting up, he shouted, 'Run, lads! Get your packs and get yourselves back to our trench. But remember, this is only some of them; there's more, so keep your heads down, and good luck.'

Running for all he was worth over, what seemed like a carpet of bodies, Albert felt the pity of it all, as he apologized a dozen times to lads that he trod further into the mud and the bloodbath beneath his feet. But, somehow, he didn't think they would mind, and he could almost hear them cheering him on: 'Run, Albert, get back for us; do it for your lads, Corporal!'

Jumping the last yard and sliding down the sandbags, he landed in a heap, his body hitting the bottom of the trench where the baked mud made for a hard landing. For a moment he stayed still and waited, unable to process what was happening in his mind. Then the sickening sound of screams for help and agonized moans penetrated his confusion once more. The gunfire had stopped. Looking up, he saw so few lads – not even a quarter of those who had gone over remained.

Orders rang out: 'Any able-bodied men, fall in for stretcher duty. Come on! We are the lucky ones, so let us help those not so lucky.'

Fear left him. He was needed and he would answer the call.

Darkness had fallen before the last moan of death hailed the end of another disastrous day. Having carried countless wounded back to the trench, whilst burial parties worked at getting the dead underground, Albert was on his last trip out. There were four lads with him. In twos, they helped a couple of wounded and set off back. 'I'll go a bit further. I'm sure I heard something,' he told them.

Reaching the barbed wire, his white flag held

aloft, he heard the sound again. Going over to where it came from, he found a young lad hanging over the wire netting. Only his torso, arms and head remained intact. Lighting his face with his torch, Albert saw it was a lad he knew: Andy Phelps.

The beam of light showed the agony and fear in the lad's eyes. 'Don't be afraid, son. Trust in God: He will deliver you to a land of peace and 'appiness.' *How I can say these words, and with meaning, when I cannot believe them? I do not know. But they give hope, and that is all that matters.* And Albert saw the hope. He saw the lad's fear go and peace take hold, just before his last breath escaped from him, never to be drawn again. 'Rest in peace, son. You've done a good job.'

Making his way back to the trench, Albert allowed his sobs to go unchecked, as his memory took him back to the time a few weeks before when he'd taken that same lad – just turned eighteen, and one of the last volunteers before conscription – to the tent hospital. He was a nice lad, who was more concerned with the trouble he thought he was causing than for himself. Edith had mended him and he'd been sent back for duty just this morning. Now he was gone.

Albert reached the trench without problems. One thing could be said for both sides: they never shot at the enemy whilst they collected their wounded and buried their dead. He looked at the huddle of defeated boys. 'Come on, lads, we 'ave to lift ourselves. This 'as been a bad day, but we are needed. We 'ave to get all our wounded brothers to the Red Cross clearing station. Look sharpish, and fall in to 'elp the medics.'

As he said this, he realized that Jimmy wasn't with them, and yet he'd seen him go over with the burial party. Calling over to a group that he'd seen Jimmy with, he asked, 'Where's Jimmy – has he come back in yet?'

'He's down there,' a shaky voice answered. 'Hurry, Corporal, he needs help.'

An alarm went off in Albert, but he stayed calm. 'Righto, leave it with me.'

Jimmy could see his pals swirling around inside his head. Most of them dead or wounded. They were his new mates – those he'd made since joining up – and Eric and Arthur, whom he'd known since birth. His mind went over and over how he'd had no choice but to step on Arthur's body as he fell just in front of him, and how they'd only gone a few feet when Eric had fallen to the side of him. But when they were burying the dead, he hadn't found either of them. At least he hadn't been able to recognize anyone he could say was them.

The images began to fade as he thought of his brothers. He'd love to feel their arms around him, or even to hear them teasing him, but at least they were at peace and finished with this lot. They weren't sitting in this stinking pit of hell.

Unable to control his limbs from shaking, he was distracted by a scratching sound. *Rats! The rats are coming!* They lurked around every corner, just waiting to pounce on him. Rats bigger than their next-door neighbour's cat back home. They would get him, he knew that. Their beady eyes shifting around in their heads always found him and focused on him.

Trying to banish them from his mind, he concentrated on thoughts of his mam and dad and a normal life: folk at the factory, a beer at the pub. Even though not of age, the landlord had served him in the pub yard and had told him to enjoy it. 'But always keep it in moderation,' he'd told him. 'Don't drink it like your dad does, Jimmy lad. That's no way to enjoy beer – swilling it down your neck, one after the other. It makes you do things you wouldn't normally do.'

Aye, Jimmy knew them things. He'd witnessed his dad when drunk, beating his mam when she didn't deserve, it. *No! That's not a good thought. Think of how good Dad is when he isn't drunk – a gentle, kind man, who is proud of me. Well, there's nowt to be proud of now, Dad, because I'm done. I can't go on.*

Now was the time. As he lifted his gun towards his mouth, a noise to his left caught his attention. Looking towards it, he saw a furry black rat standing on its hind legs. *They're coming for me! The rats – they're coming for me... Arghhh!*

'JIMMY! God, what the 'ell do yer think yer doing? Christ! Shut that racket up and pull yerself together. Fall in and 'elp the medics.'

It's Corporal Albert. He'll stop the rats. He'll stop my body from shaking. 'Help me... Help me – they'll eat me. I'd rather die by the gun.'

'No, Jimmy. No!'

His gun was twisted away from him, but he wouldn't let go; he needed it. He had to have it, had to take himself away from all the rats.

Strong arms lifted him. A shot rang out. Burn-

82

ing pain seared his hand. Corporal Albert's anxious voice penetrated the deafness that the blast had rendered on him. 'Christ! It went off. Your gun went off – Christ!'

Other voices now. 'What happened, Corporal?' 'Is Jimmy all right?' 'Move out of the way; let the corporal through.' 'You'll be reet, Jimmy.' *A northern voice. Eric? Arthur? No, they're dead!*

'DEAD! You're all going to die – the rats are going to eat you!'

'Take no notice of 'im; he's delirious. Get out of me way, lads, I'm taking 'im to the ambulance. It was an accident. He'll be all right. Doctor Edith will 'ave him back 'ere in no time.'

The words of the corporals and those of the lads wishing him well swam around Jimmy's head, as he sank deeper and deeper into the blackness that took him.

Getting into the first available ambulance to leave from the first-aid post, where they had applied a dressing to the stump that had once been his right hand, Albert decided to go with him to the hospital. The thirty miles or so to Abbeville seemed like a hundred by the time they reached it. Other cases took the stretchers, but not wanting to wait for one to come back, Albert carried Jimmy the hundred yards or so into the hospital. With each step, Jimmy's body took on the weight of a sack of coal. Albert's knees buckled as he entered the main tent.

The sight that met him pulled him up. Never in his life had he thought to witness what looked like a thousand men crying in agony. He'd heard tell of the expression 'a sea of blood' and had used the phrase himself, but not even that could describe the mass of blood dripping from the broken bodies and pooling around his feet.

Gaping holes showing flesh and bones, severed arms and legs, heads bandaged so that just eyes peered out and, above it all, the noise, the blood and the horror. Edith called out orders: 'Take number five to "Heads", and numbers six, eight and nine to "Stomachs", seven to "Limbs". Prepare the rest for immediate operations. I have sent for Captain Woodster, and he is bringing anyone he can find to help us.'

Her voice had a tired edge to it. And yet, though covered in blood and with her hair matted to her face with sweat, Edith looked magnificent. Her tiny frame had taken on the stature of a god, as light shone from her in the form of hope.

When her eyes focused on him, her face lit up. His darling girl. Once again he asked himself, *How can this wonderful woman – this lady – have feelings for me?* But she did. And though theirs was a forbidden love, one day there had to be a way they could be together.

'Albert! Are you all right? What are you doing here?'

This last question would be because Edith knew he wasn't due his rest period yet and shouldn't be out of the trenches. But he'd tasked one of the lads with telling his officer that he'd have to take Jimmy to the hospital himself, and hoped that would make his absence all right. He was sure it would, as they were used to him helping the medics when the fighting was over. Telling her about Jimmy, he was careful to add that the lad's injuries were an accident. 'He's in a bad way, mentally as well, Edi– Ma'am.'

Albert waited while Edith tended to Jimmy. Still unconscious, the lad didn't stir.

'He'll have to be operated on, but the wound is clean, so I'll make sure he stays asleep for a while, as we surgeons will be working flat out, and God knows when we will get to him.'

Comforted by the knowledge that Jimmy would be all right, he nodded. Then whispered, 'Edith, can I see you for a moment?'

Her face took on a worried look. 'I have so much to do – I'm sorry. How long now till your rest period? I know you said, but I've forgotten.'

'It didn't mean that much to yer then?'

'Oh, it did! I – I mean, oh, I don't know – all of this, it...'

'I know, it wipes out normal life; even stuff yer look forward to can diminish in its importance.'

'I – I'm sorry. I have thought about it. I've thought about it a lot. I just forgot the actual timing of it.'

'Well, it's three weeks and twenty-three hours away.'

'Ha, not that you are counting! Look, I have to get on, but I will arrange to have a day off and meet you in Beauvais town. No one should see us there – we can get separate trains. Connie went there the other day on her rest day and she brought a train timetable back with her. She said it is beautiful and has the most wonderful cathedral. It is in the province of Picardy.'

'Ah, the famous song. I'd never 'eard all of it,

85

but some lads arriving the other day came in singing it: "Roses are flowering in Picardy, but there's never a rose like you..."'

'You have a nice voice. I will get you to sing the whole song to me when we meet.'

'It will be me pleasure to do so. I'll learn the words before then. It'll be me love-song to yer.'

'Oh, Albert.'

Her blush made her look even more beautiful. He could hardly find his voice to ask, 'What time, and where, shall we meet?'

'There is a train that leaves Abbeville town centre at ten a.m. and one at eleven-thirty a.m. I will catch the ten. Connie was telling us about a cafe she found that serves delicious snacks and makes its own bread, so we will meet there. She said it is two streets away from the station. Turn left when you come out, and then take the second right. The cafe is called the Jardin d'Eden.'

Ironic, he thought, that there should be a place with a name like the Garden of Eden, so near to this hell they lived in. 'I'll be there, and I will try to get a shower first!' She didn't miss the humour of this, for at this moment they were both covered in the gore of the day. She gave a wry smile. 'You'd better! Now get off back, and let me get on with my work.'

'Before I scarper, I 'ave to tell yer, I'm worried about young Jimmy. I reckon 'is mind 'as gone. He thinks the rats are going to eat 'im, and he babbles on about death and fire and 'ell. But he didn't do this on purpose. It was an accident.' He told her what had happened. 'If the officers come to make enquiries, tell them what I've just told you, and that I'll speak for 'im.'

Her eyes had opened wide as she listened. He could see that she understood the implications. If it was thought that Jimmy had shot himself because he was a coward, he would face the firing squad.

Albert explained about Jimmy having lost two brothers at the beginning of the war. 'He's a brave lad, Edith. I've fought alongside 'im and there's none better. It's just that today's lot has turned 'is mind. Make 'im better, Edith, please make 'im better.' His plea made tears well up in his eyes. He hoped Jimmy would be okay, and thought of the lad's poor mother.

'I will – don't upset yourself. Many of the injured have mental-health problems. It happens because they are weak and their defences are down. But we have a special VAD, a girl from a family I know at home. She can work wonders with those who are suffering mentally, but don't have physical wounds to the head. She gets their confidence up and helps them to unravel their tangled minds. Don't worry. I'm sure Jimmy won't be seen as a coward by the officers. They'll believe you.'

'God, I 'ope so. They can be a pompous lot. One said to me the last time we 'ad to execute a lad, "Must keep up morale, and must keep the lads in line. Cowards and deserters are traitors!" It is as if they think the executions will keep the ranks from deserting, but it ain't like that, Edith. Most of those that run are in a bad way, as Jimmy is. I'm not saying all, but most of them that are caught are, as they can't think things through logically. I'd not object to shooting the other kind

– those who plan to go and are difficult to find.'

'I don't know what to say. Most of my colleagues are male officers and we have debated this. They understand the condition of the men, but still agree with the punishment.'

'They're of a different breed. 'Ow could someone say what that last one did, to a man shivering with fear in front of a firing squad? I'm not kidding, Edith. After he'd said about keeping the ranks in line, he turned to the lad waiting to be shot and said, "Hope you heard that, and may God forgive you for your cowardice – fire!" All in one sentence. It's sickening, Edith, and I don't think I can do it again.'

'I'm sure you won't have to. I will speak to Christian and Douglas about it. Thank you for getting a message to them for me. Now they know I am here, they are visiting me whenever they can. It is wonderful to see them.'

'I ain't met them yet. I just sent a note along the line and 'oped it would get to them, I'm glad it did. Yer know, Edith, if this were other times I'd–'

'Doctor, over here, quick!'

Edith smiled, a sad smile.

Not wanting to leave her feeling sad, Albert winked and said, 'Only three weeks…'

'And twenty-three hours! I know.' She giggled, a sound that warmed the cold place that held his heart, but what she said next lifted him even more, because her words showed him how much she cared: 'Keep safe, Albert, promise me you will keep safe.'

If only this *were* other times, he thought, and then consoled himself. If it were, she'd not even talk to him, let alone acknowledge an attraction for him.

Edith watched Albert leave. A feeling of 'if only' came over her, but she shook the silly notion from her and turned her attention to the lad Albert had brought in, because now he had stirred, his mental state was apparent.

From a foaming mouth, the boy uttered over and over again that the rats would get him. He didn't seem to be in pain and she was glad of that, because dosing him now would interfere with the anaesthetic she needed to give him later, but his distress was terrible to see and for that he needed Jennifer's help. She touched Jimmy's hand. 'Everything will be all right, Private O'Flynn.' Then she turned. 'Has anyone seen Jennifer Roxley? I need her here.'

'I passed her as I came in, so I am sure she will have heard your shout,' answered Captain Mark Woodster.

'Oh, you got here quickly. Thanks. Hope you've brought help – we're going to need it.'

His smile soothed, but what he said annoyed her. 'Had to. I couldn't ignore a damsel in distress now, could I?'

'I'm managing perfectly well, thank you, and am not distressed. Neither am I a damsel! It is the wounded who need you, not me.'

'Oh dear – sorry, old thing. I didn't mean... Anyway, least said soonest mended. What do you want me and my team to do?'

Feeling silly for giving him such a rebuff, Edith took the easy way out and went into professional mode. 'If you take all the limb amputations and I deal with the bullet wounds, that will be a big help. I have a couple of serious head-wounds that need priority, so I will start with them. Nurse Connie, whom you know, has a list of who should be first, and is in charge of pre-ops. And Nurse Nancy will take care of them post-op. Have you met her yet?'

'Once you've met one, you've met the other, with Connie and Nancy, I believe. They seem to come as a pair. Yes, I have met them both and couldn't wish for better in my team. Besides working with them a couple of times, I met them on the beach the other day, and they were having a whale of a time—'

'We've no time to chatter, Captain Woodster. I have to scrub up. Good luck.'

Walking away from him, her nerves felt in a tangle. He had a way of rubbing her up the wrong way, and she didn't know why.

As she scrubbed her arms and hands, having donned a clean white gown, Edith thought about Mark Woodster. A senior medical officer and surgeon with the South Lancashire's, he had told her that his family were all medicine- or army-orientated. He'd taken to the medical side, but found himself in both with the outbreak of war. A handsome man and a good-humoured one, he often helped out when the going got heavy. His usual job was in the first-aid station on the front line. His prompt and expert attention, under horrendous conditions, had saved many a man from dying and kept them going till they could reach the hospital.

He'd called into the hospital on his day off and

asked if he could have a follow-up on the men he'd sent there. Seeing the strain she was under, he'd volunteered to help. Now, once he'd cleared his station and battle had ceased, he tirelessly came over to help them and always answered her call for assistance. She really should treat him better, but she found it difficult even to be civil with him. Now, Albert... *Is there something in this comparison? Am I rejecting what Mark stands for: the upper crust of society that Mother has tried so hard to marry me to, and keep me chained to? Is that why I find Albert so attractive? After all, he represents everything Mother would look down on and forbid me from mixing with. Oh, I don't know...*

Hours later, Edith straightened her back. The strain of the night had worn her nerves thin, and the pain of extreme tiredness was so severe that her body felt as though every limb had been stretched from its socket.

'Come on, old thing. Connie has made an urn full of tea, and it's the best-tasting tea ever!'

'Captain Woodster, why do you call me "old thing"? It is very rude and presumptuous of you! I am not your *old thing!* I'm...' *Damn, now the tears were coming.*

'Hey, it's all right. I'm sorry. I ... I–'

'No, it's me that's sorry. I know it is just a term used by our class, I am being silly. Please ignore me.'

'You're not being silly, old– I mean, Edith. It has been a long night, and I have shed a few tears myself during it. I shouldn't have taken liberties. Oh, Edith, I...'

His words triggered more tears. His arm had come around her. The nearness of him as he held her made her feel strange. Her father and her brothers had been the only men ever to hold her before this. Stiffening, she pulled away from him and blew her nose. She couldn't cope with the confusion of feelings inside her. She'd gone from being a woman who shunned all men to being affected by two, in ways she didn't understand; men of two very different worlds – what was wrong with her? Whatever it was, she must keep it in check or it would be the undoing of her.

Mark let out a huge sigh, looked at her for a moment with a look that spoke of his own confusion and then said, 'Let's get to that tea before it's stewed, eh?'

All she could do was nod, then follow him as if she were a little girl. Maybe tomorrow – now only a couple of hours away – would bring her back to sanity. All she needed was a little sleep. Of that she was sure.

6

Ada

Low Moor, July 1916
An unexpected love

The bed creaked as it took Paddy's weight. How was it that she used to quiver with anticipation at him joining her in bed, her body eager and expectant of him possibly making love to her? And yet now it was as if she was dead inside, and she hoped and prayed he wouldn't turn towards her.

'Why do I have to feel you stiffening in repulsion at me? Can you not be forgiving me? Didn't I tell you that your sister made a prostitute of me? We needed to eat, Ada, and to pay the rent and the bills.'

'Aye, and buy gallons of beer, and bet on the horses.'

'Whisht, will you? Can you not try to forget, and have us back to how we were? I miss you, Ada. No one gives me what you give me.'

'And that says it all, you cheating, lying bastard! I'm the *only* one who should be giving that to you, but you've allus put yourself about. You've never been faithful to me. Now you want me to accept you shagging me own sister and putting her in the family way. Well, I don't, and I never will.'

'Aye, they are me failings, but I've learnt me

93

lesson. Come on, me Ada, come into me arms and let me be making you happy again.'

'No. Don't touch me!'

'Ada, come on – you know you're wanting to.'

His hand crept up her nightie, creating the usual tingle in her groin. Clenching her thigh muscles tightly, she barred his progress. 'Don't! You repulse me. I never want you to touch me again.'

'Is it not me wife that you are? Aye, and the teaching is that a wife gives unto her husband when he needs her to. I can go to the priest, if I've a mind, and he will be telling you that to disobey your husband, or to refuse him his conjugal rights, is a sin against the vows you took when you married me. So, let's have no more of this nonsense.'

With this, Paddy lifted his body onto hers. Crushed beneath him, she pushed against his chest. 'No, no! Leave me al–' Her breath caught in her lungs at the deep punch to her stomach.

'I'm sorry. God, I'm sorry, Ada. Why is it you make me do such things to you?'

A sick feeling churned inside her. Paddy was past reasoning with. Sucking in air, she tasted his beery breath and the stale lingering tobacco of the fag he'd smoked before coming up to bed 'You should take No for No. I'm not ready. I've told you that time and again, but you just take from me as if I am a whore. Whether I will get over the hurt and humiliation in time, I don't know, but I'm not ready, Paddy.'

'Oh? Is it that I have to force you again? Well, so be it, because I'm having me dues.'

'Please, Paddy, don't ... please...'

His knee prised open her legs, bruising her

94

thighs, but she fought him. She couldn't just give in, no matter what the cost to her. Another punch to her ribs took all the fight from her. The malice that came with the blow hurt her as much as the blow itself. If Paddy loved her, how could he treat her like this?

As he entered her, he called out in triumph. 'There – are you for changing your mind, now that you have me? Come on, me Ada, love me like you used to. I promise I'll not be letting you down again. Oh, Ada, Ada...'

Each thrust sickened her. Lying beneath him, she let her body go limp. His rape would not be helped by her, nor would she give him the gratification of having won her over. Nothing in her responded to him – nothing but the repulsion of all he stood for, and the hurt he'd brought down on her.

It didn't take him long. After he sighed a deep satisfaction as he rolled off her, she thought he would just go to sleep, but his mood turned ugly. 'Reject me, would you? Lie under me like a dead duck, eh? Me – your husband of twenty-odd years? You bastard!' His fist sunk into her stomach again. Vomit retched from her. Winded and unable to rise, she choked on the foul-tasting liquid. The sound brought Paddy to his senses. Grabbing her, he pulled her to a sitting position and thumped her back. 'I'm sorry. Oh, Ada, I'm sorry.' His words came out in huge sobs. As he held her to him, his tears dampened her hair. His body shook as he let go of a deluge of grief and remorse. When she could make out what he was saying, she heard the lads' names and his lament at how he'd treated her. It went on and on, but none of it touched her. Inside, she was dead to him.

Alighting from the train with the hundreds of other workers, Ada felt glad to be out in the fresh air. The carriage had been stifling. Not that the feeling would last, as she was soon inside the gates of Barnbow Munitions Factory and then inside the factory itself, stripping off her clothes and donning the special overall and cap they all had to wear.

Keeping her head down, she shuffled along with the rest of the women. The closeness of their bodies jostled her and caused more pain to her bruised insides.

As the factory doors opened, the smell of acetone stung her nostrils and made her feel giddy. The strong chemical odour of this component of the cordite that she worked with permeated the air and clung to her clothes, giving her a constant headache. But that was the least of the worries that she and the other women had, as the packing of the shells with strands of cordite was dangerous work. Explosions could happen at any time, and the cordite had the effect of turning their skin yellow. With this thought, Ada rubbed her arms, but then what did it matter what she looked like? Or what colour her skin was, because inside she was nothing. She didn't even bother to drink much of the extra rations of barley water and milk the workers were allowed, and which they were told would combat the yellowing. Instead she gave it to Betsy, for her and her young sister and brother to get the goodness of.

Poor Betsy – she pined for Jimmy. But she was a strong lass, and a grand one, too. Sometimes she seemed like the only light in this dark world. *Oh, me Jimmy lad, make it home. Please make it home!*

'Hurry up, you lasses. You've to be at the benches so the others can leave, you know that!'

The voice of their supervisor, Joe Grinsdale, didn't hold anger or aggression. She doubted he had either in the make-up of him. She'd known Joe a long time. They'd played together as kids and had gone to the same school. She'd always liked Joe.

'Ada ... Ada, are thee alreet, lass?'

Looking up into Joe's concerned face nearly undid her, but she swallowed hard and replied in the strongest voice she could muster, 'Aye, I'm grand, Joe. Yerself?'

'I'm reet worried for thee, lass. Have you been drinking your rations? Eeh, that's something of a daft question, for I can see you haven't. Well, I'll see thee at break time and make sure as you have a glass of milk. I've seen you take your quota from the churns that come up from the farm, but I never see you drink it.'

'I put it in me bottle and have it later. The smell of this place puts me off.'

'Look, lass. I – I mean... Anyroad, you'd better get to the cloakroom and get into your overall. The time's getting on.'

Too tired to wonder what Joe had been going to say, Ada filed in with the rest of the women, grabbed a set of overalls, a mask and a cap from the bins just inside the cloakroom and found a corner where she'd be least noticed.

The soreness of her limbs had her wincing in pain. Clara Lightmoor stood near her and looked around at the sound. Clara lived just up the road from Ada and always had something to say. 'He been at you again, love? Eeh, you should leave him. He's a bad 'un, if ever there was one. You know he's been after that young Lilly Blanford – her as come from Wales to work here – don't yer? And there's a rumour–'

'Shut your mouth, Clara! You'd make out that the Devil was courting God, you've such a lying tongue in your head!'

'Ha! Bloody cheek of you. Well, while I'm on, it's common knowledge as your Paddy has put your sister– Hey, geroff me!'

The thin thread that had held Ada together snapped. Her hand lashed out, but Clara's defending raised arm took the blow. Ada felt as though she was hitting a brick wall. Waves of shock and nausea sent her reeling backwards.

The sound of the horn marking the shift-change brought her to her senses. She pulled herself together and pushed past Clara.

As she took the place of Jean Dwight she was treated to one of Jean's lovely smiles. 'Eeh, glad to see thee, lass. I'm tired to me heart. Though you look worse than I feel. Are you alreet, lass?'

The same tears that had pricked the back of her eyes when Joe had asked this of her spilled over at being asked the question again. But Jean didn't comment on the drops of water running down Ada's face; she just patted her gently and said, 'It'll all come out in the wash, love. It allus does.

Concentrate on your work – it helps.'

Ada picked up the next shell on the belt, which replaced the one that Jean had just filled and hung on the moving runner above her. She began the task of filling it with the bundle of cordite, and only managed to say a quick thank you to Jean. Turning her head to do this sent pain all the way down her neck. Her vision blurred. Looking back at the shell she held, Ada clung onto it. *God, don't let me drop it, please!*

'Here, give me that, Ada. What d'you think you're playing at?'

Beads of sweat joined the tumbling tears now running down Ada's face. The burden of the shell had only just left her arms when a blackness descended on her and she slumped to the ground.

'Oh my God! She's fainted.'

In the fog of Ada's brain, the words sounded muffled, as if being said through water. But the effect of them brought her round. Opening her eyes, she looked into Joe's lovely soft brown ones. 'Eeh, Ada lass, come on – let me help you up.'

His strong arms grasped her and propelled her body upright. Vomit rose to her throat with the motion, but she swallowed it down. Her throat stung with the aftermath, but she wasn't going to disgrace herself by being sick in front of them all

'Come on, I'll take thee to the nurse. I told you, you need to eat more and drink your quota of milk.'

She couldn't answer Joe, but was glad of his help as he kept his arm around her. A few sniggers went round the room, but the implication of them passed her by until they were standing alone in the corridor. Then Joe shocked her by saying, 'Ada, oh Ada. I'm sorry, but I have to say what's in me heart. I love thee, Ada...'

'What – what are you saying, Joe? You can't. I – I...' Confusion deepened inside her. Still fuzzy from the faint, her brain couldn't process Joe's words and they didn't seem real. Had he really said he loved her? Trying to find some clarity, she looked up at him. His smile jolted her heart. *This cannot be happening!* 'Don't be daft, Joe. This is no time to take the rise out of me. Just help me to the nurse, and get back to your job – or we'll both get the sack!'

'But I mean it, Ada. I can't sleep for thinking about you. And it breaks me heart to see what is happening to you. It's like the light has gone out inside you, since Jimmy went, and I know as you're not being treated reet by Paddy.'

She had no words to answer him. Her emotions were all in tatters and she had lost control of them. A sob racked her. The concern in Joe's eyes deepened. Ada felt herself swaying towards him. 'Help me, Joe... Help me.'

'I will, me lass. Lean on me and I'll get thee to the nurse. But know this, Ada: I am here for you, and you can lean on me anytime you like, lass.'

Once more his arms encircled her. She used his strength to make her way along the corridor. Her own feelings were tangled and confusing. Something had stirred inside her when Joe had declared himself – something she hadn't felt for a long time. It was as if the young girl trapped in this weary, sad body had popped out just for a second and had responded to the love offered to her.

But she mustn't go down that road. She must stop Joe from making the mistake of his life. A man in his early thirties, he had never married. He'd been engaged once, as she remembered, but the lass had gone off with his friend and they had married within weeks. That must have scarred Joe. Some said he had a breakdown, but although he did go into hospital for a spell, it was found that he had a murmur in his heart, and his collapse had been due to that weakness. This kept him from going to war.

Joe had little that was immediately eye-catching about him, but he was one of life's nice people, who became more attractive once you got to know him. His grey-blue eyes framed with long lashes – too long for a man – always held kindness, although just now she'd seen desire smouldering in them and that had shocked her. But she still couldn't work out exactly why she was suddenly affected by him. Joe was miles away from being the type that Paddy represented. Dark and handsome, charming and strong, Paddy had melted her the moment she'd met him; but Joe, though as tall as Paddy, was on the fair side and shy, and ... well, ordinary.

His lack of confidence often had him bending over, as if to make himself unnoticeable, and that is what had happened in her case. She hadn't noticed him – not in the way a woman notices a man. Not at all. At least, not until just now. Until that moment he'd just been Joe, someone she knew and liked.

By the time they reached the nurse's office Ada

101

had begun to feel better and tried to argue that she could carry on, but Nurse Penny insisted that she was examined properly, before she would let her return to her bench. As soon as Joe had left, she asked Ada to strip off to the waist.

'Eeh, lass, is that your husband's work?'

Shame washed over Ada at these words.

'It's time we women stood up for ourselves, and men were prosecuted for treating their wives in this way – it ain't reet, Ada. Look at your bruising. No wonder you feel under the weather. But, y'know, there's them as are fighting for our rights, and when this war is done, I might just join them.'

This surprised Ada. Penny Jarvis had always seemed the quiet, studious type. She'd never married, though Ada couldn't imagine why, because although she was a rounded woman, with plenty of padding and a huge bosom, she had a pretty face and a lovely kind way about her. She'd make a good wife and mother. It seemed a shame that no one had taken her up; and now, with all the young men being killed off, there would be no one to do so.

To combat the pain this last thought brought her, Ada tried to make a joke. 'Eeh, Penny, I can just see you chained to a railing and shouting, "Votes for women", and no one down London understanding a word you're saying!'

Penny laughed. 'Aye, so can I. But understand me or not, I'd do it. All of this makes me blood boil.'

She rubbed soothing oils into Ada's skin as she spoke, which brought her some comfort. 'I'm leaving him when I can, Penny. I'm saving up me money. Paddy has no idea how much I earn, and he's happy with what I give him, so he don't ask questions as to what I keep back. Only he ... he got me sister pregnant, and that were the last straw for me.'

'Eeh, Ada, you got a bad 'un in him. And, aye, I knew about your sister. She's been having me attend her, as she's trying to keep it secret. She asked me to rid her of it, but I'm not into that game. I feel sorry for her, in a way.'

Hearing this made the pain of Ada's betrayal fresh again. 'Well, she shouldn't have took me man – she's got her just desserts, as I see it.'

'As she tells it, she were seduced; and, because of her situation, she was easy pickings for a man such as Paddy. Now she's lost you, and is likely to lose her husband and everything she has.'

'I can't feel sorry for her, Penny. I would never do what she's done.'

'There's none of us knows what we would do in a given situation, lass. Anyroad, I'm talking about anything and everything, other than the real reason I made you have an examination. I need your help, Ada. I have some bad news to give to both Mabel and Agatha.'

'No! No, no, no – don't tell me. Not Eric and Arthur, oh God...' Ada sucked in her breath.

'I'm afraid so. Killed on the first of July, the day the papers are saying was a disastrous day. They numbered the dead at around twenty thousand, with another thirty thousand wounded. How them nurses cope out there, I don't know.'

Ada blocked out Penny's words and wailed. Her only thought was: *Jimmy's mates, dead! But what of Jimmy? My Jimmy...*

'Ada, love. Oh, I should have thought on. Oh God, Ada, I'm sorry. I forgot your Jimmy's there and they were all mates, weren't they? But, lass, you would have heard by now if Jimmy had been hurt. The officer who brought the news would have known and would have told me. I just thought, as you'd been through this, you could help Mabel and Agatha. I was going to send for you, if you hadn't come through me door.'

How Penny could talk in such a matter-of-fact way Ada couldn't understand. Two fine lads were dead! Two more from the street that had seen these lads kicking balls and giving cheek when told to stop. Lads that had hung around with her Jimmy and had called out teasing words to her Bobby and Jack when they had swaggered up the street in their Sunday best, looking to pick up a couple of girls.

'Look, I'll give you sommat to calm you, then I'll sign you off for the day, Ada. I'm reet sorry, lass. Dealing with stuff, day in and day out, makes you immune to the suffering of it at times. I just wasn't thinking.'

'No. You're reet, I should be with them.' As she said this, Ada felt a calmness take her and knew that she was the right one to be with Mabel and Agatha, and to tell them the terrible news. She knew how gut-wrenching it would be for them, and how their world as they knew it would come to an end, never to be properly mended again. She knew the hollow feeling, the devastation wrought – as if everything before the moment you heard your son was dead was all for nothing. Penny wouldn't know that, or how to deal with it, as she'd never birthed any young 'uns. Standing tall, Ada said, 'Don't send me home. At least not without Mabel and Agatha. I've got meself together. I'll tell them, and then I'll take them home and stay with them. They will know that I understand.'

'Aye, that's what I thought. Y'know, I could have married. I had me chances, but it never appealed to me. And now, seeing what all of you are going through – lasses as were at school with me, suffering like you are – I'm glad I didn't. Reet, I'll have Agatha and Mabel sent up here. God, it's a cruel world, Ada. A cruel world.'

Feeling sick at the prospect of seeing Mabel and Agatha, Ada jumped when the door opened. Joe entered first, followed by the white-faced and shaking Mabel and Agatha. *They know*, Ada thought. There was no other reason they'd be summoned here, and their haunted looks told of their fear. And she was to confirm it for them.

Penny asked the two women to sit down. They did so as if someone was working them with strings. Ada looked over at Joe and felt a nerve twitch inside her, as she read the love that he had for her shining from his eyes. Unable to deal with his feelings, or her own, she concentrated on Agatha and Mildred and what she had to tell them. 'Eeh, me lasses. How can I tell thee what I have to say?'

There was no need for her to say any more. Agatha's and Mildred's screams of 'No, no!' wrenched at her heart and tore open her own wounds. She moved to be in the middle of them, and let her own tears flow with theirs. She'd never been close to either of these women, they were just acquaintances, but they now felt like kin as she held them. She didn't protest at their wails, but allowed them to vent their anguish. And when Penny tried to calm them with the soothing, inadequate words of 'Now, now', Ada quietened her by saying, 'Let them be. It is best out. Nothing lessens the pain, but this outpouring gives a little release and stops you going mad.'

From where she squatted, Ada looked up at Joe. His face was wet with streaming tears. At that moment it didn't take the jolt of her heart to tell her that he was very special; and yes, she could admit it, he had filtered into her emotions. The feeling came with the urge to run to him and be held by him; but for now she needed to be strong for Mabel and Agatha, and her own feelings had to be shelved.

Aye, and she'd shelved Paddy, an' all. She knew that now. In the context of everything, he was nothing. And it came to her that she would go and see Beryl and help her through everything she had to face. What did it matter who had fathered the babby? All that mattered was that she should make sure the babby and Beryl were all right.

She didn't know how she came to this understanding, but what Paddy and Beryl had done suddenly paled in the face of everything else. Not that she would forgive them totally. They didn't deserve that, but she could get to a place where she could cope with it. However, no matter what, she knew she would never get to a place where she wanted to stay with Paddy. No, the last thread of her feeling for him had been severed.

106

7

Andrina and Eloise

Rossworth Hall, mid-July 1916
A shocking tragedy

Andrina released a sigh of relief. Once more she'd been able to dodge Eloise and take her walk alone. This meant she could go towards the kitchen garden, in the hope of seeing Jay. The last few days since that first illicit kiss with Jay had been wonderful. Especially as Daddy and Mama had been away.

Daddy had said there was no reason for them all to return to London until the autumn, and that although he might be needed in the House of Lords from time to time, he would go back alone and would not disturb and uproot them all. Mama had been adamant that she would go with him this time, as he was only going for three days. There was some shopping she'd needed, and so Eloise and Andrina had been left to their own devices. During that time she had met up twice with Jay. They had even managed a secret picnic yesterday!

Their parents were back now and intended to stay for a week or two, making it even more difficult for her and Jay to meet. She hoped to manage it today, as her mama and papa were preoccupied and had spent much of their time locked in Father's office.

Thinking about the excitement she now had in her life was scary. Her own and Jay's intimacy had not progressed after that kiss. But she'd wanted it to, and this frightened her. Her longing had, to her shame, let feelings visit her at night that she'd tried hard to suppress. The uncomfortable guilt that she felt as a result of this had made her very strict with Jay, and she'd told him that it wasn't proper behaviour to touch her.

It was sort of working. Jay tried to restrain himself, as she did, but the brush of a hand would happen and then they would hold each other's gaze for a moment; a moment that set her heart thumping and let her know that, if Jay did go further and kiss her, or even... No, she wouldn't; she was adamant that she wouldn't!

Most of the time they talked. Jay seemed to possess so much knowledge about all kinds of subjects, such as politics, the class system, the war and even gardening. His flat tone, caused by his deafness, didn't grate on her, but rather sounded different from anything she had ever heard and had become a source of joy to her in itself.

She'd become fascinated by subjects that would have bored her before, and had listened, enthralled, as he'd taught her the names of plants and their habits – when they should be planted, when they flowered, and about the pollination process – a dangerous subject that had led to them leaning into each other and sharing a longing that was tangible.

Reaching the wall that surrounded the kitchen garden, Andrina hesitated for a moment. She could hear a voice saying, 'But why, Jay? Ain't I good enough for you, then? If her High-'n'-Mightiness asked you to take her to a dance, you'd jump at it, when she's nowt but a whore. Hey! You pushed me!'

'I'm sorry, I didn't mean to, but it was a reaction to your filthy insinuations. And how dare you call Lady Andrina a whore? Get back to your work, and leave me alone. I'm not going to look at you now, so I won't know what you're saying – just go!'

Oh God, the servants are gossiping! How long before Mama and Daddy hear of what I am up to?

The gate gave its usual creak as she opened it. As if sensing her presence, Jay looked towards her. 'Lady Andrina?'

'Yes, Jay, it's me.'

'Oh God, you didn't hear, did you?'

'Yes. It is very worrying. If Father finds out…'

'Well, you may not have to worry about that. I have news. I've learned something about the truth of my birth–'

His voice went into a moan as his body slumped to the ground. Florrie stood over him, wielding a bloodied spade, as if about to hit him again. Andrina's scream stopped her.

As she turned on Andrina, spittle sprayed from Florrie's mouth. Her blackened teeth ground together in a snarl. 'You stole me man! You're nothing but a whore. He's nothing to you. Well, if I can't have him, neither can you!'

The spade came down on Jay's head once more. Blood squirted in Andrina's direction and splattered her frock. Lunging at Florrie, Andrina thwarted her attempt to land another blow, but

109

the movement unbalanced them both. As she fell backwards, Andrina was unable to stop the full force of her body hitting the ground; a jolt thudded through her, taking her breath from her.

Florrie was quicker than Andrina to recover, and was up and standing over her before she could draw the air back into her lungs. Glancing up, she saw the sun reflect off the spade held high above Florrie's head. Venom spewed from the maid's frothing mouth. 'I hate you. I hate the stinking lot of you!'

Andrina knew that she'd screamed, but didn't hear her own voice, as darkness descended on her and all sound went into the black hole that swallowed her.

From her position in the hall just outside her father's study, Eloise listened with horror to what her father related to Mama. 'Sixty thousand casualties! Oh, my dear, what will happen, what will happen? They say that, of the sixty thousand, twenty thousand were fatal. And this all happened on the first day of the new offensive.'

As she heard him outline the battles that were taking place in Albert, Longueval and Bazentin, Eloise found it difficult to imagine the horror erupting in these towns with such nice-sounding names. She wondered how Edith was coping, and if she and her brothers were safe. These thoughts were ended suddenly as her father's voice rose in anger. 'What the blazes does that idiot Haig think he is playing at? He is responsible for the lives of our boys!'

The sound of the gentle weeping of her mama

compounded her fears. But then Father's next words put a dampener on her own plans and further upset her. 'Felicity, whatever you do, you must dissuade Eloise from going. I would prefer her to see the error of her plans to join the Voluntary Aid Detachment, but if you cannot get such a result, then I will strictly forbid her and refuse to sign the papers.'

'But, *mon cher,* you cannot do this. Eloise is a young woman with a mind of her own.'

'I can, and I will. Women do not have minds of their own! It isn't like in France, my dear. Women here have to obey their father until they are married, and then they obey their husband.'

'Ha! I abhor that stupid rule. I never obey you!'

Time to go, Eloise thought, as her father's voice became soft and held loving amusement. 'I know you don't, you little minx. Come here and give me some comfort, for I am out of sorts today... Aah! I thought you would obey that order.'

Before Eloise had taken many steps away from the door a shout halted her. 'Your Lordship, come quickly.' Eloise turned back round towards the study, only to see the astonishing sight of Jorrington, their usually sedate butler, running and hollering at the top of his voice.

'What has happened?' she asked, shouting louder than him.

'In the kitchen garden, M'lady. Hurry, hurry!'

Lifting the hem of her day-frock, Eloise fled, knowing that her father and Mama were only a few steps behind her.

'Eloise? Where is Andrina – why isn't she with you?'

Eloise's blood ran cold as a scream took the space around them and stopped her from answering her father.

Maggie, the downstairs maid, appeared at that moment as if from nowhere. 'They're in the kitchen garden. Oh my God, she's murdered him!'

Eloise sped across the lawn, desperate to find out what had happened and to shake the mounting fear inside her.

Flinging open the garden gate gave witness to a scene of horror: Florrie wielded a spade, while Jay lay unconscious on the ground, and next to him...

'No, no!' was all she could utter as she looked at her beautiful sister. Andrina lay unmoving, her face covered in blood, her eyes staring into space. Empty eyes. Dead eyes.

'She stole me man! I had to kill her. I had to kill them both!'

Eloise drew in a deep breath as she stared at the demented Florrie. With this, a pain seared her, burning her lungs and clenching her heart till it felt as though it would snap in two.

'Stop it! Stop it *now!*' Her father's command stayed Florrie's hand, just as she was about to bring the shovel down once more on Andrina. Turning towards them, Florrie's eyes flared as she stared at them in turn.

Mama stood like a statue; Father was angry and shaking with fear; several maids were crying, their bodies quivering with shock; and the butler, dear Jorrington, looked back at her with tears running down his cheeks. None of them moved or made a sound. An animal-like noise broke the silence as Florrie charged forward, dashing between the wall of people and out of the gate.

An anguished cry of *'Mon bébé, mon bébé!'* brought reality back to Eloise. Mama flung herself down next to Andrina and held her lifeless body, muttering over and over, *'Mon bébé.'*

Father moved forward. Taking Mama in his arms and prising her away from Andrina, he said, 'Come inside, my darling. Jorrington will see to things.'

This grated on Eloise. 'How can he? How can anyone see to things! Oh, Daddy. Andrina, Andrina!' Her father rose and was by her side in a flash. His strong arms grasped her just as her legs buckled. 'Make it right, Daddy, make everything right again.'

The tears raining down his cheeks mingled with those on hers, as he whispered, 'I cannot, my darling. Oh God!'

A stillness had descended on this beautiful house that Eloise had loved. A stillness that held the cloying sadness of the death of Andrina. It was a sadness that Eloise thought would never lift.

Rossworth Hall had been her sanctuary, the place she loved most in the world. It would never be the same again. Nor would she ever look on the magnificent parkland and find the peace it had always given her.

Life was unfair. *Why should Jay live and Andrina die?* At this moment she hated Jay and wanted him dead, too. He was just as responsible for Andrina's death as Florrie was. He had lured Andrina, played on her silly fantasies. He should hang, just as surely as Florrie would.

This thought had hardly died in her when the door of the drawing room opened. Her eyes hurt as she took them away from what she'd always thought of as a calming view across the lawns with their beautifully trimmed bushes and trees, but which now she'd stared at without registering. Her father, aged by many years in the few hours since the shocking event, entered the room.

'Are you all right, my dear? Your mama has been given something to make her sleep. The doctor is still here and wonders if you want anything to help you?'

'I will never be all right again, Father. But no, I don't want anything, thank you. I want to think, I want to imagine... Oh, Daddy, help me!'

He crossed over to her and she went into his arms. Snuggling into the smooth cloth of his evening jacket, it struck her as odd that he should have bothered to change his clothes, but then he must have felt that keeping things normal would help.

'There, there, my dear, try to be brave for Mama.'

'I will, Daddy. I will.'

'It will take us a long time to come to terms with it all, but if we help each other, we will get through this. Now, my dear, I want to talk to you. Are you up to it? There is further news on Jay. The doctor says he is still unconscious, but that he is improving. He can be moved now, and will be taken to hospital. His mother has been informed and she is naturally very distressed. I have arranged for her to be taken to him.'

Eloise made no reply to this. Her father gave a

little cough that she knew meant he had more to say. She cringed at what it might be.

'Eloise, I have to ask: what was going on, do you know? Andrina wasn't... No, she wouldn't. Florrie was demented. We cannot take any notice of what she said. Andrina wouldn't look at someone like Jay, I...'

'She did, Daddy. Andrina had a silly fascination for Jay, but I hadn't wanted to worry you, as I thought it would pass. He is responsible, Father. Jay lured Andrina. He played on her infatuation.'

'Good God! And you didn't think to tell me or your mother this was going on? That a servant and your sister–'

A knock at the door stopped him from going on. Jorrington announced that the police would like a word.

It was an hour later when Eloise discovered that Florrie had been found. She'd hanged herself. Eloise wasn't sure how to deal with this news. Everything seemed so unreal. Changed forever. How could a normal day end in such shocking tragedy? *Oh, Andrina, my darling sister ... how can I live without you?*

8

Albert and Jimmy

Abbeville Camp and Stores, mid-July 1916
A thread holds us to life: Jimmy's breaks

'I don't believe it was an accident. Had you not come across James O'Flynn when you did, he would have done this deed anyway.'

For a moment Albert couldn't think who this James was, then realized that the officer was referring to young Jimmy. This was a formal hearing, so they would use his proper name. 'No, sir, it wasn't like that. The lad was shaking, but not with fear; he was shaking with the 'orror of what he'd seen and realizing that 'is friends hadn't made it. We all do that. Sometimes it lasts a while, and at other times it goes as we get on with 'elping the wounded. Young Jimmy ain't a coward. He's one of the bravest lads I've fought alongside.'

'So how come his gun was loaded and ready to fire? What was he going to fire at, if not himself, to inflict an injury that would get him out of here? The battle was over, so he'd no need to be prepared for attack.'

'He must 'ave forgotten to unload, sir. He would 'ave come round. He was in a bad way mentally, but he...'

'Exactly! Afraid, and wanting to take the cow-

116

ard's way out.'

'No!'

'Yes, I think so, Corporal. It is admirable that you want to protect him, but where would we be, if we let these cowards off? All the men would be doing the same – shooting themselves just to get home.'

''Ow the fuck dare you–'

'Corporal, I would remind you who you are speaking to!'

'And I would remind *you*, Captain Blakley, that you are out of order speaking of the ranks in that manner.' General Ickmey's voice resounded around the wooden barrack room that was being used for young Jimmy's court martial. It was one of a dozen huts not far from the hospital tents, which were mostly used for stores, although some were used as rest rooms for the men and officers when they took a short break from the front. This one in particular was used as an officers' mess.

General Ickmey presided over the proceedings and was known as a fair man when dealing with the ranks, though Albert doubted that would make a difference to Jimmy's fate. But now as the general continued, his voice booming, his words made Albert feel pride – a pride that nudged the hopelessness of Jimmy's case to one side, just for a moment... 'And might I say that to address such a callous remark to Corporal Price, who has seen so many heroes from the ranks die and has been mentioned in Dispatches, is beyond the pale. Yes, there are cowards amongst the men, but to put them all under the same heading is an insult to the thousands of brave men who have

117

lost their lives and to those still willing to fight for their country.' After a moment's pause he turned to Albert and said, 'However, Corporal Price, this is a court martial, and I will not allow such language, or indeed outbursts of any kind.'

'I beg your pardon, General Ickmey, sir. Thank you for what you said.'

'Very well, let us proceed. Captain Blakley, I think we have heard enough evidence now to come to a conclusion. Please round up your questioning.'

Standing and clicking his heels, the captain narrowed his eyes. 'No more questions for this witness, sir.'

Albert rose and went to sit behind Jimmy. It had only been four days since the incident and the lad looked drained. His eyes were glazed and a dreadful trembling shook his body. *Couldn't they see the lad wasn't right?*

Albert wanted to say something to Jimmy, but knew that if he did he might be removed from the room and he wanted to listen to the summing-up of the evidence given when he hadn't been in the courtroom. Evidence that gave no hope. Evidence taken from the lad who had told Albert about seeing Jimmy in the trench. His testimony alone – relating that he'd seen Jimmy cowering in a corner, sweating and shaking and then reloading his gun – must have sealed the boy's fate. Then came a summary of the evidence from the medical staff who had treated Jimmy. Edith, his own Edith, had said that the injury could have been self-inflicted, though he guessed she would have tried to qualify that, by saying that she believed the circumstances under which she was told it had happened. But then even if that was so (and he hadn't been present during her stand, so didn't know for sure), no such possibility was permitted in this one-sided summing-up. As the officer's voice droned on, his tone mocking any idea of Jimmy's innocence, Albert listened with a sinking heart to the final nail in Jimmy's coffin being hammered home, as he heard what had been told to the court by the VAD who had worked with Jimmy. She had said that Jimmy told her he had intended suicide.

Albert's fears deepened with every word uttered by the prosecuting officer.

Once the officer came to the end of his summing-up, every man to the last one knew the outcome. There could be no other, but when Albert heard the general say the words, the bile rose in his stomach.

'James O'Flynn, you are stripped of the honour of being a member of His Majesty's Forces and have been found to be a coward. Punishment for this offence is death. You will be taken out at dawn and shot. May God have mercy on your soul.'

A sob came into the silence that followed. It was a weak sob, but the sound cut a deep pain into Albert's heart. He had to do something – anything – to save Jimmy.

As he walked back to the soldiers' rest room from the officers' mess hut Albert's heart felt heavy with dread. The decision to end Jimmy's life had been cut-and-dried for the officers. You fought or you were a coward, and that was that. Well, Jimmy had fought; he'd gone over the top without protest and had charged gallantly into

119

the fray, not faltering. And now, for a moment of madness, he was going to die at the hands of his own comrades. *Well, here's one who isn't going to fire a bullet at him. Nothing is as sure as that. I'll be called upon, no doubt, but I won't fire, and I don't care what happens to me as a consequence!*

The summons came within the hour. Albert spat on the ground in disgust. Twelve of them had received the order. Besides himself, the lad who'd testified and hadn't stopped sniffling since had also been charged to be one of the line-up to fire at Jimmy. They were in the mess hut when it came: a written instruction to fall in for firing-squad duty at 3 a.m. the next morning.

None of them spoke for a full ten minutes. To Albert, it had been settled. How come these particular men were here, ready? Some had given evidence, but not all, and not all had been due a rest break either.

The sound of the battle raging in the distance took the space around them. Albert wondered how many would die today, and knew all would be classed as heroes. Jimmy deserved that accolade. *Jimmy is a hero – he is!* 'Damn it, 'e is!'

'Did you say sommat, Corp?'

He hadn't realized that he had, but now he knew he'd sworn out loud. 'Look, lads, it's odds-on that all of us will be dead sometime in the near future. I don't know about you, but I don't want yet another one of our comrades' blood on me 'ands before I die. As Corporal, I'll be the one to prepare the guns. I'm going to make sure that I'm one of the ones with the live bullet in me gun, and I'm firing above Jimmy's 'ead.'

120

'But, Corporal, sir, you'll end up shot yourself!'

'I don't care, Brigsy. I'm not shooting young Jimmy, are any of yer with me? You all know the score, some live bullets, some blank. A daft system that's meant to 'elp us believe that we didn't shoot the deadly bullet. But we all know if we did or didn't because the live bullets give a kick-back and the blanks don't.'

'What's your thinking, Corp?' Brigsy asked.

'If you're with me I could make sure who gets the live bullets, and them as do will 'ave to agree to fire above Jimmy's head. Then he won't die. And, if that is so, then surely no one could be so inhuman as to make a lad face the firing squad twice, so I see it as a way to try to save 'im.'

'Aye, I'm with you on that, Corp. I'm not for shooting a fellow northerner, especially one who has shown the courage that Jimmy has. I'll take a live bullet and fire it above Jimmy's head, and I'll take the consequences.'

'But you'll be court-martialled.' This, from Gates, got short shrift from Brigsy: 'Aye, we knows that. But seeing as the Corp is willing to face that, then the least we can all do is to support him.' Brigsy looked around at all those called upon.

One by one they agreed. Names were put into a hat and those to have live ammunition didn't falter on their decision. The talk went to the spark of hope Albert's plan had given, as they all felt the hopelessness of their lives. And all said words to the effect that if a bullet had their name on it in the near future, they would have a better passing, knowing they had saved Jimmy. Better than dying at the top of the trench and dropping face-down into the mud, having advanced no more than ten yards in a bloody killing field.

Albert took each one's hand in a firm shake of friendship. It hurt him to realize that, in his plan, he would have to make provisions for his own safety and theirs that would mean hurting, and even maiming, some of them. But what upset him most was that he knew he would be deserting these men, as he planned on taking his chances and making a run for it, no matter what that entailed, or what the consequences to himself.

Darkness clothed the hut where the twelve slept. Albert lay awake listening to their snores, though some, he knew, were awake like himself. Safe in the knowledge they wouldn't question him, he got out of bed and dressed.

Outside, the air held the dampness he'd become used to. Making his way to the stores, he intended to retrieve some things from his box. Like all of his fellow soldiers, he had a box of sorts, holding personal belongings. Most boxes held letters, photos and memorabilia, items the soldiers had picked up, wanting to take home, to capture in some way what their life was like: empty bullet cases, German Army helmets or belts, that kind of thing; some had German weaponry. His own pride and joy was a Chauchat machine rifle. It was a brilliant gun that you held at the hip and it fired round after round, used by the French and many other countries. He'd often wondered why the English hadn't been issued with them.

Greeting the guard, he stood for a moment and smoked a fag with him. He knew Freddie well, for the two of them had grown up in the same street in the East End. Freddie turned a blind eye while Albert rummaged through his box, not bothering to look at what he pulled out of it or to question the fact that he'd walked out of the store with a long bundle.

The site of the coming execution sickened Albert as he walked up to it, but he kept focused on his plan. Already a working party was in place, preparing the site: a bench for the guns, chairs for the clergy and doctor.

Unrolling the cloth that contained his guns, Albert loaded the handgun and placed it in his pocket. It bulged out, but when his jacket was back in place, the flap covered it. Now he prepared the automatic and strapped it to his back through his jacket belt, hoping it wouldn't show.

One of the working party must have heard the click of the loading action. He stopped what he was doing, lifted his rifle and shouted, 'Who goes there?'

Coming into view, Albert answered, 'Corporal in charge of the firearms.'

'Oh, righto. How you doing, Corp?'

'Been better. Have yer the guns unloaded yet?'

'Aye, they're in that box over there.'

'Right, two of yer bring the box to the bench for me. I'll get on with preparing 'em.'

Working away at laying out the guns and loading some of them with live ammunition and some with blanks, Albert kept his eye on the men. When none of them were looking, he undid his belt and carefully pulled the Chauchat from behind him. The rattle of the bullets hanging from it made him freeze with fear at one point, but none of the others took any notice. He hid the rifle inside the empty box and covered it with the hessian that had been wrapped around the guns, before closing the lid.

Taking out his knife, he made a nick in the underside of the butts of the guns he must allocate to the men who had agreed to have those with live bullets in them. He *must* get it right. Any mistakes and Jimmy would be a dead man.

A distant church clock struck the half-hour. One-thirty. He needed to get back to his men and prepare them. There would be under an hour to go, by the time he got back. With everything in place, nerves attacked him. Adrenalin had kept them away till now. Sweat stood out on his body and his stomach churned, to the extent that he had to crouch behind a bush to relieve himself.

Jimmy stood where they placed him. Taking his last glimpse of the world through tear-filled eyes, he looked up at the cloud-covered sky just breaking into light and throwing a purple hue over the shadowy field. Then he let his glance fall on the black outline of the trees and savoured the feel of the breeze as it brushed across his skin. This field had no trenches dug into it, a fact that reassured him that at least he wasn't going to die in a trench, or on the battlefield, with his fellow men treading his body into the mud.

The prayers of the chaplain came to an end.

With the tying of the blindfold, the calm that had descended on him as they had driven him the short distance to his place of death deserted him. In its place a feeling of being strangled by his own throat muscles took him, as his breath came in short, painful gasps.

He tried to think of his ma, but her face wouldn't come to him. Then he thought of Betsy, and although at times he'd been annoyed at how she put herself in his way whenever she could, he knew he'd been pleased really, and wouldn't know what to do without her. He thought about her beauty, her golden curls, her smiley eyes and her full lips. How he longed to have her with him now. He would hold her cuddly body to his, and kiss every part of her.

'Firing squad, fall in! Firing squad, take aim.'

A trickle of warm water ran down his leg. *Please God, don't let me mates see as I've wet meself.* His breath laboured even more. His heart thudded against his chest. Clamping his teeth on his lips, he waited.

'Fire!'

The deafening crack of the rifles had him gasping in a deep breath of fear. Then he felt nothing. No pain, no falling to the ground, no blackness... He wasn't dead! The angry voice of the officer in charge broke the silence:

'What the...? How dare you disobey an order! Christ, you'll all be shot for this. Corporal, I saw you and some of your men raise their rifles. You must have planned this. You blithering idiot. What did you think? That you would save the snivelling coward? Well, that will happen over my dead body.'

A blast made Jimmy jump. Then a hot pain registered, flaming a redness through his brain, before an impenetrable blackness engulfed him. It was a swirling blackness that lifted him as if he was a feather and took him towards a beautiful light. As he floated, all fear and feeling left him, and a happiness like none he'd ever felt before settled on him. Into this happiness came a voice. A voice that he loved and had missed so much – that of their Bobby: 'Come on, lad. Eeh, you took your time; we were expecting you five minutes since.'

Nothing moved; even the breeze died. Albert stared at the crumpled body of Jimmy as he tried to process what had happened. He hadn't reckoned on the fact that the officer in charge had a handgun with which to finish the job, if the squad hadn't hit the target. How could he forget such a vital piece of information?

An intense rage boiled inside him. It took away all reasoning. Tearing at the officer, he raised his rifle and, with blood-curdling screams, brought the weapon crashing down on the cowering figure of the man, who no longer held any authority for him. Blow after crushing blow reduced the man's head to a bloody mess.

'Stop, for Christ's sake! Corp, stop!'

These words, and the hands that restrained him, brought Albert back to sanity. With the return of his reasoning came remembrance of his plan. Shaking himself free, he dashed over to the box, retrieved his Chauchat machine rifle and stood, holding them all back.

Their shocked faces reflected back to him the enormity of what he intended to do, but he couldn't change his mind.

'Corporal, for God's sake! Whatever your intention, allow me to tend to Private O'Flynn and the officer. I have to make sure O'Flynn is dead, and the officer may need my help.'

Registering the medic and the priest standing on the sidelines for the first time since before the shooting, Albert waved the medic forward. Once he'd done his checks, Albert ordered him and the now-kneeling priest to lie facedown in front of him, where he could see them.

His men had quietened. They stood like statues, gaping at him. None of them had a weapon to hand with which to stop him, having swapped theirs for the ones he'd given them.

'I'm sorry.' Opening fire, he made every bullet count. Each soldier – whether still standing in his shocked position, or on the move ready to run for his life – took a bullet in the knee or thigh.

The air filled with their screams of agony.

Cries of 'You fucking bastard!', 'You fucking traitor!' and 'Why?' came to him, and the horror of the scene with his men, his faithful comrades-in-arms, writhing in a bloodbath of pain, nearly undid him. But his reason for inflicting the pain helped him to cope, as he tried to explain. 'Shut up and listen. I'm sorry, but I 'ad to do it...'

'Fuck off, you bastard!'

'Listen, Jacky. I'm telling yer, I 'ad to. I won't be with you, to 'elp save you. I'm off. This way, I've given yer your tickets 'ome.'

As no further protests broke the moans of agony, Albert turned his attention to the prostrate figures of the priest and medic in front of him. Taking out his shotgun, he aimed it at the priest.

'Don't, Corp – don't. What you've done so far I can come to live with, but killing innocent men, I couldn't. I'd not be able to live with it. For Christ's sake, spare them.'

This plea from Brigsy didn't penetrate the hot feeling inside him, the searing hate of the officers, which he'd never experienced before. He had to kill them, he had to! He couldn't leave witnesses. The shots brought forward cries of anguish that would live with him forever, as the pain of killing innocent men pierced his soul.

Without warning, exhaustion crept over Albert. His legs wouldn't hold him. He slumped to the ground on his knees. He had to make his men understand. 'I didn't want to 'urt yer, lads, not ever, but I couldn't bear the thought of leaving yer to go through a court martial and a firing squad, when I was out of it. That's why I did this to yer and why I killed them.' He pointed at the dead bodies of the priest and the medic. 'Now, there's no witnesses as to what 'appened. Tell them that I went berserk and shot everyone. Tell them that you tried to carry out your duty, but that knowing which ones of yer I'd given the live bullets to, I must 'ave shot them first, making it so that you missed. That will explain your rifles 'aving been discharged. Say that the officer, realizing what was 'appening, shot Jimmy, and then I bludgeoned 'im to death. I 'ope you can see me reasoning and can forgive me. I'm done for, anyway. Oh, I'll take me chance and run for it, but I don't 'old out much 'ope.'

It was Reeto who spoke. Everyone called Ivan

Hardcastle 'Reeto' because of his northern accent, and because this is what he said when others said 'Righto' to an instruction,

Struggling to speak and still writhing in agony, he muttered, 'I – I reckon as I can speak for all... At this moment I could t – take a gun to thee, Albert Price, but I – I know as I am going to be thanking you in the f – future, 'cause as I see it, you've been for saving our lives and giving us a ticket home. That is, if we don't die of blood loss or some infection or other.'

Feeling his strength come back into him, Albert stood up. 'Thanks, Reeto, I'm glad you can see me intention. Now, don't worry, I told Freddie Bird to stay awake. I told 'im that if we weren't back in the hour, which is what we usually are, then he was to raise the alarm as we would need 'elp. I didn't tell 'im all of me plan, but enough so that he took notice. You all know 'im, and know he will keep 'is word, so I'll leave you now and take me chances. Good luck, and thanks for all the times you protected me back. I only 'ope you can come to see that today I was looking after yours.'

Only curses followed him, but he understood that. They gave him a moment of deep remorse, as he straddled the old bike that he'd hidden there earlier. It had been found in a ditch before all the fighting started in earnest. He and a few others had worked on it when they could – pinching stuff from the stores and doing it up and making it roadworthy. That had been a good time, a time of bonding, and the bike had provided them with a means of fun as well as transport.

Since then he'd run the gauntlet of a million

chances of death, and had seen good lads killed or maimed in their thousands, and all for nothing. Nothing for him, anyway, as he now faced a life of never going back to his beloved East End. Never to have a laugh with his mates in the Elephant and Castle, or to save up a few coppers and go up west for a night out. Nor would he ever again enjoy a cup of cockles, or juggle a handful of roast chestnuts as he swaggered down the street with a wench on his arm. All gone. And what of the new life he'd planned in his head? But then that was an impossible dream. He had to admit it: his love for Edith – the almost painful feeling for her that consumed him – was never going to go anywhere. He'd be better off dead.

Slipping his hand into his pocket, his fingers curled round the handle of the pistol. Sweat broke out from every pore of his body, and his hand shook. But then a picture of Edith's face came to him. He saw her lovely, calming smile and knew he had to live. And he knew, too, that he had to live out his life with her. He would go to her and beg her to accompany him; but if she wouldn't, though it would break his heart to do so, he would force her to at gunpoint.

Edith lay awake. Her mind was too troubled for her to find solace in sleep. Somehow she felt that all was not well at home, but she couldn't think what could be wrong. Christian had been to see her earlier and had told her Douglas was safe, so she knew they were both well.

Christian had looked pale and his cheeks were sunken. His eyes were fearful, as he'd told her that he was to command a force that would try to take Delville Wood. He'd told her that the task was going to be a very difficult and dangerous one, but that he had every faith in his men. 'That Corporal Price, who gave us the message that you were here, is to be made up to Sergeant and assigned to me. A good man, by all accounts,' he'd said, and had gone on to say, 'We are set for tomorrow, but he doesn't know yet. I am to inform him in the morning.'

She'd had to look away and had felt silly in the presence of her brother, for having the thoughts that had visited her about the corporal. After a moment she'd managed to say, 'Oh yes, a very good man. He cares about those he is in charge of, but he is suffering badly today, because tonight he has to be in the party that has to shoot one of their own. A young boy, Jimmy O'Flynn. It's disgusting, Christian. Jimmy is mentally ill, not a coward. Since when do we English put to death our mentally ill patients?'

Christian hung his head. 'I know, and I agree with you. The practice sickens my stomach. And yet I can see the value of the deterrent, and the need for one. I am sorry for the boy and his family, and I hope Price comes out of this as he always does, with his head held high. He should do, as he has always put his duty above his personal feelings.'

'Sorry for his family,' she'd almost shouted. 'Christian, Jimmy is their last son – their last child! His brothers were killed at the beginning of the war. Jimmy defied the King's orders that no more of the family would be asked to serve, by

131

coming to do his bit. He is sixteen! Is there nothing you can do to stop this?'

His shamefaced 'No, I am so sorry', and the tear she saw in his eye, stopped her from berating him further. Orders were orders at the end of the day and, a captain or not, he had to follow them and uphold them.

Her thoughts went back to Albert. She wasn't so sure he would cope and come out ready to carry on and do his duty. He had expressed extreme distress at the coming execution, but he also knew it was his responsibility to do this last act for one of his own. *Ha! Duty – responsibility! How much of that can they ask of one man?*

Edith feared for him, and her fear left her tossing and turning until she felt herself drifting off. But it seemed she'd only just closed her eyes when a hand shook her awake. Terror gripped her, and her dread of bad news came rushing back into her confused mind.

'Edith, Edith ... shush...! It's Albert. Oh, Edith.'

'Oh, Albert, you frightened me, what are you doing here? Are you all right? What's happened? Oh, my dear, you are crying.'

'Come outside. I don't want to wake anyone. Get your things on, though, as it's cold and wet out there.'

Whispering as Albert had, Edith told him she would only be a minute. Her arms ached to hold and comfort him, but this made her cross with herself. What was she thinking! Always in control of her emotions, it was disconcerting to have them run away with themselves and propel her into making decisions she might not otherwise take.

Rain soaked her the moment she stepped outside. She should have been used to it by now, but she wasn't. The mud sucked in her wellingtons, making it difficult to step towards the huddled figure of Albert waiting at the end of the dormitory tent.

A shock went through her as she neared him and his hand shot out and grabbed her. 'I 'ave to go, Edith. I've done something really bad. I want you to come with me.'

'What! I can't – don't be ridiculous. Let go of me, Albert, you're hurting my arm. What have you done that has meant you have to go? Surely nothing is that bad that you have to become a deserter?'

'I killed three officers. I – I lost me reasoning. Please come, Edith. They will be after me by now. I 'ave to leave right now. I'll tell you all about it as we go. But if we don't go now and they catch me, they'll 'ave to shoot me on sight, as I won't go without a fight. Please, Edith, I – I love you.'

Horror at what he'd said rendered her speechless, but then the thought of Albert being shot made her heart sink as if a heavy weight had landed on it. But despite this, she knew she could not desert her patients and her colleagues, who all relied on her. 'I cannot believe what you are saying, Albert. This isn't like you. My brother was here today and he said you had been singled out to go with him; he said you were known as the bravest and most loyal soldier. Why? Why are you doing this?'

'I've no time to tell you. Just believe me that if we don't go, I will die.'

133

'Then you must go, but I can't come with you. I'm needed here. I have to stay. Please, let go of me and get away as quickly as you can. I will pray for you, my dear, and send my love with you. Stay safe, and we will meet up in the future, I am sure of that.'

'You are coming, Edith! Me life is worth nothing without you.'

The cold steel of the barrel of his gun dug into her neck. Stunned, she gasped for breath, drawing droplets of rain into her mouth. 'No! No, don't do this. I will scream.'

Choking from his hand clutching her mouth, she felt her body being wrenched towards him. Not wanting to hurt him more than she was already, but having no choice, she kicked out at his shins. But she was no match for his strength, and felt her feet dragged from beneath her as he pulled her along with him.

Though her wits wouldn't give her a way of escaping Albert, she did think to dig her boots into the mud, in the hope that they would make a trail. But even as she did so, part of her didn't want him to be caught. His actions were not those of a man who is right in his mind. Something had tipped him over the edge. This was not Albert doing this terrible thing, but something in him that might have lain dormant all his life, had it not been released by some horrific trigger. She could only guess that the trigger must have been Jimmy's death.

As he dragged her with his hand over her mouth, she had to take gasping breaths. Her neck hurt from the strong hold he had around it. The sound of his breath labouring, as hers was, gave her hope; the struggle was sapping his strength. Making one last effort, she pushed at him. Albert's hold on her broke, sending her sinking into the mud. Spitting the rain and dirt from her mouth, she allowed a sob to escape her and begged of him once more, 'P – please, Albert, just go. Go!' But then her fear was compounded to horror.

'I am going. Forgive me.'

And she saw, in the dawning light, his gun being placed in his mouth. 'No, no, Albert. Not that. I'll come. I'll come with you... Please, not that!'

Lifting herself, Edith went to him and helped to take the gun from his mouth. His body leaned heavily on her, and his pitiful words tugged at the inner part of her that knew she loved him. ''Elp me... 'Elp me.'

'I will. Don't worry, I will help you.' A sudden thought came to her: *Marianne!* They could make their way to Marianne's apartment. She would help them and then, when Albert was safe, she could come back here and resume her work, telling them that she'd escaped. Wiping the tears and rain from her eyes, she took hold of Albert's hand. 'I have a friend who may help us. She lives in the South of France. We can sort out getting to her later, but for now let's just get as far away from here as we can. Which is the safest route to take?'

'I think we should keep to the coast and make our way down towards Spain. But it's going to be 'ard going, Edith, and I 'ave to make it look as though you are me prisoner, in case they catch up with us.'

'Will they be looking for you now?'

135

'I'm not sure. It's been an hour or more since it 'appened. So I think them at base-camp know by now what's gone on. They may wait for it to get lighter and send a party out after me, or they may not be able to spare the men. There's an offensive planned for later today, and it means splitting the battalion as it is – or, rather, what's left of it.'

Edith assumed he was referring to the planned offensive on Delville Wood. 'Yes, I know. I told you, my brother is leading part of it. He was relying on you.'

Albert's demeanour changed in an instant. He was once more in command of himself and the situation. His hand tightened on hers. 'I can't 'elp that. Come on, let's take the coastal road. But if we see anyone, I will grab you and make it look like you are with me against your will.'

Protesting no more, she did as he said, but inside she thought, *I* am *going against my will, but yet, at the same time, I am willing, if it will save him.* With this thought came a self-loathing at the weakness her love for Albert had given her. How could she think like that when so many relied on her to save their lives?

Everything in her wanted to turn and run, but his grip on her felt as though she was being held by an iron fist. What choice did she have? Putting her head down against the onslaught of the wind and the rain, and matching his step, she took no heed of the tears that flowed down her cheeks.

9

Ada

Low Moor, late July 1916
A heart can only take so much pain

Ada lifted the latch of her front door. The smell of cigarette smoke told her Paddy was in. Her insides clenched. He had become a monster that she feared – and fear was one of the few emotions she felt these days, as most of the time she was devoid of emotion.

Life had become something to get through, rather than to live. Somehow she got up each day and went to her work at the munitions factory. Somehow she endured Paddy's onslaughts on her body, and the pain of his and her sister's betrayal.

Peering around the door, she saw the empty scullery. There was nothing out of place except a butt-end smouldering in the tin lid that Paddy used as an ashtray. He must be out the back, as she could see the back door was ajar. As she stepped inside, the sound of Paddy crying stopped her in her tracks. By the direction from which the sound was coming, she knew he was in their loft bedroom. Her body stiffened against the pain she could hear in his sobs.

Afraid to ask, she waited. Hardly able to breathe, she clung onto the high-backed wooden chair.

'Ada, me Ada. Oh God, how is it that I should give you this news? I can't ... I can't. Christ! Why, why?'

Looking up at his haggard face, staring down at her from the top of the ladder that led to the loft, gave her heart a jolt, and an urge to scream at what she knew to be a truth. But no sound came when she opened her mouth. Her body crumpled. Barely making it to the fireside chair, she slumped into it. Vomit rose to her throat. She grabbed the empty coal scuttle and retched into it.

Paddy's footsteps resounded around the room as he descended the wooden ladder. At the bottom he staggered. Was he drunk?

Picking up the stub of his cigarette, he threw it past her and into the empty fire grate. The thought came to her, as she wiped her mouth with her pinny, that she should get the blackening out and clean up the stove. It had been a long time since it had been done. But then she was working all hours God sent her, and her bones ached with tiredness. Some chores she just had to let slip.

Still ignoring Paddy, she thought about her stash. Now, amounting to the huge sum of twenty pounds, she knew she would be able to leave soon and make a new life for herself. Twenty pounds! She couldn't believe it, and felt rich beyond her dreams. But then the long hours of shift work and piece-work and her working in the most danger-ous shop meant that she had netted just over six pounds a week. Paddy didn't know. He tried to guess, but as he got a fair whack of it, he thought she was tipping up the lot.

God knows what he would do if he found out

the truth. But she hoped to be long gone before that day.

His cries penetrated her thoughts. Why had her mind gone off on such a tangent, when there was terrible news to face?

'Tell me, Paddy. Tell me.'

'I – I don't know how to. Here, it is better that you read this for yourself.'

Taking the crisp paper from him, Ada let her eyes fall on the words: *Your son, James O'Flynn, has been killed in action.*

Just that. No 'We regret to inform you', as had been written for Bobby and Jack. Nor did it say 'He died bravely', as it was said they had. Nothing – just 'killed'. Her mind repeated the word over and over: 'killed ... killed ... killed'! The last time turned into a scream that sounded as if it came from a mad woman, as her heart ripped in two. Tears didn't come, though; this was too much for tears, but hatred came. Hatred and blame.

'You killed him, Paddy! You, with your thinking he was his own man. I could have got him off – the bloody King said I could – but no, you said Jimmy should go. I hate you... I HATE YOU!'

Paddy didn't move. His body remained bent over the table, but Ada hadn't finished with him, because while she felt like this she'd give him all the pain that clutched at her chest.

'But you don't care, do you? You can spawn as many bairns as you want, can't you? Beryl's carrying one for you already. You've shagged me own sister! So what price me lads, eh? What d'you care.'

'Will you shut your mouth? Care? Me strapping boys gone – all gone – and you are for saying I don't care!'

The strength had come back into him, as now he stood at his full height. Anger flared from every pore of him. Snatching up the poker, Ada stood brandishing it in front of her, spitting out her guts at him. 'You come near me and I'll smash your head to pieces. Murderer! Vile, wife-cheating, wife-beating bastard!'

'Enough, woman. A man can only take so much. Come into me arms and let me give comfort to you. It is together we should stand at such a time.'

'Comfort! I'd as soon jump into the fire as into your arms, you murdering swine.'

The blow came without her seeing him move, he was that fast. His hand slapped her face, shocking her and rendering her unable to see what was coming. And so, before she was ready, a punch sank into her belly, taking the wind from her.

Paddy caught her sinking body and held her to him. His tears wet her hair and her face; his cries held the agony of grief. Gasping for breath, Ada could do nothing to stop him carrying her to their bed. But if she had the strength she would kick his proud manhood – kick and kick it till it lay, never to harden again. Instead, all she could do was lie limply while he stripped her of her knickers and entered her.

She had never been taken like it, and she never wanted to be taken like it again. Howling his sorrow with every thrust, Paddy gave her no pleasure, but only increased her heartache and grief. He had been her man, and now he had gone, just as those he'd sired had. He was nothing to her –

140

nothing. His groan and the stiffening of his body told her he'd reached his end. She took his weight as he slumped down on her. He remained still, causing her further pain with the heaviness of him on her bruised body. She hadn't the strength to move him from her, but she had to, or she would suffocate. 'Sh – shift yourself, Paddy, you ... you've had what you wanted. You ... beat it out of – of ... me again. For God's – s – sake, let me breathe.'

As his body rolled off her and he withdrew from her, he muttered, 'You bitch!'

She took no notice of him as she gasped in deeply, trying to fill her lungs.

'You drive me to do what I do, then you blame me and make me feel like I've raped me own wife. You give me nothing now. Nothing. It's like shagging a rice pudding – and that's for insulting the pudding me mammy used to make me. I'm telling you, I'm for taking up the offer I've had from that young widow up the road, Rosie Parfit. She's after me giving her what she's missing, now her Dean's gone. And she ain't a bad looker, and promises to be a good little shag.'

It surprised Ada how much this hurt, but she wasn't going to show it. 'By, she'll soon ditch you. You're past it. Any man as can't keep his own wife happy ain't worth a light. Eeh, they all know as you're searching for sommat as you haven't had in a long while. They say you go from woman to woman 'cause you're trying to prove you're still the man you were. Ha, they laugh at thee, Paddy O'Flynn!'

Paddy drew himself to his full height, but this

141

stance only lasted a few seconds as he collapsed into a heap. His body hit the wooden floor with a thud.

'Paddy, Paddy...'

A growl that could have come from an animal shuddered through him. With it, Paddy regained consciousness, looked up at her and released a strangled cry. 'Our boys, our babbies – all gone ... all gone. Gone, Ada. By Jesus, how are we to go on, Ada? How?'

She could not answer him. Her anger had gone. He only had two ways of coping: one was to hit out, and the other was to take a woman – any woman. She realized that. This crying and giving up wasn't Paddy, but she couldn't help him now. She needed her own release from the pain of her loss, and from the pain of the treatment Paddy had meted out to her. Rising, she left him lying there and ran from the room.

Once down the ladder, she ran out of the door, not caring that her hair was matted, her face bruised, her stomach hurt, and that between her legs she was wet and sticky and had no knickers on, because none of these things mattered. Nothing mattered. Jimmy was gone.

Reaching the beck, she waded in. How often had she brought her lads here with a bottle of water and some butties of bread and jam? They had fished with empty jam jars, catching tiddlers, and she had let the sun warm her and had dreamed her dreams as she lay on the grass. Now she stood in the middle of the beck, with the water swirling around her, and there were no cries of 'Mam, I've caught one' or 'Mam, our Jimmy's scaring the fish

– he's too noisy'.

There were no hungry lads stuffing themselves and leaving trails of sticky jam around their mouths. There were no quarrels breaking out over Jimmy's crusts. Jimmy never liked to eat the crust of the bread, and the other two had vied for them, grabbing them from him, wrestling them away from the other. *Eeh, I shouted at them to give over, or I'd clip their ears!* 'WHERE ARE YOU NOW, ME LADS! WHERE ARE YOU!' Her screams assaulted her ears, and water sprayed over her as she thrashed the surface of the beck in her anguish. 'I WANT ME LADS. I WANT ME LADS!'

'Eeh, Ada. Ada, me lass.'

Arms that she knew held only kindness came around her. Through swollen eyes she looked into the gentle face of Joe. 'He – he's gone, Joe. Jimmy: me lad. He's gone, Joe.'

'Aw, lass, lass.'

'Help me, Joe. Help me!'

'Come on, let's get out of the water.'

Her feet squelched in the mud and her soft shoes came off. Realizing this when they reached the bank, Joe waded back in and retrieved them. 'Here, Ada, love. I've a flask just up the bank. I'd come down to do a spot of fishing. I allus bring a picnic with me when the weather's nice. When I'm on late shift, that is. Come and sit down and have a sup. It'll not be hot, but warm and sweet, so it'll help you.'

With only her empty sobs to break the silence, they sat together on the bank. As if nothing could change it, the water in the beck babbled on over the pebbles and rocks that formed its bed. A shimmering light reflected the sun and dappled its surface. A breeze tickled the air, bringing everything around them into life, making the buttercups and daisies nod to each other and the branches of the trees dip and sway.

Using Joe's huge white hanky, Ada wiped her tears and snot, but more followed in a constant stream, emptying her of all emotion. She was like the beck, she thought, rolling along, bubbling up when hitting a rock, and calming when trickling over the smooth bits. But would there ever be any smooth bits ever again?

'I'm reet sorry, lass. I know as that doesn't help, and I have a lot more to give than just being sorry, but now isn't the time to even talk about that. What will you do, Ada, love?'

'I don't know, Joe. I just want to end it all. Go to me lads and have done with the pain.'

'Naw! Eeh, naw. That's not the answer, lass. There is happiness in this world for you. You know how I feel about you, and I would work till the end of me days at making you happy again, if there was a way that I could.'

'I'm leaving Paddy, Joe. I – I don't know where I'm going yet, but I have to get away from him. He – he had me sister...'

'Aye, I know. But stay a while, lass. You need to be with him through this. You brought young Jimmy into the world together, and you have to see his passing through together. If you don't, there'll be no end to it all. Then, when this lot's done – the war, I mean – if you'll let me, I'll help you get away. I'll take you away from it all.'

'I can't... He'll kill me, Joe. He beats me and

rapes me. It's like he has to punish me for what he is. He blames me for his own weaknesses.'

'Naw! God, Ada, I had no idea.'

A voice, scathing and angry, cut him off. 'Is it a man you have behind me back, then? Getaway home, you filthy whore!'

'Paddy! Naw, it's not what you think. This is Joe from me factory, he's been helping me.'

'Aye, and I can guess just how it is that he is helping you. You bastard!' Paddy swung out at Joe, but Joe dodged the blow and caught Paddy's arm and swung it in such a way that Paddy was flung to the ground.

'Look, Paddy, it ain't what you think it is. As Ada was saying, we work together. Aye, we're friends, but that's all. I were fishing, and Ada needed help. If you were any sort of a husband, you'd give her that help. She's a grieving mother.'

Paddy had had the breath knocked out of him and struggled to get it back. In that moment Ada felt sorry for him. 'Don't be daft now, Paddy. You know you're me man and there ain't naw other. We've a lot on our plate, and fighting ain't going to make it better. Let's go home.'

'And, while we're on, Paddy.' Ada held her breath at this from Joe, but let him continue, without protesting. 'I don't want to hear as you take it out on your missus again. I'm reet sorry for your loss, but beating her ain't sommat as I'll put up with.'

Shocked that Paddy didn't answer, and that Joe sounded, well, so unlike Joe, Ada just stood there and waited. Something had happened here that she'd never seen before. Her Paddy had met his

145

match; and for that match to be Joe, who was looked upon as a weakling, made her unsure how this situation would pan out.

As Paddy went to rise, Joe offered him a hand. 'You've been through the mill, man. Both of you have. No one should have to bear what you two have had to. If there's owt I can do, let me know.' With this, he retrieved and replaced the cap that had fallen off his head in the tussle, picked up his things and walked away.

Ada stood, not daring to move.

'How is it that you're all wet, Ada?'

Paddy's voice had a soft tone, and an almost ashamed note to it.

'I ran into the water. I don't know why, but me and the lads used to come here and...'

'Aye, I know. Well, let's go home. We'll not find our lads here, or anywhere we look. We need to start to pick up the pieces.'

'You've to change, Paddy. If I'm to stay, you've to change.'

'Don't you think I know that, Ada? Me ways are not how things should be, but it is as if I am driven. But I will try. I promise, I will try.'

'There's to be no going off with others and putting it about. You've to think on about doing sommat in the way of working for the war effort, instead of living in the bookie's pocket. And the beatings and the rape have to stop.'

'Are you accusing me of raping me own wife again? Huh! I'm entitled to have you when I want you, and no court in the land will have it otherwise, so think on. You give willingly to me, and stop making it that I have to force you. That sin is yours, Ada, and it is one as leads me to look elsewhere. But the beating of you – well, that isn't something I like doing. I will swear on me lad's death-beds–'

'Don't!' Shivering as if she would never stop, Ada looked up at him. 'Don't ever use our lads' names to swear owt. I can't bear it.'

'I'm sorry, that wasn't what I should have done. Damn it, woman! How many concessions do you want from me? Let's go home, Ada. Come on, me wee lass, let's go home.'

Taking his hand felt right, but the action deepened her confusion. A big part of her wanted rid of this man, but there was still a small part of her that couldn't give up on him.

10

Eloise

London and Leicestershire, mid–August 1916
Loss and revelations

'Daddy?' Eloise's tentative address to her father reflected the morose mood the family had fallen into, since the reality of Andrina's passing, four weeks ago, had hit them. Unable to stay at their country home with the memory of the tragedy so raw, they had returned to London, but the move hadn't helped.

Her father was leaning over his desk reading a letter. Looking up, he glanced over his half-glasses at her, but didn't speak. This unnerved her more than she was already.

'Daddy, can I talk to you? I want to do something. Being idle is driving me mad!'

'D – don't ask me to let you go to France, my dear, I – I cannot.'

'No, I know, but what about helping with something here? Hospital work, or something at the War Office; anything really. I have a conscience, Daddy, and feel as though I am letting the side down. There isn't a family we know that hasn't got somebody – son, daughter, father or even mother – helping the war effort, except us.'

'I don't think you can say that. I am involved, as far as I can be, with strategies that have to be discussed in the House of Lords. And of course, your cousins... Look, my dear, we will talk about this later. I have news. It – it isn't good, and I don't know how to tell your mama. I'm sorry, but I can't give my attention to your needs at the moment, though there is something I have to discuss that concerns you.'

'What is it, Father? I mean, the bad news. Oh God, cousins Christian and Douglas are all right, aren't they?'

'As far as I know, my dear, but poor Edith isn't. I haven't wanted to tell you and your mother before, it was all too much for you, but Uncle Christopher and Aunt Muriel are coming down from the country where they have been since Andrina... Well, you see, my dear, it happened on the same day... I – I couldn't tell you, and your

148

aunt and uncle understood, but now, with them being just down the road, I have to. They are distraught, and more so as time goes on.'

'Oh God! Edith? Why? How?'

Listening to her father shocked and frightened her. *Edith dragged off by a demented corporal, who had beaten his superior to death and shot two officers and his fellow soldiers!* It all sounded preposterous, but there was no doubt. The corporal had ridden away from the scene of his terrible crimes on a bike. That bike had been found outside Edith's dormitory tent. Deep ruts in the mud showed that Edith had been dragged. No one knew why she'd dressed and gone out in the rain to him, but she had, and now... 'Oh, Daddy, the world has gone mad. Poor Edith. Is there no news of where she is?'

'No, I'm afraid there isn't. I am, of course, doing all I can. I put in a request to get the boys back on leave, and think it may be granted.'

'Oh, Daddy, I can't bear it.'

She slumped in the chair just inside her father's office. Every limb shook, and her stomach churned till she felt she would be sick. This was all impossible. It hadn't happened. Things like kidnap happened to other people. But one look at her father's face told her that it was true. *Oh God help us, and please help my darling Edith!*

'I asked this of you just four weeks ago, my darling girl, but I have to ask again. Please try to be strong for your mother and, more than anything, for Aunt Muriel and Uncle Christopher. I will do all I can to get Christian and Douglas home for them – well, for us all, really. Don't cry, darling.' But as he said the words and rose and came over to her, to hold her in his arms, he too was crying.

Tears seemed so futile and didn't release the grief and sadness trapped inside Eloise. To her, they only increased the pain, as the loss of her darling sister was still very raw in her heart. The news about Edith only compounded her grief. It seemed the only thing to do was to give up altogether or soldier on. Her father had asked her to do the latter, and she had to, for his sake. He needed help, as he had to be the strong pin that held them all from falling apart. She would give all she had and would stand by him in that.

She released herself from her sobbing father's arms. 'We can get through it, Daddy. With your help, we can all get through. I will be there for you and Mama, and my dear aunt and uncle.' And as she said this, she knew that she had undergone a profound change. She didn't know when it had happened, but she was a million miles from the girl she used to be, whose head had been full of nothing more than the pursuit of fun, fashion and a marriage partner.

None of those things mattered to her now. Her youth had been peeled from her, layer by painful layer. She was now a woman. A strong woman.

'Daddy, you said there was something else concerning me?'

'Yes, dear. It is about Jay.'

She shuddered, and her father said, 'I know, I hated hearing his name, but I don't think we can let him shoulder all the blame for what happened. As appalling as it is to acknowledge, it appears Jay and Andrina were in love.'

150

'I can't accept that, Daddy. Andrina was bored; she hated the country life and wanted a distraction. She had a silly crush on Jay. He used that to lure her in deeper than she should have gone. He knew what he was doing. And he must have known Florrie was in love with him, and what she was really like. He must have known what Florrie was capable of. He killed Andrina, just as surely as Florrie did, and he should hang!'

'My dear, I had no idea you felt like this. You're wrong – you have to see. Andrina was a headstrong girl. If she set her heart on something, she usually got it. Look, Mama found her diary. It seems she was deeply in love with Jay, but knew it was wrong and hadn't... Well, anyway, it seems that Jay had respected her wishes not to do anything other than meet up and hope, I suppose. Poor d – darling Andrina.' His voice broke once more.

She resisted the urge to go to him. 'What do you want me to do, Daddy?'

'Jay is asking for you. He is very fragile and could still die from his injuries, but this letter from Doctor Jacques, whom I have asked to continue to treat Jay at my expense, says that Jay's agitation is holding back his recovery. He is very distressed and constantly asks for you.'

'Do you want me to go to him? What about all that is going on here?'

'Once Mama sees how strong you are, that will help her. But at the moment there is nothing you can do for your uncle and aunt. I don't know why, but I can't bear the thought of Jay dying. It is as if he is family – well, servant family, if you know

151

what I mean. No, he is more than that. I – I can't say, I mean... Anyway, we have to remember that he made dearest Andrina happy. You know, h – he came to us at a very young age, and was always hanging around, helping the gardener of the time. And there is a... Oh, I don't know.'

'I do, Daddy. You are a wonderful person who cares about people. Naturally you care for someone who has been in your employ for such a long time. I will go to Jay, but not until I have been to see Aunt Muriel and Uncle Christopher and have made sure that Mama is coping.'

'Thank you, my dear. I will let the doctor know. Just knowing you have consented to come should put Jay's mind at rest. My dear, will you also call in on his poor mother – I mean, adoptive mother – whilst you are there? Tell her how sorry we are.'

'I will. Daddy, is there something else troubling you in all this?'

'Yes, a suspicion. Oh, it's nothing. I must go and see your dear mama now, Eloise. Forgive me, but I can't put off telling her the dreadful news any longer. Will you come with me?'

Eloise knew her heart was beating loudly as she waited outside the Feilding Palmer Cottage Hospital male ward, in Lutterworth, a small market town situated about five miles from her home in Leicestershire.

The nurse in attendance was making Jay 'presentable', as she put it. How could he be un-presentable?

A cry of pain made her stiffen. It had come from Jay. Eloise felt a moment of pity for him; she was not entirely without sympathy. Since arriving at Rossworth Hall the day before, she had talked to Maggie, the downstairs maid, and found that everyone's sympathy lay with Jay. Maggie had even said, 'Begging your pardon, M'lady, and I don't wish to speak ill of the dead, but Lady Andrina had no right to mix with the servants. It wasn't her rightful place, and she stepped over the line in doing so.'

Though feeling angry at Maggie, Eloise had known that of course the girl was right. The blame for the liaison had to lie with Andrina, despite what she thought about Jay luring her dear sister. After all, he would never have come to Andrina; she had to go to him. That wasn't Jay luring her, but more Andrina courting his attention.

These conclusions had helped. It wasn't nearly as painful to come and see Jay as it would have been had she still blamed him.

This thought had hardly died in her when the door opened. 'You can come in now, Lady Eloise.'

The smell of carbolic soap hit her as she walked through the door. She'd never been in a hospital ward before, and it seemed she had walked into a room of white when she first glanced around the door. The bed linen and the nurse's uniform, the bandages around Jay's head and even the small chair next to the bed were all white. But then she realized that the brick walls were cream and the bottom half of them had green tiles.

Nerves jangled in her stomach. What was she going to say to him? Would he even be able to read her lips, because his head looked as though it was completely covered in bandages, to below

153

his eyes!

'La – lady Eloise?'

'Yes, Jay, it's me.'

His hand gestured that she should come nearer and she realized he couldn't see her face. It was silly of her to have spoken until she was nearer the bed and bent over him. Doing that now, she saw that one of his eyes was uncovered. 'Are you all right, Jay?'

A tear trickled down his cheek. The sight undid her. Her legs gave way, and she abruptly sat down into the chair. But she must not give way to the clogging feeling in her chest. She had to swallow hard and compose herself, otherwise she would drown in the sorrow that had her in its grip. After a moment she stood over Jay again. 'I'm sorry, Jay, I don't know what I can do to help you.'

Through his tears he sobbed, 'Find forgiveness for me. You and – and Lord and Lady Mellor. Please forgive me.'

'We don't hold you responsible, Jay. It – it was more Andrina.'

'No! We–'

'I know, you were in love. But still, she should have known better than to have started a liaison. You – you are a servant.'

'I – I shouldn't be. I should be the rightful owner of Hastleford Hall. I am–'

'What are you talking about? Your head injury must have sent you out of your proper mind. How can you say such a thing?'

'My – my mother. My adoptive m – mother will tell you. I am a Daverly. I – I was born before Lord Daverly ... died. I am his son.'

'Oh God! You really believe this? But it's impossible. As I understand it, there were no male heirs, and that is why the house went to my aunt. You're being ridiculous. Aunt Muriel was an only child. I – I mean... Look, you have had a head injury; that must have unbalanced you and given you this preposterous idea!'

'No, it's true. P – please go and talk to my mother.'

'Very well, I will. But this is all nonsense, and she will laugh at me. Jay, my aunt's family is in turmoil. They can't take this kind of – well, fear that they may lose their country home, on top of all that is happening.'

'Th – they won't. I – I just want to prove who I really am. If it had ha – happened before... then A – Andrina and I, we could have married. I am no relation to you; only my sister – half-sister – is. She is your aunt by marriage, that's all.'

Once more his tears began to flow.

'Don't torture yourself. I am sure these are thoughts that are visiting you in your weakest moment. I'll sort it out. Everything will be fine, I promise.' She caught a small glint of hope in Jay's eye. But, for her, the thought of any of this being true appalled her.

She didn't want to open the door of the butcher's shop. The bell above it clanged as she did so. Mr Tattumby looked up from the task of chopping raw meat, dropped his cleaver and touched his forelock. 'Good afternoon, Lady Eloise. I expect you've come to see Mrs Tattumby?' Unable to find her voice, she nodded. 'Come on through,

M'lady. Mrs Tattumby is expecting you.'

Dodging the dripping animal limbs hanging around the shop, Eloise followed him. She was surprised by the brightness of the parlour; with its smell of beeswax polish still in the air, it gave a warm welcome. Pretty, hand-embroidered cushions and antimacassars adorned the two brown leather armchairs and matching sofa. The wooden legs and arms of these were carved and shone, so that they had the appearance of a deep lustre. The red-tiled floor had the same gleam, and the scattered rag rugs were of a light beige with intricate patterns of flowers and birds woven into them. They were a thing of beauty, and after greeting Mrs Tattumby and accepting the offer of a cup of tea and cake, Eloise had to comment on them. 'Did you make those beautiful rugs, Mrs Tattumby? I have never seen such perfection, or indeed any pattern in a rag rug before.'

'No, Jay made those. He is very clever with his hands, and very intelligent.'

'Oh?' She didn't know what else to say, as this answer was unexpected.

'Sit down, M'lady. I won't be a minute.'

When she opened the door to her kitchen, delicious smells of fresh baking wafted through. They gave comfort and said to Eloise that she was a welcome visitor and had been prepared for. She hadn't realized just how hungry she was, but the aromas tantalized her and she couldn't wait to eat whatever had been prepared.

'Here you are, M'lady.'

A plateful of delicious-looking scones lay on a tray with some butter and jam in little pots beside them. A china teapot stood next to these, and two china cups; no doubt the Sunday-best china, and all for her benefit. The gesture touched her and, as she had done many times in the last few weeks, she had to swallow hard. It was funny how small things like this kindness shown to her could trigger her grief.

'I know why you're here,' Mrs Tattumby began. 'I have wronged Jay. I don't know how he can forgive me, but he has. You see, I kept from him the truth of his birth and denied him his true place in life.' Her head sank so far into her neck that it almost rested on her huge bosom. A big lady in every way, including having a large, kind heart, Mrs Tattumby had a round, jolly face that was usually smiling, but now looked crestfallen and full of guilt.

'Well, if Jay has forgiven you, you should forgive yourself.'

'I know, but I find it difficult. I never did before ... what happened. I mean, I always said I would tell him when he reached twenty-five, and he could do what he wanted with the information, but none of this would have happened if I had told him earlier. He wouldn't have been a servant to anyone and could... Well, he could have had your sister's hand as he wanted to, and no servant girl would have thought of him as hers.' Again she dropped her head. 'I'm very sorry. I truly am very sorry. Me and Mr Tattumby have watched you and your sister grow up, and now I am the cause of the terrible circumstances that have come about.'

With an effort she didn't know she could muster, Eloise took a deep breath and, in the face of this woman's tears, didn't let one tear escape from her own eyes. 'No one is to blame. You couldn't have seen this as an outcome of keeping a secret. Now please, Mrs Tattumby, tell me who is Jay, really?'

'He is the son of the late Lord Daverly of Hastleford Hall and half-brother to Lady Muriel, the present owner. His mother was Lady Amelia Falding.'

'Good gracious – a half-brother of my Aunt Muriel! This cannot be true. And you say that Lady Amelia was his mother? But didn't she die somewhere abroad when she was very young?'

'No, she died in the attics of Hastleford Hall in 1891, giving birth to her son.'

'After my Aunt Muriel was already married and had her own children! I cannot take all of this in. It is preposterous! How can you say such a thing? The scandal!'

'It's because of the scandal that it was kept quiet, but it can all be proved. At least, there are folk still alive, who could be made to tell the truth. The local doctor at the time did everything the gentry wanted him to do. He is still alive, and no doubt would like to ease his conscience before he dies.'

'How do you know all this, Mrs Tattumby?'

'From a manservant – a horrible man called Horace Shepherd. He brought the baby to me, then disappeared. It was said that he stole a lot of the house silver and went off to America, but I know he was paid off. He did a nasty thing. He told me the truth about Jay's birth.'

'I think that was an honourable thing to do.'

'I know it does sound that way, but he was meant to take the baby to an orphanage in London. He was given money to do so, but he said that he thought of me, and the child. He said he'd come to love the child's mother, and he thought that one day the child should know who he was – and who his mother was. But he would never know, if he was dumped in an orphanage. Then he threatened me never to reveal the secret while the present lord was alive, or I would know the consequences. He suggested that I say the gypsies had left the child on me doorstep.'

'Why did you keep it secret, after Lord Daverly died, Mrs Tattumby? Why did you accept the child?'

'God forgive me, but you see, me and Mr Tattumby were childless, and I loved Jay on sight. I couldn't let that Horace take him to no orphanage. After Horace left, me and Mr Tattumby talked and talked. Should we, shouldn't we? In the end we decided we had no choice: we had to go along with the tale about the gypsies. It was convenient that they were in the area and disappeared overnight. Everyone accepted the story, and it gave me a reason to keep the baby I loved so much. And besides, the family would have denied it all and would probably have found a way of hounding us from the village and would have had the child taken from us and put God knows where. They were very powerful – they held positions in government and were known to be ruthless.'

'So, what did Horace tell you?'

'He told me that he had witnessed Lord Daverly and Lady Amelia together on many occasions during the time when Lady Daverly was still alive, but gravely ill. He knew what was going on between them. You see, it was well known that Lord Daverly was a womanizer, but it was said that Lady Daverly didn't care as long as he was discreet. She was a funny one. Very cold-hearted. Everyone used to say she must have shunned his attentions as she only had the one child.'

Frustration at these digressions made Eloise want to ask Mrs Tattumby to please stick to telling her relevant information about Jay, and Jay only, but she let the woman continue without interrupting her.

'Anyway, according to Horace, Lord Daverly was smitten by the young Lady Amelia, and she fell for him by all accounts. Then Her Ladyship died and the house was closed down. They brought most of the staff from London with them, when in residence anyway, but kept a few at the Hall – gardeners and such – to take care of the place. Horace was one of only two household staff retained at this time. The other was a maid, Betty Redhurst; she was something of a nurse, and had been with the family for years. Lived out her days in luxury, she did. Somewhere in the Stratford area, I heard.'

Eloise clasped her hands tightly, swallowed hard and steeled herself for what was to come. Keeping her voice steady she asked, 'And so, how did it happen that Jay was born there?'

'Horace said that one winter's night Lord Daverly arrived with a small party. He and Betty were called into Lord Daverly's office. They were told that there would be a guest arriving, but that

160

her presence must remain a secret to all. And that they would be charged with looking after the guest. They were sworn to strict secrecy, on the promise that they would receive a payment that would set them up for the rest of their lives; and were given the threat that if they told anybody anything, they and their families would be out on their ears. Their guest was the pregnant Lady Amelia. For the next five months no family attended the house, other than Lord Daverly. He would arrive in the middle of the night, stay until the next night and then leave. Betty got a room in the attic ready for the confinement, but there were complications. It didn't go well from the start, and Lady Amelia was very ill towards the end. About a week before the birth she was so distressed about having a bastard that a priest from Leicester was brought in and married her and Lord Daverly. The local doctor, Doctor Henderson, who is living in retirement in the next village, was witness to the marriage.'

'What? They were married, but then why...'

'Because it was done without her father's consent. And think about it. There would still have been a terrific scandal to face. To all of society, Amelia was abroad for a year. She was meant to be in India. How would her family live down the lie? No, the plan was for the child to be given away, and for Amelia then to go to India for a few months, saying that she had extended her time there, and then to return and marry Lord Daverly officially. But she died giving birth, poor soul. She is buried in an unmarked grave in the churchyard. In the dead of night they buried her, with no family attending. And the next thing it was said in the paper that she'd contracted an illness in India, and had died and been buried there. The only decent thing was the memorial service in London for her. At least that put her to rest, poor soul.'

Stunned into silence, Eloise just stared at Mrs Tattumby. After a moment she could take in the sorrow of all that had happened. Poor Jay, denied his rightful place in life.

'Did his father ever realize that the child you had adopted was the one he had instructed to be sent to the orphanage?'

'There was one occasion. I was walking down the lane with Jay, when he was a toddler. His father was visiting your family estate with a shooting party. He was riding along with your grandfather, who was still alive at the time, when they stopped in front of us. Your grandfather only knew the gypsy story, and so remarked what a fine boy Jay was, and that it had been a wonderful day for me when the gypsies had left him with me. Lord Daverly looked astonished and asked to be told the story. He glared at me and looked intensely at Jay. He couldn't have missed how like Lady Amelia the boy was, and is still. He spoke to Jay. Of course Jay just carried on playing with the stick he was waving about. "He is deaf," I told Lord Daverly. At which he became very agitated, begged my pardon and wanted to leave. They rode off, and that was that. Lord Daverly was killed in a riding accident not long afterwards.'

'Oh dear. Lady Muriel was taken to be the heir. She didn't know any different. It was thought that there were no known male relatives of Lord Daverly, and so she inherited Hastleford Hall and all that went with it! What do we do now? I ... I mean: what does Jay want to happen? Does he want to claim his inheritance from my aunt?'

As she waited for a reply, Eloise thought that the whole thing was despicable, and part of her felt glad that she was only related to her Aunt Muriel's family by marriage, as what they had done was abhorrent to her.

'I'm not sure. But before this whole situation, he wanted to let people know the truth, so that he could–'

'Marry Andrina? Oh dear, it is such a tragedy. My dear sis – sister.' The tears that had threatened to flow while hearing Jay's story now spilled over. Sobs racked Eloise's body. Two large arms encircled her, and although on any other occasion she would consider this inappropriate, she welcomed the comfort they gave, but did not miss the heaving of Mrs Tattumby's big body as she joined her tears with those of Eloise.

As she laid her head on the soft cushion of Mrs Tattumby's breast, exhaustion took over every bone in her body. *How am I to deal with all of this? How can I put it onto my dear aunt and uncle at such a time? Does Aunt Muriel know of Jay?* But then an even more disgusting thought entered her: *Does my father know the truth?* No, he couldn't, could he? Then it came to her that this is what Father was referring to, when he said that Jay felt like family and that he'd had suspicions. *Oh dear, it is all such a mess. Such a tragic, tragic mess... Andrina gone forever. Edith, God knows where – and even*

163

whether she is safe. And now Jay, desperately ill and having been forced to live a life that he was not born to; and all in a silent world.

'Look, M'lady, it ain't much, and it don't condone what I did, but let me tell you: Jay has had a happier life with me than he would ever have had in an orphanage – or with them lot, if I had taken him back to them. Even if they had accepted him, the moment they found out about his deafness, they would have had him committed to an institution and he would have spent his life locked up; he wouldn't have had the life he was entitled to. And that Lady Muriel would still have inherited.'

Eloise hadn't thought of this angle, but she could see it was a possibility. Many rich and powerful families did lock away any children who were crippled or maimed in any way. And, knowing Aunt Muriel's family, this was most likely what they would have done with Jay, if confronted with who he really was.

The thought brought some comfort, and she realized it was probably behind Jay forgiving this woman. Well, she herself couldn't forgive her aunt's family, and something had to be done to put right the wrongs they had done to Jay. But she didn't know what this would be, as she was not yet in control of her emotions – they were so swayed by her grief that they didn't allow for decision-making.

For now, Eloise just wanted to stay encircled in the arms of this loving woman. For no matter what Mrs Tattumby had done, she was certainly that: a loving and kind woman, whose actions might have been misguided, but who had ultimately enabled Jay to be saved from what his own family might have done to him.

11

Edith

**A deserted farm, France, mid–August 1916
Finding the depths of love**

Despite her pleas over the last four weeks, Albert had refused to listen to her. It had been a gruelling journey, tramping miles and miles across fields, eating off the land, stealing from meagre crops and accompanying those with meat from any animal that Albert managed to trap or shoot.

Edith's hair was matted and plastered to her head. Sores on her feet rubbed and oozed pus, her teeth were coated and her nails dirty. Occasionally they had washed in a stream, but her clothes were clogged with mud, and the tooth-powder and soap Albert had packed into his backpack had run out a few days ago.

'We 'ave to keep to the fields, Edith,' Albert had said on countless occasions, when she'd begged him to allow her to go into the nearest town. If only he would let her, she could try to access some money from her bank account and pay for a hotel and transport to the South of France.

She was certain Marianne would help Albert to

disappear, and her to get back to the hospital.

'If we use the roads or enter a town, we may bump into soldiers returning from the front, or others going there. My description would 'ave been circulated by now, especially as they might think I kidnapped you.'

She had been tempted on more than one occasion to scream at him, 'You *did* kidnap me! You used emotional blackmail. You dragged me away from my bed.' But she didn't. He had enough to carry on his shoulders, and seemed to her to be getting dangerously morose and paranoid. It was all she could do to keep his spirits up.

The sight of a farm in the distance gave her hope. Albert would break in and steal what they needed: food, soap, coffee – milk and eggs even. The thought of it took away any pangs of conscience she might normally have had at such actions. Tiredness seeped into her as they neared the building. Crouching low made her joints ache.

'We will 'ave to lie low until darkness, Edith. Then I will see what I can get.'

'Promise me you won't hurt anyone. I couldn't bear that, and could never forgive you for it.'

'I promise. Now come on, let's make it to that barn for shelter. We might even get some shut-eye while we wait for the owners to go to bed.'

Lying down didn't give her any comfort. Over the days they had walked and starved, the flesh had dropped from her bones and it was now difficult to position her body without something digging into her.

Though they lay together for warmth and had done on many occasions, Albert had respected

166

her wishes and had not touched her. These hadn't truly been her wishes, as many times she had lain next to him aching for him to hold and kiss her, but she was afraid and unsure.

Sometimes she'd even dreamed of Captain Woodster, and woke up longing for everything he stood for. He was of her world; he thought the way she did, he loved the same things: medicine, and devotion to the care of others. His conversation was on her level... But then she would look over at Albert, curled up and sleeping next to her, and her heart would flip over and she knew he was much more a part of her than she really wanted him to be.

'Wake up, Edith. Wake up.'

'What? Oh, I – I didn't realize I'd fallen asleep. What's wrong?' A shiver that wasn't just down to how cold she felt trembled through her.

'Nothing – everything is right. The farm 'as been abandoned. And recently, if you ask me. I waited till dark, but no lights came on in the 'ouse and no smoke came from the chimney.'

'But there's lights and smoke now – look! Perhaps you were wrong, and perhaps we shouldn't make so much noise.'

'That's my doing. I crept over there and found the house empty. Oh, it's been ransacked, but I found stuff that made me 'eart sing. There's canned food, a bottle of brandy and some wine in a flask; and, oh, soap and stuff. I've 'ad the water on the stove and 'ad a good wash down, and filled a tin bath for yer to soak in. Come on, and while yer 'ave a bath, I'll make something for us to eat.'

His breath wafted to her the evidence of him

having drunk some of the brandy already, but she didn't blame him. Nor did she care. All she could think of was how what he'd described to her sounded like heaven to her aching limbs.

'I must have been asleep for a long time?'

'Two hours in all. I kept coming and checking on you. And I put that blanket on you.'

She hadn't noticed the blanket, but now picked it up and wrapped it around her, trying to stop the shivering of her limbs as she walked with him to the farm.

It was all she wished it to be. A typically French farmhouse, just as she'd seen in pictures, and on her travels to Marianne's. Built of grey stone, all of its windows had shutters on them; some were secure and closed, but a couple blew loose in the breeze and banged against the wall and then banged shut again, creating an eerie feel in the dusk of the evening. That feeling left her as she entered the kitchen. Albert must have worked hard in those two hours, as it was no longer ramshackle, as he described, but had an order to it. The long wooden table in the centre had been cleared and washed down, and now held a lit oil lamp in its centre.

The fire glowed from the grate, joining the flicker of the lamp and giving a romantic hue to the whole room. In front of the fire, and between two armchairs, was what she thought she'd never see again: a steaming hot bathtub. Her insides warmed at the sight of it, but her clothes and hair suddenly turned into sackcloth and straw, as her longing overwhelmed her.

Taking a swig from the bottle of brandy, Albert

wiped his hand over his mouth. 'Go on – it's all yours. I won't peep.' A hiccup accompanied this and lit a tiny flame of fear inside her. *If Albert gets drunk, will he be as much in control of his emotions as he has been?* Oh God, she hoped so. She wasn't ready. Not yet.

'Will you go out of the room, Albert, please? Is there a sitting room or somewhere you can wait for me? I promise I won't be long.'

'If that's what you want, but I 'ad in mind to prepare them salad vegetables I found in the greenhouse – there's tomatoes and lettuce. Look, I'll keep me back to you and work at the sink. I've opened a couple of tins, and found one contained some sort of meat. I'll put that on the stove in some wine, with some of them bulbs hanging from the ceiling. They must be French onions or something.'

She giggled at this. 'Just one clove of one bulb will be enough, Albert. They are garlic. They give a lovely flavour, but are very strong. Anyway that all sounds delicious, and I'll even have a glass of wine with the meal. But you go easy on that brandy; when you are hungry and haven't had a drink for a while, it can have a quicker effect on you.'

'I'm all right – I can drink most men under the table.'

Another hiccup set the nerves in her stomach fluttering, but she couldn't wait any longer for her bath, so she didn't argue. Taking off her clothes, she found that the luxury of dipping her toe in the water took away her concerns. Sinking her whole body into the water and caressing it with the

169

soapsuds made her forget everything for a second – even her niggling worry over her health – for the trembling wouldn't stop, and the feeling of fuzziness in her head that she'd thought was down to having dozed off and being awoken so suddenly hadn't left her. Relaxing back, she closed her eyes.

'You're beautiful, Edith.' This had her opening them again, and relit the fear in her. Albert stood over her. His body swayed a little, his words slurred. 'I slove you more thans anyshing.'

Her hands covered the tips of her breasts and she hoped the suds hid the rest of her. 'Albert, you promised you wouldn't look. You're frightening me.'

'Edith, oh, Edith, I can't 'elp meself. I want yer, Edith. Pleash come to me and let me–'

'I'm not ready, Albert. I'm afraid. I've never…'

'I won't hurt you. I'll be gentle. You're a doctor, so you know what it's all about.'

'Of course I do. But that doesn't make it any less frightening. Besides, I wanted it to happen when I was married. I didn't want to do anything before.'

At this he turned and walked away, and her nerves settled down again. He wasn't going to impose himself on her. But she would get out of the tub and wrap herself in the blanket as quickly as she could. She couldn't dress, because all of her clothes were wet and filthy. But she would wash them in the tub and hope they would dry out in front of the fire.

Dinner was a quiet affair at first, as Albert seemed to be sulking, and Edith found it difficult to focus properly on any topic of conversation, as

170

her head ached. When Albert did speak, it was about Jimmy.

'I can't get that poor boy out of me 'ead. Why oh why? What's the bloody good of killing our own – and young lads, at that? Lads as shouldn't even be there.'

'I don't know. It's a tragedy. But one we can't change, because those who have the power think it is the right thing to do.'

'Them like your brothers, you mean? Well, you can tell them from me: they are murderers, just as I am. We've all murdered – killed young lads. Oh, it might be that we 'ad to, as we were under orders and are fighting for peace, but each one of them lads 'as a mother, and many 'ave a wife and kids. It fills me dreams, Edith. Gives me bloody nightmares, it does.'

His voice didn't slur so much as have a tinge of anger to it. She tried to soothe him. 'I know. I have seen you sweating and tossing and turning, and many times you have called out names in your sleep. When we are safe, we will get some help for you.'

''Elp – I'm not mad, woman! It ain't me as needs bloody 'elp! It's the likes of you and your class. Toffee-nosed, jumped-up buggers. You make the rules and we 'ave to stick by them. And you: you're bloody frigid. Cold as bloody ice! I reckon your feelings are as tight as your arse is.'

The trembling of her limbs increased; she felt cold, and yet sweat stood out on her body. Her voice sounded weak to her own ears when she spoke, her tone begging: 'Albert, there is no need to speak to me like that. And please stop drink-

ing. It is changing you. I told you: you are frightening me.'

'Frightening yer – I ain't going to bloody 'urt
yer. I told yer. But I can't wait any longer, Edith.
You're going to 'ave it tonight, I'm telling yer.'

'No. Albert, no!'

He must have undone his trousers without her
seeing him do so. As he rose, his need was there
for her to see. Shock held her rigid as she saw his
eyes fill with his lust. Before she could move, his
hands reached for her, pulling her to him and
holding her as in a vice. The blanket fell away
from her, and his voice, thick and heavy, compounded her fear. 'Oh, Edith. It's time. I want
you so badly that I'll 'ave to just take yer.'

His alcoholic breath repulsed her, as his lips
came down on hers. His teeth clashed onto hers.
His tongue darted in and out of her mouth. But,
against her will, feelings welled up in her. Suddenly this didn't seem wrong, but was something
she wanted. She wanted him close to her like
this, wanted to feel him pushing against her.

But then repulsion at these thoughts fought
through the pleasure. Struggling, she tried to pull
away. But she did not have the strength to do so;
she felt drained of energy.

'You want me – yer know yer do. Come on,
Edith. I love yer. I want yer so much.'

Those words, said with tenderness, softened
some of her resistance. She allowed his kiss,
revelled in the feel of his hands squeezing her
breasts. But still a little voice said: *No*. 'No, no
Albert, this isn't right. You are drunk. You–'

He took no heed of her. Unable to fight him

172

off, her body went wherever he took it. They landed on the rug on the floor. Bruised and hurting inside, Edith begged him, 'Please, Albert, not like this. Not like this. Wait. please, wait!'

Her pleas made no difference, and her tears were ignored. His weight came onto her. He prised open her legs with his knees and entered her.

A scream came from her that stung her own ears, but only had the effect on Albert of making him thrust harder and groan louder. 'Edith. Oh, Edith...' The pain of his thrusts lessened. His kisses soothed. His declaration of love and his caresses aroused something in her that she didn't want to give in to, but could not resist as she listened to his voice. His tone, different from anything she'd ever heard, was heavy with desire. 'You're me own love. Me woman. Let me love you.'

Against all she knew to be right, she did relax and knew the joy of him fully filling her. Her body moved with his; her kisses were given willingly and on every part of him she could reach. Feelings grew and grew inside her, till she abandoned herself to the sheer bliss of them and joined her cries of lust to his. Then it happened. A feeling too big for her burst inside her. She stiffened, didn't want it, and yet wanted it with every fibre of her being. When she allowed it, and it reached a crescendo, she hollered her joy to the world, clenching herself onto Albert so as to hold on to the feeling for as long as she could.

When her body came down from it, she crumbled. Tears tumbled from her. Uncontrollable weeping seized her; this wasn't the weeping of sadness, but the weeping of release. Of becoming a woman.

They lay still and quiet when it was over. Neither moved for a full minute. The mantelshelf clock that Albert had wound up and set to the time on their watches ticked loudly. Albert's breath became steadier with every tick, but Edith found she couldn't steady hers, and the headache she'd ignored came back with a vengeance, marring the feelings of joy she'd experienced. Or maybe guilt was seeping into her? She'd have to pull herself together. Maybe after a night's rest she would feel better. Another shiver took her, giving her the thought that she must have a cold coming on. Which wasn't a wonder given the conditions she'd lived under these last weeks.

Albert broke the silence. Lifting himself onto his elbow, he looked down on her. His face was awash with tears and was holding something that scared her. 'I'm sorry. Forgive me. I shouldn't 'ave done that. Oh, God! It is all too much. Go back, Edith. I – I cannot face life any more. I can't live with all that 'as 'appened, and what I've become.' With this, he rolled over and stood up.

As he fumbled with his jacket, she pleaded, 'Don't go. It's all right, I wanted it to happen... Albert? Albert, what are you doing?' The flicker of a flame from the fire caught the barrel of his pistol. 'Albert! No!'

The explosion ricocheted off the walls, deafening her. Blood and flesh and bits of brain slapped her body. 'Noooooooo! No! Why? Why...?' Her breath held painfully in her lungs as she finished screaming, and as the shock of his action settled in her. Kneeling, she stared at the body, with only one side of a head and a grotesque eye staring at her.

The trembling of her body was uncontrollable now. Its severity caused her teeth to rattle together. Her throat dried. The zinging inside her ears increased, and a blackness enveloped her.

The light was momentarily hazy and then became bright again. Edith found it hard to break through the fog that was clouding her brain. Images clawed at her. She couldn't breathe without feeling pain. *Where am I?* Something felt very strange. The smells that surrounded her were not familiar, and she could feel the presence of someone in the room, but not someone she knew. Her head hurt. Her lungs didn't want to take in their full capacity of air. Sweat dampened her body. Weakness had taken every limb, rendering her unable to move. Forcing words through a sore and dry throat, she asked, 'Wh – where am – am I?'

An answer came in French, but with an accent Edith didn't recognize. Memory exploded in her brain, forcing an agonized cry from her.

'*Non, non. Ma chère, vous êtes en sécurité.*'

Nothing about her felt safe; she felt so weak, so ill. But she had registered that the woman had called her 'my dear' and she didn't sound threatening.

'My name is Petra Tolenski, and my husband is Aleksi. We are from what used to be Poland.'

It seemed Petra needed to tell her story. She continued, talking about how she came to be living in France. Much of it went in and out of

Edith's focus, but from what she could glean, these people were from the Russian sector of what had been the independent country of Poland just over a century ago.

'Eleven years ago the Russians recognized us as a country and liberated us, but we could see that the German and Austrian hold on the partition of our country was very unsettled, and we feared for what would happen in the future. And so, with our new freedoms, we took the chance to get out. We have a daughter, Marcelina, who went back to marry her long-time boyfriend. She would not listen to us and is now caught up in the terrible regime of the German Reich and cannot leave.'

Petra's voice droned on, spinning around with the pain in Edith's head. It was a pain that threatened to take her back into the blackness, which held nightmares she didn't wish to visit. But eventually Petra told her how she came to be here. Her husband, Aleksi, had seen lights and smoke coming from the deserted farmhouse whilst he had been in his top field, bedding down his herd of cattle. That had been three days ago. He had gone to investigate. He had taken his barrow and brought her here, and had gone back and buried the young man.

Dizziness sent the room spinning again, as memory tore through Edith's mind. She wanted to ask: why? Why had they just buried Albert and not fetched the police? But fear that the symptoms she'd been suffering had escalated stopped her, as a realization came to her that she was on the verge of pneumonia. The very word terrified her – she would face the prospect of her own imminent death if she wasn't treated immediately. If she'd been in an unconscious state for three days, then her brain's initial coping mechanism must have shut off from reality. Now, it would seem, her body was taking the impact.

A pause in Petra's story gave her a moment to ask, 'C – can you g – get a doc – doctor, p – please?' A fit of coughing almost suffocated her and produced the dreaded frothy sputum she knew to be an indication of how serious her condition was.

'It is thirty kilometres to the nearest doctor, and our donkey is lame. It would take Aleksi a day or more on foot, and he cannot leave the livestock at this moment; also there is the harvesting. We have been hoping that the goat-herder, who comes along at this time of year, would arrive and take a message for us. But he hasn't come.'

'I – I can pay f – for your l – losses. Plea – please.'

There was a splitting pain in Edith's head and her breathing was agony. She knew it wouldn't be long before she entered the disease state of crisis. Her terror intensified.

'Pl – please,' she said. It came out as a desperate cry.

Still Petra hesitated.

'I – I need...' Once more a fit of coughing left her gasping for breath. 'St – steam ... roo – room. Fill with st – steam and – and...' Her mind jumbled. Nothing made any sense. A sinking feeling took her. It offered relief from all the pain in her head and chest. Letting go, Edith sank into unconsciousness – a place of swirling peace.

12

Ada

Low Moor, late August 1916
The munitions factory explosion
brings change

Finding no solace in anything she did, Ada had come to the conclusion that to carry on working towards her goal was the only way to cope. Oh, aye, she'd thought of doing herself in, and would have done if it hadn't been for Joe's love. Not that she could return his feelings, as everything inside her had died with the letter's arrival, but she found something to grasp onto in the friendship and support he offered, and felt a need to be where he was. This meant doing the daily grind at the munitions factory.

Today, Monday 21st August, it was three weeks, four days and twelve hours since she'd read the terrible words. She felt weary through to the bones of her as she stepped off the train after an early shift at the factory and began the trudge up Clackheaton Road. Agatha and Mildred were by her side, and Joe was just behind.

The station clock had shown it was two-thirty. The sun beat down on them. Children, on holiday from school, ran around, some of them rolling balls with a stick. One of a group of girls

178

threw a stone into a pattern of chalked numbered squares and hopped into where it landed. All of them chatted and laughed.

Women stood in the doorways of their houses or sat on their steps. Flowered aprons covered their long skirts, nets kept their hair in place, and fags hung from their mouths as they called out to one another. It was a chatter that stopped, as if as a mark of respect, as she, Agatha and Mildred walked by, for the three of them were known as the mothers of the lost 'pals' and, as such, held the admiration and awe of their fellow mothers.

Smoke billowed in the distance from the Low Moor Munitions Factory. How Ada longed for a position to become available there, so she didn't have this daily journey to Leeds. As they turned into New Works Road and she caught sight of the factory, and of her cottage, her longing to work there increased. But then she remembered that if she moved jobs, she wouldn't be near Joe. That thought had her turning her body to look at him, but as she did so, an intense force hit her, taking all control from her and flinging her backwards. She thought she'd bump into Joe and send him flying, but his own body was propelled away from her, as if a giant hand had picked him up and thrown him. Seconds later Mildred and Agatha flew past her, in much the same manner.

Debris fell from the sky; bricks, bruising and cutting, bits of wood and a roof tile hit her face, and dust stung her eyes. But it was a huge piece of wooden beam that gave her a pain that seared through her. It crushed her and left her unable to move, as it pinned her to the ground. The boom –

a sound like nothing she'd ever experienced – blocked her ears and made the noise of crumbling houses, shattering windows, women's screams and children's cries come to her as if they were far away from her, instead of surrounding her.

The munitions factory – oh God, it's exploded! Please God let everyone be all right. Let Beryl be safe. Oh, why didn't I go and make me peace with her? And where will Paddy be? What about our home? Me things – me lads' stuff!

Then Ada's panic died, as there was a terrific bang and a huge fireball shot into the sky above her. The ground beneath her shook. Something hit her head. The pain from it was only momentary, as she was sucked into a welcoming darkness that took her to a place where she could feel nothing and knew nothing.

Waking to a world of whiteness disorientated Ada, as did the strange shapes around her: distorted figures of people, a swirling curtain and a trolley shape that wobbled.

'Oh, me Ada, are thee alreet, lass?'

Joe's lovely voice. He was here with her. He hadn't been killed. 'Oh, Joe. I can't see thee, but I feel your presence.' It was a feeling she had never experienced before. A good feeling: a feeling of great love, and not in any way related to the sexual attraction that she now knew was all there was – and had ever been – between her and Paddy.

'I'm here, lass, at the side of you. No, don't turn your head. I'll lean over you. One of your eyes is bandaged, and the other has been washed out and some drops put in it, so you might not be

180

able to focus.'

A dark shape came into view above her. 'There, lass, is that better? Now, you're not to worry. You're in Leeds Hospital. They say you've broken a few ribs and need monitoring, in case one of them pierces your lung. But you are going to be fine. Everyone is okay – cuts and bruises mostly. It was the munitions factory. It exploded and set off a secondary explosion in the gasworks.'

'Is – is Paddy ... and me house...'

'I think Paddy's all right. I asked around, and it turns out he was in the Black Horse when it happened; a few were having an after-hours game of poker with the landlord. He wasn't hurt, but no one seems to have seen him since. I thought he would be with you, so I took care and was ready to turn away if he was here.'

'And me house?'

'I'm sorry.'

'Naw!'

'Look, it's not reduced to rubble, like some. But it ain't liveable in, either. I'm sorry, lass.'

'Oh God, Joe – me stuff!'

'Stuff's only stuff; it can be replaced.'

'But me memory box of me lads' things, and the money as I've been saving. I have to have them! Do something for me, Joe. Please go to me house and get them for me. Please, Joe.'

'Don't fret yourself, Ada, lass. I'll do what I can.'

'Go now, Joe. I can't lose me boys' things, nor me money.'

'You won't. Just tell me where to look. But I can't go now – there's coppers and firemen all over the place, stopping folk going into their houses until they are deemed safe. I'll go in the early hours of the morning, under the cover of darkness.'

This calmed her. If the police were looking after the properties, none of those likely to thieve from her house when she wasn't there would dare go near it. But she wouldn't rest properly until she had all her things here with her.

Exhaustion took over her, as the worrying wearied her. Her eyes closed without her bidding them to. But there was something she was determined to say. 'Joe, I want you to know that I love you...'

His kiss on her lips was gentle and only lasted a second, but it sealed her feelings and brought a smile to her that hurt her face. She didn't care. She felt safe. But that feeling had only just settled in her when Paddy's voice shook her.

'What the feck are you doing, eh? That's me wife! I knew there was something between you.'

Joe's body shot away from her. Paddy must have grabbed him.

'Naw, Paddy, naw. Don't! Leave him alone!' But as her words died, it was Paddy she saw being flung past the end of her bed. His landing shook the bed, as his head hit the iron bedstead.

Screaming as loud as her dry throat would let her, Ada called for help. Footsteps came running. A male voice shouted at Joe to back off.

Ada held her breath. Turning her head gave her pain, but enabled her to see Joe. His face looked shocked as he stared down towards the floor.

'Get a porter, Nurse. Let's get him onto a stretcher and into a treatment room!' It was the same male voice, which she was convinced belonged to the doctor. It had an urgency to it that increased her feeling of trepidation. Still Joe didn't move, but he did speak.

'He attacked me.'

No one took any notice of this. But the male voice asked, 'What is the injured man's name?'

'He's me husband. Paddy O'Flynn.'

Coming over to her, the man, whom she could now see dressed in a doctor's uniform, looked down on her. 'Your husband?' His question held disdain as he looked from her to Joe.

She closed her eyes against the accusations she knew he was forming in his mind. A tear squeezed through her eyelids. It ran down her cheek, leaving a cold trail, but she wouldn't let others follow it. That would mean an avalanche of them, so she swallowed hard and told herself that it didn't matter what folk thought. What did anything matter, any more?

But this changed to a deep anxiety as the doctor said, 'Nurse, go and fetch one of the policemen here.' Then turned to Joe and said, 'This looks serious – he could die. I advise you to stay here until the policeman arrives, which shouldn't be long, as the hospital is crawling with them. They are dealing with the aftermath of the explosion. I am sure they will want to talk to you.'

As they left the room with Paddy on a stretcher, Joe sat down heavily in the chair he'd vacated. Ada didn't know what to think or feel, and even less what to say. All that had happened in the last twenty-four hours had left her stunned. Now Paddy, her husband of twenty-odd years, could

183

die! God, what next? What next?

'I'm sorry, Ada. I only acted in self-defence. I – I didn't mean to hurt him badly. It was just one of me throws that I'd learned. You see, I often get called names for being here and not over in France, and on occasions it gets nasty and someone will attack me. If it's a bloke – say one in middle age that hasn't been called up, and they look strong enough – I defend meself by throwing them and then, when they are disabled, I tell them why I can't go and what I am doing instead. That seems to sort things out. I promise, I never meant–'

'I know. I saw what happened.'

'I doubt anyone will take your word. You only have a small amount of vision in the one eye. And it is well known that I am sweet on you, Ada. They will say I attacked your husband because of that!'

'It's alreet, Joe. Nothing can happen – it was self-defence. Paddy's strong; he'll come through. It'll take more than a blow on the head to do my Paddy in.'

'You said "my Paddy". I thought you didn't have any feelings for him, lass, I thought...'

'I do have feelings for him, but nothing like I have for–'

The ward door opened and a policeman marched in. 'You. What is your name?'

'Joe Grinsdale, sir.'

Turning to her, the policeman said, 'Ada O'Flynn?'

'Yes, sir.'

'I understand the man attacked in here just a

few minutes ago is Paddy O'Flynn, your husband?'

Something in his voice frightened her. She could only nod her head.

'Well, I'm sorry to say he died of his injuries as they were carrying him to the emergency station.' A painful gasp choked Ada. Her ears wouldn't give her the truth of the words the policeman was saying. But the reality of it hit her as she heard him say, 'Joe Grinsdale, I am arresting you for the murder of Paddy O'Flynn...'

Murder! Paddy dead! Naw – naw! Her voice took on a mind of its own as, following a low, agonizing moan, she said, 'Naw, he didn't do it. Paddy swung at him. Joe just threw him in self-defence!'

'More concerned for your lover than your husband, eh? Sounds like the poor chap had a reason for taking a swing. Anyway we'll let the judge and jury decide whether he's guilty or not. All we know is that we have one dead man, and standing in front of me is the man who is responsible for his death.'

The clink of the handcuffs resounded around the room. Joe looked at her. His expression showed both fear and sorrow.

'It'll be alreet, Joe. I'll tell them it was self-defence, I'll tell them!' But before she had finished saying it, the policeman had manhandled Joe out of the door.

Resting her head back, Ada looked upwards and cursed God. *Why? Why? What have I ever done to deserve all you throw at me? Well, you can take this as me last prayer, 'cause all me others have fallen on your deaf ears. From now on, it's me. Me, on me own, but I'll show you. You'll not beat me!*

Her tears, and the desperate feelings inside her, didn't go with these words, but she meant every one of them. God had taken the last of her family, and in circumstances that meant the man she loved had gone as well. She dared not think about how she would face the future, if Joe hanged.

Without Paddy? Oh, aye, I'll feel his loss, but he deserved what came to him. Now he'll be with the boys. This thought gave her more pain. *All of them together.* A deep loneliness settled inside her and brought forth a cry of, 'Naw ... naw. I can't bear it, I can't!'

'Now, now, you have to keep calm. Crying will give you more pain and may exacerbate your condition.' The posh voice of the nurse held kindness, but what she said next sounded judgemental. 'I have heard it said, up here in the North, that you can't have your chips and have a pie, too. I don't know your circumstances, but from what is being said...'

'I didn't have naw pie, and I had very few chips, come to that. All I've ever had since this war broke out has been heartache. You don't know me, lass. When you've given three sons to your King and country, been beaten from pillar to post and raped by your husband, been blown up, and dared to seek a little happiness from the man that loves you, then – and only then – can you stand in judgement of me!'

The nurse was quiet for a moment. When she spoke her voice sounded shocked. 'I – I'm sorry. Oh, that is awful. I have never had anything like that happen to me. I – I shouldn't have spoken to you like that. I had no right. My name is Irene, but I am called Rene. I hope you will forgive me, and if there is anything that I can do to help you, I will.'

'There is: take care of me. Make me better. And then I can cope and can help me Joe to cope. It ain't that I am saying I'm not sorry about me husband – I am. I feel his loss, though it pales on top of the loss of me lads. A body and soul can only take so much. I have no reserves. But, even if I had, I wouldn't waste them on Paddy, but use them to help me free Joe.'

Rene patted her gently. 'Tell me all about it. Then I will see what I can do.'

Though the telling caused pain, it also helped. Rene had that air about her that made you want to trust her and confide in her. And, though it seemed unlikely as they were worlds apart, Ada felt as though she had found a friend, someone who would be on her side. 'Where are you from, Rene? You ain't from round here.'

'No, Leeds is a long way from my home. I'm from London. I came to work here, as this is a training hospital. I want to go to France to help, but as a fully qualified nurse. I didn't want to be a VAD.'

'What's that?'

'It's short for Voluntary Aid Detachment. There are some spiffing girls working for them – some of my friends are attached to hospitals over in France. They try their best, but they told me in their letters that more often than not they are ridiculed by the real nurses. I wouldn't be able to take that. I am a fiery person. Besides, the war has given me a chance to show that I am really talented at something, and I have found that I love being a nurse. My parents would never have agreed to me training as a nurse in other circumstances. They just wanted to marry me off.'

'Well, I think you will be an asset to them out there and will save many lives. And you will do so brilliantly, without causing pain or suffering, which is how you've just treated me. Ta, love. And while I'm on, you've a good bedside manner, as they call it, as you've soothed me. Though I could still scream and scream at the injustice of it all.'

'Well, you just do that, if you have to. I will make sure everyone knows that you should be allowed to, and they should just offer you quiet comfort, not words of chastisement or anger. I won't tell them your story – it is yours to tell – but I will say that you have been to hell and back, and that you deserve our respect, not derision.'

'I can't say as I'm back from hell, Rene, as I am still living it! Every day I'm scared with a hotter and more intense pain than any hellfire could inflict on me. But I turn the pain into strength. I draw from it to sustain me, so that I can carry on.'

'You are a remarkable woman, Ada. And an inspiration.'

'Aw, I don't know about that. But ta, lass. Do one thing for me, will you? Will you try to find out what happens to Joe? I need to know.'

'I'll try. Now I'm going to give you something to make you rest. The doctor prescribed it for you. Here, take these.'

With Rene's help, Ada swallowed the tablets.

After a while she found it difficult to keep awake.

As she drifted off she noticed the moment when Rene left her bedside, but somehow she thought Rene would never leave her, not really. Because, even if she never saw her again, she would never forget the slim, pretty girl with the beautiful dark, kind eyes.

13

Eloise

London, beginning of September 1916
Everyone's shoulder to lean on

Leaving her Aunt Muriel's side wasn't easy for Eloise as her dear aunt was distraught. It had been seven weeks since Edith had gone missing, and still no news of her had filtered through. Coping with her aunt's constant breakdowns was difficult, not least because she didn't seem to register that Eloise herself was grieving – and for Edith as well as Andrina. And now she carried the burden of Jay's birthright, too.

Her father was the only person she could talk to. For him, Jay's story had been a confirmation of his suspicions. Father had told her that he remembered an incident that had taken place at Hastleford Hall when he was a young man.

Father had visited Hastleford Hall, Aunt Muriel's home, with his brother Christopher and his parents since a young boy, as their ancestral homes were in nearby villages. Their families had socialized a great deal. Father had been very vague in his knowledge, but said that what Eloise had told him fitted with what he had always suspected, even though it shocked him to the core.

'You see, Eloise,' he'd said, 'we all knew that your Aunt Muriel's father, Lord Daverly, was carrying on with Lady Amelia, though we were all surprised when she went off to India not long after Lady Daverly died. Some said it was to give propriety to them marrying when she returned, as there would be a suitable lapse in time and, being apart, they couldn't be accused of acting improperly during the mourning period. But a few months after Lady Daverly's death I was visiting my father on our estate in the next village and went for a walk. I was a week off marrying your mama and I wanted to have a little space to myself. Your Aunt Muriel and Uncle Christopher were already married and had their three children. I was late in meeting the love of my life. I walked over to Hastleford Hall and went into the grounds through the back gate near the river. It was dusk by the time I reached there. Not expecting to see anyone but the servants, I was surprised to see a lady walking across the lawn. She was heavily pregnant, and I thought it was Lady Amelia. I was shocked rigid for a moment, but then got my wits about me and made myself scarce.'

Father had gone on to tell her that, a few weeks after their wedding, he and Mama had spent time in the country, and had heard that a baby had been left on the step of the butcher's shop, and that the butcher and his wife were of a mind to keep the child. It was talked about by everyone – the vicar, the gentry and the peasants – as all things that happen out of the ordinary are, in such tiny villages as Stanford, where Hastleford Hall is, and Market Bosworth, where their own ancestral home was. Father even knew the tale about the gypsies being the culprits.

Father's suspicions had eventually led him to give Jay a position on his estate, but not to speak out or do anything further.

This lack of action made Eloise feel angry and frustrated. Nevertheless, her father had reasoned that he couldn't prove Jay's parentage one way or the other, and he hadn't been able to challenge anyone about it, because such accusations would have been deemed scandalous.

These thoughts went round and round Eloise's mind as she walked the five hundred yards along Holland Park from her aunt's house to her own. As she reached the gate she had a sudden urge not to go inside and instead instructed her maid, who accompanied her, 'Dorothy, follow me. I'm going for a walk, but please don't attempt to engage my attention in any way, or stop me from anything I may be doing.'

'No, M'lady,' said Dorothy, which made Eloise feel a little pang of guilt. Having once been her nanny, Dorothy loved to recall stories from walks out when Eloise was a child. These would always be to the park, as they were now, and so Dorothy had a lot of memories to convey. But Eloise just needed to be alone with her thoughts today.

The afternoon was a pleasant one. The flowers

and trees were still in their summer bloom as the two of them walked towards the Earls Court gates of Holland Park itself.

Passing through the gates, it only took a few minutes' walk to bring them to the fountain at the back of Aunt Muriel's house. Cousin Edith loved this fountain and, by being near to it, Eloise felt as if Edith was close to her. She was certain Edith was still alive. She would have known if she hadn't been. Something would have told her; besides, she had to keep hoping that Edith would soon be found.

Poor Edith; apart from what might be happening to her now, when she returned she had a lot to face. Things Eloise couldn't visit at the moment. If she allowed herself to, she would lose the purpose of this time to herself. She did wonder, though, what Edith would think of her now, because just a few short months ago Edith had seen her as a silly girl, and that is what she had been. How she would love Edith to know that she had changed, and that she shouldered everyone's problems and stood strong for them all. Edith would never believe such a transformation could happen.

She sat on a bench near the fountain. The spray from the tumbling water sent little droplets to wet her hair, cooling her after her walk and clearing her mind. Only for it to start clouding over the next minute with her worries. *What will happen if Jay changes his mind and wants his inheritance, as surely he will? How will Lady Muriel take that? Will she be able to stand it?* So much hung in the air.

Her initial feelings about Jay had changed, and now she wondered if the nice young man she'd found him to be wouldn't want to take away her Aunt Muriel's inheritance; and if he did, then, as Aunt Muriel's half-brother, he would surely look after her, perhaps even make her a generous allowance. But still, that wouldn't help matters, as it wouldn't be the loss of the money so much as the shame of losing her standing that would injure poor Aunt Muriel the most.

Eloise shrugged and resigned herself to deal with each thing as it happened, rather than worrying about them all now. She had her own future to think of and, with this thought, she remembered Rene's letter. It had arrived in the late-morning post. The scrawling handwriting and the postmark had made it easy to identify. Tucking it into her bag, she'd wanted to wait until after her visit to her aunt to read it, desiring a moment to herself when she could absorb and savour the news and snippets of Rene's life that she always wrote to her about. A free life, and one Eloise longed to live for herself.

She and Rene – Irene, really, but she hated that name – had been friends since birth. Rene's father, the wealthy industrialist Thomas Cooper, and Eloise's father had been at Eton together, and the two families were very close.

Eloise had written to Rene for advice about the kinds of war work available, and, what she should do to get accepted for it. Not that Rene's advice would be much use now! It just wasn't possible for her to leave home as things were at the moment. But she did want to do something to help the war effort.

Some of Rene's news was the usual chit-chat

about her colleagues' antics and her own progress towards her final exam. But a part of it concerned a patient, and it moved Eloise almost to tears as she read: 'Oh, Eloise, I have met the most courageous woman. Her name is Ada O'Flynn.'

Letting the letter fall to her lap, Eloise found that Ada's story had greatly affected her. *Oh God, there is so much pain in the world – how are we to bear it?* A lump constricted her throat. *I must not give way.*

Dorothy's voice broke into her thoughts and helped her to control her emotions. 'I'm sorry, Lady Eloise, but I can't sit silent when I see you troubled. Is there anything I can do?'

'I wish there was, Dorothy, but who can mend the world? Will it ever be as it was?'

'I don't know. Have you had more bad news? Is Miss Rene all right? I recognized the handwriting and knew the letter was from her.'

'It is. Yes, she is fine and sends her love to you.' Rene loved Dorothy as much as she herself did; many times when they had been children Dorothy had been in charge of them both. 'It is the pain and suffering she is witnessing that is upsetting.'

As she finished telling Dorothy about Ada, Dorothy said, 'Poor woman. Sadly, she is just one of many, many grieving families, M'lady. Some, like this Ada, have lost more than one loved one, and others have lost their only breadwinner and are facing the workhouse. Then there are those young men who have come back maimed and unable to work, reduced to begging in the streets...'

'That's it! I – I mean, you've given me an idea,

Dorothy. Something that I can do to help, whilst still remaining at home to be a support to Mama. I will set up a charity to help anyone who has been damaged in any way by this war. I'll provide funds to feed and house them, and help the maimed to make their life more bearable! Dorothy, I have no need for the advice given by Rene, which is advice I couldn't follow anyway after... Well, we won't talk of that. My new venture will help me to bear that, too. Come on, Dorothy, we have work to do!'

'Oh, Lady Eloise, it would be wonderful if you could help, but what use can I be? And have you considered your father? He won't allow this – you know he won't. He doesn't like the thought of you working, unless it is something genteel like sewing cushions or knitting socks.'

'You can be my right-hand man. I know no one better. And together we will tackle Father. But first I must plan it all, so that he can see we know what we are doing. Our first case will be Ada. We'll visit her and bring her some money, so that she can engage a lawyer to help save her new love. I can't bear to think of him hanging. Rene has said that although she didn't witness the fracas, she believes Ada's account of it. And if she does, then I do too, so we have to do something to help.'

Father paced up and down the upstairs sitting room, a room all the family loved because of the peace it afforded; somehow it felt detached from the hustle and bustle of the downstairs rooms, which always felt unsettled as the servants went about their business and visitors frequented them.

A large room positioned at the back of the

house, the upstairs sitting room overlooked the park. It had many windows, which displayed spectacular views and could make you forget that the house was in London.

Furnished in the French style, with heavy furniture and a large collection of paintings on the walls, the soft decor of blush-pink and ruby velvet provided a lush, yet restful feel.

Eloise looked over at her mama, sitting quietly on one of the three sofas in the room, and felt at a loss. Mama had her head down and didn't look as though she was going to be the champion of Eloise's cause that Eloise had hoped she would be.

So far Father had been very accommodating about her idea and had helped her as much as he could in raising funds and sending out a letter of appeal to all of his contacts. But now, faced with the reality of how much involvement she personally wanted to give to the project, his objections were making her worry that he would halt her plans from progressing any further. 'No. Eloise, it is a ridiculous idea! I can't have you going up to the North of England with just Dorothy to chaperone you!'

'I have to, Daddy, otherwise all my efforts will have been for nothing.'

'Look, my dear, I do admire the way you have planned this charity, and think that dedicating it to Andrina's memory is a fitting tribute to her and is helping us all, by having something positive come out of the dreadful tragedy of her loss. Plus, the money you have raised is very commendable in such a short time. Your hastily arranged garden party was a huge success, and our friends have been most generous in their donations. It has been good to see you so occupied, but–'

'Daddy, please! I will be safe. Dorothy will look after me, and we will be with Rene in the cottage her parents have rented for her. She has a maid with her, too. So we are not on our own. If this is to work, I can't just be a figurehead who raises the money. I have to see it through. I have to be seen to be supervising the projects the charity takes on. Then everyone will feel safe, and happy to donate towards it.'

'Look, this idea is only three weeks in the making. Carry on raising money, by all means, but wait a while before you take on any projects. This one in particular may harm your efforts. Funding a murderer, to secure a lawyer to get him off – it will damage your credibility and mine, too.'

'But he's innocent, Daddy.'

'So you believe, but what if he isn't?'

'He still has a right to be represented, as he would be if he was a rich person.'

'Yes, but is he really the best person to be focusing your efforts on? Your money has been given to you in the good faith that it will be helping victims of the war.'

Eloise remained quiet for a moment. Then a solution occurred to her. 'Very well, Father, I take your point. But I still need to go up to Leeds and then to Low Moor, to see Ada. She is someone who has lost everything: her three sons to the war, her home to an explosion, which was due to the war. Of course very few know about that, because of the reporting restrictions necessary to safeguard

197

the location of the munitions factory. Neverthe-less, it happened, and the devastation it has wrought is something that I can address from our funds. As for the man accused of murder, I will personally pay for a lawyer for him, from the money Granny left me. I believe strongly in his innocence, as related to me by Rene. I can't stand by and let him go to the gallows for something he didn't do.'

'Eloise, Eloise, where has all this come from? I want my silly, empty-headed little girl back. My two silly—'

'Oh, Daddy, don't. Don't!'

Hurrying to her father's side, as did her mama, who had remained quiet throughout the debate, Eloise felt tears begin to tumble from her and asked herself, *Am I doing something wrong? Is this new 'me' too much for my parents to take, so soon after their loss? One daughter gone forever and the other changed beyond recognition?*

Her mama's voice cut into her thoughts, as she spoke to her husband. *'Mon cher,* don't. I know all of this is having an effect on you. It is on me, too. But we need to be strong for Eloise. To ad-mire her, and to support her. She is not wallow-ing in her grief, but turning it into strength and a desire to help others. I, for one, am standing by her and will support her all I can.'

'Thank you, dearest Mama, thank you.'

Her father blew his nose loudly, signalling his resignation. 'Go with my blessing, my darling. But you are not going on the train. I will buy you a car and find you a trusted chauffeur. That will give me some peace of mind. A male accompanying you will give you added protection. And, I will fund the lawyer...'

'Oh, Daddy, thank you.'

'No, wait while I tell you my conditions. I will need satisfying that the man is innocent. To do that, I need to have the full story. Then I will engage one of the best lawyers I know, to talk to the accused, and to the dead man's wife; and to anyone who had a part as a witness, or who has an opinion because they were on the scene soon afterwards; and to those who could be character witnesses. If, after all that, my man is of the mind that the accused is innocent, then I will go ahead with the funding.'

'They are good conditions, Daddy, and I agree to them. But everything must happen with haste. I want to go within the week, and the wheels of justice are already in motion. We have to act quickly to make sure they turn in the right direction.'

Her father shook his head. 'My little Eloise, you have grown into a wonderful woman and I am proud of you.'

No words could have been more musical to her ears; for her father to be proud of her made everything worthwhile. Going into his arms, and having those of her mama encircle them both, created another poignant moment for them all, but one that spoke of hope for their future and of their ability to go forward, with just the memory of Andrina to sustain them.

As Eloise broke away and left her parents to continue to console one another, the sudden weight of what she had taken on hit her. Was she up to it? Could she – a spoilt young rich woman –

make a difference? Well, she would soon find out, but nothing would stop her from trying. She had just broken down the last threads of resistance from those who had the power to prevent her from continuing. For her now to have their backing meant that the world was waiting for her – she hoped it was ready, because she certainly was.

14

Edith

France, mid–October 1916
A discovery keeps Edith lost to all

Edith had spent much of the past nine weeks living in a strange and unfamiliar world. A world that held pain and a half-life, where she functioned, but didn't care about anything or anyone. A world where nightmare images visited her and made her want to hide away behind the comfort of a veil, which she brought down to blot out everything whenever she chose.

The sheer guts of Petra and Aleksi had brought her through the pneumonia that she'd almost succumbed to. They had, they told her, nursed her around the clock until the crisis had passed, washing her and her soiled linen; feeding her with drips of food that they had whisked and whisked until it became fluid; and talking to her, in an effort to encourage her to live, for her loved ones.

Her recovery had been hindered by this foggy place that had enclosed her, which she knew was due to her mind blocking out what it couldn't cope with. But in the moments when she could think and allowed herself to talk and ask questions, Petra and Aleksi had avoided answering anything about the night they had found her. Until now this had suited her. But now she had an urge to contact her family. She wanted them to know she was safe. She needed to be with them, and she needed the Red Cross to fetch her and help her to recover completely, so that she could go home and eventually get back to her job. *That is, if I am wrong about being pregnant... No. I cannot even think about it. And I won't!*

Wandering around the farmhouse felt familiar. She must have done this many times over the last few weeks, without registering that she had.

Neat and clean, the kitchen smelt of baking and gave off a shabby but homely appearance. Sofas that had seen better days had been patched here and there, but were of the rounded style with soft feather cushions that always welcomed and comforted. There was other furniture, too – a table and chairs, and a huge sideboard made of heavy pine. The table had a scrubbed look that rendered its top paler than its matching chairs. Well-beaten rugs were scattered over the polished flagstone floor; and a huge range, taking up almost one wall, with shining pans hanging around it, dominated one end of this large, and only, downstairs room.

She knew the routine of the place, too. She knew that Petra helped Aleksi outside for most of the

201

morning, fitting in her housewife chores around feeding the hens, collecting the eggs and milking the two cows they had, whilst Aleksi worked the fields and saw to the other livestock, the pigs and sheep. Their days were long and hard. How they had found the time and energy to look after her she wasn't sure.

Seeing Petra coming across the yard, Edith determined to tackle her about everything. It wasn't right just to bury Albert. The police should have been called. And her family should have been contacted, and she should have been taken home. Nervous and feeling queasy at the thought of what she might learn, she sat down at the table. From there she would be facing Petra as soon as she entered.

Petra's face looked fearful when Edith asked why the authorities hadn't been called. With a voice that shook and held obvious terror, Petra answered, 'I – I... We could not. The truth is that we don't own this farm. We are illegal immigrants. It's true that we came here fearing for the future of our own country. We travelled with our daughter over many kilometres with a horse and cart, living like gypsies. Though we had money, and could pay for what we needed, we feared everyone. We were afraid to call the police when Aleksi found you. They are looking at foreign nationals with much more scrutiny than they have ever done before.'

'But you live openly, and you sell your produce, so how do you keep yourself unknown?'

'This is a very remote place. We rarely come into contact with anyone, and to those we do see, we have passed ourselves off as the cousins of the man who owned this farm. The owner was dying and almost penniless when we came across it. We knocked on his door and asked for water, and whether we could buy some vegetables and maybe a chicken. Not that he had much, for the farm was neglected. He took us in, saying he needed help. We invested our time and our savings in the farm and looked after him. He was of Polish descent, so folk who did know him accepted our story that he had sent for us. He had no family, as far as we knew. Aleksi travels a long way to market, much further than he needs to, but it is safer, as no one questions him there or knows where he comes from.'

Petra's head drooped with the weight of confessing this. A moment's anger visited Edith, as she thought the decision they had taken greatly affected her and her future. But then, these people had saved her life. If she gave them away, they might be in danger of being jailed for living here without registering, and for disposing of a body in an improper way. She made up her mind that she couldn't do that to them.

'I must contact my parents and let them know that I'm alive and well. But please don't worry. I won't expose you, as you have been so kind to me. I – I won't like lying, but I'll say that Alb – Corporal Price – abandoned me here when I became sick.'

She didn't know how she was going to carry this off, but somehow she felt she had to. It wasn't as if she would be hurting anyone. Albert had told her he had no family that he knew of, as he'd been brought up in an orphanage, so there was no one

203

who would suffer the agony of not knowing whether he was dead or alive. Otherwise, she would never even have considered doing this.

'What happened to the people who owned the farm where you found me?'

'They were German. They were legal residents, as far as I know, but upped and left once war was declared. It's a shame, as they were nice folk. They helped us a lot and we felt bad about deceiving them. And I feel bad about the position you are in, because of us, and the hurt we have caused your loved ones. But please believe me: we had no choice.'

Suddenly Edith wanted to take this woman in her arms and thank her, and stop her feeling guilty. She rose to do so, but a feeling of nausea took her and she had to hurry past Petra to the outside privy.

'What is wrong? Oh, *ma chérie*, are you falling sick again?'

Edith retched again. As she did so, Petra stroked her back. It was a soothing gesture, but one that didn't give comfort. What she feared was beginning to seem like a reality. She was pregnant; there was no other explanation. The dread of it had lain in her since her first conscious memory of what had passed between her and Albert: the sometimes awful recollection of him raping her, but then the wonder of how that had turned into an act of love, before the extreme horror of what he did afterwards.

The signs had all been showing themselves to her. She was conscious of having missed a period, perhaps two – she didn't know, and she dare not

204

ask if she had menstruated during the time she had left her life in Petra's hands. *Oh God, if it proves to be right, what will happen? I couldn't go home. I couldn't even contact my dear mother and father, for they would be so ashamed of me!*

Straightening up, she wiped her mouth on the cloth Petra handed her and gratefully took the glass of water she had fetched. After sipping a little and feeling less queasy, it shook her to hear Petra say, 'You are having a child, yes?'

Defeated, Edith said, 'Yes, I think so.' With that admission, a weakness took her. How soon her new-found strength had disappeared. A tear fell down her cheek.

'No, *ma chérie*, this is not to cry over. You loved the father, yes?'

'I did. We were miles apart in our standing, but war threw us together and yet–'

'Standing? What is this standing? Are you talking of a class system, because you are rich and he was poor? I know he was so, because if he had not been, Aleksi said he would have been an officer. I assume you are rich, by how you speak. Poor children are not taught to speak French in your country, nor do they become doctors.'

'You know I am a doctor, and about Albert and our lives?'

'You told us many things, *ma chérie.*'

'Oh, Petra, what am I to do? I will bring disgrace on my family. The scandal would kill them!'

'Have you no one you could go to?'

'No – well, maybe. But no, I couldn't. I – I... Look, it is complicated. I have a ... a kind of aunt, she is my cousin's aunt. She lives in the South of

France, in Nice. But no, I can't burden her. I couldn't put her into the position of deceiving those she loves. Oh, I just don't know what to do!'

'Then do nothing – stay here. We're glad to have you. It's like having our daughter back.'

Edith didn't know how to answer this. It was a kind offer and one she welcomed, but could she hide herself away here for the rest of the months she had to carry her child? *And what of my parents, and my brothers and cousins – all the family? They must be worried out of their minds!*

The choice was a difficult one and rendered her quiet for some minutes. Petra didn't speak or try to persuade her. Edith's mind went from thinking she would face it all and go home, to thinking: no, she would stay here, hidden away. In the end she decided it was better to remain missing than go home a shamed woman, bringing untold pain and embarrassment to her family, and maybe even being struck off the medical register.

If only she could receive news about how everyone was doing. Were her brothers safe? This was what worried her most, because, apart from missing her and worrying about her, she was sure her lovely cousins were fine. How could she ever have thought of them as silly? They were just being girls, and it was she who was the odd-bod. But what of Mama and Daddy? *Oh, dear God, I have no choice but to leave them in the no-man's-land I have put them in. I have to save them from the shame. I have to. But then, what of the child when it is born?*

As if this thought had conveyed itself to her, Petra said, 'If you stay, you can go home as soon as the birth is over. I will take care of your child and bring it up for you. You can visit whenever you want to. No one need ever know.'

Unable to think of any other solution, and feeling herself going into a haze once more, Edith nodded. 'Thank you, Petra, I will think about it. Oh dear, I'm tired. So very tired.'

'I will help you, *ma chérie*, come on. Let us get you back to bed.'

Once in bed, the enormity of her problems hit Edith, and her heart ached just to be held by her mother and father, and to exchange silly conversations with Andrina and Eloise. Then to go on a holiday to Marianne's, and even to go back to her post as a doctor in Abbeville.

Captain Mark Wooster came into her mind with this last thought, and she knew she had thought of him many times during her illness. Perhaps he would help? If she could somehow contact him, perhaps he would present a solution: help her to get rid of the child even... But no, that thought was repulsive to her. No doubt, if she wanted to, she could induce the baby herself; there were ways. Dangerous and illegal ways, but she knew, when the thought first entered her head, that it was something she could never do. Never! And just as surely as she knew that, she knew she already loved her baby. Rubbing a hand over her slightly rounded stomach, she said out loud, 'I love you already, little one, and wouldn't harm you. But I don't know how I am going to take care of you, without causing pain to those who don't deserve it. That is the question that is frightening me. But I will find a way. I will.'

Part of her wanted to curl up in a ball and sob

207

out all the pain, but she didn't. Instead she let her thoughts wander to her passion: women's rights. It frustrated and angered her to think that, even if Albert had lived, he wouldn't have carried any shame concerning his child. He would have been congratulated by his mates and looked on in wonder, that he had wooed a lady of her standing and had actually 'given her a good shagging', as she knew that was how the ranks referred to making love.

He wouldn't have to be sent to some convent in shame, cast out from the society he was used to, or banished from his home. If he'd had family, they probably wouldn't even have chastised him. How different things were in this world for a man, compared to what they were for a woman. That had to change. Somehow she would find a way of working towards that change after the war. Somehow she would try to make it possible for unmarried mothers to live in dignity with their child. Imagine if they took her child from her at birth, as they did from the poor souls who had no say in the matter! Oh God, that could still happen to her, if she changed her mind and contacted her parents. Suddenly she knew she had made the right decision.

However, she didn't know what it would cost her family not to have any news; or what it would cost her, to continue to live in exile.

She started to imagine how she might implement such help for women: perhaps she could set up a home for them to stay in during their pregnancy? Or a kind of 'bridging' home to move on to, where they and their child would receive continued support until they found their feet and were able to live an independent life?

These ideas came tumbling one on top of the other, and they lifted her and in some way united her with other women out there in the world, going through what she was experiencing. And they gave her strength, which she could hold on to to sustain her.

Looking up to the ceiling, she said, 'Our child will be safe with me, Albert. I forgive you for what you did. I want you to rest in peace.'

When she thought of Albert, a picture of the young boy he had tried to save from the firing squad came to her. So she added to her prayer, 'I promise, Albert, that one day I will do as I said, and as I know we would have done together. I will find Jimmy O'Flynn's mother and father and tell them about his bravery, and assure them that he wasn't a coward, but a very brave boy.'

She felt the sadness of the world weighing her down, but she stayed strong.

She would not cry. Yes, she was imprisoned in a place she had no choice but to be in, and the world was closed to her, but crying would play on her weakness and put her right back where she'd been. For the sake of her child, she would get through this, she would... *Please God, help me. Help me...*

Looking in on Edith, Petra found that she had drifted off to sleep. She felt glad, as she needed to think. An idea had come to her, inspired by her daughter Marcelina's desperate situation, but it needed planning and discussing with Aleksi. Just maybe, though, they could pull it off.

Aleksi looked at her across the kitchen table. His eyes were weary, his attitude one of suspicion and fear. 'What is it you want to discuss so urgently? Why can't you listen to me and get rid of the girl. She is well now and can only bring us problems. Let me take her to Paris, then she can find a way home from there. She will bring trouble to us, if we keep her here.'

'She cannot, and does not want to go home. I've told her the truth and she will not betray us. You see, she is with child.'

'What?'

'I know it is a complication, but one that we can turn around to help our beautiful Marcelina. Edith is from a high-class family. If her parents find out that she is pregnant, they will see it as a disgrace brought down upon them. Edith's society will reject her. She may not be able to continue to be a doctor, so who knows how she'd make enough money to keep herself and the baby alive. No one will marry her. She will be an outcast. I have said that Edith can stay here, and that she can leave the baby here with me. Then she can go home. She can say that she has been very ill and lost her memory. I have told her that we will take care of the child, and she can visit whenever she wants.'

'And how does this benefit– Oh my God, Petra, you are not thinking what I think you're thinking?'

'I am. And why not? When Marcelina last miscarried, she had everything taken away from her.'

210

'But why didn't you tell me this, Petra? Our own child undergoes an operation as serious as that, and you keep it from me?'

'I was afraid of your reaction. I knew we couldn't go back there. I tried to shield you. The agony of our separation, and not knowing when we will see our child again, is enough to bear. I decided to keep the operation from you for that reason. Marcelina was devastated, but we can bring her happiness again.'

'But how? By stealing a child? And how will we get the child to Marcelina? You have just said that we can't go back, and you know she can't get out.'

'The letter that you brought back from town this morning is from Marcelina. She disguised it in an official envelope. I've been waiting for the right moment to share the news it contains with you. Marcelina is back in Russia. She and Feodor have made it back to where his parents fled to. Oh, Aleksi, we can go there. We can cross the border and go to Russia. We can take a child to our daughter. Marcelina has said that there is still travel in and out of there by boat. You know that Feodor's parents are very rich; they have orchestrated Marcelina's and Feodor's escape and they will help us, too.'

'Why didn't you tell me this sooner? You could have discussed it when you came out to the field with me. You are a mystery to me at times, Petra. But what you do not realize is that this is *not* good news. On my travels I pick up news of what is happening in the world. There is a great deal of unrest among the students and peasants of Russia. There is likely to be another revolution, far bloodier than that of 1905. It's not safe to return there, and I am heartsick that Marcelina is in Russia. Tsar Nicholas does not take any heed of how his warring tactics are alienating his subjects. There is a great deal of unrest.'

'I didn't tell you because I hadn't read the letter then. I too thought it was an invoice or some such. Oh, Aleksi, every joy is counteracted by a step back into fear. But surely, if Feodor's family know of the unrest, they will act. We should wait until we hear again from Marcelina. It is months until Edith's baby will be born. We have a long time to plan.'

Though her heart was racing with fear at what Aleksi had told her, Petra still felt hope. Feodor's parents had at last done something to get their son and Marcelina out of Poland, and she felt certain they would make plans to save the young couple and themselves.

15

Eloise and Ada

Low Moor, late October 1916
An unlikely friendship that brings hope

'Rene, it is good to see you.'

'Well, I can't believe you're here. I don't know how you managed this, Eloise. And, though I don't mean to sound rude, never in a million years did I think I would ever be sitting in a teashop with you, in the North of England, discussing ways of helping others! What happened to change you?'

'I know. I was an empty-headed, silly girl, but war gives you food for thought. I've been working through a gradual process of wanting to do something to help, as you know, but when Andrina died it – it did something to me, and quite the opposite to what I expected. It made me stronger, and it made me think more of others.'

'I didn't want to mention Andrina, but I'm glad you have. It broke my heart when I heard the dreadful news from my mama. I'm so sorry. I didn't believe the stories passed through the servants' grapevine.'

'They were probably true.'

Talking to Rene seemed to help. Rene was an independent ear, someone who hadn't been involved and, whilst she was saddened and shocked, she was not knocked off-balance by it all.

'Oh dear, poor Andrina. I wanted to come down for the funeral, but I couldn't. I had no leave due, and a friend's death didn't come under the rules for compassionate leave.'

Eloise understood, and told Rene that all of her family had known she would have been there, if she was able to. They talked about the funeral, and discreetly dabbed away tears over the loss of Andrina, before the conversation turned to Edith. Rene had met Edith on a couple of occasions, and her way of looking at things gave Eloise some hope as she said, 'I'd say that Edith is all right. From what I saw, she was a determined woman, who became a doctor against all the odds of a woman achieving this. Why you haven't heard anything could be down to a number of things, not least poor communications due to the war. The Army has taken over most of the services, and has priority. Edith will find a way to survive, and a way to get in touch when she can.'

Rene's reasons for not hearing from Edith sounded plausible, given how long it took for letters from her Aunt Marianne to arrive from France. The last one was dated months prior to its delivery.

'I think you are right – of course you are. Now, let's talk of other things. The reason I am here, for one.'

'Yes, of course. Ada. Poor soul, she's lost and doesn't know which way to turn. She's staying with her sister Beryl, but there is a bitterness between them. I think I told you about Ada's husband's affair with the sister, and it resulting in a pregnancy?'

'You did. How awful for Ada.'

'Yes, well, she needs to get out of there. Her cottage was destroyed and she lost most of her things, but thank God she found the mementoes of her sons. She is a proud woman, Eloise, so your charity won't be easily accepted.'

'Have you spoken to her about me?'

'No, I didn't think it wise. She might not have agreed to come. I just wrote to her telling her that I had time off, and would she meet me here? She'll be along soon, I am sure.'

Ada released a sigh of relief and frustration as she closed Beryl's door behind her. The atmosphere

214

between Beryl and Bill made for an uncomfortable life in their presence. Beryl – rounded as if she was carrying a dozen young 'uns, and about to drop her babby at any time – moped around, not wanting to do anything, whilst Bill was in a permanent bad mood.

Trying not to be alone with Bill was a strain, but if she didn't dodge him, he would start on the same subject. And he asked questions, always questions: did she know about the affair? Couldn't she tell Paddy was having it off with another woman? Oh aye, she could answer that one, as suspecting it had been part of her daily life, or even knowing he was at it, and suffering the humiliation it wrought upon her.

In some ways it would have been better if Bill had left Beryl and let that be the end to it, because what he put her through amounted to cruelty. It had shocked Ada to find that he had a side like this to him, as he'd always seemed such a nice man. Not that she blamed him altogether; she had little sympathy for Beryl at times, and forgiveness hadn't come wholeheartedly from her, and probably never would. But, in her condition, Beryl didn't need the constant aggravation and reminder of her sins that Bill subjected her to.

Leaving the house and the troubled folk inside it behind her, Ada walked down the hill. Every step caused her pain, as many of the ribs broken by the force of the explosion still weren't fully healed. Biting on her lip, she tried to ignore the discomfort and decided she would make it to the tea rooms, which were about a mile away.

It would be lovely to see Rene again. Ada didn't

know how someone of her standing could look upon her as a friend. Her experiences of moneyed folk in the past had led her to believe they were all a toffee-nosed lot, who'd rather look down on you and label you as scum than talk to you. But, in Rene, she saw someone who cared.

Her thoughts went to Joe. Poor Joe. If only she could visit him, but they had put him on remand in a prison down south, to await a trial date. His case seemed a helpless one, and in her nightmares the gallows loomed. So often she awoke with sweat running down her body, her hands clawing at herself and unreleased tears and screams strangling her throat. Would she ever see Joe again?

'Hey! What world are you in, Ada? I've shouted at the top of me voice to you, and you haven't acknowledged me!'

Looking up, Ada was shocked to see Bill. He'd pulled up in his car, a huge Ford Roadster that thought itself a Rolls-Royce, and was treated like one by Bill. How he afforded it, let alone afforded to run it, she had no idea.

'Climb up. I know you're not comfortable walking, and I thought it would sit well with your new friend to see you arrive in a car.'

'Ta, Bill. That's kind of you, but I wouldn't have bothered you.' But as she said this a little tickle set up in her belly, at the thought of riding in the open-topped car.

'Let me give you a hand.' Before she could object, Bill was out of the car and coming round to her. 'Put your foot on the step and I'll give you a push.'

His push enabled him to place his hands where

he shouldn't. Swinging her bag caused her deeper pain than walking had, but also caught Bill a glancing blow that had him stepping back in astonishment.

'I – it were a mistake, Ada, I didn't mean to...'

'Oh, aye, your bloody hands slipped a bit low and then forward, did they? Don't play them games with me, Bill. Anyroad, I thought you couldn't do owt!'

'Not with Beryl, I can't. She's too demanding. She's like an animal grabbing me and expecting it every bloody night, despite her having it off with your Paddy at the same time. Not that I knew that. But she got me in such a state with her demands that I... Well, I couldn't perform at all in the end. But with you, Ada, I–'

'No, you bloody can't! I ain't like Beryl. Oh, aye, me Paddy were a passionate man and I were willing, but I ain't for having another woman's man. I'm a loyal person. I have me Joe now, and will be his until the end of me days. You just try them tricks on me again, Bill, and I'll knock your block off.'

'Sorry, Ada, I didn't realize. Come on. I'll be good, I promise.'

Unable to refuse the lift, she allowed him to help her climb in, and was glad that, this time, he kept his hands on her waist.

'I'll say something, though, Ada. I married the wrong sister.'

Ignoring him, Ada had thought she'd never see the day she'd sit in a car. *Eeh, it's grand! Though the seat is harder than I thought, specially with me having no padding on me rump now. I've to feed meself up and get back me figure, just in case Joe gets out.*

She shook herself in disgust. These thoughts must be the result of what Bill had just done. She hadn't wanted her feelings to be reawakened by such an incident, but had to admit that the touch of a hand there brought back memories of the pleasure it gave her, and she realized she missed coupling with a man. Aye, and at times she missed Paddy. He was larger than life, and with a sexual appetite that could satisfy many women at once. But mostly he had been hers. She would think of that when she remembered him, and not of the many times he had strayed.

'You're quiet. Enjoying your ride in a car then?'

'I am, Bill, but I wish you hadn't done what you did. It changes things between us. I won't feel comfortable around you now.'

'You can't blame a man for trying, Ada. We have our rights, and you gave off something that said you liked me, so it was your own fault.'

Bloody men! Give them a smile and they think they can have you. And it's your fault if they try when you don't want them to! Some things need to change in this world. 'So, if I ask you to take me to visit Joe, you'll expect to be in me bed by the neet? Well, I have news for you, Bill. Friendship from a woman isn't a reet to take her down. God, you men think with your cocks, and that's why the bloody world is in the mess it is.'

'Ha, you'll be bleating "Votes for women" next. God only knows what state we'd be in, if that ever happens. You'll all be voting for the most handsome man, whether or not he has any brains. God help us and save us from such a fate!'

'Bloody cheek. You know, you are a handsome man, Bill, and well set up, but I don't see the ladies braying at your door. So that knocks your theory for six. I hope those fighting for women's rights win through. I don't agree with how they go about it, but I'm with them and would help them if I could.'

Bill was silent and concentrated on his driving. Ada glanced at him. He was a handsome man. His tall, slender figure gave him an elegance and made him look good in his bespoke tailored suits; and his dark hair, parted in the middle and held to his head with some cream, suited him, as did his handlebar moustache. His brown eyes were attractive and had a look that said, 'I'm an all right bloke.' They made you trust him, but now she wasn't so sure and wondered if she'd seen the last of his advances towards her.

'Yes, I'll take you to see Joe,' he said, after a moment. 'I'd like to meet the fellow. He must be something special, to have taken you from Paddy. Oh, I know Paddy was a wild one, but he was the kind that could get any woman, and a woman felt privileged to be wanted by him. I have often wished I had half what he had, in those stakes.'

Ada thought it best to let this go. Bill was hoping for a compliment, but he wasn't going to get one. She was happy that she was being driven in his car. If it meant she had to deal with his advances, well, she'd be ready for him. Nothing she could say would change his, or any man's, ego; they'd still think every woman wanted them. Theirs was a culture that made them think there was no such thing as rape. Well, she knew there was. Many times Paddy had forced her to open her legs when she hadn't wanted to. Though she had to admit that sometimes, when he had, she'd been glad. But then that was because he was her husband and she held a big sexual attraction in her for Paddy. Those men who took a woman against her will in different circumstances: that was rape by any name and repulsed her. *Aye, there's a lot that needs changing, but whether any of it will happen in my time, I don't know.*

Her nerves jangled when the car drew up outside the teashop. The shop looked the same as every other time she'd passed it. Its net curtains were draped in immaculate folds and were a pristine white. The windows gleamed. A posy of flowers sat in each window, and the white paint of the window frames was set off by the black paint of the outside sills and the door.

It wasn't a place she'd ever thought to come to. Hettie Baxter, the owner, thought herself higher than other people, and didn't want the likes of Ada and other working-class women on her premises. Her cakes were for the toffee-nosed lot who lived on the hill. Well, she lived on the hill now and could be classed as one of them. This made her giggle a little.

'What's amusing you then, Ada? First time in the teashop, is it?'

'It is, Bill, and I can't wait to see Hettie's face. She'll not like it.'

'She'll have to lump it. You're as good as the next one, and the lady you're meeting with is above most of them, from what you tell me. Go in with your head held high. You look lovely in that frock

220

that Beryl has lent you. Blue suits you – it sets off your red hair. And, with Beryl's fur wrap, you look the business. Beautiful!'

Once he'd finished, Bill cleared his throat. Ada gave him a warning look and he held his hands up and shrugged his shoulders, but didn't argue with her.

'I'll park up the road a bit and wait for you. That hill is enough to kill anyone, let alone some-one who's still carrying an injury.'

Ada wasn't sure she wanted this, but knew it would be difficult to climb the steep hill to his and Beryl's house. 'Ta. That's kind of you, Bill. But no funny business.' She slithered off the seat, missing the step, and winced with the pain the movement caused her.

'You should have waited. I was on my way to help you out.'

'Aye, I know the kind of helping hand you give. I'll see you in a while.' Glad to escape the dis-turbing banter, Ada hurried inside, nearly jump-ing out of her skin at the loud clang of the bell over the door. All eyes looked her way. But those that held hers – the piercing, disapproving ones of Hettie – made her cringe with embarrassment. A voice saved her.

'Oh, Ada, you made it. Here, we're over here, my dear.'

Hettie leant heavily on the counter in front of her. Her over-plump frame, fed on a million of her freshly baked cakes, shook the structure and she stood back quickly, letting out a loud huff.

Ada smiled sweetly at her and then turned to-wards Rene. Hettie was getting her comeuppance, and that felt good.

But this feeling soon died when she realized Rene had someone with her. Her nerves fluttered in her stomach once more as she walked in between the mostly occupied white-clothed tables, with dainty china set out on them.

'Oh, Ada, it is good to see you, and you look lovely. How are you?'

Ada's voice seemed stuck in her throat, so she just nodded and smiled.

'This is my friend, Lady Eloise Mellor.'

A lady! Oh God, I shouldn't have come. The lovely smile the lady gave her settled Ada some, as she took her outstretched hand. She gave a bob, then reddened as she felt sure that wasn't the right way to address a lady. 'Pleased to meet you, Your Ladyship.'

'Just call me "Lady Eloise". Don't try to get your tongue around anything more, or you will just make me giggle, and then I will feel rude.'

This was said with a grin. Lady Eloise had a sense of humour. Rene giggled, which set Ada off. She was always prone to the giggles when she was nervous, and she tried to swallow down the one that threatened to escape now, but didn't manage it. All three of them joined in the laughter, despite receiving a few disapproving glances and similar huffs to the one Hettie had uttered.

'Oh dear, we had better behave ourselves. It is so nice to meet you, Ada. Please sit down.'

It shocked Ada to know that she could sit in this lady's presence and feel comfortable doing so. 'Thank you, Lady Eloise. It is nice to meet you too, and to see you, Rene. Eeh, you look bonny without your uniform on, lass.'

'You do, Rene dear. But not as pretty as you do, Ada. That dress is lovely.'

'Thank you. It's me sister's – she married well.'

'Good to hear she is doing something nice for you. Oh, I mean...'

Now Rene was the one to look embarrassed, thinking she had said the wrong thing. Hoping the moment would pass, Ada straightened the skirt of her soft woollen frock, which had a sort of fishtail-style hem that hovered just above her ankles, and was in the prettiest peacock-blue. 'Aye, she's trying to mend her ways. But she ain't happy, and hasn't been for a long time.'

'Ada, I hope you don't mind, but I've told your story to Lady Eloise, including your plans for the future. You see, she is here for a reason. She wants to help you, and other victims of the explosion. She's set up a new charity to help all victims of war.'

'I don't need charity, Rene.'

'Rene said you would be averse to accepting my help, Ada. But please think about it. I can get you a new home and furniture and–'

'I have money. A neighbour went back into me house and found me lads' possessions, and he found me money. I'd hid it in a tin under the floorboards of me bedroom. I had a dream to start me own business, but now I will use it to help meself. Well, I know it's soon after the death of me husband, but I have a man-friend and he is in trouble. I hope to help him an' all.'

'That is admirable – well done. I do know about Joe, as Rene has told me your story.

Lawyers are very expensive. But, Ada, I can help you with that.'

'Thank you, but I do have enough. I was earning six pounds a week at the factory.'

'Six pounds! Good gracious, I thought the national average was more like ten to twelve *shillings* a week.'

'It is, but working on the munitions is dangerous work, and the workers face death every day. Besides, we do long hours. A friend of mine went to the pub with her mate, and they treated a corporal who was on leave and bought him a pint. He couldn't believe it when he saw how much money she had, and she found out that she was paid ten times what he was – and he faced having to climb out of the trenches and dodge a thousand bullets. We do all right. You won't find many among the munitions workers around here that need your help.'

'Well! Ada, I'm as shocked as Lady Eloise is, but very pleased for you. But why don't you listen to what she has to say. It may mean that you can use your own money for what you originally intended it.'

'Yes, Rene is right. My father, Lord Mellor, is prepared to look into Joe's case...'

As Ada listened, a small ray of hope warmed inside her. 'He would do that for me? For Joe? Oh, ta. Ta ever so much.' Without her bidding it to, a tear dropped onto her cheek.

'Here, Ada, my dear, wipe your eyes. Everything will be all right, I'm sure of it.'

The dainty handkerchief Rene handed her smelt of violets.

'You keep it. It's a present from me.'

'Thank you, Rene. I'm sorry I blabbed, but no one's ever offered to do owt for me before – not without some sort of payment. Me sister used to help me out, but she took much more in return, as you know.'

'I do, dear. Let's not talk about her. Give the details about Joe to Lady Eloise, and then leave it to her. Soon a lawyer will be in touch with you. He will ask you a lot of questions about how it all happened, but just be honest with him. Don't be afraid.'

Hettie stood in front of them now with a pen and little notebook. 'What can I get you, ladies? And you, Ada O'Flynn?' she asked in a mincing voice:

Ada felt as though she could spit in her eye, and would have done, if she wasn't in the company she was in. Looking directly into Hettie's eyes, she chose the same as Rene: a scone with jam and a pot of tea. Ada hoped that she looked and sounded dignified, as if she was used to sitting in Hettie's tea room with two ladies. Hettie gave her a sly smirk, but Ada ignored this and turned her attention back to Rene.

'It all looks so bad, Rene. Folk think I was having a thing with Joe, but I weren't. I knew he loved me, but apart from thinking about him, I was never disloyal to Paddy. Not physically. I did tell Joe I loved him. But that wasn't until every shred of love I had for Paddy had died, following all that he'd done.'

'I know. Like you say, yours and Joe's affection for each other will be a big issue, as it gives Joe a motive. But the truth will be seen, I'm sure. I believe you, and so does Lady Eloise.'

'I do. I truly do, and I believe the lawyer will too. And if he does, he will defend Joe and, with any luck, get him out of prison and back with you, where he belongs.'

Ada had to use the hanky again. She still felt quite weak at times, and very vulnerable when it came to talking of Joe's plight.

Without mentioning Ada's tears, Lady Eloise said, 'Now, let's talk about this shop you want to run. What kind of shop? Where would you like it to be? And, if you need it, will you accept my help along the way, including financial help? My fund is for just such an event – someone who has been stricken by what the war has brought to them and who wants to build a new life.'

Ada told them of her dreams of owning a dressmaking shop, and felt cheered by the conversation. It felt as if talking about something that she wanted in the future actually gave her a future. A much brighter one than she had thought possible, and with that came hope. A hope that one day the dreadful pain that clutched at her heart, from the loss of her lads and what had happened to Paddy and Joe, would lift. And maybe, just maybe, in this new future she envisioned she would find happiness with her Joe.

But she knew one thing: she'd found another friend in Lady Eloise. She liked her as much as she liked Rene, though it still felt strange to have posh friends. She couldn't call them mates – that wasn't a word that fitted these ladies. But somehow she knew they were in her corner and that gave her comfort. And she knew that, with their help, she could climb a mountain. That's what saving Joe would be like: climbing a huge mountain.

16

Ada

Low Moor, early November 1916
A bitter revenge is taken

Beryl's screams filled the house, bringing back to Ada the memories of the pain of giving birth. With these memories came the stark emptiness of the loss of her sons, but she had to be strong for Beryl, and for Paddy's child.

Steam billowed from the kettle on the stove, lifting its lid and giving off a hissing sound that comforted. She placed three heaped spoons of tea leaves, plus one for the pot, into the china teapot – something she never did without thinking how lucky some folk were to be able to afford real tea, and not the blended muck she and her like had to make do with. Suddenly she was stopped in her tracks. A car door had slammed. Bill must have returned. He'd gone out the moment he realized Beryl was about to have her baby. Where he'd gone to at two o'clock in the morning, she could only wonder at; but now it was going on five and he must think it would be all over. Well, he had another think coming, as there were hours to go yet.

His face had a pinched, ashen look as he entered the kitchen. Ada motioned with her head towards the stairs. 'Well, as you can hear, it's not over with.'

'God! How long does it take?'

'Well, He is the only one who knows, but He ain't telling. Though it can be anything up to thirty-six hours or more for a first. And Beryl is no spring chicken, so there could be complications. The midwife said she has informed the doctor that Beryl is in labour, and that he will drop in later to check on her.'

'Will she be all right?'

'Oh, it matters to you, does it?'

'Of course, Ada, I'm not that callous. But I don't mind saying, I don't know how I'm going to live with her bastard. You must understand that. You're in the same position as me – with it being my wife's and your husband's baby that's on its way.'

'Put like that, I am. But I have found some forgiveness in me. You'd do well to do the same. It happened. You know why it happened. I knew my Paddy and can accept that he would give himself to anyone who asked... Beryl had reason to ask, for she was deprived.'

'That's below the belt. I told you the reason. But I can assure you that problem never bothers me now. I've found an outlet for my needs, seeing as you refused me one.'

'You're disgusting, Bill. You've changed beyond recognition. For you even to ask me puts you just as low as you view my Paddy. Have you no respect for Beryl at all? And if you haven't, then at least have some respect for me. I'm no whore. I'm the sister-in-law you've known since I was a lass.'

'Sorry, Ada, but I just can't help myself. You've got under my skin, and I want you. I need you. Can't you look beyond Beryl being my wife and your sister? She betrayed us both. It would serve her right to know we got together, and that I could give you what I couldn't give her.'

There were no words Ada could say to this. It seemed that Beryl's and Paddy's actions had somehow twisted the nice Bill she had known and made him into an evil-minded, selfish man, whose only wish was to get the ultimate revenge on his wife by committing the exact act that she had.

With Beryl quiet for a moment, the silence between them was broken only by the sound of the water as it gurgled onto the tea leaves, sending an aroma towards Ada that she welcomed. How much a cup of tea healed the surface of things and helped everyone to cope!

Passing Bill, with two steaming cups in her hand, left her no defence. His hands came onto her waist from behind. She stiffened. 'Let go of me!'

'I can't, Ada. I have to touch you.'

His hands travelled up to her breasts, pulling her into him, so that she could feel his need. Shock moved through her. To her disgust and horror, she felt a sensation of pleasure, but a piercing scream brought her straight back to reality and, with a deft movement, she lifted her heel and kicked Bill's shins. His cry as he let go was drowned by the noise Beryl was making, a noise that propelled Ada forward and up the stairs.

Once in the bedroom, she spilled more of the tea

than she had done during and after Bill's assault, as she took in the sight of what looked like a river of blood coming from between Beryl's legs.

'Oh God! Eeh, what's to do? Nurse, what's going wrong?'

'Run for the doctor, and be quick, Ada. She's haemorrhaging. Here's the babby, now. Oh dear, I need help. Ada … hurry.'

The teacups landed on the dresser with a slam as Ada dropped them and ran onto the landing. 'Bill, Bill, we need the doctor, urgently!'

Forgetting that Beryl and Bill had a telephone, she ran down the stairs, grabbed her coat from the hooks behind the door and was about to go out, when Bill said, 'Stop! It will be quicker to phone him. What's going on? Is Beryl going to be all right?'

There was fear and concern in his voice, which registered with Ada. This brother-in-law of hers was lost. She realized it now. He'd been hurt beyond his own endurance and had used whatever method he could to muster some dignity and to lash out and hurt back. Sympathy for him made her talk to Bill as she'd never intended to again. 'Make the call, Bill, love. That's the best thing we can do for our Beryl at the moment. Get the doctor here, and quick.'

The baby snuggled into Ada, its little mouth trying to suckle on her breast and wetting her blouse in the process. But she didn't mind. The little lad had the look of Paddy, even had his black curly hair, and he had wriggled into her heart the moment she'd held him. Putting her finger into his

230

mouth soothed him. His gentle sucking took her back down the years. But this time to a happy place, where her memories sat well in her and brought her a little peace.

Beryl lay like a little doll, shrunken in size and with pinched features that expressed the pain she had been through. She was clinging onto what little life-force she had left. Ada prayed she wouldn't let go. The doctor had stemmed the flow of blood, but had said that Beryl was critically ill and needed to go to hospital. They were waiting for the ambulance.

Bill paced up and down the hallway below.

Going to the landing, Ada looked down on him. Unsure whether to take the babby to him or not, she swayed gently, a natural movement when holding a child.

As if he sensed she was there, Bill lifted his head. 'What will happen? Is he all right?'

She hadn't expected this. 'Aye, he's bonny. Do you want to take a look at him?'

'No, I'm not ready for that.'

She understood.

It had been two weeks since the birth. Ada sat by Beryl's hospital bed, worrying about her sister's state of mind. Since the birth Beryl had been a different person. Weak in body, yes, that was to be expected, but weak in her mind, too. She babbled a lot about things that had happened in the past, but her memories and thoughts were all mixed up. She seemed to think that Bill had murdered their dad, when he'd died of the consumption when they were just children, and she kept asking for

Mam. Their mam had been dead this good while since. She'd had a bloating illness of some kind, which made her body swell with water.

Telling Beryl these things distressed her further. 'This kind of confusion is often the case after such a trauma,' the doctor had said, 'and her weakness will improve. The blood transfusion was successful and her blood count is normal now. Give it time, and you will have your sister back as she used to be.'

But that had been over a week ago and now they were talking of psychiatric treatment. Oh, dear God, how much more can you send us?

Beryl's pitiful voice broke into this prayer. 'Mam, mam, don't go…'

'It's not Mam, it's Ada. I have to go – your son needs feeding. Beryl, please try to get better. Your little one hasn't got a name yet. He needs to be registered and baptized. Try to think about what you want to call him.'

'I haven't got a son. Don't want one. Bill can't give me a child. What are you talking of?'

'Eeh, Beryl, love, it's pitiful to see thee like this. Get some rest. I'll be back later.'

On her return to the house, Ada felt her stomach tighten as she heard Bill doing something in the kitchen when she opened the door. He was getting hard to handle, with his persistent advances, but what could she do? She had nowhere to go and couldn't leave the babby.

Hitching the huge pram up the step disturbed the child and his squeal told of his annoyance and his hunger. Agatha had minded him while

Ada went to the hospital, but had shied away from doing anything other than rocking the pram if he cried. It was too painful for her. Ada knew that feeling.

Agatha and Mabel had recovered well from the explosion that had ripped their worlds apart. Both back at work, after suffering bruising and eardrum problems, they had each managed to get back into their homes and were picking up the pieces of their lives, as much as they could. At least they were trying to get back to normality. They were an inspiration to all.

'Is that you, Ada? I'm just making a sandwich. Do you want anything?'

'No, ta, Bill. I have to see to young 'un.' Walking through to the kitchen with the babby in her arms made her realize that the child was acting like some sort of shield. Bill didn't like going near him, and so he left her alone if she was seeing to him.

One-handed, she went through the motions of making up the feed, but pouring the milk into the banana-shaped bottle wasn't something that could be done with just one hand. Knowing it was useless asking Bill, she didn't even attempt to. 'Come on, my little babby. I'll have to put you back in your pram while I sort your bottle.'

Going back into the kitchen, she held her breath. *Please don't let him start his tricks.* Trying a distraction, she said, 'Well, aren't you going to ask after your wife?'

'What wife? Oh, you mean Beryl. She forfeited the right to be my wife when she took your Paddy to our bed.'

'Eeh, give over. That's yesterday's news. Forget

233

it, and get on with your life and help Beryl to get on with hers. She talks about you all the time, you know.'

'Ha! I'll believe that when I hear it – not that I will. As far as I'm concerned, she can rot in some institution. I like things as they are. You and me–'

'There is no "you and me", Bill. When are you going to get that into your head? No, don't come near me. I'm warning you. Bill...'

He moved across the kitchen towards her as if he was an athlete. Trying to get out of his way, Ada bumped into a chair, sending it flying. Tripping over it, she landed on the floor. Winded and feeling the pain of her still-bruised ribs, she could do nothing to stop him coming down on top of her. His weight crushed her. His voice, low and deep, said her name over and over again. It disgusted her.

'No. Please don't, Bill. I'm begging you, don't do this.'

'You want it – you know you do. Well, now you're going to have it.'

'I don't. I don't... Nooooo!'

Her frock was above her knees, his hand probing her while his body weight was across her, trapping one of her arms. With her other hand she hit out at him, but the pain in her ribs was too much to bear.

Her begging went unheeded. The wailing of the babby made no difference to him as he struggled to undo his trousers.

Hot tears ran down Ada's face. Sobs racked her body. 'Don't, Bill. Don't!'

As her last plea died, she felt him enter her.

'Oh, Ada, Ada, you know you want it. Let me ... ooh. I love you, my Ada.'

His movements were those of someone inexperienced, thrusting and thrusting, slipping out and having to enter her again. Each time she struggled he lost his grip, and then it happened. He could no longer enter her as his erection folded. Flopping down on her, his sobs heaved his whole body. But she had no sympathy for him.

'You bastard! Get off me.' Pushing him, she rolled from underneath him. As she rose, a temptation came to her to kick him where it would hurt, but she didn't. Making it to the sink, she turned on the tap and swilled her head and face, whilst flushing her vomit away. The babby continued to cry and cry. She had to see to him, though all she wanted to do was go to the bathroom and scrub herself clean.

The house was in semi-darkness. Not long after he'd raped her, Bill had gone to the bathroom and then disappeared out somewhere. Having settled the babby, Ada lay in the bath, allowing her sobs to come out, as she longed for Joe and an end to the difficult situation she found herself in.

It was then that the idea came to her. She would ring Rene at the hospital.

The quietness gave her the courage to dial the number Rene had given her to use, if she ever needed help. The voice at the other end told her to wait. The line crackled. Ada prayed she would stay connected. Then Rene's lovely voice came to her. 'Hello, Ada.'

'Eeh, Rene, help me.' Telling her what had happened was easy; as a nurse, Rene had a kind and understanding manner. Ada wouldn't have been able to tell Lady Eloise.

'Don't worry, Ada. We'll get you out of there. Get some things together and try to catch the last train to Leeds. I'll be at the station, as I'm off-duty in ten minutes. You can stay with me at my cottage.'

'What about the babby? I can't leave him.'

'Bring him along. Bring his things. I have a deep drawer I can make into a cot, but nothing else, so bring the essentials for him that you can carry.'

'Oh, ta, Rene. I don't know how to thank you. I know there's a train just before ten, as I used to catch it to go to work.'

'Can you catch that one?'

'Aye, if I hurry. Though hurrying isn't something I can do, given that he's bruised me. I'll do me best, though.'

'Good. And don't worry; you can stay with me permanently, if you have to. I don't know why I didn't think of it before.'

Ada couldn't answer this. Instead she just said, 'Ta, Rene,' and hung the telephone back on the wall.

What Rene called a cottage turned out to be bigger than any cottage Ada had ever seen! It was a double-fronted, bay-windowed detached house in its own grounds, and grander even than Beryl's. It stood among other similar properties, all imposing and all seeming to ask what the likes of her thought she was doing on their street.

'Come on. Annie will have the supper on and a

fire lit. Oh, by the way, Annie's my maid – you haven't met her yet.'

It didn't take long to do so, as the door was opened by a round-faced woman that Ada judged to be in her late forties. Plain, yet with jolly features and twinkling eyes, Annie had a rounded figure that gave the impression she scurried rather than walked, as she led the way along the wide entrance hall.

At the bottom of the stairs Rene said, 'Annie, will you get Ada a nice hot drink? Make yourself at home, Ada, I'll be with you soon. I didn't have time to change, before picking you up, and was only able to come back here to inform Annie about what was happening. I need to wash off the smell of the hospital. I love it when I am at work, but not in my own home.'

Rene ran up the stairs facing the front door and disappeared.

'Let's 'ave a look then.' Annie pulled the blanket from around the babby. 'Lawd love us, 'e looks a laverly chap. 'What's 'is name?'

She nearly said 'Jimmy', but the name caught in her throat.

'Cat got yer tongue? Oh well, there's nothing to be frightened of 'ere. Make yerself comfy in that little sitting room there. It's where Miss Rene likes to sit in the evenings. I'll get you a cup of Rosie Lee.'

'A what?'

'Oh, don't mind me. I'm from Landon, the East End. We 'ave our rhyming slang. Rosie Lee – a cup of tea!'

Annie's laughter was infectious. Giggling with

her eased some of the tension inside Ada. 'Eeh, I've never met anyone from London before. And if they're all like you, then I've missed a treat. Nice to meet you, Annie.'

'And you, love. I won't be a mo. Take a pew.'

The fire crackled in a homely way and sent warmth around the room. Ada would call this room cosy. Four wooden-armed chairs were placed around the fire and the central occasional table. There were two sideboards holding knick-knacks; one stood against the back wall, and the other on the only other wall that didn't have a window. Lamps and a bookshelf completed the furnishings. The rust-coloured upholstery was complemented and lightened by the bright cushions in yellows and reds. It was a warm and lovely room, Ada thought, and began to feel relaxed as she trod the soft ivory, red and gold patterned carpet to seat herself on the chair nearest the fire.

At least the babby had slept through it all and, though awake now, was still undisturbed, despite the noisy, draughty train carriage, the car journey and, now, entering a home he wasn't familiar with.

Looking down at him, she thought his eyes would be a beautiful blue colour, as they lightened every day. And this, together with his sweeping eyelashes, made Ada see Paddy in him more than she had in any of her own.

'As no one else is going to name thee, lad, I think I'll have to. Well, your dad was baptized Patrick Brendan, and that will be your name – only I'm going to reverse it, so no one can shorten it to Paddy. Brendan Patrick O'Flynn. Eeh, I wish you could have another surname, as that one isn't a lucky one, but Paddy O'Flynn fathered you, so you are stuck with it. Aye, and you might be stuck with me an' all. But I'll do me best for thee, lad. Me little Brendan. I love you as if you were me own. At least no war can take you away from me, as this is the war to end all wars.'

Excitement squeezed the muscles of Ada's belly as she waited on the platform for the train. Not even the bitter cold could dampen her spirits. So much had happened in the last six weeks since she'd landed on her feet at Rene's. On top of that, Lady Eloise had offered her a job! She was to coordinate the charity work needed in Low Moor. *And by, there was a lot of that needed!* There were still folk camped out in the school rooms, unable to get back into their own homes after the munitions explosion, poor things. And it looked like it would be years before all the houses were made safe, or pulled down to make way for new ones to be built. Her first job would be to provide some sort of Christmas for these folk, and to that end she had already set up a delivery of food parcels and toys to the school as well as to those who had managed to stay in their homes. It had been a mammoth task, but Eloise had been on hand to advise her and so it had all gone smoothly. Next she would concentrate on providing decent shelter in the interim period before proper homes could be found for those left homeless.

Swinging her bag, Ada realized that she was the happiest she'd been in a long time, though she doubted she could ever say she was truly happy and really mean it, as nothing could brush away

239

the sad parts of her and give her unscarred happiness. But she'd settle for what she had, and knew that in the near future it would increase threefold or more, if Joe was acquitted. A lot of the joy she felt at this moment was because Grayson Berry, the lawyer who had been looking into Joe's case, had given her hope. He had taken on the defence of Joe. He'd said he knew an honest man when he met one, and he'd never met a more honest one than Joe Grinsdale.

It had made Ada proud to hear it. And to know that Joe's case had been helped by her telling how it all happened and Grayson Berry believing her; and also by all the folk in the community speaking out about Joe's good character – and how the same couldn't be said for Paddy.

Now it was the first day of Joe's trial in Leeds Crown Court, and Ada could attend however many days the trial took, as Annie had taken to little Brendan and would look after him for her. Things seemed to be panning out at last. If only she hadn't the continuing worry over Beryl's health.

Bill had filed for a divorce from Beryl, on the grounds of her being insane, despite him having promised he wouldn't do so, if Ada kept quiet about him raping her. *The rotten sod!*

There hadn't been any improvement in Beryl's condition, either. If anything, she seemed to lose her grip on reality more and more as the days went on.

Somehow, I'll have to find a way to help her. And I will. Whatever it takes, I will. But first, let me get me Joe home and settled. Then I can sort out everything else.

17

Edith

France, mid-December 1916
An encounter

Edith ran her hand over the bump of her stomach. From her training, she remembered the drawings of what a baby would look like at four months' gestation and smiled, even though she was sure she shouldn't be as big as she was.

Expanding every day, she had begun to wonder if there was more than one baby. That thought frightened her. How was she going to sort a future for herself with one child, let alone two? She spent hours thinking about it. Should she leave her child with Petra, as Petra had offered? Should she just leave her child for a short time, and then set up a secret home somewhere once she was back in England? She could engage staff to take care of the child between the times when she could visit.

None of the scenarios she thought about were ideal, but at least she'd come to terms with what was happening and was trying to make plans. For the first weeks after her discovery, weakness had taken away her ability to cope with the idea of having a baby.

She looked over towards the field where Aleksi was beginning the winter turning-over of the almost solid ground, and pulled her coat further around her before walking towards him. She called out as she did, to tell him she was going for a walk.

He answered with a wave. She wouldn't walk far, but inside her she'd felt an urge to go to the farm where she'd spent time with Albert, and to say a few words to him. Somehow she felt that his spirit would be there. She would tell him she was sorry, that she hadn't realized the extent of his trauma and what it had done to him mentally. She would also tell him that she was carrying his child and ask him to help her to find some kind of solution.

Thinking of him buried there in an unmarked grave hurt, but it was how it had to be. Those who were still living were more important, and so she had to protect Petra and Aleksi. She didn't know what she would have done without them, but it frightened her that, as a doctor, she hadn't reported Albert's death. Now she could never reveal it, as the repercussions would be enormous for her.

Loneliness seeped into her. It was always her companion, as she longed to be with her family and friends again and to let them know she was safe.

Seeing the farmhouse in the distance made her heart drop. Could she do this? Could she revisit the scene? *Oh God!*

Clutching her stomach, she retched. Nasty-tasting bile stung her throat. Spitting out the residue, she straightened, only to look into the face of a man standing a few feet away.

Gasping with fright, she stared at him. Tall and slim, he wore a hunting jacket and carried a gun. His hat, a deerstalker, made him look British, but his words belied any hint of an English accent. *'Hé, qu'est-ce que vous faites? Qui êtes-vous? Pourquoi êtes-vous ici? Vous allez bien?'*

Somehow, upon hearing him, she was no longer afraid of him. He had kind brown eyes that showed concern. Answering him with care, she said, 'I am just out for a walk and I felt sick. My condition...' She patted her stomach and then pointed in the direction of the farm as she went on, 'I'm staying with my late husband's family at the farm along the way there. And yes, I am fine, thank you. May I ask you the same questions? What are you doing, and why are you here? Though I don't have to ask if you are all right. I can see... I mean, well, you're not being sick.' *Oh dear, what am I blabbing on about, and where did those lies come from?*

'You're English?'

'Yes, but I don't like my questions answered by further questions.'

'Pardon.'

She waited. He took off his hat, revealing hair that was very dark and shining with blueish lights. Then he answered her, his English perfect. 'I'm a French officer. To say I'm all right isn't quite true. My last few months have been hell. Maybe you will understand if I tell you that I've been fighting in Verdun. Then again, why should you? You're an English lady in France and well away from the fighting, so you can't have any comprehension of the war and what it's really like. I've been given a

243

rest period of two weeks. I – I couldn't go home. I couldn't face it, and so here I am, camping in the wilderness, hunting, fishing, trying to get things out of my head – not that it will help, as I'm returning very soon. It's difficult to reconcile the peace and tranquillity here with what is happening just a few miles away, where it is a completely different picture. But I won't taint your innocence with all of that. It's better that you don't know.'

She wanted to say that she did know, but she kept quiet, letting him speak. It was so good to hear her own language.

Then he surprised her by asking, 'Would you like to sit a while and just talk?'

'Yes, I would, thank you.'

'Over there is a little hill. If it would not be too much for you, we could sit on the top, where there is a rock that is dry and you can see for miles. I was there yesterday and it is where I was heading for. Though you may be cold and wanting to get on with your walk. I shouldn't ask.'

'No, my coat is very thick and keeps me warm.' Though not very fashionable, and well below the quality she was used to wearing, as it was one of Petra's, the coat was made of thick wool and had a flare to its cut and thus accommodated her shape.

'I have a flask of coffee in my haversack. My parents sent me some good coffee beans and I have boiled them in a pan. We can share it.'

Following him, it occurred to her what a strange encounter this was. She could never have imagined that she would meet a French officer whilst out walking in this remote place, but she could see why he would make for it. Though mostly flat, the terrain was lush with foliage. The trees were stark against the skyline, with many evergreens stubbornly declaring their resistance to the winter. It was a beautiful area – even now, when the ground was hard and crusty from the frost that bit it at night, its landscape spoke of peace and soothed the senses. But then a thought occurred to her that disturbed her. *Wouldn't any soldier rather go home, if he had enough time? Is this man telling me the truth, or has he deserted his post?* Dismissing the idea, she realized he would not have said he was a French officer if he had deserted. He would have made up any story he could think of, and would have shown fear at being discovered.

Helping her up the hill and then to sit down, he asked, 'Did you lose your husband to the war?'

Gazing ahead, she didn't speak for a moment. Panic had set in. What could she tell him? If she said 'Yes', he would want to know where and with what regiment, and she might slip up and reveal too much. He might be French, but as an officer he could have spoken to English officers – maybe even her brothers. *Oh, my dear brothers, I hope you are safe.*

'No. He was a doctor and became ill. It was a mystery what ailed him, but he died very quickly, just under five months ago.' Visions of Albert shooting himself came to her and made her body shudder. With it came the sadness at what the war had cost them – Albert had been a nice cockney chap; he hadn't been given the best start in life, and then he'd found himself in charge of young lads, seeing them shot, blown to pieces or maimed and broken, till his mind couldn't deal any longer with what he'd seen. She thought about the millions who had died already in this war. She thought of her brothers, in constant danger, and of all the families torn apart. Her own family – distraught, she imagined, over her continued absence, and not knowing if she was alive or dead. She thought of herself in a predicament that she had no idea how to cope with... *Oh God!* A sob escaped her.

'I shouldn't have asked. I'm sorry. Here.'

She took the khaki-coloured handkerchief from him and wiped her face. 'I – I'm all right. It is such a sad world. How did we come to this?'

'Let us not talk of the war. I need to escape it, just for a little while. I'm Laurent Pevensy. I will tell you about who I am, in my real life. I'm a scientist studying the disease of cancer. It is a struggle, but we aim to beat this killer disease, and we have hope. Especially since the German zoologist Theodor Boveri discovered that it has a genetic basis, as now we have something solid to work on. I am in constant touch with my colleagues and they keep me up to date with progress. I also have some of my books here with me, and study in my rest periods, as well as working on theories and working out problems they send to me. I should have taken my immunity from war service, but I wanted to help my country.'

Without thinking, Edith gave away that she too worked in medicine, as she said, 'I find that fascinating. I have seen many of my patients die in agony from cancer, and as a doctor you feel powerless to help. We need you scientists to unravel the mystery behind these diseases, so that

246

we can find treatments. Yes, you should have stayed; you would have saved many more lives in the future than you can at the moment.'

'A doctor, too! And you have no idea what killed your husband? Give me his symptoms and I will work on it. You didn't give me your name? Where did you study? What kind of doctor are you: a surgeon, a practitioner, a specialist?'

With a shock, Edith realized how much she had revealed. Her thinking went into overdrive, trying to come up with a cover story. She couldn't risk discovery. 'My name is Enid Reed.' Elsie Inglis came to her mind, and her story gave her further material: 'I studied in Scotland at a school set up by a woman who found many stumbling blocks for women in the profession. I am a surgeon. We surgeons do try to help cancer sufferers by removing tumours, but we need something to help halt its progress – or even to know more about how it spreads through the lymphatic system. Though of course the Curies' radiation discovery has helped, and radiotherapy is giving hope to those who are diagnosed very early on in the disease.'

'Edith!' She suddenly heard Aleksi shouting for her.

'Oh, that is my father-in-law.' She stood up. For a moment Edith was grateful for having chosen a false name that was very similar to her real one.

They had spent the past two hours talking. She had been lost in a world she truly knew, and with someone who understood and who gave her fresh insights, and she hadn't realized the time had flown so quickly.

'I'm here,' she shouted as loudly as she could, in an attempt to stop Aleksi repeating her real name. She saw him in the distance and waved.

He waved back, calling, 'Are you all right? We were worried.'

'I'm fine. I'm coming home now.'

Thankfully Aleksi just waved and turned away. Whether he had seen Laurent or not she couldn't tell, but thought it likely, as he didn't wait for her, but hurried away. He would be afraid. She should not have engaged so deeply with this stranger, but should have excused herself in the very beginning and returned to Petra and Aleksi. She had put herself, and them, in danger.

'Your father-in-law has an Eastern accent. Is he from Russia?'

Suddenly she felt she could trust Laurent. 'No, but nearby. The Russian section of Poland. He is afraid. He – he escaped here.'

'A refugee? Well, he has nothing to fear from my countrymen. He should register, and then he will be accepted.'

'It is complicated. Please forget about it. I – I...'

'You are afraid, too. What are you frightened of?'

'N – no, I'm fine. Once my child is born I will return to England. It is just that I cannot travel at the moment. There are complications.'

'You need medical help, is that it? Oh, Enid, take care of yourself. Don't put yourself, or your unborn child, in danger.'

His concern touched Edith more deeply than she wanted it to. It triggered a tear.

'Oh, *ma chérie*, what is it. What troubles you?'

Still holding his handkerchief, she used it once

more to mop her eyes. She wanted so much to tell him her story and ask him for his help, but she couldn't, and that made her feel lonelier than she had ever felt in her life.

'I'm being silly. Talking to you – another professional – has made me miss talking to my husband. I have to go. It was nice meeting you.' She was lying again, but whereas when she had first concocted them, the lies hadn't mattered, now somehow they did. 'I – I hope we meet again.'

'We must. I will not let you go out of my life. Where can I contact you? What is your address?'

'Please don't. It would hurt my parents-in-law; they wouldn't understand. I will have to explain now how I came to be talking to a man, and a stranger at that. They are grieving for their son. I'm carrying his child.'

'I understand. But what about when all this is over? You say you will go back to England? Perhaps I could write to you there?'

'No. Look, give me your home address and, when it is safe for me to do so, I will write to you there. I promise.'

'Safe? You are very mysterious. I am most concerned for you.'

'Please don't be. I'm fine. I'm just worried about how it will look, if you contact me. I can get in touch with you when I know it's safe to do so.'

'Very well. I will wait and look for the post every day. And, until I'm home, I will badger my mother whenever I can, to let me know if any post arrives for me.' As he said this, he pulled out a notebook and flicked through the pages. She could see that some pages had drawings of birds and others of woodland animals.

'You draw beautifully. But it's strange that you then hunt down and kill those same animals.'

'Only for food. I love to camp in the wild and be self-sufficient, be at one with nature. Now, here's my address. Enid, I'm sorry, I don't want to scare you or disrespect you, but I have to tell you: you are the most beautiful woman I've ever met.'

A blush crept over her cheeks. A twinge in her stomach shocked her. She looked up at him. 'Thank you. For a lady to receive such a compliment, in the condition I am in, is very special.'

'You are special. May I kiss you? I know that is forward of me, but it is the way of life now. I may never get another chance.'

'I would like that. I, too, do things that I wouldn't normally do, driven by the thought that so much may pass me by.'

His lips felt soft and wonderful as he kissed her lightly. She wanted more – a deeper kiss – but couldn't make the move to make it so, and knew that Laurent's good manners would prevent him from taking that liberty.

They came out of the kiss, but Laurent's arms still enclosed her. She looked up into his eyes. 'I really hope that we will meet again. And I … I need to tell you that my real name is Edith, not Enid. I was afraid to tell you the truth. Please don't ask me why, not now. But when I write, we will all be safe and I will tell you everything.'

For a moment he stared at her. She could see that he was confused, but she couldn't leave him without mentioning her real name and letting him know there were things he had to learn about her.

'I am mystified by you, but understand. The times we live in dictate what we can do and say. Edith. Edith – I like that; and it's what I thought that man shouted. Just tell me that you are in no danger.'

'I'm in no danger, but I am not in my rightful place and where I want to be. Something happened that I can't speak of, for fear of betraying others and putting them in danger of losing everything. Once the war is over, then I can speak. Then you can make up your mind if our … our friendship can continue.'

'Edith, I want more than friendship with you, and at this moment I can see nothing that would prevent it. At least, I mean, if you feel the same way?'

She knew that she did. That somehow she had met her soulmate, in the middle of nowhere, and whilst she was trying to cleave herself from the guilt she felt about Albert.

'I do feel a connection to you. Keep safe.'

'Edith...'

His arms tightened around her once more, crushing her bump as his lips met hers, this time setting off an explosion of the feelings he had awakened in her. And she responded with all that she was.

She pulled away, unable to take any more. 'I – I have to go. I – I'm sorry. I wish this is all there ever was, for eternity... You, me – this peaceful wilderness. Oh God!' A shiver rippled through her. Into her mind came a picture of Albert.

'Edith, I'm so sorry, forgive me. You must still

251

be grieving and in need of comfort. I didn't mean to take advantage of that. It was very bad of me. Please don't be afraid. It won't happen again until you are ready.'

'Goodbye, Laurent. Goodbye.'

He went to protest, but let her go. Silent tears wet her face as she walked away. The hateful deceit she had played out added to her guilt.

Once out of sight, she realized she still had his handkerchief. Squeezing it tightly, she sat down on the cold grass and called out softly, 'Mama, Mama, I so need you. I want to come home. I want to come home. I'm sorry.'

18

Ada

Low Moor, mid–December 1916
The cross she bears becomes heavier

Just as joy had been Ada's companion as she'd stood on the platform a week ago, hopelessness was now. The prosecution had dropped the charge of murder and entered one of manslaughter. It didn't matter how much Grayson Berry pleaded against it; the judge allowed a full acquittal of the charge of murder on the grounds of self-defence, and agreed to the lesser charge of manslaughter, saying that the defendant would know from his training that the technique used in the throw he subjected the victim to could result in serious injury or death. Aye, it was better than the one of murder, but as Grayson pointed out, it would be more likely to attract a 'guilty' charge, as the jury would feel they had somehow given a just verdict on the loss of a man's life. Whereas with the murder charge, if they weren't sure, they would have to bring a 'not guilty' verdict and Joe would have been free.

From her position, sitting stiffly on the wooden bench of the public gallery, Ada could see Joe. He stood facing the judge. A hush had descended. Joe's face showed the strain of the last few months. New lines had appeared around his mouth and he'd lost weight. His cheekbones protruded, leaving hollow dents beneath them.

The first time she had been allowed into the courtroom to watch proceedings, after her own testimony had been heard and cross-examined, Joe had glanced up at her and had given her a reassuring wink. Grayson had told him off for doing so, as it had been seen by the jury and could be construed as saying, 'We are getting away with it!'

This had horrified her, and wiped away all the pleasure the wink had given her. Now, as she remembered it, she thought, *Oh, Joe. How I long to hold you.*

The judge's words droned on, but the only ones she heard were 'detained at His Majesty's pleasure for a total of five years'. In that moment she thought it was a long time to wait to hold him, but she *would* wait. No one else would take his place. She allowed a tear to plop onto her cheek, as she saw them take Joe down to the cells. The clanging of the chains around his ankles and wrists grated on her, making her want to scream at the injustice of it all, but she stayed still.

She didn't know how long she was waiting there, but when a voice called her name she realized she was the only one left in the courtroom.

'Ada. Ada!'

Looking down, she saw Grayson.

'Come on, I have gained permission for you to speak to Joe, but you will have to hurry, as they don't hang around. They'll take him to Leeds Prison overnight, and then tomorrow to wherever his sentence is to be served.'

She was happy just to be close to Joe for a moment. 'Oh, Joe, I'm sorry. I've brought all of this down on you.'

'Eeh, lass, you haven't. I should have taken Paddy's blow and not attacked by way of defence, or retaliated. I have a lesson to learn. Not being able to go to war when all of me pals went was a big blow, and then the jibes of "coward" got me down. Sometimes the jibes came with violence and so, despite me bad heart, I trained in self-defence, and that gave me reactions that I didn't think twice about using.'

'Why didn't Grayson use that in your defence? It would at least have given a reason for why you acted like you did. As it was, the jury were left thinking you were defending yourself and did so in an angry way, and with hatred, against the husband of the woman you love.'

'I know. I just didn't want to use it as an excuse.

Paddy is dead because of what I did. What if I killed someone else who thought of me as a coward? No. I'll be safer in prison until this war is over.'

This made her cross, but she wasn't about to show it. These moments were precious. 'Joe, you've never held me. Not really held me.'

'And I can't now, with these irons on me. Oh, me little lass.'

'But I can hold you, my darling.' Reaching out to him, she held his head to her breast. 'The memory of this embrace has to last us a long time, Joe. Always think of it, and I will remember the feel of it and be waiting for you. The first thing I'll do when you come out to me will be to hold you. Keep thinking of that, Joe, and we will get through this.'

Her words belied how she felt. She wanted to scream and scream, but his bravery stopped her. He was prepared to take his punishment – a punishment that extended to her, as the next five years would be a living hell for her. But she would follow his example and face it with courage. She would be as courageous as he was.

On the train home Ada read everything she could see on the newspaper that her fellow passenger opposite her was reading. It kept her mind occupied. Each time he turned the page and folded it back over the others, she would see headlines like 'Lloyd George to Form a Coalition', or others to do with the war's progress. Another read: 'Woman Burned to Death in House Fire'. There was no good news in the newspaper – nothing to hold on to. But then one headline hit her and shook her body: 'Miss Edith Mellor Still Missing'.

Looking out of the window, Ada tried to imagine what it would be like to be kidnapped by a murderer. Rene had told her the story of Edith one night as they had sat together talking. Ever since, Ada had remembered Edith in her prayers, and had even asked her lads to do what they could by asking some of those saints that they must know by now to help this courageous female doctor.

Edith was a heroine. Rene had said that this is what all the papers had called her, and had outlined Edith's work in a hospital on the front line of the Somme. They had written about how much her colleagues had loved her, and thought her the bravest person. This courage would bring her through, wouldn't it? God, she hoped so.

When she turned back to the newspaper, shock trembled through her. There, in large letters, was the headline 'Cowards Shot at Dawn Should Be Named and Shamed!'

Something about this headline had her recoiling into her seat, yet unable to take her eyes off the article. For some reason it triggered the memory of the letter that had come about Jimmy's death, and made her question why the death-penny had never arrived. Nor his last letter – a letter each soldier wrote before they went into battle. A letter that was sent to their family, if they were killed. Why hadn't any of his personal belongings arrived, either?

Her blood ran cold. Her thoughts gathered pace. *Not me Jimmy. Please God don't let that be what happened to me Jimmy!*

As this thought died, she remembered that young Harold Smithward had returned home injured. She hadn't known him as well as she'd known Eric and Arthur, as he lived a few streets away, but she had known that he was one of the pals who left at the same time as Jimmy. She would stay on this train, instead of getting off at the first stop near Rene's, and travel to Low Moor and visit him. Maybe Harold knew how Jimmy had died.

Her thoughts went back to Edith and to her courage. *Well, the same applies to you, Edith, as does to Joe. I will bind what courage I have to yours, as well as to his, and even though I have never met you, Edith, I know doing so will help me. Aye, and I'll pray every night for your safe return, lass.*

Letting out a deep sigh, Ada hoped and prayed that, whatever she learned from Harold about Jimmy's death, she'd find strength in the binding of her own courage to Edith's and Joe's, and that doing so would help her to bear all she had to face.

The trudge up the hill to where she remembered Harold and his mother lived tired her. But Ada's determination didn't waver. She had to know the truth.

It shocked her to see the big lad that Harold had been reduced to a gangly, gaunt-looking young man with one arm. She'd not known about the injury he'd sustained. After greeting him, she asked outright, 'Tell me the truth, Harold. What happened to me lad? Was he shot for cowardice?'

A look of astonishment and shock crossed Harold's face, but then he stood tall and said, 'I'm sorry, Mrs O'Flynn. I would never have said owt, if you hadn't asked. And I've told no one, but aye, Jimmy was shot for cowardice. Oh, he weren't a coward. There was no one braver, but it looked bad, him shooting his hand off.'

'What! Oh God!' The impact of this last knocked her sideways. Her Jimmy shooting his own hand off – why?

A small woman appeared at the door and stood next to Harold. Ada assumed it was Mrs Smithward, Harold's mother. 'Here, Missus, I don't know you well, but I know of you, and you're welcome to me home. Come on in and sit down. I'll make you a brew.'

Harold helped Ada into the small parlour with the one arm he had left, and she was grateful for this. It was an airy room, with its scant furniture lovingly cared for, yet it felt welcoming, which she was grateful for. Sitting in the stiff-backed fireside chair, Ada found that she couldn't speak for a moment. Then the door to the side that led to the backyard opened, and Ada was shocked to see young Betsy standing there.

'Hello, Mrs O'Flynn. I – I've missed you since you moved.'

'Eeh, lass. I'm sorry. I had such a lot to deal with and – well, no time left on me hands, with the work at the factory and everything. Are you alreet, lass?'

'Aye, I am. I've been helping Harold. After you left, he was me only link to Jimmy. We've been a sort of prop to each other.'

Harold smiled across at Betsy. It was clear that he saw her as more than just someone who was helping him.

'I'm glad, Betsy, love. We all need a distraction, and I wasn't there for thee. I hope you can forgive that.'

'There's nowt to forgive. I understood. Me and Harold, we ain't... I mean, I still have Jimmy in me heart.'

'I know you do. But, lass, you have a life to live, and I reckon as Jimmy would be reet pleased to know you're helping the one pal as returned. Aye, and if owt comes of it, then the pair of thee would have his blessing, as you have mine.'

'Ta, Mrs O'Flynn.' This time Betsy grinned at Harold, and Ada knew that Betsy was going to be all right. She'd found happiness, and it was no more than she deserved.

A cough brought Ada's attention back to Harold. When she looked at him, he asked, 'Shall I tell you it all?'

'Aye, please. Tell me everything you know about what happened to me Jimmy. God, it beggars belief that me own countrymen could kill me son.' A sob escaped her, but she swallowed it down.

Listening to the horrific story gave her heart-ache beyond endurance. No wonder she had felt an affinity with the kidnapped lady, Edith Mellor. Edith's kidnapper was a man thought of as a murderer, but she had now learned that he had tried to save her Jimmy.

Though it was difficult, Ada managed to keep calm whilst Harold spoke. She felt nothing for the murdered officer – he had got his just desserts; but the priest and the medic? Their deaths horrified her and made her think twice about admiring Albert Price. But more was to come, and as Harold came to the end of his recollections and spoke about how the lads of the firing squad were all injured and had come home, she let loose a wail that she'd been keeping inside her for a good while.

'Eeh, love, I know how you must feel, but give over, or you'll be ill. Hang on to what Harold told you. No one thought Jimmy guilty, and the corporal and the lads tried to save him. God knows where that corporal is, or the poor lass he took off with him, but he is a hero, despite him murdering them as he shouldn't have. Our Harold says so, and he never lies. Here, sup your tea whilst it's hot; it will help.'

Ada let go of the hand that held hers, a hand that she hadn't even realized had taken hold of her. But, as she took the mug, the same hand came around her. Betsy, dear Betsy. She was a young lass with a heart of gold, who knew the suffering Ada was going through.

The mug burnt her fingers, but Ada didn't care, for the pain lessened the one searing her heart, as it took her attention. Taking a sup gave her some relief and helped her to control herself. Answering Harold's mam, she said, 'You're reet, only what that corporal did wasn't the reet thing to do. That young lady's family must be out of their mind with worry. I'm assuming you are Harold's mam, so you know what it must be like for the mother of Edith Mellor – the lady doctor he kidnapped.'

'Did you know the lass that was kidnapped?'

'No, but I know of her. Me friend is a friend of the family.'

'By, lass, fancy you having friends in them circles.'

'I met her in hospital – she's a nurse. All of them posh lot are trying to help the war effort, and this is what me friend is doing. She trained at Leeds Hospital and will soon go to France.'

'Well, lass, I'm glad for you. You'll need some friends to help you. And if them friends are in high places, all the better. I must say, I had wondered how it was you had come to be living in Leeds. Oh, aye, I've heard your tale. But, mind, it isn't spoken of as a scandal. All the folk round here understand, after all that's happened to you. That sister of yours...'

'Look, it's good to hear me name has not been blackened. But me sister's needn't be, either. A lot happened that led her to do as she did, and now she's paying for it.'

'Aye, we never know what drives folk to do bad stuff, but often it is sommat as they can't help. I'm sorry, lass, real sorry for you. I was told as you were a strong one, and I'm glad that is so, as above all you need strength to cope with everything, and to find forgiveness – and not bitterness – for them as wronged you.'

'You're nice, Mrs Smithward.'

'Grace. Me name's Grace. And I like you an' all, lass. I admire you. And if ever I can do owt for you, you only have to ask. You have me address.'

Ada left after receiving a hug from Grace and a real cuddle from Betsy, and she could feel a little happiness seeping through her pain. Looking into Betsy's face and seeing hope there, not despair, helped that to happen, as did seeing Harold and

Grace put their arms around Betsy as she wiped away a tear. *Eeh, it is good to know that lass is alreet. In me grief, and in all that has happened, I have neglected her.* But Ada knew that Betsy understood. And, though it was early days, she could see that Betsy was loved and would have a happy future.

As she'd travelled back on the train to Rene's, Ada had come to a decision about her future. When she'd arrived back at Rene's house, Annie had greeted her. 'Oh, Ada, you look all in. Come on, me sunshine, tell me all about it.'

'I can't. Not yet, Annie,' she'd told her. 'How's me little Brendan? Has he been good?'

'Not altogether, but it ain't 'is fault. 'E 'ad colic, bless 'im, but I've settled 'im now.'

After looking in on the sleeping child and feeling the love she had for him, Ada had taken a bath, telling Annie that she needed time on her own. When Rene came in, she would tell them both what had happened.

Rene sat listening quietly, as did Annie, as Ada told them she'd decided that she wouldn't take the job offered by Lady Eloise, but would instead move to London to be near Wandsworth Prison, where they had told her Joe was being taken, so that she could visit him.

'I'll look into starting me business up somewhere near there.'

'What has changed your mind, Ada, dear? You said you would stay here, no matter what happened to Joe.'

'I need to get away. I can't bear all the reminders.

262

Not now. And there will be those that point their fingers. Not just because of what Joe did, but because of me Jimmy.'

Rene broke the silence, 'Oh, my dear, my dear.' She rose and came to her, but Ada warded her off.

'I can't – not yet. I'm trying to keep me emotions contained so that I can function. Your sympathy will undo me. I know you care about me, Rene, but I need your help, not your sympathy.'

'I understand, but know that I am here for you. And if this breaks you, I will help you to pick up the pieces.'

'Thank you, Rene. I know that. And I know as Lady Eloise will be able to help me as well. I have someone to suggest who might be able to take on the position she was offering me. Harold, the lad as I've just been speaking of. He's a good, kind lad. It will be hard for him to get a job, with only having the one arm, and coordinating the charity would be reet up his street.'

'That sounds like a good idea. I will put it to Lady Eloise. And yes, you are right, she will help you all she can.'

'And I will too, love,' Annie said. 'I live in a 'ouse not far from Shepherd's Bush. Being in semi-retirement, I'm only called on now and again, when Miss Rene needs me. Though she pays me a retainer, bless 'er. Me granddad left me the 'ouse. It was given to 'im by 'is employer on 'is retirement, for years of good service. It ain't far from Wandsworth – about five miles away, I reckon. You're welcome to live there with me. And I could maybe 'elp yer by taking care of Brendan. Yer see, me and

Miss Rene 'ave already spoken about what will 'appen when she goes to France. I've said that I don't want to work for the family until she returns, but if she needs me then, I will take up me position again.'

'Oh, Annie, ta. It'll be grand to be with you, as I'd be lost in the big city.'

They chatted on about how the living arrangements would work, and whether Annie thought the area was a good one for a dressmaking shop.

It was Rene, who had sat quietly by listening to their plans, who answered this one. 'Well, it is on Lady Eloise's doorstep, Ada. I'm sure she will help you by sending clients your way, and with setting up the business. You will need a lot of money, so please don't refuse her help. This is what she set the charity up for: to help war victims.'

'But I don't consider meseif to be a victim.'

'Well, you are. And if it doesn't sit right with you to take the charity money for your purposes, then look on it as a loan and pay it back. I'm sure Lady Eloise would agree to that.'

'Well, put like that, yes, I will see how she can help me.'

A short silence fell. Once more Rene was the one to break it. 'I have news, too. I'm going into special training very soon, and that won't last long. They are desperate for nurses at the front, so I will soon be heading to France.'

'Oh, naw!' Ada looked over at Annie. Annie hadn't spoken much, but now a little sob escaped her.

Rene put her arm around her. 'Annie, dear, it will be all right. You have your plans, and now

264

you will have Ada and Brendan to take care of, so you will be fine. We knew this was coming.'

'Knowing it's coming is one thing; you actually going is another. I'm scared.'

'I know, Annie, and I can't say that I'm not. But I'm excited as well. I go next week, so you will be hectic, closing this place down and supervising the removal of my things back to my home. You will have no time to think about it all.'

Again there was silence. Ada thought she'd heard all she wanted to hear about France, and didn't want to admit that this was the place the lovely Rene was going to. She would think of her as being on holiday – that way she could cope.

Rene interrupted this thought. 'Ada, dear, I don't know if this will be of any consolation to you, but I think the information you've heard from Harold will greatly help Edith's family. I will contact them. To think that the man who took their daughter is a kind person at heart, who cared for his men, will give them hope that he won't hurt Edith. They have been given very little information, and what they know suggests that the man suffered a breakdown and was in a poor mental state. This didn't give them a good feeling, or anything to hold on to. Now they will have something. They will know that his actions weren't those of a demented man out of control, but of a man acting in a manner to save the life of an innocent boy. Oh, Ada. Ada, my dear...'

This time Ada did allow Rene to hold her. As she cried, her world didn't seem such a lonely place. She had Rene, and she had Annie. Who could feel alone with such wonderful folk to care for them?

And she had Joe, too.

Five years was a long time, but she would visit whenever she was allowed to, and she would throw herself into her work. She'd cling on to the courage she knew Edith had, and let that help her. She'd get by. She had to.

19

Eloise

Holland Park, London, and Rossworth Hall, Leicestershire, Christmas 1916 The past catches up

Gazing around the ballroom, Eloise thought how wonderful it looked. Despite everything that had happened, a little Christmas spirit and joy seeped into her. This was the only part of their house in London that Father had allowed to be decorated this year. Though there were to be no family parties, the servants' ball had taken place the night before, and tonight would be Eloise's charity ball.

Most of London society that she'd invited had said they would attend. This would be the last event of the season's calendar before they all left to go to their country homes for the Christmas season. Tomorrow the servants would begin the task of packing for her family's move to Rossworth Hall, in Leicestershire. Once there, she would see Jay – something she was looking forward to more than she ever thought she would.

It had both shocked and pleased her when her father had said they would go to Leicestershire for Christmas and New Year, which was a tradition and was usually a wonderful time, as she'd thought her parents might not have wanted to go there this year, given recent memories.

She thought about the village ball, when all the locals were invited to the Hall and a bonfire was lit. She could almost smell the aroma of delicious roasted chestnuts mingling with that of the branches and garden waste burning brightly and lighting the sky.

Mother and Father would give a present to each of the children at the ball, and a hamper to each family. Then the young girls would come in, led by Christian and Douglas holding her own and Andrina's hands and Daddy taking Edith's, before the young men would dance with them. *Oh, they were such wonderful, innocent times. Where did they go? Andrina is now lost forever. And Edith, Christian and Douglas … I want you all home safely. Please, God, please bring them home.*

This year there were to be no parties, and Eloise had been tasked with distributing the toys and hampers in the village hall the day before Christmas Eve. Jay had promised to help.

Something in her lifted at the thought of this. Over the last couple of months, since she first heard the truth about Jay, their friendship had deepened. Letters had gone to and fro between them, and she had made a couple of visits to see

267

him. His health had improved and he was now almost as strong as he had been. He hadn't returned to his job. Instead he'd helped her with her charity, seeking out returning wounded and the bereaved, to see if they needed any assistance.

Jay had surprised her. Her impression of him, before she knew him properly, had been of someone uneducated and a little simple. But now she found him full of fun and very intelligent. He had taught himself such a lot from books. But then she should have realized how clever he was, for hadn't he taught himself to speak just by lip-reading, despite never having heard a word spoken in his entire life?

He did a wonderful job for the charity and, because of his own affliction, he was accepted by those who had been wounded and bereaved. Being accepted was something she found difficult herself. By most of those she tried to help she was looked upon as 'one of those born with a silver spoon, who can't possibly know what it feels like to be in need – a do-gooder'. So she concentrated on raising the money required, and had coordinators working in most areas of England, especially London, where there were three people working flat out, due to the bombing raids carried out by the Zeppelins, which had devastated certain areas and caused much loss of life. The coordinators' salaries were a massive drain on the charity, and something that the committee she had formed objected to. But she always found a way to reassure them, explaining that the majority of employees were soldiers who had no hope of getting another job, due to their injuries, which meant that the charity was helping them to help themselves and to help others! It all made sense to her. She was particularly pleased with Harold Smithward, who had been recommended by Ada. He was a gem, and in the few days since it had been agreed that he was a good choice for the job, he had already submitted his ideas for many new projects that would benefit the stricken Low Moor area. Ada had let Eloise know about them by telephone from Rene's house, before she had left for London.

Thinking of Ada, Eloise wondered how she was settling in. It had been a few days since Ada and Annie had arrived in London, but they had been busy days for Eloise and she had found no time to visit them. She would put that right today. Everything was organized for tonight: her gown was laid out for her on her bed, a chiffon, soft green-coloured, ankle-length creation, with peacock feathers printed on it, giving it a vibrancy that she loved. Her hair was already styled, so she would just have a quick bath, then half an hour for her maid to dress her and to apply some make-up, and she would be ready in plenty of time.

Ada opened the door to Eloise and greeted her in a way that Eloise loved. 'By, Lady Eloise! Eeh, it's good to see you – come on in.'

Somehow Ada made you feel loved. Just as Annie did. They were two women from opposite ends of the country, and yet similar in nature: down-to-earth, strong women who took all that life threw at them and got back up and tackled whatever it had in store. She so admired them

269

and was lifted by being in their presence.

Giving a little bob curtsey, Annie gave Eloise a welcome that was just as breezy. 'Oh, M'lady, fancy you comin' fer a visit. Sit down and I'll make a cuppa – or a "pot", as Ada calls it.'

The curtsey unsettled Ada. In a fluster she bobbed up and down with almost every word as she apologized, 'Eeh, I beg your pardon, M'lady, I'm not used to such company.'

Laughing in a way she had thought never to laugh again, Eloise begged her, 'Please, don't worry. Oh, dear Ada, you look like a jack-in-the-box. I mean...'

Mortified this might be taken the wrong way, Eloise tried to retract her comment, but there was no need. Both Ada and Annie were giggling, and then Ada said, 'More like a daft ha'porth!'

Eloise had no idea what that meant, but as their laughter increased, she had to join in with them. 'Oh, dear. It does help to laugh and engage in merriment. It is so nice to see you both, and in good spirits, too. Is everything going well?'

'It is, M'lady. We're getting on like a forest fire in the wind. And Ada 'as such plans, she's got me as excited as she is.'

'I know. Miss Rene telephoned about them. I'm so happy for you, Ada. As soon as I return after the Christmas holiday I will help you all I can.'

'Ta, M'lady.' Another bob accompanied this.

'My dear, you have no need to curtsey every time you speak to me. Well, you have no need to at all. I think it a silly custom.'

'Oh no, I don't agree. Sorry, M'lady, but we all 'ave our place in life and 'ave to keep it. It is the order of things, and 'ow it was meant to be.'

Eloise could only smile at this from Annie. Her father had long since said that the class divide was perpetuated by the poor, far more than it was by the upper classes.

The sound of a baby gurgling had Annie scurrying off in one direction.

'It's time for little Brendan's feed. I won't be a minute, M'lady,' said Ada, as she scurried off in the other.

Sitting back in her chair, Eloise reflected that she couldn't remember when she'd last felt like she did at this moment: cosy and warm and welcomed. It wasn't all down to the two nervous women making her feel that way; it was her surroundings, too. This room had a welcoming, home-made feel to it: the two fireside chairs – which she would call nursing chairs, as they had no arms to them – were a beige colour, and had crisp white antimacassars over the backs of them. Each was embroidered with intricate patterns of violets and daisies, entwined in a heart shape. On the polished wooden floor there was a beige pegged rug, with a pattern of dark-brown swirls around its edges, which looked like many half-moons intertwined.

The rug triggered a memory of days when she had visited Rene's home as a child – Annie would be pegging this very rug, as she watched them playing. Often they would stop what they were doing and watch, fascinated, as Annie pushed the peg, loaded with wool, through the netted base and back again, leaving the wool looped at the back. Then, with a pair of special clippers, she would clip the wool so that all the strands at the front of the rug stood close together and all were of the same length. It sounded simple, but Eloise knew there was a process whereby the strands were secured in place, which Annie had never explained to them.

It had taken years to complete the rug, as she remembered it being in progress from when she was about eleven years old. She and Rene had been seventeen when they held a little ceremony as the last piece of wool was pegged into place. It had been very funny to see Annie do a little dance of joy. Eloise and Rene had gone into a fit of giggles at how Annie's bosom had jigged up and down – such things amused seventeen-year-olds. At this thought, the same feeling that had visited her earlier came to her. *Those were such innocent, carefree days!*

Looking around at the rest of the room, Eloise thought that every corner of it reflected Annie's personality and her handiwork. The table that stood against the wall with four chairs neatly tucked around it was draped in a cloth just as white as the antimacassars, and with matching embroidered hearts. A dresser in the corner displayed pieces of china, and next to the very welcome, glowing fire a brass coal-scuttle stood, shining with pride at its prominent place. It was a lovely room, lovingly kept.

'Here's your pot of tea, M'lady.' Ada came back into the room carrying a tray, on the corner of which lay a banana-shaped baby's bottle, which she picked up, saying, 'I'll just take this into Annie for little Brendan. I won't be a mo.'

'Oh do tell her to bring the baby in here to feed

him. There is no need to hide him away. I would love to meet him.'

'Eeh, ta, M'lady, that's grand of you.' Opening the door to the hall and stairs, Ada called out to Annie to bring Brendan down. Then she turned back to her and said, 'He loves to be with folk. He's a little charmer, just like his da– I mean...'

'I know. I'm sorry, he must be a constant reminder for you of that painful time.'

'No. I don't put any of it on his shoulders. And I'm fine with it all now, and have been ever since I met Joe. I can remember Paddy without anger, and I accept and love his son. I just felt embarrassment at bringing the subject up.'

'I understand, but you have no need to. I've nothing but admiration for you. May I ask how your sister is?'

'She's not good, and hasn't been ever since the birth. Her husband has put in for a divorce, and that has devastated her. She has no interest in Brendan, and won't even have me take him with me when I visit her. I'm going to see if I can get her transferred nearer to here, and will keep trying to get her to accept her babby. By, it were a wrench coming here and leaving her, but I had to think of meself for a change. But eeh, that place she's in. It ain't fit for pigs. And that's how those in there get treated. There's a few soldiers in there that could do with your help, M'lady, I can tell you.'

'Oh dear, I'm sorry. I hope things improve for her. I wonder sometimes how we are ever going to help all those who need it. It seems an impossible task at times.'

'Aye, but at least you're trying. You haven't turned your back on us, as most of your class do, using us to clean up after them, fight their bloody wars and then kicking us in the gutter.'

'Oh, Ada, I didn't know you felt like that. I'm so sorry. We're not all like that.'

Annie coming into the room with the baby stopped the conversation, leaving Eloise feeling down for the first time since she had arrived. But Annie saying, 'This little man is demanding 'is food; I tell yer, the male species starts the process of domineering us as soon as they are born,' made her smile again.

A silence fell, once the baby was happily sucking on his milk. It didn't hold any comfort, and Eloise was beginning to regret coming. Annie was the one to lift the feeling, in her usual direct way. 'Well, I've a knife in me drawer. Once baby is fed, I'll use it to cut the atmosphere. What's made you both clamp your lips?'

'Eeh, it were me, letting me tongue have its rein on them as least deserve it. Forgive me, Lady Eloise. I don't deserve what you've done for me, in giving me the confidence to break away and make me feel worth sommat.'

'Please forget it, Ada. In your position I would feel the same. But I do want you to know that a lot of my class *are* concerned. Not many can physically do anything about the social imbalance, but most rally round to give funds to my cause. And my father tells me that many social issues are being discussed in Parliament, especially since the new Prime Minister, David Lloyd George, took office. Father says he has some very forward-thinking ideas, which, if implemented, will bring about change in all areas, especially for the lower classes.'

'I spoke out of turn, M'lady. No class of people deserve to be lumped together. I don't like it when it's done to me own lot, and I shouldn't have done it to yours.'

As she finished talking, she slumped into the chair opposite Eloise. The sight of her look of defeat brought a lump to Eloise's throat. She swallowed it down. 'Don't ever suppress what you want to say, Ada. There is too much of that, especially amongst women. And it is by talking to each other that we find a solution to what is wrong at the heart of our country. We women should stand together.'

'You're a special person, M'lady, and you have a wise head on your young shoulders. You're different to any I've ever come across. You're a saint.'

'Ha! I've never been called that before. It's a good thing Ada doesn't really know me, don't you think, Annie? I rather like being looked on as a saint!'

'Proper madams – that's what they were when they were growing up, I can tell yer, Ada. But I agree with yer. Lady Eloise and my Miss Rene 'ave turned out champion.'

'Ooh, I can feel my head growing and bursting out of my halo!'

They all laughed at this and Eloise felt the tension lift. 'Let's talk about the future, shall we? Tell me your plans, Ada. I'm so excited for you.'

Ada outlined her plans to become a seamstress, and her fears about what might go wrong.

'Your plans are attainable, Ada. Tell me, where did you train?'

'Mostly at me mam's knee – she was a time-served seamstress. She was taken on by a French lady, who ran an exclusive gown shop in Leeds. Mam were that good that, when she married and had me and Beryl, Madame Camilla installed a sewing machine in our house and had a sort of cage built in the corner of our parlour. Mam used to sit in this cage working away for hours, while we played around the outside of it. As we got older she taught us her skills. Not that Beryl took to it, but I did. I inherited an old treadle-machine that Madame didn't want back. I used it for years, earning a bit here and there by making things. I never retrieved it from the rubble of me cottage, though, and I reckon it's ruined now.'

'Well, my advice to you would be to get a new one, and to make up some samples that I can show to my friends for you. They do all have their own favourite outlets, so they will need winning over with something very special.'

'I will, M'lady, but I don't know where to start.'

'Leave it with me. I know several industrialists and can ask amongst them. Enjoy your Christmas as much as you can. It's been a terrible year for all of us, and we have ongoing things that worry and upset us, but hopefully we will have a little joy over the next two weeks.'

'Aye, things like war and death are great levelers. We're all in the same boat, when hit by the devastation they cause. I'll be thinking of you, M'lady, and hoping you and your family can find some peace an' all.'

'Thank you, Ada, we will try. And I will be thinking of you and praying you find some peace, too. I feel much happier that you have Annie and are here in London, away from all the sad reminders of the life you used to have.'

Ada seemed to hesitate. 'M'lady, can I tell you sommat? I've told Rene, and I know she will have told you, about the connection between your cousin Edith and my Jimmy. Well, even before that, I felt sommat between me and Edith. From the moment Rene told me about her, I knew we were linked in some way. I knew she must be a very courageous lady, to do what she set out to do. Anyway, from then on I've felt a kinship with her, of sorts. It helps me to think of her courage, and to try to be the same as her. It is something to cling on to. When you think about her, think of the strength and courage she has and latch onto that. It might help you an' all.'

Feeling the lump rise to her throat again, Eloise smiled through tingling tears. 'That's lovely. Thank you. I will, and I will tell Edith's mother your story, and how Edith helps you. Just maybe she can find a way of doing the same.'

The party was in full swing, and the ballroom was fit to burst with the number of people in it. The heat, despite having all four French doors open, was stifling. A three-piece music group played tunes that had the hardier amongst them dancing reels and waltzes. Eloise thought the atmosphere was wonderful, until a commotion near one of the French doors caught everyone's attention.

'It's Lady Muriel – she has fainted!' This cry

277

alarmed Eloise. She had been most surprised when her aunt and uncle had accepted her invitation. It had been sent out of courtesy, and she hadn't expected them to come. But Aunt Muriel, in one of her brave moments, had said to her, 'I have decided that yes, we will come to your charity ball, Eloise, my dear. Life has to go on, and it won't stand a chance of doing so without the magnificent effort our young people are making. We will support you, darling. Your work is much needed, and I admire the way you have found yourself a niche to do your bit, despite the restrictions the family grief has put upon you.' Eloise had been astonished. 'Thank you, but you really don't have to attend if you would rather not. Your donation is more than generous enough.' But her aunt had been insistent. 'No, we will come. God knows we could do with some light relief from all the pain and worry. As this is a charity ball, it is socially acceptable for us to attend, which makes it easier.'

Now, looking down on the pale, crumpled form of her beloved aunt, Eloise felt guilt at even putting her aunt in such a position, knowing how frail she had become.

'Give her air, please!' the commanding voice of her Uncle Christopher boomed out. Holding a distinct, doctor-in-command tone, the order didn't offend, but made everyone move back. Lady Davina Fortescue even took hold of the door and wafted it backwards and forwards to create a draught. It was something Eloise would have expected her to command one of the servants to do, rather than take on the task herself.

The seconds ticked away, each one deepening Eloise's concern as she watched all of her uncle's loving ministrations to revive Aunt Muriel have no effect. Gradually her face drained of the little colour she had had and took on the look of white porcelain, making her rouge all the more obvious.

No one in the vicinity spoke. The music had stopped, and only the hushed tones of those who could not see what was happening could be heard.

The initial guilt Eloise felt had been banished by a deep fear that had taken its place. Her mind filled with prayers: *Dear God, no. Not Aunt Muriel. Please not Aunt Muriel!*

Looking around and finding her parents close by, she read the same terror on their faces. Eloise looked back at the horror of the scene in front of her. Her uncle's voice penetrated her panicked mind.

'No, Muriel, my darling, don't leave me. Don't leave me.'

Another voice took charge. It belonged to the Duke of Cumbria, who voiced what they all wanted to hear. 'Tell us what to do, Christopher. Do we need an ambulance? Do you want us to help you get Lady Muriel home? Can you treat her yourself? Just tell us what to do!'

If Eloise lived to be a hundred she knew at that moment she would never forget the words her uncle spoke, or his tone of utter despair. 'It is too late. Oh God, my Muriel. My life. My love.' His sob ripped Eloise's heart from her. He crumpled and lay beside the unmoving wax-like figure of his beloved wife. 'My family, my family. My Edith missing, my sons in danger, and now my darling

279

Muriel gone.' But nothing affected Eloise more than when his voice rose in pleading anger, 'Why? Why? God, tell me, why?'

On the day that Eloise was meant to be giving out the hampers and gifts in the church hall of Rossworth village she stood looking into the gaping, dark hole of the family crypt, set in the centre of the parish-church cemetery, next door to the hall.

The unreality of the situation hit her, as she saw Andrina's coffin inside, still looking brand-new and sitting on a shelf above that of her grandmother. All the caskets were made of lead and, apart from discolouring, hadn't deteriorated. She could see several of her ancestors' caskets from where she stood. Aunt Muriel's casket was placed on a shelf at the back, where there was room for one more. *Who will that be? Eventually there will be room for two there.*

The surreal discussion that had taken place a few days ago, as the plans for this funeral were made, came back to her. Uncle Christopher had wanted Aunt Muriel in the Mellor family crypt, as opposed to her own family one, so that he could be near her after his own demise. Eloise's father had agreed, but had expressed his concern that the crypt might not be big enough and that a new one would have to be built for Christopher and his descendants. There hadn't been any time to implement the plan, and so it had been agreed that Aunt Muriel should start her repose in this crypt and then be moved to the new one when it was ready. Special permission had already been gained for this to happen.

The new crypt would be built on the plot of land that Eloise stood on. Andrina's death had been just the start of this journey, she thought, as she wondered how many of them would still be alive by the time this war ended. Although Andrina's death hadn't been due to the war, all of their lives were in danger because of it now: her cousins through direct action there, and those of them at home through the Zeppelin bombing raids. Even Aunt Muriel's death was, she felt, a consequence of the strain the war had put on her. Unbeknown to Eloise, her aunt had had a weak heart, and the condition had been aggravated by her fear for the safety and welfare of her children, and Edith in particular.

Poor Edith would never see her mother again. *How will she bear it...? But then, will we ever see Edith again? Somehow all hope of anything good happening in the future has deserted me today.*

As he stood next to her, Christian's body shook with sobs and something told her he was having similar thoughts. She took his hand in hers. On his other side stood Uncle Christopher, staring at the crypt in the same way she had been, his face telling of his heartbreak. On his right stood Douglas, who appeared not to feel anything, as his face was devoid of any expression. But she knew his pain cut just as deeply into him as it did the rest of them. Douglas had always been like a closed, locked door – there was no getting through without the key. Sometimes, when she had been much younger, she had seen it open when he'd played games with her and Andrina. She knew that behind what looked like an uncaring, serious young man lived a kind-hearted soul.

Worry seeped into her as she watched him. Other discussions had centred on his inheritance and the fact that, being the male heir to Aunt Muriel's family seat, Douglas would become the new lord of the estate.

At that moment a figure in the shadows caught her eye. Jay! *Oh God, why hadn't her father spoken up?*

When she had spoken to Jay the day after they and the cortège had arrived, and after the carrying of Aunt Muriel's coffin into the parish church, he was undecided about what to do. Whereas he had been adamant that he would not stake his claim while Aunt Muriel was alive, he now felt differently. She had told her father this, but he had cautioned her that until Jay said one way or the other what he wanted to do, the subject was best not broached.

Why do men think they know it all? Father could at least have talked to Jay!

How would Douglas feel, finding out he was not the rightful heir? How would he react to having the position and wealth that the title would bring him snatched away from him?

Douglas wasn't materialistic, but he had been schooled in the responsibilities that he thought would be his; and he had been studious, even as a young boy, in preparing himself. He knew, and had the respect of all the leaseholders of the farms belonging to the estate. Before the war he'd taken on his shoulders the setting-up of a monthly meeting of the tenants to discuss new farming

282

methods, and how they could implement them and share the cost as a team. He'd never liked London and had already made plans to live permanently in Hastleford Hall once the war was over.

Jay moved out of the shadows and walked forward. Several of the family glanced at him. Looking at her father, who stood holding her mother's arm a little to the left of her, Eloise saw a look of shock and fear cross his face.

No one said anything, but an uncomfortable ripple of disapproval went through the mourners as Jay came and stood between her and her father. She didn't dare look at him. The heavy wooden door of the crypt was closed, and then came the grating, screeching sound of its outer gate, as it too was closed.

The click of the key being turned in the rusty lock made her tremble.

Life was never going to be the same again. Jay's appearance had told her what his intentions were – intentions that would shake the foundations of everything she and her family had come to expect.

What had happened so far had shaken the rock that her family, and that of her cousins, was built on. But what was to come – if Jay did declare himself – would surely crumble it.

20

Jay

Leicestershire, Christmas 1916
Rightful place

As the funeral party turned away from the family crypt, Jay took hold of Lady Eloise's arm and turned her to face him. He could see that she was embarrassed and a little afraid. He needed to see her face to know what she had to say. How he longed to hear her voice – any voice.

Sometimes, since Florrie had attacked him, he had heard sounds. They had frightened him at first, as he had no concept of what they were. Now he dreaded them coming, as they were high-pitched zinging noises that drove him mad. They lasted for hours once they started. Unsure if they meant anything, he hadn't told anyone about them and it was all he could do to try and cope with them.

Lady Eloise's mouth formed the words, 'Not now, Jay. It is not an appropriate time.'

'I can't leave it, Lady Eloise. As is the custom, you will go back to the house now, to listen to the will being read. I cycled to Rugby the other day, as soon as I heard of Lady Mur... my half-sister's death. I contacted your family solicitor. I know of him as I've often posted letters for your father and have seen his address on envelopes. I told him my story. He has looked into it and, just this morning, has verified it by talking to Doctor Henderson. He had no time to contact your father before the funeral, but will inform him the moment the family arrives home. I needed you to know. I didn't want it to be a shock to you. It is likely the rest of you won't be told until you are gathered for the reading of the will. A will that is null and void now, as the estate belongs to me and cannot be disposed of as my half-sister wished.'

'Why now, Jay? Couldn't you have waited?'

'No. I would never have revealed the truth whilst Lady Muriel was alive, but now I have to. If I don't, there will never be a good time. I want what is rightfully mine.'

'I can understand that. But when Douglas has just buried his mother? It can't be right.'

Jay shrank away from the look she gave him. Her expression showed disgust. Maybe he should have consulted her. But when he did, she did nothing. She only wanted to save her aunt from shock and humiliation. Oh yes, he could understand that, but right is right. It was right that he was the owner of Hastleford Hall and the estate, and not Douglas; and that he, Jay Tattumby – or whatever his real name was – was the new lord.

Lady Eloise had been silent for a moment. She let out a release of breath. 'I will speak to my father. Look, he is waiting for me. I have to go.'

'I'll come with you.'

'No, you can't!'

'Then I will make my way to the Hall and wait outside. The solicitor has told me to attend.'

'How could he do that, without first consulting my father? Please, Jay, give me time to speak to him. Please.'

'You will have time to speak to him on the way. The solicitor told me that the wake is to be held at Hastleford Hall, my ancestral home. I will cycle straight over there now. You will all be there before I arrive. This will give your father time to inform everyone, so that it isn't a shock at the formal will-reading.'

'Jay! You have been planning this? Why do it in such a cruel way? Why didn't the solicitor ring my father and warn him what was happening, so that he could prepare my uncle and my cousins?'

'No, I have been left with no alternative. At first I just had a quest to learn the truth. The undeniable truth. I... You knew that. Didn't you speak to your father?'

'I – I, yes, I did. Look, I'm sorry, Jay. In all fairness to you, my father should have done something, but as you were not willing to declare yourself whilst Aunt Muriel was alive and none of us dreamed she would die as soon as this, my father can't be blamed for not acting.'

'No, and I can't be blamed for acting the moment she did die. At least if the family had been made aware as soon as she died, it would have helped. What was your father thinking of?'

'What does anyone think of on a sudden death? The shock is—'

'It was a shock to me, too. A tremendous shock. You see, though it was unlikely to happen, I had hoped that if Lady Muriel was told about me, we could have got to know one another and arrangements could have been put in place. I would have signed something to say that nothing should change until after her death, other than my acceptance into the family. I have been let down – ignored by your father. He should have acted once he knew the truth, even though he knew I did not intend to take up my rightful inheritance. As it is, it is going to be such a shock that it could cause a chasm in the family that will be irreparable. Though I do have plans to try to avoid that.'

For a moment Eloise hesitated, but then he saw that she was coming round to seeing his point of view, as she lifted her head. 'None of this is your fault, Jay. No one can deny you what is your own. The family will see that you were prepared not to do anything to hurt Lady Muriel, by claiming your just rights whilst she was alive, and will respect you for that, I'm sure. They may be angry and hurt and disappointed at first, but they will come to terms with that. As you say, my father should have done something, once he knew the truth. He has always suspected, and that is why he has treated you so well. But how will you go about things so that there will not be a split in the family?'

'I don't intend to abandon them. I will need their help. I won't even take their beloved home away from them, but will have one built for myself and my family nearby, on my land. I want Douglas to run the estate with me, and to have the standing that he would have had as the lord. I'm not sure of the details, as I don't know the extent of my inheritance.'

'From what I know, it is extensive. Come with me – we will have to speak with my father.'

As they reached the car, Lord Mellor climbed out and looked from his daughter to Jay. His anger was evident in his red face and in the way his words formed on his lips. 'What's going on? This is very bad behaviour, delaying the family in this way, Eloise. Your cousins need our comfort. We should have arrived back at their home just after them.'

Eloise made sure that she faced Jay, so that he could make out what she said. And he felt very grateful to her and watched carefully as she answered her father. 'I am sorry, Father. But the conversation Jay and I have just had is of great importance. Jay has seen the family solicitor, who has verified everything. He is waiting to talk to you and Uncle Christopher. Jay is going to claim his rightful ownership–'

Lord Mellor struck Jay's shoulder with his glove, bringing his attention to him. 'What? Don't you dare, young man!'

Before he had time to answer, Jay felt Lady Eloise grasp his arm. Turning towards him, she kept her face to him as she made her angry retort to her father. 'Father! Compose yourself. You should have acted before now. But at least you can take Uncle Christopher and the boys to one side and tell them, before we all gather to hear this formally from the solicitor. Jay has plans that will make this all a lot less painful than you imagine. It is time to give him the respect he should be afforded. He is mortified it has happened like it has. But we need you to deal with it with as much dignity as you can muster. Getting angry with Jay is not going to do any good, and is undeserved.'

By the look on her own face and her father's, Jay surmised that Lady Eloise had never spoken to her father in this manner before. Something in him recognized that she had put her duty to him above her respect for her father – something that, he hoped, wasn't all down to duty, but due to a much deeper feeling she might have for him.

These thoughts didn't stop the fear he felt, as Lord Mellor looked angrier than Jay had ever seen him. However, what Lord Mellor said belied what he must be feeling, as his words told of a calmness. 'Get into the car, Eloise. Jay, make your way to the Hall, but have the kindness to give me time to deal with the situation as best I can before you arrive. Nothing formal will be done until you do so. And I hope to God you are going to deal with this with compassion. I apologize for not having acted when Eloise told me of your rightful claim, but I–'

'Please don't apologize, sir. You have always been good to me, and I appreciate that. I – I hope you believe that I would never have taken anything from Lady Muriel, and that I intend to make sure things don't change too much for my family. It will take them time to get used to everything, but once they see that I am not going to lord it over them and leave them penniless, I am sure it will help. None of us are equipped to deal with such a situation. Mistakes have been made, but we couldn't know they were mistakes until we had the hindsight to see what has happened. Lady Muriel's sudden death has brought everything to a head.'

'Thank you, Jay. It doesn't excuse my behaviour, but it does help that you understand. Now we must get going, as they will all be worried about us. We will see you back at Hastleford Hall. And may God help us all through the next few hours.'

As he watched them leave, Jay reflected on how his feelings had changed. At first, when Lady Andrina had died, his inheritance was no longer of any importance to him. Loving her, or at least thinking himself in love with her, had made him want to be accepted in her society.

But since he'd begun to know Lady Eloise, he had known what real love is. Every minute of his waking day he pined for her. That hadn't happened with Lady Andrina. What he felt then was excitement as a result of his burgeoning sexual feelings, though he would never have let it materialize in that way. He'd had a love and respect for Lady Andrina, and her death had affected him greatly. But Lady Eloise was part of his being. She was in his soul. If he was ever to ask for her hand, he had to pursue his rightful heritage.

By the time he was called into the house Jay thought that he would freeze solid. He couldn't believe that, after learning who he really was, Lord and Lady Mellor had still shut him out to wait, as they would one of the servants. They had even left instructions for him to wait in the kitchen, but his pride had not let him do that, and so he had stood by the front door and waited.

When Woodacre opened the door, his words grated on Jay. 'What do you think you're doing, standing here at the front door, young Jay? You should have waited in the kitchen. Go round

290

there now, and they will let you in and bring you through.'

'No, I would prefer to be let in through the front door, as is my right. You and the others will learn why very shortly, Mr Woodacre.'

Woodacre's mouth dropped open, showing his toothless gums, but he opened the door and, without a word, showed Jay through the huge hall to the room where the family were assembled. As he went to open the door he said, 'Well, I never thought this day would come. Good luck!'

Jay stared into Woodacre's blue-rimmed hazel eyes 'You knew?'

The old man nodded. 'What does it matter now?'

Anger made Jay want to shake him, but the door was open and Woodacre was announcing his name.

For a moment he stood with all eyes on him – even those of Lady Eloise, whom he had not expected to be there, thinking that maybe only the male members of the family would be in attendance. He was glad that she was.

Douglas and Christian stood together, stiff and tall, every inch the soldiers they were. Their expressions told him of their devastation. Mr Ramsey, the solicitor, was there too.

'I'm sorry, but I think we should all begin with the knowledge that I couldn't help what your grandfather – my father – did,' Jay said.

Douglas said something to the solicitor.

'Please look at me when you speak, even if you're not addressing me. You all know that is the only way I can hear.'

'I apologize, Jay,' Douglas responded. 'I said, "This is preposterous!" There must be a mistake, or some rule of possession or something. I am the new lord, and I will not allow you to take that away from me.'

'I am not taking it. It is rightfully mine. I expect you know that I would never have done anything whilst your mother – my half-sister – was alive, may God rest her soul. But now I must.'

'Why *must* you? I will appeal against this... I will fight you in the courts. There must be something I can do.'

It was Ramsey who answered him, and again Jay had to ask him to look at him as he did so. 'As I see it, there is nothing that can be done. Mr Tattumby is the new lord. As a male-line successor, before your grandfather died, he has precedence over you. Your mother should never have inherited. I have spoken to all those who are still alive whom I could contact, and who witnessed Mr Tattumby's true identity, and I have their written testimony.'

'IT CAN'T HAPPEN!'

'Douglas, my dear, please. Please try to accept it, and hear Jay out. It is not as bad as you think.'

'It is worse than I think, Eloise. Nothing can make it better. We – Christian, Edith and me – and Father ... we will be penniless, and homeless!'

'Please tell me what Douglas said, Lady Eloise.'

After she had finished telling him, Jay walked over to where the solicitor stood. 'From here, I can see what you are all saying.' His eye caught the figure of a broken man, that of Sir Christopher sitting in the corner. 'Listen to me. You're my family. Douglas and Christian, I am your uncle; and I am your brother-in-law, Sir Christopher. As such, I will never see you penniless, or homeless. I don't know the size of my fortune, but I am hoping that my plans are well within my means.' As he outlined how they would be gifted this house and the one in London, and how he would build a new mansion for himself and his family, they began to look at him with interest, rather than disdain. 'I will settle a sum on you all – a generous one. The title is nothing. Your friends will hear that an unknown heir came to light, as is indeed the truth. It will be up to you how little, or how much, you tell them. They will see that your status has not diminished, so there will be no talk that would harm your name.'

When Jay finished speaking, no one moved. After a minute Douglas flopped into the nearest chair, and Sir Christopher sat up straight and looked at him with an unreadable expression, before standing up. 'You were wronged by my wife's father. For that I apologize. And I would like to thank you, Lord Daverly – because that is your true name.'

'Thank you. I appreciate you saying that, but no fault lies with you, or any of you. My status has come as a deep shock to you all. I only hope we can go forward in a manner that will unite us, and not divide us.' Turning towards the solicitor, Jay asked, 'Please can you tell me if what I propose is within my means?'

'It is, Lord Daverly, you are an extremely wealthy man.'

An excitement that he hoped did not show clenched in Jay's stomach. *Me, rich!* He tried to maintain his composure. 'I'll leave you now. You have a lot to come to terms with, not least the reason you are gathered together today. Your guests must be wondering where you are.'

Then the most surprising thing happened. Douglas came over to him and shook Jay's hand, saying as he did so, 'I can't pretend that I'm not bitterly disappointed and hurt, and that it's not painful to see my plans for the future of the estate rendered worthless, but I accept that this was not your fault. I want to thank you for your generosity.'

'None of your plans will be wasted. I would like you to work alongside me to manage the estate. I can't do it on my own. We could form a partnership.'

'Good God, man. I am trying to hate you, but I can't. Of course I accept your offer, for this estate is all I know. Christian has his scientific studies; and Edith – poor Edith – has her medicine. But as for me, well, this estate is in my blood.'

'Yes, you are right. It is in your blood as it is in mine, for we are of the same line.'

Sir Christopher came over to Jay and placed his hand on his shoulder, getting his attention. 'Your father's family were bankers and politicians, Jay. And I would say you have the latter in you, as you also have my late wife Lady Muriel's kindness, and that of your niece, Eloise.'

'Lady Eloise is my niece? I – I thought... I mean, how are we related?' Looking over at her, he saw Eloise blush. He'd let his guard down, and they must all know how he felt, or maybe thought

294

he was determined to have one of the sisters and, as Lady Andrina had gone... Oh God, why had he shown such surprise and disappointment?

'I'm not your real niece, so you needn't worry. I am only a niece-in-law. And you needn't look so horrified at being related to me. I am still your boss, Jay Tattumby, I – I mean Lord Daverly! You have to give me notice before I release you from that shackle.'

Everyone laughed and the tension broke. It was funny how they could laugh when they were there for such a sad occasion, but Jay knew that often happened at a wake. There was always more laughter than tears.

Christian, who hadn't spoken until now, came over. 'I echo my brother's words, Jay. Thank you for your generosity.' And then he said to his father, 'Father, Jay is about the same size as me. I propose that he changes into something of mine and we introduce him right now as the heir. What do you think, Douglas? Could you cope with that?'

'Yes, better sooner than later. What do you think, Father?'

'I agree.'

They all still stood around him and, as they had addressed each other, Jay had been able to turn his head to look at the speaker of the moment. His own concerns now came to the fore.

'But what shall we say about me – where I came from? I wouldn't want to start a scandal for you all.'

Looking from one to the other, he saw that it was Douglas who spoke. 'We will just have to tell the truth. After all, it will come out eventually: the villagers all know you, the staff all know who you are. Besides, sometimes just coming out with the truth stems any scandal.'

'Won't they think me a ruffian?'

'Not at all. I know you cannot hear yourself, but although you have a flat tone to your voice, due to your deafness, you speak like an educated man otherwise. How you have learned to speak so, I can't imagine; it must have come naturally to you. Your mother... I mean–'

'No, it is all right. Mrs Tattumby will always hold the rank of my mother, and I know you were going to say that she did a good job. She did, and she has devoted her life to me. And I suppose, as she knew who I really was, she made it her duty to make me speak properly: the King's English, she called it. Thank you, Douglas. You've given me confidence to meet the people I will be mixing with.'

Lady Eloise came up to him and touched his arm. 'Would you be so good as to take me into dinner when you are ready, Lord Daverly?'

'I'd be delighted to, Lady Eloise.'

Again a chuckle went around the room. Then a serious note overcame the company. Jay felt confused.

'It is my uncle,' Eloise told him. 'He said that he is dreading the dinner. Poor soul. Convention can cause a great deal of pain at times. Why can't it be that just the family are together at such moments?'

Looking around, Jay saw Sir Christopher being comforted by his brother, and his heart went out to him. As he watched, Douglas and Christian took over from Lord Mellor and supported their

father, and Lord Mellor came over to him. 'Well
done, Jay. I take everything back, and apologize for
my outburst earlier. If you will excuse me, I need
to go and inform Lady Felicity of what has happened. Come along, Eloise. We will wait in the
drawing room until all the family is gathered together and then go into to dinner as one, with Jay
heading us.'

A little squeeze of his arm from Lady Eloise
gave him encouragement – something he needed,
along with courage, to face the room full of
aristocrats and dignitaries. But he would have her
by his side, and that is how he hoped it would be
for the rest of his life.

21

Edith

London, first week of May 1917
Only hell awaits

'Edith, I still can't believe you're home. Has it
really been a week since you arrived? Are you feeling a little better, darling? I have so much to tell
you.'

Tell her. My God, hadn't she been told enough
already? Andrina, her lovely cousin, and her own
dearest mother were dead!

'I'm sorry, Eloise, but I can't cope. Please leave
me alone for a while. I know you are doing your

best, but this situation is too much for me at the moment.'

'I won't leave you, Edith, but I will stay quiet. I will just sit with you until you're ready to talk.'

Would she ever be ready to talk? Could she ever tell Eloise about all that was tearing her apart inside? The premature birth of her darling twin girls had drained her. Leaving them had wrenched her soul from her.

In the end she'd had no choice. But, once she felt strong enough, she would sort out a secret home for them, and a nanny and other staff. Once that was done, she would visit Marianne and collect her adorable girls on the way home. It wasn't a good plan – it was sketchy and not fully formed yet – but somehow she would be reunited with her darling daughters.

So many frightening questions visited her, but she had no answers for them. Questions like: How would she keep them secret? How would she be able to stop them wanting to be a part of her life? Her real life, not the life she would lead when she visited them, but her normal life. *Oh God, I feel so weak.*

'That was a big sigh, darling. Can I get you anything?'

'Just peace and quiet, Eloise! Is that too much to ask?'

'Forgive me. I only speak out of my love for you.'

'Oh dear, I'm sorry, please don't be offended. I'm not myself.'

'I will fetch Aunt Marianne. She can always settle you.'

Edith felt relief when Eloise left the room. In the week since she and Marianne had arrived back in England, everyone had wanted to celebrate. But how could she, with the dreadful news she had returned home to? Marianne had told her as gently as she could, but the impact of it all hadn't really hit her until she'd stepped through the door of their Holland Park home. Oh, how she wished the family had been at Hastleford Hall. *How did it happen that Douglas is not the new lord? How is it possible for life to have been turned so topsy-turvy, and in just a few short months! How can I ever call Jay Tattumby 'Lord Daverly'? It's just ridiculous, unbelievably ridiculous!*

Getting up from the chaise longue that her mother had loved, she walked over to the French doors. Mama had loved this room. *Oh, Mama, wherever you are, do you know my suffering? Do you understand? In life you would have condemned me, and maybe even have banished me from home, but in death do you accept me?* She allowed her tears to flow and through her wet eyes saw the early signs of summer vying with a winter coating as the sun banished the last of the slight ground frost. An unusual occurrence for this time of year, but although it was dry and sunny the temperatures remained low and produced an overnight covering that whitened the world, when really it was blood-red, churning pain into everyone's hearts. She didn't know what was more painful: thinking about the death of those around her, or thinking about the two tiny babies she'd left behind.

Born on the 19th of March, her twins had arrived a few weeks early and she'd had to fight to help them to survive. When she'd left they had been thriving. She had asked Petra to name them, and she had called them Elka and Ania – such lovely names. Dear Petra and Aleksi, she owed them so much; and now she had taken even greater advantage of their kindness, but she knew they loved the girls and would care for them until she could return. As promised, she'd transferred a large amount of money to them, to pay them back for all they had done for her and all they were continuing to do. She would always keep them close to herself and the girls.

Petra and Aleksi had been afraid and heart-broken when the Russian Revolution broke out in March, thinking their daughter would be lost to them forever. But they had been happy when they'd had a letter telling them that Marcelina was safe and had returned to the eastern sector of what used to be Poland. *Safe?* Edith wasn't so sure about that.

Frightening things were happening in that area, she had discovered. Having access to the up-to-date news, once she reached Marianne's, she'd heard of the terrible losses and displacement of people in Eastern Europe and had feared for Petra's daughter.

But she also had another niggling worry: she hadn't heard from Petra and Aleksi since leaving them. She had given them Marianne's address and had written to them, but although she had been at Marianne's for two weeks before returning home, no letter had come in return. This just didn't fit with how they had been when they said farewell. Petra and Aleksi had taken her to Paris in their battered old car. At the station she had held her twins to her. Her despair had been so deep that, when her train was announced as arriving imminently, she'd turned and said, 'I can't go. I will stay lost forever. I cannot choose my old life over my girls.'

Petra had seemed afraid at first, but then she was probably just feeling anxious. 'But you must – you cannot change your mind now!'

Aleksi had stepped in. 'Petra, my dear, whatever Edith chooses to do will be the right thing. It is very hard leaving one's children – we know that.'

Petra had calmed, and her outburst had become more understandable. 'That is what I meant. Think of your family, Edith; your poor mother, not knowing if you are alive or dead. Her heart must be breaking. Elka and Ania will be safe with us. You can come back for them, as you plan to do.'

With reluctance, Edith had told them that she knew they were right and that she had to go back, but it was the hardest thing she'd been called on to do in her whole life. The couple had put their arms around her, and the hug the three of them and the girls were in lasted for several minutes. During it Petra said that Edith had become a second daughter to them, and that they would never do anything to hurt her; whatever they did or said, she was to know that they did so in her best interests. Edith had worried about this comment. Was Petra trying to tell her something she couldn't voice? But the train had come in, and in the hustle and bustle of getting on it and the heartbreak of saying goodbye to her girls, she had forgotten her concerns.

Marianne had been ecstatic at seeing her and had accepted Edith's story without question. She'd told Marianne that Albert had abandoned her after she'd had a fall. The fall had knocked her out, and she had supposed Albert thought he could fare better without her. She said that she'd only learned what had happened from the farmers who took her in, because the concussion she had suffered had resulted in her losing her memory.

When her memory came back quite suddenly, she told Marianne, she'd made her way south immediately. What she hadn't planned on was the news awaiting her at Marianne's. Feeling strong, she had intended to travel home alone and visit her babies on the way, but what Marianne had to tell her rocked the core of her and sent Edith into a pit of despair she never thought she could climb out of – a despair that still had her in its grip. If only she'd had news of her girls before they had left Nice. That would have been something to hang on to. But now she was in limbo and didn't know what to do or which way to turn.

The door opened, jolting her out of her dark thoughts. Marianne glided into the room. 'Darling Edith, Eloise tells me you need help. I don't know what I can do for you, for your pain will take time to lift. I can only be a shoulder to cry on. But I've had an idea that might help a little. I've been wondering if you would like to go to Hastleford Hall for a few days? Felicity has suggested that she and I spend some sisterly time together; and I thought, with Hastleford being so close, that she and Eloise could go to Rossworth and you and I could go to Hastleford. What do you think?'

'Oh, Marianne, I don't know what I want.'

'I know you don't, darling, but one thing I know you do need is to visit your mama's and Andrina's graves. You need to say a proper goodbye. We could have a service in the church for them while we are there. I am not used to such things, but Felicity told me it is a tradition over here, and it might help you.'

'Yes, it would. It all seems so unreal. It is as if Mama and Andrina are there, in Leicestershire, and I only have to go there and all of this will have been a dream. This perception will leave me, if I visit Leicestershire. I will see the truth for myself. But how I am going to face it all, I just don't know. There will also be the ordeal of meeting up with Jay. I just cannot come to terms with it all.'

'Then you must face it head-on, my dear. As cruel as that sounds, you have to go to where your dear mama and Andrina are. And, yes, you do have to meet up with the new lord. I am quite fascinated by it all. I think it makes a wonderful story. I cannot believe how easily your father and brothers have accepted it all. In France there would have been duels of honour fought, and feuds opened up, with sides being taken and loyalties divided. You English are so calm and gentlemanly about these things. No fun at all. I will write a romance around it, but set it in France – it will be my best novel yet!'

Her laughter sounded alien in the sombre atmosphere of the house. But it was also infectious, and Edith found herself smiling.

'That's better, my darling, though I feel there is something troubling you far deeper than the terrible losses we have suffered. Can you not tell me about it?'

This shocked Edith. Marianne had always had second sight. She desperately wanted to tell her the truth, but she couldn't. Oh yes, Marianne would understand, but she couldn't burden her with such a secret and force her to deceive all those she loved. God knows it was tearing Edith apart, having to do so. She couldn't inflict that on this lovely lady; nor could she share the way her guilt was wearing her down. Mama had died because of the stress she was under, and most of that stress had been due to Edith's disappearance. But then what could she have done? Coming home pregnant would have killed her mother, just as surely as her absence had. *Oh God, I want an end to this pain!*

'Darling, tell me. Please tell me what is really troubling you. Let me help you.'

These words undid Edith. Falling to her knees, she felt her body heaving as she sobbed, loud sobs that echoed around the house. Bending with the weight of them, she beat her fists on the edge of the rug. Mama's rug. As she crawled towards the roses in the centre of it, her fists burned as she pummelled the pattern, which had no right still to be so vibrant when her mother, who had loved it, was gone.

'Edith, Edith, my dear, stop. Please stop.' Marianne was on the floor beside her. Her lovely face was wet with tears. 'Don't do this to yourself.

Whatever it is – no matter how bad – I will love you and help you through it.'

'I – I can't... I – I have done... I mean, no... No, don't make me; please don't.'

'All right. Come on, my darling. I don't have to know what it is. Just knowing there is something, I can be by your side, supporting you in it, even if I'm not here. You will feel my presence, my darling, and I will be your strength. Bind yourself to that, dear. All that I am is there for you.'

These words made Edith feel calmer. The burden of her secret was strangling her. The pain of her loss, and of parting from her little girls, was threatening to break her. But she would hang on to what she still had, and what Marianne was offering her: someone to turn to.

'I – I... Thank you. I feel better now.' Rising, she went into Marianne's arms and found a warmth to banish the chill from her, and reassurance in the strength offered to her.

Now she could go forward. She would visit Hastleford Hall and say her goodbyes to her dear mama and the beautiful Andrina. She would meet the new lord with dignity and acceptance, and then she would return and start to organize a plan for Elka and Ania, her darling babies.

And she would write to Laurent Pevensy, who had never been far from her thoughts since their chance encounter. She would write again to Petra and Aleksi. And when all this was done, she would beg a visit to Marianne's, where she was sure a letter from them would be waiting for her. On the way back she would pick up her children and begin her life again.

With these thoughts, a new determination entered her. She could go forward. She could, and she would!

22

Edith and Eloise

Leicestershire and London, mid-May 1917
Friendship crosses the class divide

'Ooh, bad luck!'

'Bad luck? I'm hopeless at croquet, and always have been. It's all right for you; being a surgeon, you have a steady hand and a good eye!'

Edith laughed at Eloise, but knew it was true. She also knew it had been too long since she'd practised her skill and her calling, and that she should be thinking of putting that right. Of going back to the front even. Today she had received letters from Connie, Nancy, Jennifer and Mark. It was so good to hear from them.

All the letters had come together in one envelope, and all expressed their joy at her return. Each said how much they missed her. Jennifer's held a surprise and gave a little twinge of regret:

I know you won't mind, as you were never interested in him, but Mark and I have fallen in love. Oh, Edith, he is just the best and makes all of our lives out here bearable. He has moved to take over your posi-

tion and is keeping up the good work you began.

For a moment Edith felt sad. It had been good to feel the attraction that she knew Captain Mark Woodster had felt for her. But she was being silly. His attention had stroked her ego, that's all. She hadn't felt anything for him like she had for Albert, or Laurent.

This thought had her standing and drawing in her breath as though she'd been thumped in the chest. Eloise's antics soon settled the feeling as, scoring a hoop point, she did a jig around the lawn calling out, 'Ha, not so good now, are you? I might even win!'

Laughing at her, Edith said, 'Oh, poppycock! Anyway, I give in. I need a drink. Darling, be an angel and summon Woodacre. Tell him to bring refreshments to the river's edge.'

'You're not going all morose again, are you, Edith? You are jolly hard work at times. Oh, I didn't mean to offend you.'

'No. Don't worry, I know what you mean, and I am. But I've had enough of being frivolous and living on the periphery of life. I want to take hold of life again. I'd like you to tell me about your work. I am so proud of you, and I want to help.'

'Oh, Edith, that would be wonderful, and I know it will help you. It did me, when I lost Andrina and had to cope with you being missing. I know what you've been going through. I went through it too, but I turned it into something very positive, and now I'm too busy to dwell on things.'

Edith could only nod. What she'd said about being proud of Eloise didn't really sum it up. She

307

had been astounded by the change in her, and admired Eloise more than she could say.

As she walked down to the river she passed the cherub statue that she loved, and stood for a moment looking at it. What would she have done if Jay hadn't given them this house? They were very lucky that he'd recognized it was theirs, and that his settlement to each of them had been so generous. He had treated her the same as her brothers, so she was now rich in her own right, which endeared him to her even more!

When she reached the river she stood for a moment, gazing around her at the beauty of the countryside – land that they had thought belonged to them, but which now belonged to Jay. Somehow she had to come to terms with this. After all, Jay was family – he was her half-uncle – and so she must stop thinking of the estate as passing to someone else as if they no longer had a stake in it.

Jay had been wronged by her grandfather, but now all of that had been put right. She had to accept that. It would be wonderful for Douglas still to have the management of the land, and to be able to live in his beloved Hastleford Hall.

It was time she met up with Jay. He had been generous and had said that he wouldn't encroach upon her until she was ready to speak to him. He still lived with Mrs Tattumby, and was remaining there until he could build the mansion he wanted. And he still carried out the charity work he was doing with Eloise, which kept him busy and meant that Edith hadn't come across him yet. Well, she was ready to now. In fact she was ready for a lot of things. She would suggest to Eloise that they invite

Jay to dinner. Just the three of them. Marianne and Aunt Felicity would understand.

Seeing Eloise in the distance coming from the house reminded her that she had wanted a little respite to think over the letters and their content, and to give some attention to her own feelings.

Connie and Nancy hadn't changed. Their letters were full of the funnier side of life at the hospital. It touched her, though, when Connie spoke of how she'd missed her and had prayed every night for her safe return.

Mark's letter had an apologetic tone to it:

Dear Edith,

I hope this letter finds you well. We are all more delighted than we can say at your safe return.

I know that Jennifer is telling you the news about me and her, and I hope you will wish us well. I did show my feelings for you, and they were real at the time, but you never returned them or gave me a second of hope that you would do so.

After going through hell at your disappearance, I took the comfort Jennifer offered – you know how good she is at counselling those who need it. Before long I found myself falling deeply in love with her.

We are very happy and intend to marry once this war ends. We would love to have your blessing.

My fondest wishes,
Mark

Bloody men! Huh, who does he think he is? But then she laughed as she imagined Mark agonizing over how to tell her that he'd switched his attentions to Jennifer. As if she cared! Typical male ego. But then she *had* felt a moment of regret. It was silly really, because her own feelings had been turned upside down by the lovely Albert – an uneducated cockney who was so far removed from her own life and standing that it seemed almost impossible she had even looked at him.

Her heart twisted at the thought of what had happened to him. *This bloody war, it's tearing the guts out of people all over the world.* Albert would never in a million years have murdered someone, or committed rape, or taken his own life, if he had been able to live his life in his natural environment.

A smile played around her lips as she thought of how he might have been. He'd have met a brash, heart-of-gold cockney girl, married her and had a few children; he'd have worked at his job as a mechanic, had beach holidays in Essex, enjoyed his pint of beer at the local and been a happy man. *Oh, Albert – and all young men like you – my heart bleeds for you.*

Despite thinking fondly of Albert, she had long since recognized that the feeling she'd had for him had been no more than sexual attraction. He'd awoken in her feelings that she never thought she'd have again, once he died; but she had, and more deeply. What would Laurent think when he read her letter?

A blush swept over her face at the thought of it; but, as he had said, things could not be left unsaid in this unstable world. She knew, beyond any doubt, that she was in love with him. She longed to be with him, almost as much as she longed for her babies. What would he think when he read the truth? For no love can be built on lies, though she had omitted to say what had happened to Albert (just that he had left her), and had sworn him to secrecy with the truth about her children. Now all she had to do was wait to hear from Laurent, and wait for her intended visit to Marianne's, where surely she would hear from Petra.

In the meantime she was strong enough now to sort something out for her children, and she had more than enough funds to do so. She would do this when she got back to London.

Eloise had joined her by the river and they had been chatting about Eloise's charity work for a few minutes when Edith said, 'I haven't said anything before, but I was shocked when Daddy told me that you all knew a small amount about the man who had taken me, but at the time I didn't give much heed to it. He said it was through someone you had come across in your charity work?'

'Yes. Ada O'Flynn. Oh, Edith, her story is so harrowing, and yet she is such a strong person.'

When Eloise finished telling her Ada's story, Edith couldn't speak for a moment.

'Are you all right, Edith, my dear? I'm so sorry – has it been too much for you?'

'No, I – it's just that I knew Ada's son. I knew Jimmy! I treated him. And I vowed that I would tell her the truth: that he wasn't a coward, and that his hand being shot off was an accident.'

'She knows that from the young man who told her about his death. He was a friend of Jimmy's. If you could tell her too, that would be spiffing. It isn't that she doesn't believe it, but – well, she could do with you telling her, too.'

'When can I meet her? It's a long way to travel up to the North.' She thought about her plans. 'But that doesn't matter. I will go as soon as I can.'

'You don't have to go that far, dear. You remember my friend Rene? Well, Ada is living with Rene's old nanny, Annie. Annie has a house in London.'

How strange the coincidences that are thrown up in life, and even more so in war, thought Edith. Listening to Eloise speaking about Ada's connection to her friend, and how Ada now lived virtually around the corner from her own Holland Park home, it all seemed incredible.

'I will visit her, Eloise, I promise. But, you know, there is something else that I think is important too, and I have been putting it off. Jay: I need to meet up with him. And once that is done, we should return to London and I will visit Ada. Do you think you could fix it up so that I could go on my own to see her? I – I ... well, I think it best. It isn't going to be easy for her, hearing what I have to say.'

'Of course. And, Edith, I am so glad you want to see Jay, too. Look, there is no easy way to say what I want to say. You will think me silly, or disloyal to Andrina.'

'I will never again think of you as silly, Eloise.'

'You did once, then?'

They both laughed, and it felt good. 'Yes, I did. The pair of you were very silly, in my eyes. But you are not now, my darling cousin. You are one of the people I admire most in the world. Now, tell me what you were going to say.'

'I think I'm falling in love with Jay.'

'What? My, I didn't expect that! But, darling, I am not disapproving. I know more than anyone that love can strike at any time and can link the most unlikely people.'

'Jay isn't unlikely now. He is above us, in standing. But it isn't that. I have been attracted to him for a long time. Oh, I know that when Andrina was attracted to him – God rest her darling soul – I was most disapproving, but I didn't know what love felt like then. You don't think I am being disloyal to her memory, do you?'

'No, darling. Andrina would be so happy that you, the sister she loved, and Jay, the man she loved, have found happiness. He does love you, I presume?'

'I don't know. I think so. I hope so. But he may not want to speak, even if he does. He may feel guilty about it. Oh, it's so frustrating!'

'It will work out. Love finds a way, they say. Let's go and find Woodacre and ask him to see that a message gets to Jay to invite him to dinner tonight. And I will watch for signs of his affection towards you.'

'Oh no, you mustn't.'

'Ha, I'm only teasing. Come on. I think we should also make arrangements to go back to London very soon; tomorrow even, if it can be arranged.'

It had been a surprisingly pleasant evening, and Edith had found herself warming to Jay. It had been embarrassing to her to have to thank him for his generosity, but he had put her at ease.

He'd been the gentleman personified in his dealings with them both, though his attentions to Eloise convinced Edith that Eloise's love was indeed returned. Not that she had done anything about it, as she didn't agree with interfering in such matters and preferred them to take their course. She was sure Eloise and Jay's relationship would progress in the near future.

Now, two days later, Edith was on her way to meet Ada. She'd liked what she'd heard of her, and wanted to tell Ada about Jimmy's last hours. Though wanting to and doing so were two different things, and she wondered just how she would find the courage to do it.

Ada stood up from her seat next to the table when Annie showed Edith into her parlour. Edith kept her gaze steadily on Ada's. In Ada's eyes she read an agonizing hope.

'I'm pleased to meet you, Miss Edith. I hope I'm doing reet calling you that, but Annie said it was how I was to address thee.'

'Yes, and may I call you Ada?'

'I would like that. Ta. And ta for coming to see me. It means a lot to me. You don't know it, but I've felt a connection to you for a long time.'

'Oh?'

'Aye. Ever since Rene told me of you, I have thought of you as a hero, and have tried to hang on to some of your strength and use it to help me. Then, when I heard that Corporal Albert Price, who took you, was the same man who'd tried to save me son Jimmy, I felt the connection even more. It sort of bound me to you. Oh dear,

314

you will think me mad.'

'No, I don't. I'm glad I was able to help in a small way. But, you know, I'm not the hero you think I am. I have many failings. Shall we sit down?'

'Oh, begging your pardon, Miss Edith. That should have been me first thing to do, instead of babbling on. Here, sit by the fire. It's reet nippy out there today.'

'Thank you.'

'Can I get you some tea? I mean, Annie will get it. She said owt we want, I'm only to shout.'

'That would be very pleasant, thank you. Like you say, it is chilly outside.' Edith knew that Ada was chattering on out of nerves, but she felt a deep warmth towards this woman, whose honesty shone from her.

After requesting the tea, Ada said, 'Lady Eloise left a message that you were coming. She said as you have ... well, that you knew me lad, Jimmy?'

'Yes, I met Jimmy. And, as you have said, it was his corporal who kidnapped me. Look, this isn't easy. I – I don't know where to begin.'

Annie walked in with the tea just then, inter-rupting them. 'I had it all ready; just had to add the boiling water, so that you didn't have to wait, Miss Edith. Shall I pour?'

Ada jumped in before Edith could answer. 'Naw, I'll do that, Annie. Ta ever so much.'

'Well then, I'll leave you to it. I 'ave to pop out, so you'll 'ave your privacy, but I'll be back in an hour. I'll take Brendan with me; he's sleeping now. I'll say me goodbyes to you, Miss Edith. It is nice to see yer again. I would love to 'ave time

315

with yer, if yer can spare it sometime, so that you can tell me what kind of situation me Miss Rene will be going into, and what I should send her, and what I should write to 'er about.'

Annie's accent brought memories to Edith that hurt. Hers was a female version of Albert's voice. She banished the thought. 'I would like that, Annie. I'll try to sort something out for next week, if that will be all right?'

As Annie left, the sound of the tea being poured into the lovely china cups resounded around the room. Nerves at the thought of the coming ordeal shook Edith. Talking about anything to do with what had transpired always put her in this state, and talking about her time with Jimmy felt so close to her own ordeal that she wondered if she could cope with it.

'Do sit down opposite me, Ada. It will be easier than looking across to the other side of the room at you.'

Ada sat down. The rattle of the cup in her saucer showed how nervous she, too, was feeling.

'Before I begin, I want you to know that I understand your loss. I came home to find that my mother and my cousin had both passed away whilst I was lost in France.' *Lost? Yes that was the right word, because that is what I have been. Lost in my own world. The worst thing is that I still feel lost.*

'I'm sorry. I did know. I wondered what it would be like for you, coming home to such news. Me heart goes out to you.'

They were dancing around, not wanting to get to the point. Edith drew in a deep breath. 'Jimmy wasn't a coward.'

'Aye, I know that. I know about his hand, but how did that happen? Harold, the lad that told me, didn't know. Only that his corporal had said that it was an accident.'

As gently as she could, Edith told her what Albert had told her. She did not change a thing. As she listened, Ada's features elongated and her mouth opened in shock. When she spoke, she sounded incredulous with disbelief. 'Me lad? Me Jimmy? Going to shoot himself? Naw, that ain't reet; he wouldn't. Naw... Naw!'

'My dear, it wasn't Jimmy's decision. I mean, not a decision that he would take in his right mind. He was traumatized. He'd suffered a breakdown. In that state anyone would contemplate, and maybe even carry out, suicide. But that doesn't make him a coward. It just makes him a sick boy who needed medical help. Albert went to stop him and lifted him, but the gun went off. Albert hadn't thought Jimmy meant to do it, so didn't think the gun was ready to fire. He was mortified and did all he could to persuade the court martial, but–'

'Oh God. Oh God!'

'I'm so sorry, Ada. I shouldn't have come, but I wanted you to know that Jimmy wasn't a coward. I – I thought it might help.'

'Me Jimmy! NAW... Naw!'

Getting up, Edith went over to the distraught Ada, who was rocking backwards and forwards. 'I'm sorry.' Her own tears choked her. Kneeling beside the doubled-over woman, Edith put her arms around her, trying to hold her, but Ada was like a stiff board, rejecting any such comfort. *Oh God, why did I think it would help her to tell her? Why?*

Unable to stem her own sobbing, Edith knelt close by and cried with Ada, keeping her arm round the back of her. Gradually Ada's wailing stopped and she asked in a steady voice, 'Was me Jimmy afraid?'

It was time for some lies. The truth hurt too much. She couldn't tell Ada how her son screamed in fear, when told that he was to be taken away and tried for cowardice. 'I don't think he really realized what was going on. He was very calm when they came to question him. I stayed with him. I am sure he didn't know what they were saying.'

'Did Albert tell you what he was like when... Oh God!'

More lies. 'Yes. He said he stood straight and was quiet. Albert said he'd never seen a braver lad. Albert was distraught, as he thought he could save Jimmy. He did try. He did all he could.'

'I know.' Ada's body had calmed. Some of the stiffness went from her. 'I can never have him back. But to know he wasn't a coward, and yet was shot by his own side as if he was, hurts so much. A sick boy! What were they thinking?'

'It's a tragedy. So many sick boys shot. They know about shell shock, but still they pardon very few. I will write a report and ask for it to be put on Jimmy's file. I will also ask my uncle to bring this question up in the House of Lords. He is on so many committees. We need to get Jimmy pardoned.'

'Them things don't happen for the likes of us. Look at my Joe: in prison for sommat as was self-defence. I know it were me husband that died

318

that day, but it was still self-defence. None of your fancy lawyers could save him.'

Edith didn't know what to say. The whole experience had opened up a wound in her. She fought hard for control over her feelings. But Ada's next words showed she wasn't winning that particular battle.

'Eeh, don't take on, lass. I – I mean, Miss Edith. None of this is your fault. I shouldn't have upset you like that. Me grief is the grief of a mother, and that cuts deep. Deeper than you can understand at the moment.'

'I do understand. Oh, Ada, I do.' Nothing could rein back the emotion that compelled her to unburden herself. 'I have twin girls. I left them hidden in France. Oh, Ada, the pain of not being with them, and of living a lie... Oh God!'

Ada got up out of her seat and then knelt beside Edith. 'Eeh, poor lass, come on. Let's get you to a chair, and then you can tell me all about it.'

Somehow Ada took on the role of comforter, even though she was in dire need of comfort herself. Allowing Ada to help her to her chair, Edith sat down. 'Promise me you will never tell anyone – not even Annie, or Rene, who I know you are close to. And, please, never breathe a word in front of Lady Eloise.'

'I won't. But you sound as though you have a burden too big for you to carry alone. Tell me all about it.'

Once she'd finished telling Ada her story, Ada was silent for a moment. Her hand rubbed up and down Edith's back. 'I'll help thee, lass. I'll do owt in me power. I'll look after them for thee. I can think up some story or other. I don't know what: sommat along the lines of them being related to me... That's it! When were they born?'

'March the nineteenth.'

'Would it be possible to pass them off as five months old?'

'I don't know – I wouldn't think so. They were born six weeks early and were very tiny. Why? What are you thinking?'

'I could pass them off as Jimmy's. He went in January, last year, but had a few days' leave in March when his training was completed. So any child he fathered then would be five months old by now. No one knows me here, so they wouldn't have a clue me story weren't true. I could say as me son's girlfriend had contacted me and said she couldn't cope, and that she was giving the twins up for adoption, so I took them on.'

'But if no one knows you, what will it matter, as you can put them at their right age? Oh, Ada, would you? Would you do that for me and my girls? But how would you cope? You already have your little nephew.'

'I'll find a way. Besides, I'll have your help. You will visit and–'

'Wait a minute... Look, yours is an excellent plan, but will put a lot of strain on you, and I can't see how I could feature in the girls' lives in the way I would want to, without raising suspicion. But there is a way. I have been thinking for some time about starting a place for girls in my situation. I think there will be many, because war makes people act differently from how they would normally. The place I have in mind will be a place of love, and its aim will be to help unmarried girls keep their child, if they want to. The children will be looked after, and mothers can visit and will be helped eventually to be in a position to make a home for their child. Of course there will be adoption help, for those who can't have their child with them, for whatever reason. How does that sound to you? Do you think – with me overseeing it all – you could run such a place for me?'

'It sounds grand, and I'd like to give it a go, but what would it mean? What would I have to do? How will it help you and your girls?'

'I met someone. And I have written to him. I have told him everything. I am hoping with all my heart that he will still love me, despite everything that has happened, and will ask me to marry him. Then I'm hoping he will agree to adopt the girls. I could bring them back here, and we can take care of them in the home we will start, until – if Laurent is willing – the time comes when they can come to live with me as my own. Oh, that would be wonderful.'

'It would. But eeh, Miss Edith, there's such a lot as could go wrong. What then?'

'I will still have them near me. In the home. And I can see to their welfare and their future. I have to do this, Ada. Putting them in your charge, in the way you describe, would leave me knowing they are well, but that is all. I could never adopt them, or even visit them, for what excuse could I use?'

'Reet. Your plan it is then. It will mean me giving up my own plans, but I don't care about that. It was daunting me anyroad. But me talent needn't be wasted. I can teach the girls we have in the home how to sew. That would be sommat for them in the future. We could have a sewing room, where we make things for them; and as the children grow, they can learn how to do it for themselves. We could take older children in – those that have been orphaned.'

Edith felt lightened by Ada's enthusiasm. It fuelled her own, to the point where she decided that she would speak to her father about her plans as soon as she could. Tonight even. Yes. He had said he would be dining with her tonight, and there was only the two of them. She would put it to him that it was this, or going back to France. She knew which option he would choose for her. Plus her training would not go unused. She would work on a part-time basis at the hospital, when they needed a surgeon with her skills, and would be the chief medical officer for the children and mothers in the home. She was sure now that this home could be established.

Despite Ada's sorrow, she too laughed. 'Eeh, I feel as though me future is sorted, because I was worried about starting a business up. I don't knaw much about business, but I do know about young 'uns and what they need, and I have that knowledge in abundance to use.'

'Thank you, Ada. I'm so glad I came. We have shared things today that will bond us in friendship, despite our different backgrounds. Ada, what do you think about calling the home "Jimmy's Hope House"?'

Ada gasped. 'By, that would be grand. It would be like giving him his honour back. Ta, Miss Edith.

You don't knaw what you've done for me today.'

'Nor you, for me. Just to unburden myself is healing me a little. If it hadn't been for Jimmy and the love Albert had for him, the twins wouldn't exist, so it is a fitting name.'

'Aye. Though I'll never breathe a word as to where Albert really is, I'll allus pray as he has found Jimmy and that they're mates, wherever they are.'

'I am sure they are, Ada. And thank you for your promise. I hope I haven't burdened you by telling you the truth. But it really must never get out. I have sworn that Albert left me and went on his way.'

It was with a much lighter heart that Edith left Ada than when she came to meet her. It wasn't just that there seemed, at last, to be a solution to how she could be with her twins. But, in Ada, Edith felt she had found a true and lasting friend.

23

Edith

London and France, July 1917
A journey of hope, eternal despair

Anxiety dogged Edith. It came out in her irritation. 'Oh, just pack what you think, but remember, it will be very hot in Nice!'

Denise, who had been her mother's maid, had

flapped around, asking this and that question until it had driven Edith to distraction. Never one to have a maid, thinking it an unnecessary luxury when she could very well do things for herself, Edith had felt compelled to keep Denise employed. Mother would have expected that of her. Father had paid the woman a retainer until her future could be decided, or in the hope that she would find other employment, but the latter hadn't happened, and now Edith felt stuck with her.

'Sorry, Miss Edith. I am just unused to what you need. I knew exactly what your–'

'Yes, yes. All right. Look, I'm the one to apologize. Forgive me. I'm being most rude. I trust your judgement, Denise. You have packed many times for Mother's visits to Nice and have got it just right. I will leave it to you.' Bobbing a curtsey, Denise left the room.

Thank goodness, now I can concentrate. I must write to Laurent. Why haven't I had a reply to my last letter? Is he safe? Did he feel disgust at my story? Did I do the right thing in telling him the truth about my babies? She was full of questions and uncertainly.

Taking her pen and ink, she began to write:

Dear Laurent,

I hope this, my second letter, finds you safe. I will not say I am well, for how can anyone be well in the circumstances in which we find ourselves? And I have worried about you ever since I heard the news about the failed Nivelle offensive, in the Second Battle of Aisne. I have wondered if you were part of that. However, I continue to hold hope in my heart. I believe I

324

would know if anything had happened to you.

It seems strange that such a short encounter between us could bind me to you as it has done. I pray that telling you the truth about my circumstances has not meant that you no longer wish to know me.

In my other life, I would not have been writing this letter, or have a memory of a kiss that changed me forever. But these are not normal times, and we must allow our hearts to lead us. I hope yours leads you to me...

Continuing to tell him of her plans, and giving him Marianne's address, Edith finished the letter with the endearment:

My darling... Can I call you that? I know I am being most forward in doing so, but that is what you are to me. I am forever yours, Edith x

She blotted the page with her roller ink-blotter. A silly notion came to her. She would sprinkle the letter with her perfume. Laurent had no idea what her normal scent was. The day she met him, she must have had the smell of sweat and even vomit on her. A shudder went through her, as her intended journey that day came back to her. But then she allowed thoughts of Laurent to take her senses, as the memory of him holding her and the touch of his lips on hers came to her. *Oh God! Please let him be safe!*

In the six weeks since her conversation with Ada she'd made a great deal of progress in setting up her charity. She'd established an account in the name of 'Jimmy's Hope House' and had made

Eloise a trustee, along with Jay. She knew she could trust them to oversee the setting up of the home. Jay had even donated enough money for her to purchase a building, a disused warehouse in Hancock Street, Kensington.

Plans had been drawn up for its conversion and subject to their permission being granted – which was just a matter of rubber-stamping them as her uncle had used their standing to push them through – the purchase would be completed. Builders had already been engaged – again, Lord Mellor had seen to this – and were ready to move once the plans were approved.

In the meantime Eloise, despite being busy with her own charity, was finding time to work on engaging some old-school nannies to care for the children who would be housed in the home. And Jay had taken on the task of finding the right furniture and was doing a sterling job, choosing from catalogues and then showing his choices to Edith who, so far, had loved every one and had placed orders for their delivery on a date to be decided. Edith, meanwhile, had set about finding the equipment she would need for the clinic that was to be an integral part of the home.

All that remained was to find the children and young mothers who needed such a facility. She had thought about placing a discreet advertisement saying something along the lines of 'Are you alone and expecting a child?' or 'Do you have children and can't cope, through being made a widow?' That kind of thing. She'd also thought about dropping leaflets into local doctors' surgeries, or approaching the local papers about running a story about her home. Somehow she would get it off the ground.

Ada was working hard, learning about aspects of childcare so that she could command the respect of the nannies she was to manage. She was rising to the challenge, and the love she held inside her endeared her to the more experienced nannies that she was meeting as they were engaged. Ada had proven, too, that she was up to the admin side of the general management of the home, because already she had worked out the shifts that would be needed and had even put some rosters in place, marking the number of workers she would need on each shift. She'd said she would like the nannies and cleaners and cooks to choose which hours would best suit them. Edith had thought this might cause Ada a few problems when she actually put it into practice, but was willing to give her free rein and allow her to sort it out if it didn't go to plan.

It all seemed possible now that Jimmy's Hope House would really and truly come into being. For Edith, too, there was a sense of great relief and excitement about her own children coming to live there.

Descending the stairs, she went to place the letter to Laurent on the tray for posting, but thought better of it. She would enjoy the walk to the post office. A letter addressed to her lay on the platter. It looked official and held the stamp of the Guild of Surgeons. Opening it, she read the phrase 'Shepherd's Bush Military Hospital'. As she scanned the words, her heart lifted to see that she had been accepted to work on a part-time basis as

327

a surgeon at the hospital. Built to care for wounded soldiers, Shepherd's Bush Military Hospital had been largely founded due to the efforts of the noted surgeon Robert Jones, a friend of her father.

It seems everything is falling into place for me. If only I could hear from Laurent. And, even more so, from Petra! But whether she heard from Petra or not, she would call there on her return home and collect her twin girls. Nothing would stop her doing that. Her heart thudded at the prospect of holding them again.

Edith's return to France shocked her. The peace had gone, and the reality of war was all around her. Now, everywhere she looked, there were gaunt-looking older men and wounded younger ones, plus women and children who looked as though they were on the verge of starvation. Buildings had a tired, uncared-for look about them, as if the life had been drained from them.

'My beloved France – how she suffers.'

Edith did not say anything to this comment from Marianne. She knew the mutiny of French soldiers after the disastrous Battle of Aisne had greatly affected Marianne and so she did not want to open sore wounds. The French were once again enthusiastically engaged in battle with the Allies at Passchendaele, so the refusal to fight had passed.

Instead, changing the subject, Edith thought this a good time to broach the matter of the length of her stay. 'Marianne, I hope you won't think me rude if I only stay for six days, instead of the promised ten?'

'What? Why is this, *ma chère fille?* I had hoped to persuade you to stay longer, not to cut short your visit!'

'I'm sorry, but there is so much to do. I give a great deal of importance to my charity, and if I am not there, then the extra responsibility on Jay and Eloise is too much to ask. Eloise has her own charity to run.'

'Oh, you girls! You are wonderful. It is no more than I expect of you. I should be doing work to help the war myself. I may well do so, now that travelling through my beloved France has shown me the devastation this war is wreaking on my people. I hadn't realized. We're so protected in the South.'

'So, you won't mind?'

'Of course I will mind. But I understand.'

The six days passed at a snail's pace for Edith. No letter had awaited her arrival, and none came during her time in Nice. Not from anyone. Her worry increased each day. Part of her wanted to go to Laurent's mother, to try and find out how he was and whether he was still alive. But although he had worked, lived and studied in Paris, his mother lived in Perpignan, which lay towards the border with Spain, at the foot of the Pyrenees – in the opposite direction to where she must travel.

As Edith boarded the train to Bordeaux – a necessary ploy to prevent suspicions arising in Marianne – her heart felt heavy. She had no idea why Petra hadn't contacted her. Checking with her bank before leaving England had told her that the cheque she had sent to Petra and Aleksi had been cashed. So why had there been no word. *Why?*

Changing trains en route, Edith boarded one for Paris. Once there, she would stay the night before finding a suitable mode of transport to take her the thirty miles or so to the farm, which lay in the remote countryside of the Chaumont-en-Vexin area. The remoteness of the farm also made her journey difficult; it was only accessible by horse-driven vehicle or car, or on foot. No train went within miles of it. If she couldn't hire someone to take her, then she would have to buy a car, if that was possible. What if she got lost? If only Petra had answered her letters; through contact with them, she could have told them of her plans and Aleksi would have come to pick her up in Paris.

Letting her head flop back and shifting her bottom, which had become stiff like a rock, she allowed her eyes to close. It would take another four hours to get to Paris. Her bones ached with the strain of the journey, and her stomach churned over and over with trepidation. *Please don't let anything have happened to my babies ... please!*

The night in Paris was a restless one. After a welcome and delicious dinner, during which Edith had seen that, as a lone woman, she was the subject of much speculation among the other guests, she had taken a bath and tried to relax. But her thoughts and fears had given her no peace.

Now, having risen at seven, she had breakfasted in her room – a plush, overbearing suite, with its dull beige walls a backdrop for even duller pictures of Parisian scenes in heavy gold frames. Add to this the purple silk drapes around the bed and adorning the windows, and the overall impression was that of a funeral parlour. Sighing, Edith realized how tired she felt and was unsure of her next move. Crossing over to the window, her feet sank into the over-patterned, thick beige and purple carpet.

Outside the sun shimmered weakly, shrouded in misty, floating clouds. The street below bustled with people, horses, carriages and cars. How strange the contrast in life was. Not two hundred miles away, men fought valiantly, dying in their thousands, to preserve this way of life and save this city from occupation, and yet life went on. As it must for her. *What to do next? How am I to get to the farm?* Her eyes rested on a cab. Horse-drawn, it would take at least two hours to get her to the farm, but it seemed her only option. It wasn't a prospect she relished, as much of the terrain was very rough going, and it would mean she would be bruised and sore by the time she reached her destination. Once there, though, Aleksi would hopefully bring her and her children back to Paris, to begin her journey home.

Her mind now made up, she tugged on the bell-cord and instructed the porter who attended her to engage the cab and take her luggage down for her.

At last Edith could see the farm. Her heartbeat quickened, her body shifted to the edge of her seat and, sliding the window down, she peered out. Where were the cows? Had Aleksi not let

331

them out of the barn yet? They were just yards away from the farm now and yet she could not hear the hens. But then would she, over the hooves of the horses?

Reining in the horses, the cab driver looked down at her and asked in bewilderment, 'Is this the place? I have followed your directions, but it looks deserted. Are you intending to stay here, Madame?'

Fear held her silent.

'Madame?' He was at the door. He was a stocky man in his forties. 'Madame, I have to get back. Are you alighting or not?'

'Yes. I – I... Thank you. Please unload my cases.'

'But, Madame, there is no one here.'

'I – I'll be fine. Thank you.'

'But–'

'Look. Will you return for me in two days' time? I will pay you well. I must stay. I must make enquiries in the area as to what has happened to my friends.' Somehow she managed to compose herself, even though inside she was screaming in panic: *Where are they? Where are my babies? Where are Petra and Aleksi? Oh God, my babies, my babies.*

Thankful to have found the key where Aleksi always left it, hanging on a nail behind an old coat that hung in one of the outbuildings, Edith was at last alone The kindly driver had been like a father-figure to her and had wanted to check that there were supplies for her before he left.

Oh yes, there were supplies. The pantry held enough food to sustain her for days: cheeses, preserves, flour and yeast, a ham even, hanging from

332

the ceiling. Cured and dried, it would have lasted for months, but combined with the freshness of the cheese and eggs and the lack of growth sprouting from the potatoes, Edith knew Petra and Aleksi couldn't have left the farm many days before her arrival. But they must have planned it, as all the livestock had gone – they must have sold everything.

As she moved frantically from room to room, her cries of pain and anguish echoed around the empty building. But nothing gave her any clues. There was nothing to tell her what had happened, and no leftover clothes or possessions of Petra's or Aleksi's, or her darling children's personal belongings. Most cupboards, drawers and wardrobes were empty.

Going back down the rickety stairs and into the living and kitchen area, she saw, through tears that stung her eyes, a letter propped up against the still-ticking clock. Her name was scrawled across the front of the envelope. As she ripped it open, hope rose inside her, but it wasn't from Petra:

My dearest Edith,
I am leaving this here in case you ever return. I have not heard from you, but I will not give up hope. I came here just as soon as I could. Today is 17th July 1917...

Oh God, two days ago!
With shaking hands, Edith read on, hoping for a clue as to where Laurent might be now:

When I found the place deserted, I searched around

333

*the usual places for a key and found it. I have to con-
fess it lifted my heart when I also found fresh food.
This must mean that you haven't left long ago, and
that someone plans on returning. I hope whoever lives
here does return and, if it is not you, they will make
sure you receive this letter.*

This last line Laurent had repeated in French.

*By now your child will have been born, and I hope
he or she is safe and well. I guess you may have
returned to England?*

*One day, my darling girl, we will be together. What-
ever troubles you will be behind you.*

*I am joining my regiment, and the British and Allied
forces at Passchendaele. I hope this Third Battle of
Ypres will end this bloody, senseless war. If it does, and
I survive, I will seek you out and I will not give up on
finding you, even if it takes me the rest of my life. For
we are nothing when we're not together.*

*Love needs no time. Love comes when we least
expect it. Love is eternal.*

Laurent x

'Oh God... Oh God!' Her fists thumped the
table, her tears soaked her face, but she did not
care. Her open-mouthed sobs racked her throat.
Her pain deepened into despair. Laurent hadn't
received her letters and still didn't know the truth
about her. What would he think when he did? *Oh,
Laurent ... Laurent. And my babies – my babies...*

24

Jay and Eloise

London, September 1917
A love declared

'I can't believe Edith has abandoned this project, Jay. It is bad form of her!'

The now completed Jimmy's Hope House had been up and running for two weeks. They were sitting together in the office. It had been ten weeks since Edith had left for France.

'My dear Eloise, she hasn't abandoned it. She has asked us to continue with it, until the war ends.'

'But how could she not tell us her plans? It's as if she has duped us into taking care of things here. It was only going to be for a few weeks, and now she writes to tell us that she won't return until her work is done – whether that coincides with the end of the war or not! I mean, who knows when the war will end? Let alone when the field hospitals will close. Why couldn't she have been satisfied with helping the war effort by working in Shepherd's Bush Military Hospital and continuing what she started here, instead of returning to Abbeville? This is all too much work for us, on top of our work for my charity.'

'I can't answer that. I somehow don't think she

planned it. Her letter said that she didn't, and I believe her. I think it happened how it happened: being back in France, and so near to the war, she felt compelled to return to her post.'

Eloise fell silent. Jay could see from her face that she was very cross. Much of this, he knew, was down to her being tired. Ada did a wonderful job of heading the nannies and had recruited a team of cleaning and maintenance staff, but Jimmy's Hope House was filling up rapidly and the administrative side had so far been down to himself and Eloise. Much of its success had been due to the contacts made through Eloise's charity. All of her coordinators made referrals, on an almost daily basis, of orphaned children and widowed mothers in need of a break. This meant that the workload had increased at that rate too.

The unmarried-mothers unit hadn't developed at all, however. In some ways that was a good thing, but in others it was a worry that they weren't reaching those who might need their help. And if they did, without Edith here to take care of the medical side of things there wasn't a lot they could offer. It was also strange how Edith had thought there would be genteel ladies in need of the charity. He couldn't imagine ladies like Eloise and Edith ever being in the position of being unmarried mothers. But then there had been Andrina. Yes, Andrina could well have ended up in that position. He himself had been on the verge of... *Oh God, how wrong that would have been!* Yes, he had known his true position in life by then, but Andrina wasn't the right person for him; he knew that beyond any doubt now.

She had just been accessible, and her attentions had flattered him. But how long would it have been before he discovered his true love?

'Eloise?'

As she looked up at him, he read the words, 'I'm sorry.'

'I know. You're tired. But we will find a way. I have heard that the Military Hospital plans to rehabilitate the wounded by finding them jobs. Why don't we approach them and see if any of the soldiers have administrative skills? We could appoint an administrative manager and a secretary. We could advertise for a nursing sister to oversee the health of the children, and recruit a governing board to vet potential adoptive parents for the children. What do you think?'

'Yes, of course we can. I'm being silly. I'm cross with Edith, but mostly I'm afraid for her. Oh, why did she do this?'

'Eloise, don't. I can't bear it when you are upset... It – it hurts. Eloise, forgive me, I have no right to speak to you of my feelings, for it is only just over a year since Andrina's death. Such a short time.'

Her hand touched his face, quietening him and sending waves of desire through him. Her eyes held his: her beautiful hazel eyes that danced when she smiled, but which now held a depth of feeling that he dare not hope was for him.

'Eloise, you must know how I feel?'

'I do, Jay. I have waited...'

'You return my feelings? Oh, Eloise.' Neither of them seemed to move, and yet their bodies were now close. He could feel her breath on his face and her, breasts brushing his chest as her breathing deepened, but still he felt afraid to do what he most wanted to do in all the world: hold her, kiss her.

'How do you feel, Jay? I need you to tell me.'

'I – I love you, Eloise. I love you with a love that fills me with joy and desire and happiness, but that would burst into something I feel I could hardly handle, if you felt the same for me.'

'I do,' she said in a breathless tone.

Her eyes closed, and her lovely full lips lifted to his. The moment he'd longed for had arrived. The touching of her lips with his own made a passionate feeling shudder through him, which he fought to control. The kiss, though beautiful and threatening to overwhelm him, wasn't enough. He needed – no, he *had* – to take her to him and join his life to hers, in the ultimate act of love.

Her desire matched his own, and her hands caressed his back with a pressure that pulled him even closer to her. Now their bodies were moulded and he couldn't hide his need, or prevent her from feeling it pressed against where he most wanted to be.

He knew he must pull away and calm the situation, but he couldn't. Eloise was so willing, so giving and loving. His hand found and cupped her breast. The deep intake of breath that he felt her take told him of the pleasure this gave. Encouraged, he caressed the tip, felt the hardening of her nipple beneath her blouse.

Prising her lips open with his tongue, he savoured the delicious thrill of the feel of her tongue, and moved his own in and out of her mouth. He was lost. Lost in a world so removed from any he'd known that he needed to go further. Had to.

Pulling away from her, he guided her to the chaise longue under the window. But, halfway there, shame washed over him as Eloise positioned herself in front of him and said, 'No. No, Jay, I can't!'

'Oh, my darling. I'm sorry. I shouldn't have done that.'

'No, darling, it wasn't your fault. My love for you is so intense that I allowed us to lose control. I love you, Jay. Please make me your wife.'

Her words calmed him. The disappointment was only going to be temporary, because she loved him. She had asked him to marry her. 'Now?'

Oh, how he wished he could hear her laughter. But he joined his with hers and the moment lightened.

'Let us post the banns right away.'

'But what about Father?'

'I know he'll agree. He's spoken to me about our feelings towards one another, and has said it is about time that I did something about it.'

'Really!'

'Ha, no. I wish it were so. But surely he must suspect, and your mother, too. I have a feeling the whole world knows.'

'I didn't. I knew I loved you, but...'

'And I knew I loved you.'

'Oh, Jay.'

They laughed together. But Jay knew he would feel no peace until he could complete what they had started, and he could really make her his.

Taking his handkerchief and using it to wipe her smudged lipstick didn't help. Once more they were closer together than he could handle. The door opened and they shot apart. Looking at Ada as she entered, Jay read what she said.

'Eeh, caught you red-handed! I beg your pardon, I just wanted some more of those ordering pads and another pen. Though I can't get used to these posh nibs. I get into a reet mess. Ink all over me, and blotches on me paper. Give me a crayon any day.'

'Er ... er...' Words failed him.

'Carry on,' said Ada, looking at them directly. 'It's about time you two got together, and if you want a bridesmaid, I'm your girl.' With a bob and a bow, she left the room.

It took a second for the shock to wear off, but then the ridiculousness of the situation hit Jay, as it did Eloise. At just the same moment they doubled over in laughter. When they calmed, he had a happiness in him such as he'd never known.

'You know, Eloise, I think loving someone is such a huge thing. It encompasses so much, and we have it all. We can work together, talk about anything together and laugh together, and now I know that the deeper side of love is going to be fantastic, too.'

A blush swept over her face, and a smile lit her eyes. Coming into his arms, he knew that she had spoken, but her head was snuggled into him, making it impossible for him to decipher what she had said, although he knew her words would be words of love. His world was almost complete.

25

Edith

Abbeville, late September 1917
Trying to heal

Edith, Connie, Nancy and Jennifer sat on the sand dunes looking out to sea. A ship glided along the horizon in the distance.

'I reckon that's the one our wounded will be on soon. It's 'eading up towards Calais, and they are well on their way there by now.'

No one answered Connie, but Nancy spoke, changing the subject. 'Well, you're a morose lot. Come on. Let's have a dip in the sea!'

'Ooh, no, Nancy. It will be freezing!'

'It's always freezing, Edith, even in high summer. But it is a lovely day today and we'll soon warm up. Come on!'

Nancy stripped off her jumper as she said this, revealing the top of her knitted swim-dress.

'Oh, you came prepared then?'

'I did, Jennifer. Didn't you?'

'No, I thought the same as Edith, that it would be too cold.'

'Uh, soft like Joe-suds, you two posh bitches are. Come on, Nancy, I'm game. Though I'll 'ave to swim in the nude, as I 'aven't come prepared, either.'

'You wouldn't!' Jennifer sounded astonished, but emitted a girlish giggle.

'Watch me!' said Connie.

Laughing like she thought she would never laugh again, Edith rolled her head backwards. Connie's huge bosom, when let free, bounced up and down as she jiggled out of her long skirt, but that wasn't anything compared to what her big bottom did when, naked as the day she was born, she ran towards the water.

'Oh, Edith, have you ever seen anything so funny and yet so beautiful?'

This pulled Edith up. With those words came the realization that it was beautiful to see these lovely girls having fun, and hearing them squeal with delight. Suddenly she wanted to be part of it. 'Come on, Jennifer, let's join them.'

'Oh, I couldn't!'

'Yes, you could. The lads know not to come down to the beach while we are having our time down here. It's a court-martial offence to intrude on our privacy when we have our bathing dresses on, so no one but us will know.'

'Ha, it's a good job no one sees what goes on during the night!'

'Jennifer! You and Mark?'

'Yes, me and Mark.'

'Well, be careful, old thing, you know where that can lead.'

'Mark knows what he is doing.'

Yes, Mark knows. I knew too, but in the heat of a passionate moment I permitted it.

'What's that look for? I'm only human, Edith. I love Mark. And God knows I can't wait for when all this is over and we can be married. Neither of us can wait. You wait until it happens to you!'

'Oh, Jen.'

'It has, hasn't it?'

'I don't want to talk about it.'

A shout of 'Hey, come on, it's not so bad once your body gets used to it' carried on the wind, and Edith shook the sad thoughts from her and stripped off her clothes, shivering more and more as she disposed of each layer.

'Oh God, Edith. I didn't know you had once been fat!'

'I – I...'

Pulling her skirt back down over her stretch-marks, Edith wished the ground would open up. Jennifer could be very outspoken; she should have known Jennifer wouldn't let anything pass. She'd been a fool to bare herself.

'You can talk to me, Edith. I know there is something wrong. I have sensed it since you came back. You have to talk to someone, and I would never divulge anything you said.'

There was something about Jennifer that made you want to talk to her. Even though she had never received any training, she was a skilled counsellor. But no, if she needed to talk, Edith did so to Ada, in long letters in which she poured out her heart. 'There's nothing to talk about. I'm fine. I went through a bad experience. And yes, I did put weight on – a lot of weight. During that time when I suffered memory loss the farmer's wife just fed and fed me, as she did her husband. But it came off, though sadly it left me with these marks. I seem to be a pear-shape and to put it all on around my bottom half. They'll fade with time. Now, I don't know about you, but I'm going in – stretch-marks or no.'

The cold water took her breath away and masked her weeping heart.

It didn't weep for long, as Connie started to splash her. Joining in the fun lifted Edith's mood, and she found she could laugh. There was so much to cry about, but that didn't make things better; laughing did. It healed you and made you able to cope.

Too cold to care what anyone else looked like, neither Connie nor Nancy seemed to notice the red weals on her thighs and stomach. She made no attempt to hide them. She didn't care what Jennifer thought, or any of them. The marks were all she had to prove that, she was a mother; that she had carried and nurtured two beautiful girls in her womb. She'd wear them on her body with pride.

When they were back on duty later that day, an influx of badly injured men kept them busy. The stench around her brought the bile to her throat. She could stomach most things, but the awful smell of rotting flesh on living humans turned her stomach and her heart.

She looked up over her mask at Mark, who was helping her to amputate a leg. 'Mark, some of the wounded are having to travel too far to get help. There doesn't seem to be a good clearing station at the front any more.'

'I know. These poor devils start off as the walking wounded. They have come back across the border from the Passchendaele battle. There are

so few trucks now that it is a case of some walking while others ride, and then they swap over.
The progress is slow. Too slow to get to us, and
very few seem to have had first-line treatment.'

Over the grinding noise of the saw, and with
drips of her sweat running down her face, Edith
said, 'Those girls who brought them look exhausted. Will it ever end?'

'No. It never will, for some of us. We will always
carry scars.'

Not wanting the conversation to go the way
Mark was leading it, Edith butted in. There was
something she needed to discuss with him, as he
was now the senior medic. 'Why can't we set up
a halfway post? I could run it. We should speak to
the Red Cross administration about it. It could
be on the border of Belgium and France. I am
sure it would save lives.'

'You may be right. I'll look into it. There, that's
done. I'll leave you to stitch it up. I need a break.
I may have to go over to the French quarter later,
as they are very short-staffed.'

As if *she* didn't need a break! But then he had
agreed to talk about her idea, so that was something. Plus, if it came off, she would be so much
nearer Laurent. Maybe she could get a message
to him! She would go over to the French quarter
herself later on. Mark had told her how snowed
under they were. It would be a distraction, and it
would be good to hear the French language
again.

The post the next day warmed her heart: Eloise
and Jay were married. As no one was there, or

345

likely to go there for a while, they were going to honeymoon at Hastleford Hall and then use it as a retreat until their own home was ready, although they would spend most of their time in London. Edith couldn't have been happier for darling Eloise. She had seen where her cousin's heart lay a long time ago. And they had put her mind at rest as regards Jimmy's Hope House, saying they had recruited wounded ex-officers and rank soldiers to fill the posts they had held, and that they and Ada were doing a wonderful job and that everything was ticking over really well.

'Doctor Edith, Ma'am, Captain Woodster asked me to ask you if you could go over to the French quarter. He is over there and has been there all night. It seems there is a soldier – an officer – saying your name over and over.'

Edith's heart jumped in her chest, giving her a painful jolt. *Could it be...? Oh God, if it is, please don't let him be badly hurt!*

'Where is he, Mark?' Mark's eyes were rimmed with black shadows. Her guilt made her snap at him. 'Why didn't you call me? I thought you were coping, and that you had been in your bed all night, as I was!'

'I was. Then they brought in a late batch of wounded and they couldn't cope. I couldn't wake you. You needed your rest.'

Shaking her head and tutting at him, she didn't argue further, but asked, 'You said someone was saying my name?'

'Yes. I'm afraid he's badly injured. And of

course he could mean any Edith, but at one point he did say, "She's a doctor."'

Hardly able to breathe, Edith asked, 'Do you know his name?'

'Pevensy. Captain Laurent Pevensy...'

Her body swayed.

'Hey, hold on, old thing. Are you all right?'

'Tell me he isn't going to die. *Please* tell me he isn't going to die.'

'I'm sorry, Edith, but he doesn't stand much chance. You should go to him. He is in the second tent along from here. Good luck, old thing. I've done all I can for him. I'll have to go to have a lie-down now. Other patients could come in, in the next few hours.'

'No, tell me. Tell me what has happened to him.'

'He's lost a leg and has stomach injuries from shrapnel. His leg was infected. I don't know how far the gangrene has spread or if I've got it all. And he has facial injuries. But he had some treatment before he got here, so that helped, otherwise he would have bled to death. I'm so sorry, Edith. He obviously is someone very important in your life, but I won't ask how.'

'Thanks, Mark. One day I will tell you about it. And, Mark, I am happy about you and Jennifer, but please take care.'

He thanked her with a wry smile. She knew he would know that she meant him to take care in all ways, because fraternizing wasn't allowed among the medical staff – let alone what could happen if they took their love too far. The disgrace for Jennifer would be too much for her to bear. As she knew only too well.

She felt crushed as she looked down on the still figure of Laurent. Life had almost left him. His pallor made his eyebrows – something she hadn't noticed before – look as black as coal. His moustache was gone. His left cheek had a hole in it, exposing his broken teeth and jawbone. But his lips were intact... A brush of memory gave her his soft, beautiful lips. Now, as she bent to kiss them, they were hard and crusty.

'Laurent. It's Edith. Laurent, darling, don't give up. Fight, my darling. Hold on to life. I am waiting here for you.'

The still form didn't move. Taking his hand in hers, she held it gently. 'I am here for you, Laurent.' Stroking the loose skin, she wondered how he would cope with having lost his leg, but then he was courageous. He would find something within himself to help him. But what about his work? *Funny I should think like this after all, for what does that matter? All that matters is that he lives!* 'Oh, Laurent, I love you.'

His head moved. His eyes opened. He went to speak, but couldn't.

'Don't try to talk. Your face is injured, and they have operated on your jaw, darling. It will heal. You will heal. I won't let you die.'

Hope came into his eyes. 'Edith.'

Her name was formed; not perfectly, and she wondered how Mark had deciphered it, but Laurent had said her name!

'Rest, darling. I will be by your side. You can get well – you *can*. I have seen miracles happen here.

And usually it is down to the will of the person. Be strong, darling; fight!'

He nodded his head. Then closed his eyes.

26

Petra and Aleksi

Chiswick, October 1917
A different view

Steam engulfed Petra. Working in the Acton Road Laundry helped to keep the rent paid and put bread on the table, but it was a million miles away from the farm that she used to look upon as a grind, but now thought of as paradise.

The money Edith had sent them had funded their escape. They couldn't go to Poland, not yet. But soon. The government of Poland was now recognized by the Germans and Russians, but was still under their rule and was a client state of Germany. But there was a new constitution. Everyone knew it was only to legitimize the military occupation, but still, it would mean a kind of peace, and that she and Aleksi could return there soon. A lot of inducements were being given to move people from the Baltic area; and their daughter, Marcelina, and her husband Feodor and his family had settled back into the new state of Poland.

Petra had written to Marcelina and Feodor and had told them of the babies she was bringing to them, and of where they were now living. Marcelina's reply had been very moving. She spoke of the prayers she sent up for the girls' poor dead mother, and implored Petra to try and find the girls' mother's family, before bringing the children to Poland.

At the sound of the hooter, Petra moved away from the press she had been working on and another woman took over. Their only exchange was a nod of the head. A tram ride took her to the flat they had been able to rent on the border between London and Chiswick.

'I'm home.'

A tired-looking Aleksi came to greet her. Kissing her, he said. 'The little ones have been good. I was just going to change Elka's bottom. That one does everything with great enthusiasm – even filling her nappy is loudly proclaimed.'

They laughed at this.

'You get yourself to bed for an hour or two, my dear. I will wake you in plenty of time to catch the tram for work.'

'But I wanted to spend some time with you. I wanted to talk.'

The wail that set up in the next room interrupted them. Petra hurried to lift Elka and hoped that Aleksi wouldn't follow her. She knew what he wanted to talk about. Edith!

With Elka cleaned and comfortable, peace reigned once more and, with a weary sigh, Petra returned to the kitchen. 'Oh, Aleksi, you should have gone to bed. The time that you can rest is ticking away.'

'My conscience troubles me.'

'But we have been over and over it. Those darling babies will have a much better life with Marcelina and Feodor, and with us. Edith told us that she couldn't recognize them as her own children. Oh, yes, she would have provided for them, but where would they have lived? With some nanny or other! And how often could they see their mother, especially if she married and had other children! Look at how she allowed herself to linger with that stranger you saw her with. And she let him kiss her! You saw her, from that tree you hid behind. That is not correct behaviour! Edith is one of those women driven by her passion for men. I have seen how her class is here. They do not mix with the working class, and yet she did. She allowed herself to be taken by a murderer. A deserter. And I do not believe that he took her against her will. Is this the kind of woman you would entrust our precious Elka and Ania with?'

'I know you are right, Petra, but Edith adored them. It hurts to think that she will never see them again. How will it be for her, when she returns to collect them and finds that we have gone?'

'It will be very painful for her, but she has her work. And, like I say, her love of what the menfolk have to offer will soon distract her. We left her supplies, so she would have been all right for a couple of days while she came to terms with it all, and I don't think it would take her much longer than that. Her kind flit from one thing to another. It will be a relief for her. The burden has been taken care of. Besides, she might not have returned, and might never have done so in the future.'

'How can you say that? She sent money.'

'Money appeases conscience! Now, get to bed, stop worrying and earn all you can at that munitions factory, to get us back to Poland!'

Not convinced that was the last she would hear on the subject, Petra watched Aleksi go through the door to the bedroom. She had a letter to write and to get into the post. She would do that now, and put Aleksi's objections and concerns out of her head. She was on a mission, and one that she was determined to win. Her darling girls would be loved and cared for, if her plan succeeded, and that was all that mattered. Not the flirty Edith!

More lies poured from Petra as she wrote:

My darling daughter,

The girl's mother had no family – not immediate family anyway – and that is why she stayed with us when she found that the rape had caused her to become pregnant. She had plans to leave the children with us, and return to her work in the field tents until the war was over and she could make a life for her children. Sadly her death changed everything.

Where would I look for family that is remote? And if I found any family members, would they want to know? Yes, I could go to the Red Cross, but my fear is that these beautiful girls would end up in an orphanage. I have not seen or heard of a good one here in England. It is better that we – you, my darling daughter – take them as your own, where they will have a loving home.

We have been accepted here as refugees of the Kingdom of Poland. We told them that we escaped to France with our newborn grandchildren when our daughter died during the birth, and then found our way to England. I hated saying that you had died, but we had to have a legitimate reason for having our grandchildren with us.

As they didn't have any certificates, the authorities here have made us register them. Here the authorities are strict on papers; in France they didn't care about the babies having papers – only us. So now they are British citizens, but I gave them the name of Feodor's family: Dranansk. Once home, we can make them citizens of Poland and have them taken into the Jewish faith.

We have made friends with another Polish refugee, Endixsi Grothan. He is from mid-Poland. His English is good and he is helping us with the language, and he secured the job in the laundry for me and in the munitions factory for your father.

Your father works nights, and I work in the day. Father is an amazing grandparent to little Elka and Ania. We both get some rest when they sleep, which is often, as they are such contented children. Elka shows tendencies of being the forthright one. She is much more demanding, and it is very funny how cross she gets if Ania is getting the attention. Ania is very calm and takes everything as it comes. She will only murmur if she has a need, whereas Elka will scream the place down!

This town is on the banks of a great river called the Thames. It is a growing town in the suburbs of the magnificent city of London. I wish you could see it, my darling. It is a good place to live.

It would be a good place to bring the girls up, but I know Feodor would not hear of it. His family is one of the most respected Jewish families in Poland, and their jewellery business has established them there.

But, oh, how my heart wishes that they had used their influence and riches to move away. They could build a new life here, or in America. A safe life, for I fear for the future of the Eastern countries of Europe. You must too, as the unrest and the unjust way that Germany and Russia deal with our country can only lead to there being an uprising of protest sometime in the future.

But we have to deal with things as they are. We are working hard to get to you, my darling, and hope to do so in the near future. In the meantime I have something special for you. We took the girls to a photographer here, and I enclose a photo of your darling daughters. I love you, Marcelina, and can't wait for the day that we are finally together again.

The knock on the door startled her. No one had ever called here before!

Opening the door, she looked into the faces of two young men. One of them held himself up on crutches and it was this one that asked, 'Are you Petra Tolenski?'

This much she understood. Her 'Yes' came out in shaky tones. Fear gripped her. How could this man know her?'

'I am Tom Frith.'

The young man with him spoke excellent Polish and interpreted everything the one called Tom said. 'We are checking up on all refugees to see if there is anything we can do for you. We understand you are coping with your grandchildren – twin girls?'

'Who told you this?'

'We have the approval of government bodies.

They identify possible needy cases for us to approach. We work for a charity set up by Lady Daverly to help anyone affected in any way by the war.'

'We don't need any help, thank you. We both have jobs and are waiting for the time we can return to our homeland.'

'But who looks after the children and is in charge of their welfare?'

'We do.'

'Are you able to afford medical care? Have you had them weighed and their weight checked, to make sure they are making progress? We are not here to interfere, just to help. We can give vaccinations against smallpox and make sure you have a supply of cod-liver oil to prevent rickets.'

'Oh, I – I don't know of all these things. We feed the babies milk and they are well. Why should we do anything more?'

'We are sure you are doing your very best for them. But wouldn't you like to be sure they are in good health? And that they continue that way? Here is the address of the home that is run for the welfare of children. It is in Kensington, which is about five miles from here. You can catch a tram to it. It is primarily an orphanage, but they run a weekly clinic for all children and babies. There is a nursing sister in charge, and a doctor is there once a week on a Thursday afternoon.'

Taking the paper he handed her, she read, 'Jimmy's Hope House, Hancock Street, Kensington' and thought that yes, she would take the children along. It would be good to have the girls checked over and to make sure they were healthy.

She was about to say that she would come, but what the young man said next panicked her and stopped her. 'Jimmy was a young man who was shot in the war. Our patron, Miss Edith Mellor, treated him in the field hospital, where she still works.'

'Oh... I – I mean... Look, I have to go. Good-bye!' Slamming the door, Petra leant heavily on it. *Oh God, Edith had found her! They would have to leave. She would send a telegram to Marcelina.* 'Aleksi, wake up! Wake up!'

'What is it, my dear? I haven't been to sleep yet. I heard voices.'

'We have to go. We have to leave. How much money have we saved?'

'What are you talking about?'

Explaining about the visit, Petra began gathering things they would need. 'So, you see, we must go – and go now!'

'Wait a moment. Didn't you say Edith is working in a field hospital in France?' At her nods, Aleksi said, 'Well, then, how could she have found us? This is what it is: the English gentry are very big on their charity work. It is like you said earlier. Money appeases conscience, and they feel better about themselves if they are helping others. I don't think you have to panic. We will go along to the clinic next week. I am sure no one there is going to connect us in any way to Edith. It will be good to know the girls are really well and that we have some preventative medicines. I haven't enough money for the trip to Poland, and it is still too dangerous to go. We may have to wait for the war to end before we can travel. So let us not make a fuss, but do what is expected of us.'

Sitting down and trying to calm herself, Petra could see the logic of what Aleksi had said. 'Very well, but we must be careful at this clinic. We must be careful how we answer their questions.' *Oh dear, why did this have to happen? Why?*

27

Ada

Wandsworth Prison, October 1917
A visit that sets the future

Ada stood at Shepherd's Bush station and for the umpteenth time checked her route to Wandsworth. Excitement mingled with trepidation and made her feel almost sick. People milled around her: confident people, all appearing to rush somewhere important. But none could be on a more important mission than she was. At last she had permission to visit Joe – now, ten months into his sentence, and telling her in his long letters that he was settled in and resigned to his punishment. *Aye, he may be, but what about me? I'm being punished too, when neither of us should be. But then Paddy paid the worst price of all, so what me and Joe have to bear is nowt, compared to him losing his life.*

When she thought of Paddy she tried to remember the good times and the good things about him. She missed his love-making to this day; and aye, she knew there was many a lass that probably did, too. But Paddy had been a good daddy to his lads, in the way he'd loved and cared for them. Even though he didn't provide well for them, they were his world. Though it was always in his character to be a rough diamond, and selfish with it, she had to admit he hadn't been that bad until he lost his lads. He couldn't handle that, and she should have been more understanding. Well, he was with them now. *Eeh, me lads … me lads.*

The smoke from the train swirled around, reminding her of other memories: catching the train to the munitions factory, the long hours, the danger – *and the explosion!* She still had nightmares about it. But it was good to know that Lady Eloise's charity was making a difference to all those who remained in Low Moor.

There were times when she missed Low Moor and the lasses there, and she often missed Beryl. Not the Beryl of today, who sent her vile letters. But the sister of her youth, before she found out about the affair Beryl was having with Paddy.

Taking her seat on the train didn't stop the thoughts. She supposed it was because she was at last going to see Joe. It had triggered her memories of the past and made her mull over what was happening now.

Looking in her handbag once again, to make sure she had her visitor's pass safe, the crinkle of paper as she moved Beryl's latest letter out of the way reminded her that she hadn't finished reading it. Pulling it out, she smoothed it and read:

So you think you're rid of me, our Ada. Well, you're

not! I'll get out of this hellhole and, when I do, I'm coming to get you.

Murderer! Child-stealer! Eeh, you've had your revenge, but that's nowt to what I've planned for you and your murdering boyfriend.

A shudder of extreme sorrow went through Ada. *How did Beryl become so ill?* But then her feeling changed to one of horror, as she read on and wondered just what her sister was capable of doing. She feared that Beryl had truly entered a state of madness, for now she seemed to think she was writing to their mam:

Eeh, Mam, I miss you. I wish you would come and see me. I ask for you every day, but these cows here, who call themselves nurses, say as you are dead. Well, I know you're not. Please come, please.

This tugged at Ada's heart. What must it be like to have some of your past wiped away and to think that your dead mam is still alive, and to long for her to come and see you? She felt such pity and she determined to find a way to have Beryl near to her, so that she could rebuild the loving relationship they used to have, as far as that was possible with Beryl's altered mental state.

She would ask Lady Eloise to help. *Eeh, it was nice to see Lady Eloise and Lord Jay so happy.* She blushed at her forthrightness when she'd discovered them kissing. *Ha, they didn't ask me to be a bridesmaid!* Better than that, she and Annie and all of the other workers and volunteers had attended a wonderful party held in the ballroom of Lady Eloise's home in Holland Park. *Eeh, it were grand as owt.* The family waited on them all, as the servants of the house and of the family's Leicestershire home were guests, too. *By, it were the best thing I've ever been to in me life!*

The lift these thoughts gave her spirit didn't last long, as she read more of Beryl's letter:

Mam, our Ada has changed. She's bad, evil. She took me man and she took me babby and had me incarcerated here! But don't worry, I'm going to get her. I know where she lives. Can you believe she's moved to London? Well, nowhere is too far. If I get out of here, she had better watch out. I have a plan. She is going to die!

I love and miss you, Mam. Please come to see me.
Your loving daughter, Beryl xxx

Ada could only guess at what their mam would have thought. *Eeh, Mam. Like Beryl, I wish you were still here, though I wouldn't want you to go through what I've been through. Or what any of us are going through, for that matter.*

Edith came to her mind then. And the twist in the tale that might mean Edith's twins were right here in London! *Oh God, what shall I do if I don't hear from Edith?* Ada had to admit it was highly unlikely that she would hear from her in time.

It had been a shock to be preparing the list of possible attendees at the clinic next Thursday and to see a note asking that a Polish lady be added to it. There was some doubt as to whether she would attend, as she had appeared to be afraid when the charity workers went to her door. But her notes had said that she was caring for her motherless grandchildren: twin girls! The notes also said that she had escaped Poland via France.

That hadn't given Ada any thoughts that these could be Edith's girls, but the woman's name had: Tolenski! Searching through Edith's letters, she had found a reference to that name, as Edith had written, 'The Tolenskis have gone.'

Oh, the heartbreak that letter had contained!

But if this was the same couple, what could she do? The torment of this question had visited her many times over the last couple of days. She couldn't confront them, as they didn't speak English. She couldn't use the lad who spoke their language, as that would mean telling him about Edith! There was no one she could turn to – no one. If she did, she would break Edith's confidence, and the secret Edith so wanted to keep would be out.

Anguish over the situation made every muscle in Ada's body tense. *How can I save those children for Edith?* Her heart thudded as she remembered reading that the Polish woman intended taking the children back to her homeland when the war was over. Would Edith be home in time?

As soon as she could, she had written to Edith. Now she had no choice but to wait for her reply. If Edith confirmed that these were her twins, by describing the couple who had care of them, then Ada would do all she could to befriend the couple and appear as someone who wanted to help, and maybe find out all she could about what their intentions were.

At last Ada was in the line of visitors. Her pass,

which she had at times thought might not be valid for some reason, had given her admittance without any problems. Once the search of their bodies had been completed, an indignation that Ada endured but hated, the main gates were opened.

They clanged as they closed behind her, and the grating of the key in the lock filled her with trepidation. But her excitement won out. There he was: her Joe, behind a grid, but smiling his lovely smile. Oh, aye, she could see it was a watery smile, as hers was, but it was grand all the same.

'Eeh, me little love, at last.'

Stretching out her hands, she caught hold of his.

'NO TOUCHING!' The shout made her jump.

'Take no notice, love. Keep hold of me hands... Agh!' A whack on the back of Joe's head cut into his words and made him pull his hands back.

'Obey the rules, Grinsdale, or go back to your cell and 'ave all visiting passes cancelled for the next year!'

'Sorry, sir. It was me excitement at seeing me lass. There'll be no more rule-breaking, that's not me style.'

'See that there's not!'

'Eeh, Joe, Joe. How do you bear it?'

'I bear it because I knows thee's waiting for me, lass. And because me slate will be wiped clean when I come out.'

They didn't speak for a moment, but just gazed into each other's eyes. She didn't miss the slow trail of a tear making its way down his cheek, but she didn't comment. Instead she told him of her new life and friends. All the bits that she couldn't put into a letter. And especially about Brendan: how he was growing and what he got up to, now that he was crawling all over the place. And about Rene. Rene had left for France, but as yet Ada didn't know where she was. But she didn't tell Joe about the woman she was to meet on Thursday. Or about Beryl. Not even to her Joe could she divulge Edith's secret, and Beryl's antics would only worry him.

Joe had tales to tell, too. Most made her laugh, although others brought a sadness to her. Like the one about the prisoner whose daughter had been killed in France; she had been driving a truck carrying the wounded, when a bomb had hit. She and all her passengers had perished. He'd asked to be allowed to spend a few days with his family, but had been refused.

'That's a sad tale, Joe. Tell him I will be thinking of him and praying for his wife and for his daughter's soul. He should be very proud of her.'

'He is, but he knows that part of what motivated her to join up was to escape the shame he'd brought down on her, so it's like a double punishment for him.'

'Aw, naw. Poor fella. Anyroad, let's talk of happier things, like the future, eh?'

'Aye. I've been told that if I behave meself, I could be in for having me time shortened!'

'Eeh, Joe.'

'Aye, I thought that would please you. And it could be by as much as a year and a half, so I could be out of here by mid-1920! By, it sounds like a lifetime away, as time passes slowly in here, but it will pass. It will.'

'It will. And, I'm asking you now, Joe: will you marry me on, let's see, the first of August 1920? I'll get everything arranged.'

'I will, Ada. And thank you for asking me, as I didn't feel I had the right to ask you, with the position I'm in.'

'By, just think, our Brendan will be coming on four years old then, and he can be a pageboy!'

'That'd be grand, lass. Grand.'

As the train took her home, Ada was filled with mixed feelings. There was extreme sadness at leaving Joe and not knowing when she would see him again, and trepidation about the situation with the Polish woman, and about Beryl. But there was also the joy at having had her marriage proposal accepted, as she knew, as Joe had said, that he would never have asked her while he was in prison. Oh yes, he'd hinted about her becoming his wife in the past, but this was a firm commitment. She'd buy a ring and wear it on her left hand. It would show that they were engaged. It wouldn't matter that it hadn't come from Joe. All that mattered would be what it stood for. *Oh, Joe, my Joe...*

28

Ada

Jimmy's Hope House, Kensington, late October 1917
Ada meets the twins, Elka and Ania

Ada couldn't keep her eyes off the door of the rooms they used for the clinic. These were the basement rooms. There were four in all: a surgery, a waiting room, an examination room and a kitchen.

In the corner of the waiting room was a booking-in desk. It was here that Ada hovered. 'Michael, I can't tell you why, but will you help me to speak to Mrs Tolenski?'

'Of course I will, but what brings you down here? You don't usually get involved with this clinic.'

'I knaw. I – I had some spare time, that's all. Anyroad, her story touched me. I read it when I made up the list of those attending the clinic today.' She thought quickly for an excuse for her interest. 'It – it set me wondering if we couldn't do something for refugees. Many of them have lost their husbands or, as in this case, a young 'un. They must be very lonely. I thought that, with the help of you interpreters, we could teach them English, so they're not so isolated.' She thought this sounded plausible.

'You never stop, do you? You are one of the kindest people I know, Ada, especially after all you've been through. Of course I'll help – between my job as an interpreter for the War Office and my voluntary work for Lady Eloise's charity, that is!'

'Aw, you're a gem, Michael.'

'Look, Ada, I know that you have a fellow, but how about you come out with me one evening? You don't seem to have any fun.'

'Ta, Michael, that's reet nice of you, but when I'm done here I can't wait to spend time with me little lad and Annie. We have a lot of fun together. I'm alreet, honest. Besides, what does an educated man like you want to take a working-class girl like me out for?'

'I – I don't mean... Ada, you can't think I meant that.'

'Naw, I don't. I'm just joking with you. I'd never think that of you, Michael.' She laughed at him as she pushed his shoulder. He was a tall man who towered over her. His dark good looks had him catching the eye of many of the lasses who worked in or visited the building, so she was flattered that he'd asked, but a little embarrassed as well.

'Well, I'm glad. And the offer stands, and with no strings attached, I promise.' He was back to his relaxed, self-assured self. 'Though I have to say that I do find you very attractive, and would hope you might turn your attentions to me.'

'Michael! You've just knocked yourself off the pedestal I put you on. There's no chance of that happening. I'm engaged to be married!' To soften this she laughed and said, 'Now, stop taking the rise out of me.'

'I'm not–'

Ada cut him off as she spotted an older, foreign-looking woman enter, pushing a pram. 'Eeh, there she is! I'm sure it's her.'

'Now you have got me suspicious. I think there is more to this than you wanting to start a group for refugees?'

'Naw... Naw, don't be daft. I – I were just pleased to see that she had come, after you saying she was afraid when you visited, that's all. Come on, she's booked herself in. Let's go and chat.'

A look of fear crossed Mrs Tolenski's face as they approached. Her eyes shifted from Ada to Michael.

Ada's heart thumped in her chest as she glanced at the twins. Though they had the reddish hair that she believed Albert had had, they looked so like Edith. One of them smiled at her, and the other glared from under a cross frown. 'Eeh, they're bonny.'

Michael said something in Polish to Mrs Tolenski. Realizing that she was frightening the woman even more, Ada asked Michael to explain her idea.

Mrs Tolenski's head shook from side to side as Michael spoke, and she clung on tightly to the handle of the large pram. The twins, one sitting at each end, stared at Ada. The one who had glared started to scream.

'Elka, you will upset Ania!'

Oh God! Elka and Ania. Eeh, they are Edith's for sure. But what can I do? What can I do?

'Are you all right, Ada? Mrs Tolenski is scream-ing that you are scaring the babies.'

'What? Oh, yes. Tell her I don't mean to. By, the young 'un has a grand voice on her – she shocked me!'

As Mrs Tolenski picked up Elka, Ania began to cry, only her little sobs sounded fearful rather than angry.

Ada picked her up and held her to her. 'There, there. It's alreet – naw one is going to hurt you.'

Hardly able to believe she was holding Edith's child in her arms, she had to swallow hard not to let her emotions get the better of her. Panic shook any trace of them away, as Mrs Tolenski put Elka back in the pram and grabbed Ania. Though she didn't understand the words she said, Ada knew the woman intended to leave.

'Tell her she must stay. Michael, tell her ... tell her!'

'But...'

'Do it, Michael: tell her it is the law!' Past car-ing what he thought, Ada only knew that she must keep them here, and that she must gain the woman's confidence.

Sitting back down with a look of defeat, Mrs Tolenski dabbed at her eyes with a rag she'd fetched from her pocket.

'Ada, that was bad form. What's going on?'

'Nothing. I'm sorry. I just felt that I had scared her away. Eeh, Michael, I couldn't have that on me conscience – these babbies need us.'

'Look, I'll talk to her for a moment. Explain that you only want to be her friend and help her with the children. You leave us for a minute and, if she is willing to talk to you, then I will fetch you.'

Knowing that he was right, but finding it difficult to lose sight of the children, Ada moved away.

Half an hour passed before Michael came to her. 'I couldn't find you. I never thought to look by the entrance! What *is* your intention: to barricade them in or something? What is going on, Ada?'

'Eeh, Michael, I can't say, but I need your help. I need to stop them leaving the country, at least for a few weeks.'

He stared in astonishment and disbelief. 'How am I going to do that?'

'Is she still saying that she is going?'

'Ada, I am losing my patience with you and will speak to Lady Eloise about this. There is something dreadfully wrong, for you to be behaving like this.'

A feeling of despair came over her. Edith would be disgraced if her secret got out, so Ada would have to make something up. 'I'm being silly. I just have a funny feeling about those twins. As soon as I heard about them, I thought of me friend back home. Her husband was killed, and the shock and distress caused her to lose her twin babbies. They came too early and died at birth. I thought that if Mrs Tolenski couldn't cope, I could get me friend to adopt them, and the Tolenskis could still be their grandparents; they could all help each other.'

'Of all the ridiculous notions, Ada! Mrs Tolenski loves those babies and lives in fear of anyone taking them off her. She would never agree to such a plan.'

Ada's despair deepened and she could think of nothing to say.

Sensing this, Michael said, 'Sorry, old thing, but it just isn't on. Oh, here they come. Now don't go upsetting her. She was quite happy by the time I had settled her, and she went in to see the doctor without a murmur.'

Standing close to the wall, Ada waited for Mrs Tolenski to reach the exit. When she did, she smiled a friendly smile. 'Was everything alreet with the babbies?'

To Michael's interpretation, the woman smiled back and nodded, saying in English, 'Thank you, yes' and then switched to Polish, which Michael told Ada meant, 'Her little darlings were very healthy, and she was grateful for the help and the vaccinations.'

Smiling widely at her, Ada thought to get a better response by doing as the woman had done and speaking directly to her, rather than to Michael. 'I wondered if I could call on you and help you out? I have a little boy. He is a little older, about a month or so, and it would be good for them to play together.'

The woman's reply, given through Michael, was disappointing. 'No, that is not possible. We can't understand what you say, and I don't want to confuse the children. We will be leaving very soon for Poland. Thank you very much, but no.'

Ada felt as though she had a lead weight in her chest at having let Edith down. She watched the woman walk away. There was nothing she could do. *Nothing!*

Trying to allay Michael's concern, she turned

370

to him and said, 'Well, you win some and you lose some.' It was a flippant remark that didn't speak of how she felt at all, or of the determination inside her to get those babies back to Edith. Somehow she would find a way of keeping the Tolenskis here as she felt sure that, once Edith received her letter, she would come home and claim the girls as rightfully hers.

29

Edith

Abbeville, late October 1917
An acceptance of life

'Edith, we must talk. You're worn out. Every night for weeks and weeks now you've sat by Captain Pevensy. You're not getting your rest, and I have to tell you that we must now send him to the French Military Hospital in Shaftesbury Avenue, London. It is where we send all our special cases. He is fit to travel and needs more than we can offer.'

Edith knew that what the French matron was saying to her was true. Laurent had made many improvements in the four weeks since he had arrived, even though he remained very ill.

Laurent looked up at her. Still only able to say a few words, he mouthed, 'I love you.'

She smiled through her tears. 'I know. I will not abandon you, my darling. I will travel with you.'

His face lit up.

She didn't feel any concern about leaving; during her long absence the team had taken on new doctors and had reshuffled their responsibilities. It wasn't that she wasn't needed, more that she wouldn't be missed too much, as there was a full team without her.

Seeing a smile on the matron's face, Edith asked, 'You understood what we said to each other?'

At the matron's nod, a little laugh escaped Edith as she voiced her thoughts. 'You French are amazing. If I had said that in a British hospital, I would be in trouble for fraternizing!'

'Ah, but we French love lovers. I will leave you a while and go and make the final arrangements.'

Turning back to Laurent, Edith told him, 'I'm glad this day has arrived. There is something I haven't told you yet; nor have we broached the subject of my true status when I met you. I only know that you at last received my first letter to you, and you gave me no indication that its contents changed things between us.'

His eyes closed and he shook his head. The gesture told her it didn't matter to him. When he opened his eyes she read compassion there and felt emboldened to continue. She chose to speak in English, in the hope that the soldiers around them wouldn't understand, and told him of her pain at finding that the Tolenskis had moved and taken her children.

'But I have had a letter which gives me hope that they are in England! I don't know why the Tolenskis have done this, but it is important for me to catch up with them and claim my girls back.'

His attempt at a smile tore at her and made her feel sad. She looked away, determined not to show her distress. Laurent had not yet seen what had happened to his beautiful face. It would be a shock to him, but there was hope it could be repaired; at least she was sure the gaping hole could be covered and, though scarred, wouldn't look so distressing.

As soon as she arrived in England she would contact her dear friend, Wilfred Young. They had done their basic training together as surgeons, and he had gone on to specialize in plastic surgery. He now worked in Cambridge Military Hospital, where his expertise was used to help disfigured soldiers returning from the war. She knew he would be able to help Laurent.

Saying her goodbyes to Connie, Nancy, Jennifer and Mark had become an emotional affair. All knew that Edith wouldn't be returning this time. From what they said, they imagined that she intended devoting her life to Laurent. There was nothing for her to deny in this, but part of her wanted to tell these wonderful friends the truth. Not being able to do so left her feeling a little out of the close-knit circle they had formed.

She had, however, told them about her charity, and they had all spoken of a reunion once this bloody war was over. Connie and Nancy thought they might like to work for her charity. 'That's if the pay's right. I'm done with being an angel of mercy. I'm going to line me pockets when I get home and set meself up proper,' said Connie. Then Nancy had said, 'Well, I don't care about money. I just hope there's a bloke waiting some-where for me. I'm not for being a spinster. I want a proper life with kids and all of that!'

This had deepened her own feelings of longing: longing for Laurent to get well, longing to be reunited with her little girls and even deeper still, a longing for the day to come when she could marry Laurent and they could adopt the twins and become a proper family, without the scandal of their birth ever getting out.

The ship looked magnificent. A liner, HMS *Opulous*, had been commandeered as a hospital ship at the beginning of the war and had served well. Her interior still displayed the grandeur of her intended working life, showing the luxury of an age Edith thought would never return.

There had been no objection to Edith travelling with her patient, though settling him in had been taken over by the medical staff, leaving her to wander around the ship and find her cabin. She found that she was sharing with an Irish nurse, a bubbly girl who lifted her spirits. 'It's nice to meet you, Doctor. I'm Helen. I'm from Belfast, where it is sure that the girls are all beautiful and the men are as hopeless as the day they were born.'

Laughing out loud, Edith said, 'Pleased to meet you too. Are you working today?'

'I am that. I'm on duty in an hour, when we sail. We are doing the first bit in shifts as it is very tir-ing. The staff who do the reception of the patients need a break as soon as that is done. I'll be on duty at twelve noon, till we dock in around three hours' time. We'll not be far offshore by then.'

'Well, here's to a safe crossing.'

Within half an hour Edith was by Laurent's side again. His face showed the strain of the journey. 'Try to sleep, darling. It only takes a little under three hours to reach Southampton. Then an ambulance will take you to London. I'll come to you just as soon as I can.'

The journey had gone without a hitch and Laurent had been made comfortable. It was a wrench to leave him, but Edith had a pressing need: to get to Jimmy's Hope House and see Ada.

One look at Ada's face told of bad news. After coming out of her welcome hug, Edith held her at arm's length and asked, 'What is it? Has anything happened?'

'There's no easy way of telling you, Miss Edith, but they're gone.'

'Gone? Gone where?'

'Eeh, I don't know. Mrs Tolenski told Michael – he's a bloke as works for Lady Eloise's charity and speaks languages – that they were planning to go to Poland. But I reckon, with how things are, they would find that an almost impossible task. I'm sorry. I tried to keep them here. I visited them and tried to make friends with Mrs Tolenski, taking her food parcels and gifts for the babbies, but it didn't make any difference.'

Edith backed onto the chaise longue in the window and plonked herself down. Her legs wouldn't hold her any longer, as the shock had ricocheted through her. Looking around the office to which she had summoned Ada, it was as if she was looking for something to anchor her, as her body took the full blow of this news.

'By, I'm reet sorry, Miss Edith. I wish I had different news to tell. I've done all I can to find out sommat about where they've gone, but those living in the flats the Tolenskis were staying in are a close-knit bunch and no one would tell me owt.'

'It's not your fault, Ada. Oh God, my girls – my babies are gone again.'

'I don't knaw how you're to cope with this, Miss Edith, but I do knaw as you can. You're strong, and you have your young man who needs you.'

'I won't cope, Ada – not ever. This pain is too deep ever to be reconciled with. I have no one to turn to. I can't hire an investigator, for fear of the truth coming out. I can't go looking myself. Why? Why did they do this? They knew my intentions. They knew I would return. Oh God, it is unbearable.'

Ada's look of worry deepened. She crossed the room. Somehow it didn't feel as if she was taking liberties as she sat beside Edith and took her hand. They had shared pain before. They were friends.

There was very little comfort in the gesture, but what little there was Edith would hold on to. She would throw herself into this charity and fighting for the rights of women, a cause still close to her heart; but most of all, she would concentrate her efforts on getting Laurent whole again, and their future together. That would bring her happiness. A marred happiness, but happiness all the same.

'Ada, when we are alone, drop my formal address. You are very dear to me and we are friends.

You must just remember to use it when we are in company.'

'Ta, Edith. I can think of nothing better than to have you as me friend – well, except me Joe coming home and us getting married, that is.'

'I know. We are both suffering in different ways, as most people on Earth are.'

'Aye, we're all in same boat. But we have to find a way of going forward towards the future. What kind of future that'll be, none of us can knaw, but we have to keep going and to maintain hope.'

'We do, Ada, we do.'

As Ada left her, Edith leaned back and allowed the tears to flow. It was better to shed them now, and then she could compose herself for her visit to Eloise and Jay's new town house, and then to her own home. It would be good to be surrounded by those who loved her. From them she would draw strength. She would give all that she could to help others, and more especially to help Laurent recover. As Ada said: they must. She would join the march to the uncertain future. She would have Laurent by her side, and Eloise would walk with Jay. Ada would have her Joe. If God was good, Christian and Douglas would come home and pick up their lives, and life would have some normality and happiness to it.

But she knew she wouldn't take the road forward as a follower of others; that wasn't her nature and would leave her too much time to dwell. No, she would be more of a worker for change and would work to shape whatever future they were left with after the war ended. She only hoped it would end in the victory that looked likely, now that the

Americans had truly arrived and their full might was behind the rest of the Allies.

Ada hesitated as she left the room, but then decided that Edith needed this time to herself. *Eeh, that Kaiser bloke has a lot to answer for. But then this war is meant to end all wars, so if that is achieved, sommat good will have come out of it.*

Soon her life would change. Lady Eloise had looked into Beryl being moved nearer and that was now likely. So she'd get a chance to rebuild their relationship, and settle Beryl some. She'd devote her spare time to that. It might even, one day, be possible for Brendan to see his mam. She hoped so, as mams shouldn't be separated from their young 'uns. The anguished cries she could hear coming from Edith, and her own knowledge of the agony it caused, told her that.

One day soon there would be peace and they could all go about the task of rebuilding their lives and those of others. She couldn't wait for that day, and neither could she wait to see Joe again. She'd take five minutes to fill in another visitor request form. This would be her fourth request since she last saw him. All these requests had been refused, but she wouldn't give up. None of them could ever do that...

30

Petra

Poland, March 1921
Salving a conscience

'Marcelina, look at them! Our darling girls. How happy they are!'

Elka and Ania, just two days away from their fourth birthdays, ran around the table containing the celebration meal. At last peace had come to Poland and she was once more a recognized country. The Soviets had been defeated, and today – 17th March 1921 – the Second Polish Republic had adopted a constitution based on the French one. The constitution expressly ruled out discrimination on racial or religious grounds. An end to anti-Semitism was in sight.

So many of their friends had been murdered. Often accused of being in league with the Soviets, and on their return to Poland in 1917, Petra and Aleksi had feared for their lives and had regretted their decision to leave London. England had now enjoyed peace for two years, although the Spanish flu pandemic had wreaked havoc on an already weakened nation.

Squeezing Marcelina's hand, Petra tried to gain comfort and to impart it. They had both been widowed by the pandemic, just under three years ago. Neither they nor the twins had succumbed, although darling Aleksi and Feodor had been nursed, and had died, at home.

Soon afterwards the Russians had become troublesome. Beating the White Russians, the Soviets had wanted to conquer Poland, and so another war had raged.

Feodor's father had been adamant that he would not leave Poland again, and now they all lived in Warsaw. This decision had left Petra and Marcelina helpless, stranded with two babies and living in fear. But today was a good day. A day to celebrate. A day to remember the past too, and to look back with sadness. But, more importantly, a day to look forward with hope. At last the Jews in Poland were going to be able to live, work and worship without anxiety.

Petra watched as Marcelina played with the children. She could see the light inside Marcelina brightening and her sadness melting away. *I did the right thing,* thought Petra.

What did it matter that Gos and Miriam, Feodor's parents, wouldn't accept the girls, or believe the story that Petra had told them about how they came to be with her. The girls were safe, and her beloved Marcelina had some happiness in her life.

Her thoughts went to Edith as she watched the little red-headed Elka and Ania running away from their mama and their cousins, Jhona and Isaac – Feodor's brother's children – who had joined in the game.

What had become of Edith? Had she found new love and forgotten the girls? Petra doubted she'd forgotten them, but did think that, when she remembered, it would be with relief. Her problem had been sorted. She'd probably gone back to her society life a heroine, without a smear on her character. *Yes. All in all, I did a good job and brought peace to two women: my beloved daughter, and Edith, whom I have to admit I became very fond of.*

She thought about her secret box. Hidden away, it held the true facts and papers pertaining to the children's real identities. This gave her an inner peace. It secured in her a knowledge that if ever it became necessary to do so, she could reveal the truth about their dual nationality, as their registration here in Poland would perhaps be the saving of them one day – who knew? With this thought, she packed her sometimes troubled conscience into the deep recesses of her mind and went to join in the fun.

31

Ada

London, March 1921
A wedding to remember

'Oh, Ada, darling, you will look wonderful. Your frock is beautiful. Joe is going to be so proud of you when you walk up the aisle towards him.'

'Ta, Edith. I only managed to finish me frock last night. I left the hem undone till I was sure Joe was finally coming home. I didn't want to jeopardize his chances by having everything ready. A bit of superstition, but I thought that if I didn't leave something undone, I might put a jinx on things – what with his release date having already been put back five times in the last nine months!'

'Well, he is home now. And Annie has rung and said he is as nervous as a kitten.'

'I can't wait to see him. But I thought it best not to, till we meet in the church. When I saw him three weeks ago I told him that the next time would be as I walked up the aisle. Eeh, it were funny posting the banns in the prison chapel. But the prison chaplain said he would duplicate them in his parish church and wed us there.'

'St Anne's is a lovely church, with its pepperpot spire and majestic pillars. A wonderful place for a wedding. Now, come on, let's slip your dress on.'

Taking the beautiful turquoise-satin dress by the hem, Edith slipped it carefully over Ada's hair for her. Then Ada took over. 'Eeh, I'm not used to being dressed. I can manage.'

They were in a bedroom in Edith's Holland Park home. Edith had insisted that Ada stay the night before her wedding and went from there to the church.

Ada hadn't felt out of place, as she visited often, often sitting with Christian when his nurse was off-duty and Edith needed to be working.

Christian had returned home badly wounded. He'd been blown up when the vehicle he was travelling in hit a mine. All the others in the truck had died, but Christian survived. If you could call the almost vegetative state that he was in, and being totally blind, surviving.

The last six months of the war had been terrible. When the war ended it should have been a time for rejoicing, but Edith hadn't felt that she could. She was still going through so much heartache and torment. Though her elder brother Douglas returned home all in one piece, the shock of what happened to Christian had quickly been followed by the death of their father; and on top of that, poor Edith was coping with the broken Laurent. The love of her life.

Ada had loved Laurent on meeting him. His bravery shone from him. He courageously took on the battle to walk again, and didn't allow his facial injuries to daunt him. Because of this, everyone accepted him as he was. He and Edith had married as soon as he could stand on his false leg. It had been a quiet affair, but a lovely wedding, and one that had helped to smooth over some of the sadness within Edith.

'Ada, when I see the light on your hair, like it is now, I think of my girls.'

'Aye, they had lovely hair.'

'Oh, Ada. Will this pain never go away?'

'Eeh, lass. It will be like a wave. Receding at times, then crashing over you at others.'

'I'm sorry. I shouldn't have brought it up today. This is your special day.'

'I know, but those are the times when the wave crashes. It hit me this morning when I woke. Me lads came to me, and I had to fight not to tear me heart from me. But I focused on what the day is going to give me. Me Joe is finally going to be me husband. He has his freedom, and our life together begins; and somehow that happiness cushioned the sadness and I could cope. You have to think of something to do the same for you, Edith.'

'Yes, you are right. I will focus on the fact that I have at last engaged a Polish-speaking investigator. I didn't think I could at first, but I realized that to break my confidence would mean the agency would never again be commissioned by anyone, so why would they do so? He has had a lot of success in tracing people misplaced through the events of war, and has reunited many families. He has agreed to take my case up and search for my girls.'

'There you are then. All will be well, I know it will. Now, is that husband of yours ready? If he is to be best man, he needs to be on his way to the church.'

'He is. Ready, that is. I don't think he has gone yet, though. Ha! He moaned about having to wear a starched collar. He said we British have always been known as "stuffed shirts", but should have been known as stiff ones!'

'Eeh, Laurent's a good 'un. He's what we would call a joker, but Annie would call "a right card"!'

'Yes, it is his sense of humour that gets him through. Well, both of us really.'

Edith's voice was wistful again, so Ada pulled her up sharpish, before she sank back into her morose mood. 'Reet. How do I look?'

'Beautiful. Darling Ada. That colour really suits you, and having your hair plaited up like that is a stroke of genius; it looks so pretty. Oh, Ada...'

'Now, now.'

'These are tears of happiness, I promise. I am so happy that at last you and Joe will be together.'

'We have a lot of hurdles to jump yet, but we'll jump them together. And, Edith, ta for offering Joe that maintenance job. He's reet handy, and will keep Jimmy's Hope House up to scratch, you'll see. We'll have no leaky roofs this year!'

'I know. And it's going to be a real treat for them all: you having your wedding party back there. The children are so excited. And all the young mothers are working their socks off getting the wedding breakfast ready.'

'Wouldn't have it anywhere else. Me Jimmy is honoured and remembered there. And that's down to you, Edith. The young 'uns all look up to him as a hero.'

'He was. Oh, Ada, come here.'

Ada went into Edith's outstretched arms and took comfort from the hug she received, but didn't stay long, for it was too much for her. 'Reet, I'm ready. Let's do this.'

'Your carriage awaits you, Madam.'

'Eeh, fancy me riding in a Rolls-Royce. I never thought I'd see the day. Lead the way, my maid-of-honour.'

Laurent was waiting for them at the bottom of the stairs. He had his false leg on, but sat in his wheelchair, no doubt conserving his energy for his duty as best man. He gasped as he looked at Edith. *'Ma chérie,* you look beautiful.'

Edith wore a dress in a style similar to Ada's. But hers was cut just below the knee, where it gave way to white stockings and satin pumps with a little heel. The dress flowed from the bodice in gentle folds. The colour – a darker blue than Ada's long, flowing frock – enhanced rather than paled Ada's dress and suited Edith's very dark hair and olive complexion so well.

'Oh, and look at you! Ada, you are gorgeous. The prettiest bride since my own Edith.'

Ada blushed. Somehow, when Laurent complimented her, it sounded so delicious – if that was a word you could use for a compliment. But it was one that fitted, as his accent and his lush tone seemed to sweep all over her and make her feel special.

'You should have left by now, Laurent. You need to be at the church to greet and support Joe. Go along with you! Your driver is waiting outside for you, and has been for fifteen minutes.'

'Don't chastise me, my darling. I had to see you both before I went. I will go now. Call the chap in to help me.'

At the church, Jay was waiting outside for them. He was to give Ada away, and she could think of none better.

Excitement knotted her tummy muscles as she took his arm and drank in his compliments. She felt, and was sure she looked, like a queen! This was going to be a good day for her. She'd not had many good days in her life to count, and the total of them could be summed up on her ten fingers and toes. But right now she'd only think of them, and not of the terrible days she'd suffered.

Joe turned as she walked up the aisle. His smile warmed her through and gave his face a lovely look, as his expression combined both love and happiness.

As they left the church and the bells rang out, filling the air with joy, and the rice rained down on them, Ada thought she would burst with happiness. Looking around she caught sight of Rene. Eeh, if only Rene could find a nice man. But there were so few to choose from and Rene seemed settled into her work. She worked as a sister in Shepherd's Bush Military Hospital where Edith also worked. It must seem to them that the war hasn't ended, she thought, as they tend to those badly wounded that still need their care. Rene came over and held her, wishing her congratulations. Annie was with her, holding on tightly to little Brendan's hand. 'Ma, ma, me want up.'

'Ha, Brendan, lad, I can't pick you up, it would ruin all me finery.'

'Huh! If she don't pick you up, I will, lad!'

Beryl! Ada couldn't believe her eyes. How did she get here? Had the asylum let her come on her own?

'Beryl, lass. Eeh, it's nice to see thee. Ada said as you weren't able to come. Glad you changed your mind. Now, you've not much on and look cold, so I'll get you a lift sorted to Jimmy's Hope House, eh?'

'I'm going nowhere, Joe. Eeh, you've got some side. Murdering her husband and then marrying her. Still, she'd not get anyone else, whore that she is. You know that she went with my Bill, don't you? Well, she did. He told me he had her on the kitchen floor. Well, I reckon that's best place for her!'

Joe looked shocked. Ada had never told him about the rape. She hadn't wanted him upset;

he'd enough on his plate. Avoiding his eyes, she looked at her sister. 'Beryl, lass, don't do this. Not today. I'm glad as you've changed your mind and come to be with us. But don't make a scene. Please.'

'Scene! What else am I to do when you stole me babby, and had me man, eh?'

Beryl lunged towards Brendan as she said this, but Annie was too quick for her and grabbed the little tot and held on to him. 'If yer try to lay an 'and on 'im, you'll 'ave me to contend with,' she said.

Beryl hesitated. Others began to stand in front of Annie and Brendan. Looking from one to another, Beryl looked like a frightened, cornered animal.

'Come on, love. Let Joe sort you a seat in one of the cars. You'll be warmer. And if you promise to calm down, you can come to the wedding breakfast. I'll take you to Annie's house and get you something to wear. Come on.'

'I don't want to, our Ada. I want Mam. Mam. MAM!'

It was a pitiful cry and one that wrenched Ada's heart.

Edith moved forward, speaking in gentle tones that held authority. 'Beryl, I will take care of you. Now, nothing is going to happen to you, and you can choose what you want to do. I'll take you back to your hospital or on to the wedding breakfast. I won't leave you until you feel safe.'

'I'll come too, Beryl. I'll help to take care of you. I'm Sister Rene, and this lady is Doctor Edith. We will look after you. Come along with us.'

Beryl's body seemed to fold as she slumped to the ground. 'I want me mam.'

'Yes, we know you do. Now, take my arm with this hand, and Sister Rene's with your other one. That's it. Now, stand up, but keep hold of us.' Once Beryl was standing, Edith turned to Jay. 'Jay, can we take your driver, and you and Eloise go in with Laurent?' Jay said that would be fine, and Edith turned to Ada. 'Don't worry, Ada. Try to carry on as you would have done. Beryl will be fine. We will be with you as soon as we can.'

Ada could only nod. The action spilled a tear from her, but she wiped it away. Her heart wanted to go with Beryl, but, to her immense pain, she had to accept that if she made a move to do so, it would upset her sister again. In Beryl's tangled mind, Ada knew that she looked on her as the cause of everything that had dragged her down.

As the car pulled away, a hand rested on Ada's arm. Turning, she looked into the lovely, kind eyes of Eloise. 'We have a wedding breakfast to get under way. Come on, beautiful bride. Lead the way.'

With a heavy heart, Ada took the hand Joe offered and went towards the gleaming Rolls-Royce. Once her body had sunk into the deep leather seat, Joe climbed in next to her. 'Well, Mrs Grinsdale, that were a good start! Now I don't want you worrying about what Beryl said – none of it. I can imagine the circumstances, and I love you more than anything for shielding me and coping with that. Eeh, there's nowt like a fracas at a wedding – good old northern tradition that!'

She couldn't help but smile. 'Aye, we'll show

these southerners how it's done, eh?'

'That's the spirit. Now, try to put it behind you. Everyone knows that Beryl is not well in her mind. None of them are going to hold what happened against you.'

'Oh, Joe, will she ever be well? Will she ever stop thinking of me as someone that ruined her life?'

'You never know, lass. It could happen. But if it doesn't, it's one more cross we have to bear, and we've borne a lot worse.'

'We have, Joe. As everyone has. You're reet. Let's put it behind us. No matter what, we'll allus support Beryl as much as she'll let us. And we'll work towards the day when she is well again.'

'Good, lass. Now. How about you give your husband a kiss?'

It was a kiss Ada had thought would never happen. All the years they'd loved one another they'd never shared a kiss, not a real one – one that was their right to take and give. With it a warmth came into Ada that blocked out all she'd been through. It unlocked her heart to the possibility of hope: hope for the future, and hope for herself and Joe and little Brendan. From now on they could build a life together, one never again to be shadowed by war.

She wished she could make things right for everyone. She wished that the scars cut deep into people's souls could heal; and that Edith, especially Edith, could be reunited with her little ones. Something Edith had once said told her there was no possibility of her having any other babbies, as her marriage wasn't likely to be consummated. That was what Ada would call a deep love – a love that had to be platonic, and yet was so strong the couple were bound together forever. Poor Edith. Poor Laurent. *Please, God, bring little Elka and Ania home to them. Make their lives complete. They have done everything they can for their country, and for those hurt by war. It's time they had sommat in return.*

Leaving this prayer behind her, Ada turned her attention to Joe. Her Joe. Her man. A happiness settled in her like she hadn't felt for a long, long time. Leaning towards him, she pursed her lips again. But just before his lips touched hers, she whispered, 'I love you, Joe.'

Acknowledgements

First and foremost I would like to acknowledge Nicholas Fothergill, owner of the beautiful, historic stately home Stanford Hall, near Lutterworth, Leicestershire. An English Heritage building, the house was built between 1697 and 1700 by William Smith for Sir Roger Cave. Nicholas Fothergill is a descendant of Sir Roger. Stanford Hall, besides being Nicholas's home, is now also a stunning venue for many events held in its grounds and in the house. I am honoured that Nicholas allowed me to model the country home and estate of my fictional Mellor family on Stanford Hall. Thank you.

And a special thank you to two wonderful ladies, my editor at Pan Macmillan, Louise Buckley, and my literary agent, Judith Murdoch. You are both always there for me, and your belief in me supports and helps me more than you can know.

I further thank Louise, along with Laura Carr and the rest of her team, for their sensitive editing of my novel – the difference you make is amazing. Thank you.

Thank you too to my beloved daughter Christine Martin and son James Wood, for reading and rereading my manuscripts. Your advice on what is and what isn't working as the manuscript develops is invaluable.

And to my much-loved nephew, Chris Olley. For your knowledgeable input on the First World War, I am truly grateful.

To 'Gungeek' on YouTube, thank you for answering my questions on cordite with such in-depth knowledge of your subject.

And to my dear friends Pat and Den Payne, who have a knowledge of the areas of London. When I told them the type of setting I needed for the London homes of my fictional Mellor family, they took me to Holland Park and there I found the perfect location. Thank you too to my dear friend Jacqueline Lacey for your help with the few French phrases used in the book.

And, as always, my heartfelt thanks to my beautiful family. To my darling husband, Roy. To our children, Christine, Julie, Rachel and James, and their husbands/partners, Nick, Ed, Rick and Scott. To all our grandchildren and great-grand-children. To my Olley and Wood families. You all bring me joy; you support me and enrich my life. You climb mountains by my side and catch me if I fall. I love you all with a special love.

The publishers hope that this book has given you enjoyable reading. Large Print Books are especially designed to be as easy to see and hold as possible. If you wish a complete list of our books please ask at your local library or write directly to:

Magna Large Print Books
Magna House, Long Preston,
Skipton, North Yorkshire.
BD23 4ND